TWILLEY

OTHER WORKS BY BRUCE FLEMING

An Essay in Post-Romantic Aesthetics

Caging the Lion: Cross-Cultural Fictions

Structure and Chaos in Modernist Works

Modernism and its Discontents: Philosophical Problems of Twentieth-Century Literary Theory

TWILLEY

A NOVEL

For Bob
with thanks
Bruce

BRUCE FLEMING

Bruce Fleming

TURTLE POINT PRESS
NEW YORK

Library of Congress Catalogue Card Number: 96-06-09-20
ISBN: 1-885983-20-4

Portions of this book first appeared, in different form, in the *Wissenschaftliche Arbeiten der Gesellschaft für Angewandte Kunst*, Wien/Brno

First Printing

Printed in the United States of America

To
Keithie, Bryna, Rinda,
and
the old days

The world of the happy man is different from the world of the unhappy one.

—Wittgenstein, **Tractatus**

I

The Journey Home

THE GRID OVER THE SUBWAY VENT obstructs his view of the spongy floor below, of the crumpled candy wrappers and the cigarettes smashed nose-on or flattened like a reed made from the tall swaying grasses which turn golden in the sun and rustle and brush the rippling white hem of our lover's dress as if exchanging whispered secrets, obstructs his view of the paper cups whose bellies have been knocked out and which now lie deflated, the air having escaped through the gaping wounds, flaps with jagged edges between which the interior stuffing whooshed at so rapid a rate that no amount of gasping from the hideously distended mouth on the other side could replace it. **Analogy:** The vent is like a tic-tac-toe board set up by a compulsively neat and prissy people, a gigantic three-dimensional grid with squares upon squares upon squares, and then handed over to their sloppy neighbors to play on, people who mark not with tiny neat black x's and perfect white o's but in loose balls of brightly-colored paper and with broken-backed bottle caps and pieces of long limp twine that drape spinelessly over the discarded pieces of paper, the cellophane sleeves on the cigarette packets unshucking themselves like spirits half-pulled from the bodies they inhabit onto adjoining squares by the bony hands of a too-eager death.

Sloppy though this arrangement is already, it is made even less precise and clear-cut by the rain which is pouring down and flowing over the edge of the grating, covering every bar of metal near that edge with a sheath of fuzzy thick clearness, the liquid form of the ice that occasionally in the winter coats all the twigs with smooth vests of glass. The effect is to further obscure the right-angle neatness of this so-carefully constructed grid and to change the surface beneath from something akin to several layers of gray felt to a hopelessly soggy mess, half puddles and slushy slime which, as the rain pocks it directly or falls from the metal in great ragged sheets, sends shooting upward in reaction unevenly-shaped drops and gouts of the muddy water which splatter the pieces of trash that are becoming more and more deeply imbedded in the slush, coloring them a uniform gray-brown so like the surrounding background that soon it will make no difference to anyone that they are not aligned with the precision they might be.

Soon the only thing that is not gray or brown in the subway vent will be the startlingly white lichen that crawls up the cement sides with its ruffled pseudopods and is cleaned and made whiter by the water pouring down on it that works loose from anemone-like grips any pieces of entangled dirt. If they were immersed for an appreciable amount of time in an undisturbed pool of water, these lichens could lose their close-cropped whiteness and flower into colorful blossoms like pills that open into multi-hued tissue paper blooms in a windowsill goldfish bowl. **Concession:** It is not probable that the sides of this hole would become shaggy with such beautiful streaming strips under the varying flow of this rain, which cannot provide the still pool of liquid necessary to such a transformation. **Historical analogy:** The vent is like a vertical burial chamber from Mesopotamia sunk in the city sidewalk much as fragments of a medieval church are re-set into the plain brown walls of museums where the daylight never penetrates and which are completely still but for the far-off sound of someone walking slowly several galleries down. Nor do they smell of the musty odors of age, dust, and dampness, but of the slightly metallic air of the circulation system which makes the candles lit on the ravaged altarpiece in a stroke of exhibition realism flicker slightly rather than beating huge wings in the corners as they would if this room were less brightly lighted.

His shoes reach out every so often and touch gently at the edge of the vent, patting their dark crèpe soles in the cataract flowing over the edge. They are wet, and the darker area of matted-down pigskin that only seconds ago looked like the thin frosting dripped on the top and down the sides of an oblong cake has enlarged to the point where the whole shoe is colored dark with the rain. With a sigh—for he is getting wet standing out in the rain, even though he cannot have been here more than a few seconds—he bends as if he were going to tie his shoelace and then seems to change his mind and curves back upwards before his head is much below rib-cage level, perhaps feeling for the first time on his scalp some water held off by the thatching of his hairs which had caught and strung the small liquid pearls as if thinking that such riches were real, not knowing that these perfect little globules would soon be gone or smashed into an unpleasant and useless wetness. **Aside:** In their ignorance, the hairs are like the characters in fairy tales who discover to their dismay that because of their unworthiness their gold and silver have turned to ashes, or dream kings who find the treasures they had accumulated during the night dissolved into the disappointing midday air. **Lesson:** Always expect the worst, be suspicious of anything that looks like good fortune, for it will always turn out to be bad, live convinced that this world is a great rolling ball that crushes all people beneath it, that our time on earth is a period of constant destruction of the human spirit and our hope less firm than the ephemeral whispering of the wind through the diaphanous green veils of the weeping willow's leaves draped upon the trees like the moldering undergarments of the sylphs hung up one spring afternoon to dry and abandoned through heaven knows what causes.

He sees the vent suddenly shudder back and forth and realizes that he has been bumped by someone on the edge of the flow of shoes that rustle and swirl around his own soggy ones. He turns his head from the spot directly in front of him to get a longer view which is filled with the wet sidewalk from which grow the stalks of tan legs and dark trousers. They seem in the density of the thicket not so much to change position as to be merely fluttering back and forth in patterns of random motion. Occasionally he can catch a glimpse of a stem or two of a primary color that is soon covered again, and then it is as if the wind blows clear a space and he is able once again to see the cement pock-marked with tiny depressions filled with water that remains unaffected by the rough concrete digging into the sides of the pool's water. **NB:** Liquid has the capability of taking into itself all wounds and being none the worse for them. Water acknowledges the presence of the knife by nothing more than a graceful parting and a slight ripple on its surface which takes several seconds to damp down to flatness as if these disturbances were the motions of sub-surface needles sewing the wound instantly together into a perfect and invisible seam. **Application:** Like some people, water manages to survive by virtue of its great malleability, remains safe by virtue of never presenting any resistance to the weapons of its enemies, though also like these people the price it pays in return is that it makes no effect on the world around it, plays the role of the neutral substance on which everything else acts.

As he follows his gaze upwards, the stems flower into people the way telephone wires outlined against a clear water-blue sky or one fleecy with billows, when looked at with slightly crossed eyes from a rapidly moving car, seem to rise and fall between the supports of their poles and suddenly evaporate into the air. Certain legs have aged before others, those that have begun to take on the darkish cast of the wet so that their outer skins cling to the solid structure within rather than hanging straight. **Conjecture:** This may be the evidence of some sort of sticky mucous emission put out by diseased stems that gums together the hairs on these legs into a thick patina made more solid by the addition of small bits of lint from the trousers and in some cases made sticky enough to glue this same cloth to the leg so firmly that they outline a muscular calf or a thin and wiry thigh.

Development: It is at this point that we will know the thing is nearly done for, for soon it would be unable to limit its oozings to a mere several drops a minute. It will begin to lactate the rotten paste and its clothes will become damp and crusted dry with the unhealthy lymph and begin to smell of the sick sweetness of illness and bacteria. Finally it will become so abhorrent to itself that it will run through the house systematically smashing all of the mirrors into piles of glittering and deadly sharp shards which it longs to drive into its body or use to sever an artery which would only bleed more of the sticky sickness that now pervades its entire being.

In its frenzy it smashes all things that can reflect its bloated face and purpling hands, breaking glass doors, scratching the bottoms of pots with handfuls of pins, destroying anything shiny without a thought to the multiples of seven years of bad luck to which it is sentencing itself, for it knows that it cannot possibly live to complete the first of these terms, will probably not live until tomorrow. It will spend the night in the shower training upon its body a continuous stream of lukewarm water to wash away the terrible slime, water that soon turns it to a mass of wrinkles which, when its much-wasted and now nearly drained corpse is picked up from the floor of the bathtub the next morning by the police called by a neighbor kept awake by the continuous sound of running water, is hardened to the texture of walnut shells that not even the undertakers with their proficient fingers will be able to smooth. Instead, its body will be painted pink and powdered with a layer of make-up so thick that the skin is filled in and elevated to the height of the highest wrinkle ridge, though the morticians would not be able to hide the tightening of the skin around the mouth except by sewing it shut and producing a tight, determined expression surrounded by skin stretched flat and hard.

He is getting wet around the shoulders and pulls his gaze from the vent and studies the crowd into which he must maneuver himself. In a moment he is in their midst, assured of protection from the rain on all sides but his top. The few umbrellas held higher than his eye level are like ambitious lily pads pushing themselves up by their crisp green stems to the light, cheating the frogs which had counted on an accessible sunning spot held stable by the water surface onto which they could pull their slimy green bodies trailing the wet tendrils of plants that make the dull green pad shiny for a few minutes until they are evaporated.

Around him he smells damp fabrics warmed by body heat. He senses the compulsion of the motion around him to continue in the direction he is going, the pressure not to break loose or to let himself go limp. **Reflection:** His body on the sidewalk would trip those around him and cause a knot or hole in the flow to which he now contributes only a small bit of energy and which acts on him with hugely magnified results. He is powerless to break the momentum alone and by force. Still, it is made up of the combined powers of many more people like him who, could they be reached and affected individually, would be able to stop simultaneously in their tracks without causing or receiving harm. Perhaps what he needs is a bull-horn, the better to begin audible persuasion to that end.

Alternately, if he were to worm his way to the edge of this stream of humanity he would be able to transfer himself to the opposing current which moves along under the striped canopies of the department stores, switching his body to the equally insistent but contrary flow of people. **Note:** Those in the stream he has left would not be convinced, by seeing the other people on the sidewalk who are equally insistent about running in another direction and who seem equally happy in the pursuit of this opposing goal, that their determination is ridiculous and their perseverance futile, any more than we can be made to see that life is without purpose by the fact that so many people so different than we have found happiness doing things that are anathema to us.

He feels elbows in his sides and the hot breath of a pair of determined housewives on his neck. In front of him are the greasy hair and slightly frayed collar of the man ahead whose scalp shows white both through his thinning thatch and at the base of his skull, where the hairs have been clipped short. The head moves less and less and then becomes still as the crowd stops at the corner for the bright red of the traffic light and for its translation into words, which has blinked on.

This box that advises one so gruffly not to walk is made of a light shining behind a sheet of glass painted black except in the spaces of the letters. **Reflection:** Were this glass to be shattered, the box would be merely a red glow that has remained on the corner instead of undertaking the acrobatics of its more adventurous brethren that hang on a wire over the busy street. On the other hand, if the mostly-black screen were completely opaque, the result would be just as disappointing and as uncommunicative as if it were non-existent. What could a yellow-painted metal box covered over with a dark black front ever mean to anyone except possibly to a trained interpreter of signs, who might understand it to explain our habit of turning a somber and unreasonably black visage to the world through the fact that the rest of our souls are yellow with cowardice and fear? **Lesson:** The initially very bright glow of the red interior is necessary to the effective working of this contraption; just as necessary is that part of it which controls and tempers the light, blocking out some of the blinding rays and permitting others passage in a rational pattern. It is only the combination of this original fire with its almost instantaneous control and the channeling of its heat that produces something which can be at all functional or pleasant to look at.

He shuffles his feet impatiently and in his motion catches a glimpse of the metal box by his elbow, which does not contain the newspaper it speaks so clearly of on its side, looking at the bars which lock nothing out and nothing in, and in fact are serving as balancing beams for insects trying to escape from the rain. This is lessening in intensity and no longer threatens to squash them with the strength of a single drop; now it only dampens them with its spray and the mist it has created in the air, causing the wings of the more fragile ones to stick closely to their bodies and giving them the look of corpses enclosed in a sleeve of blown glass, albeit moving corpses and ones with electrified or mechanically powered heads which turn inquisitively towards the Japanese beetles beating an irregular tattoo against the metal corners in their ineffectual attempts to liberate themselves through the solid walls, though they could leave so much more easily the same way they came in.

Concession: The correspondence is too tenuous, what with the motion of their feet and heads, to ever let us imagine the bugs encased in a coffin of gold beaten by the emperor's most skilled slave-smiths who were promised their freedom if they did well and their instant death if they did not but on whom the threats are without effect since the alternatives were equally agreeable. The coffin in this case would be inlaid with squares of carved ebony as black as the hair and jade as red as the lips of the princess who lies within, her smooth white eyelids suffused with a slight flush as if they could open at any moment and her mouth curving as if it could break into a smile when she awoke. **Note:** She will never awake, at least not in this vale of tears, for she is gone beyond the barrier of existence into that world of gauzes and silks and white linens which dance in serpentine undulations around the newly-liberated soul, welcoming it to its dwelling place far from care, far from worry, far from woe. And so the tears of the king fall upon the fourth and final casket of the heaviest and most brilliant crystal that lies with its contents for three months in a room open to the white-capped mountains sending chill breezes down from their icy summits that become warmer as they float over the cherry trees frothing pink in the dark night and warm daylight.

He suddenly feels more hemmed-in than before. The light has changed and people behind him are pushing in their attempt to hurry him along or get him out of the way. He casts one last look at the coin cylinder of the newspaper vending machine with its small and seemingly jagged slit at the top, shudders slightly—perhaps in sympathy with the coins which must risk scratching or worse injuries as they slip by these jaws—and steps onto the asphalt between the two guidelines of fluorescent yellow paint.

He stands for a minute in front of the department store window wondering if he should go in and looking at the chalk-white dress mannequins whose jointed hands are bent into attitudes of surprise and whose abdomens are thrust out over their carefully pointed feet as if to seduce any plastic males who might have escaped from other store windows and be walking among the crowd on this wet afternoon. **Bad news:** Try though they might, the males would be unable to do anything to prove themselves potent or satisfy their temptresses. For they are made without genitals, and thus no matter how closely they might press their hard chests against the females' unfeeling breasts, they would never be able to bring their brittle preludes to any sort of consummation. Nor would any stiff flicks of their barely moveable fingers bring the women any sort of surrogate relief, for the females too are smooth and without orifices the entire length of their torsoes.

Thus: There would be no point in the elaborate preparations necessary to one of these alluring females maneuvering to the floor behind the sofa on which her sister models are reclining, moving the potted palm in the small hitches that would be the limit of the capabilities of her hollow arms, and turning up the air conditioning to cover any uncontrollable sounds. Nor would the male need to make gestures to the other females in the window to convey the message that, if they contain their impatience, they will be next in line and that he is quite capable of taking them all one after another if they are only willing to help in the dissimulation and maintain their poses so that the people in the street do not suspect that something untowards is happening in the showcase and that the jolts the sofa seems to be making are not, in fact, their imagination.

Reflection: The mannequins are condemned to perpetual longing, to a love-hate of the body that calls them insistently to such sweet pleasures and then denies them satisfaction. Never will the molded fingernails of these females dance across the solid backs of the males, sliding suddenly off their hard buttocks as the result of an attempt to dig into them in a moment of ecstasy, never will these thin jointless fingers twine in the stiff hair of the males or pull their wigs from their plastic scalps with an uncontrollable spasm of pleasure. **Lesson:** The action of these plastic creatures is clearly noble, an example of the greatness that beings are capable of attaining in the blackest and most terrible moments of existence, an example of the virtue that can only be exhibited in the midst of suffering and adversity. For the mannequins to stand straight and seductive on the outside when inside they are neuter must be regarded as true greatness, since the position is endured for the sake of those who pass by in the street. **The greatest irony but how typical of life:** Those for whom the mannequins are making this sacrifice will never know how much suffering forms the foundations of their own few seconds of pleasure in the window display.

There is no point in remaining here before this window filled with the still, brightly-lit air of an arranged domestic tableau and populated by these plastic women against whose chalky skin the colors of the clothing appear so startling. He need not even get wet in order to go through the door: the awning reaches out to him and he is getting tired of the stiff plops of the rain drops against the canvas and the noise of the stream from the edge hitting the pavement, the darkness created there by the gray sky and the shadow of the building in contrast to which the fluorescent brightness of the window seems all the more stark.

He stands for a moment inside the doors, trying to brush some of the water from his coat, and succeeds only in pressing it in more thoroughly. Two women pass him, chattering brightly and shaking, from the translucent coverings they now trail limply from their painted fingernails, the drops of water that seep into the rug where they are devoured by hungry fibrous tongues. The rug has been discolored in a trail directly down the steps and on the sides by the railings which support a steady stream of unsteady people who hang onto each other as well as onto the metal bar burnished shiny by hundreds of hands that imparts to them in return the faintly bitter smell of the metal which lingers on their palms and soft white gloves.

The store's collected odors permeate the whole floor and form a marbled cloud in which he can catch occasional whiffs of perfumes, leather pocketbooks, and cloth. The odors have diffused up to the doors where some escape each time the doors open, changing places in their passing with the moist and gray air of outside.

He stands in the half-and-half area where the two air banks have begun to break up but are not completely intertwined. They send by his head alternating wisps of smells, ragged curls that encircle him only to come to sudden ends as the last small unfurled tail detaches itself from him. Abruptly he is enveloped in a cloud of scent that cannot have survived intact from the perfume counter. He does not turn, but closes his eyes a moment and feels the woman's warm vapor reach out to him, and then the central core of her body heat stroking him and suddenly evaporating into a brisk tail wind. He breathes quickly and more deeply as if to compensate for the rapidly fading strength of the smell. As he feels himself losing it he relaxes, the tingling on his body dwindling down into a mere roughness and disappearing entirely. He sighs and opens his eyes, catching a mouthful of air that tastes like candy or books, he cannot say which.

Directly in front of him hang racks of pocketbooks gleaming dully in the light that reflects off their crinkly leather surfaces. The pressures of hanging cause the softest of them to collapse slightly as if afflicted with a sort of debilitating weariness that cracks the edges of their stiff youth under its slight but insistent weight. Their rigid carrying straps grasp the metal hooks and seem to pull against them in an attempt to lessen the pain in the bodies they support, but those that have continued to resist misshaping under the strain show no trace of the fantastic struggle that is taking place beneath their leathery skins.

In the long glass-front counter lie rows of equally undemonstrative wallets, contortion artists which have folded themselves in halves and thirds and now lie in display boxes of cardboard made to fit their reduced sizes that act as unyielding reminders of their goals. **Conjecture:** Without the constant consciousness of the shape they must maintain, they might otherwise be tempted to glut themselves of their own volition and become fat and smooth, as unbearably well-fed-looking as those wallets that are not so fortunate to be able to choose their futures and are snatched from their ascetic and orderly life and stuffed to bulging with dollar bills, faded pictures of small children, and old love notes fraying at the edges, their betrayal to the enemy accomplished by an exchange of the very currency they are forced to carry.

Reflection: The wallet whose choice of whether to remain slim or to be satiated is taken from it is in fact the luckier, for then it is free to succumb totally to temptation, free to give in to greed and to gastronomic delights without any qualms of conscience. Who, once having accepted the inevitable fact that the thing could not possibly fight the will of the human that now controls it, could blame it for taking pleasure in that which gorges it, that which lines the silken insides of its maw and fills it to bursting? Who could recommend that it refuse to enjoy the delicious tickling feeling of the smooth money along the sides of its pouch, insist that it think of things other than the pleasure of feeling the shiny-surfaced but delightfully rough-backed pictures slip into its cellophane windows?

Doubt: Yet would there not be something odd about this sudden abandonment to that gorging which they have denied themselves all their lives? Is there not something strange about the alacrity of their surrender to desires of the flesh when once they were so concerned to maintain their ascetic regimen? **Implication:** Those who are so happy to claim control by stronger powers than they which, they think, eliminates all questions of responsibility, must have been rather unwilling self-deniers to begin with. The regimen designed to produce leanness of body and quickness of mind in the service of peace of spirit must have been torture to one who throws off its bonds with such a glad cry of joy. **Lesson:** Those few who succeed in integrating into themselves the ritual of a rigid training program designed to toughen body and soul are the happiest of all beings, for they demand of themselves the most difficult goals and have the pleasure of approaching them more nearly every day. Among such creatures it is not so much the actual achievement of their goal of being folded into the positions we see that constitutes their life—indeed this final folded state is a sort of sleep under the lights that suffuse the counter with a bluish glow—as rather the process of limbering their initially stiff limbs to the point where they are capable of taking the folds of 360 ° without crying out in pain.

The aisle that opens before him and seems to part the store in half as absolutely and neatly as a white line of scalp down the center of the patent-leather hair of a tenor in a barbershop quartet is like a runway crowded with people threading their way around each other or resting at one of the counters, a few moments for respite or for the diversion of acquisition before re-entering the race. In exchange, they must accept the packages that slow them down but that are the price they pay for the pleasure of their dalliance. **Oddity:** Surprisingly, there exist customers whose masochistic instinct is so great that they try to load themselves with merchandise they have never given themselves the pleasure of buying. But at this the store draws the line: even with its unrelenting efforts to lure the racers into taking time off at its counters, the management is not quite so cruel as this. To prevent such masochism on the part of shoppers, the store stations men whose sole purpose is to ensure that the walkers do not take a package without being given an opportunity in return to buy it. **Precept:** The desire for self-punishment such as this lurks deep in the recesses of the human soul, feeding off its host. Thus it is no surprise that our lives are permeated with symbols of parasitic plants and animals. We need only note the popularity of noodle dishes to assure ourselves of a societal fascination with the tapeworm, need remark only the direct translation of the symbol of the mosquito into the fragile and airy mobile sculptures our century has popularized and that float over many middle-class cribs, need only be aware of the age-old identification of the color white with purity and its ubiquity at weddings to trace the influence of the berries of the mistletoe, that Druidic parasite transmuted into holiday decoration.

His left foot has begun to go to sleep. He steps on it with his right, feeling not the warm gushing into his veins of the fresh blood that he had expected but only the thud of his shoe on the bones of the foot serving as protectors to the stale blood and uncirculating juices **Reflection:** Smashing this fragile curved cage would bring about a sudden explosion and movement of the stagnating juices, which would surge by the shattered white chips in a flurry of activity breaking new pathways and pressuring through old ones clogged by misplaced pulp and newly-formed clot. However, the end result of this effective sort of energizer would probably be a solid dried mass of bruises and hardened scab which would bring to a halt any motion whatever for a long time. **Action:** None. Clearly such a course is injudicious. He wiggles his toes and feels the stuffed sleepiness begin to disappear, then moves his legs.

He pauses before the oval mirror of the lipstick counter which is set at such a low angle that it shows a cameo of his shirt front and the top of his pants. His belt buckle plays the role of a shiny-lipped mouth with its dark teeth clenched on the flattened tip of an equally metallic tongue. Above this rises a column of vertically stacked shirt button nostrils colored translucent white as if they produced not dark slime from their interiors but cotton wool. Bit parts are turned in by the eyelid shirt pockets, which are closed in seemingly perpetual but rather angular sleep. He pulls the curtain shut on this scenario by zipping his jacket up the front and looks in the mirror again as if daring it to try to mount another theatrical spectacular on the front of the coat. It remains mute, showing him in return for the glare he gives it merely the uniform blue of the jacket front which reflects not only in the glass but in the silver frame around it as well and on the thin shiny arm that holds it above the glass counter top.

Analogy: This uniform reflection gives the mirror the look of having suddenly gone blue from lack of air, but there is no evidence of any throttling going on around the metal stalk and in any case it would be hard to imagine any hands made of flesh and blood having much of an effect on such a hard windpipe. **Concession:** It is not clear whether this mirror is only a disembodied portrait bust, or whether it is a living part of the entire body that reclines under it, the long glassed-in counter on which it had seemed merely to be resting but from which it may well be growing. At any rate, it is no wonder that the mirror was so eager to arrange the elements of his shirt into a face, for it is quite possibly the thing's greatest regret that it was born without features of its own.

Alternative explanation: It may be that the counter with its mirror is one of the two sisters of the nymph Echo, all three nymphs being condemned to the same punishment of mimicry but assigned to different senses. It may be her of the silver hair and the sparkling clear eyes he sees before him, her whose own eyes and lips and cheeks once glowed with the fire of the joy of life, whose eyes were capable of expressing the infinite sorrow and infinite mystery of existence and who was sentenced to a lifetime of reproducing the expressions and features of others in her now-blank face. As punishment, her chaste body has been turned to clear glass so that anyone may possess her at a glance and see her vari-colored innards which, horrifyingly enough, have become ointments and paints for the faces of customers who take no notice of the transparent nymph herself, a creature who never needed the artificial aids that these people find necessary for the enhancement of their eyes, lips, and cheeks.

Silver lining: Still, it may be that with her reduction in station has come humility, and that the nymph's once overly-proud and arrogant spirit has been humbled to a near-tolerable level through her prolonged period of enforced mimicry. If so, she is the only one of her sisters to have learned anything. Golden-tongued Echo still grits her teeth as she repeats the last few syllables of the nonsense that vacationers and their bored offspring call into gorges, sometimes adding a few grumbles of her own in defiant but fruitless protest.

As for the third sister, the nymph of touch and feeling, the sister who was once so polished a harlot that the merest brush from her silky smooth fingers was enough to send her customers' phalluses bounding up in joyous anticipation of what was to come and whose own skin, it is said, was so sensitive that had she been the princess who slept on the pea buried beneath the dozen feather mattresses, she would not have emerged the next morning bruised merely by the vegetable, but black and blue all over from the threads of the silken sheets—this sister was changed into a bruise and sent to live in the buttock of an overweight but good-hearted waitress in the barely-civilized wilds of North Dakota.

A row of lipstick tubes poke their scarlet heads from metallic shells in which, it seems, they would much rather have stayed, for they have that bland shiny sheen common to those who are a bit puzzled by the world and not at all sure they are glad they have been born. Behind the lipstick are heaps of fluffy powder puffs, their velvet surfaces settling comfortably one into another and digging their piles into the puffs above and below them so as not to overbalance and fall onto the counter with a delicate plop and a sigh of regret that they were still virgin and unable to send billowing from their limp sides whole clouds of odorous pink. The top one moves a bit and the fingers of the woman behind the counter withdraw. These fingers end in long red nails which balance themselves out over the edge of the flesh and are prevented from teetering over only by the filings the woman must give them regularly to keep their weight in alignment. The fingers are smooth and pale and move along the counter, touching the glass occasionally or straightening the bottles and tubes that are displayed there.

Through the frosted back of the counter he sees the red blur of her dress that becomes more distinct when she stops a moment and leans forward and is almost indistinguishable from the background when she stands away. Such distancing is the exception rather than the rule, as there are many women picking up atomizers and crushing the soft and vulnerable bulbs between their fingers, or upending the scent bottles onto their palms and releasing into the air another puff of strong smell when they reverse their motions and then snatch their hands from the top with a tiny pop of broken suction before smearing a curved index finger in the small wet dot and sending it upwards to flutter about their necks. These women beckon to the girl and to each other with swift and sharp movements, talking and whispering. As they move, the counter is revealed and hidden, giving him short glances of feathery black eyelashes in plastic coffins as if, like the viscera of an Egyptian king, they had been removed from the corpse to which they had once belonged and were to be interred separately.

Suddenly he catches a glimpse of rows of glass bottles lined up in clusters around the bases of advertising cards on which gloriously Technicolor starlets bring their faces close to the camera and hunch bare shoulders that are stained brown by the bottles standing prudishly before them whose faceted tops seem to hang from the ears of the photographic woman like extra-dimensional and overripe earrings which will soon distend their lobes from sheer weight. **Conjecture:** The women must be made of steel or be reinforced with bones in places where most of us have only soft flesh, flesh which can be stroked gently and quietly with the tip of a finger and made as firm and fat as a fuzzy caterpillar that will one day wrap itself in silk and become a beautiful butterfly or moth flexing its wings and flying away over the summer flowers and grasses, turning somersaults in the joy of its new-found freedom and power.

Où sont les papillons: He had once found such a sleeping beauty, one hot July morning when the dew on the grass caused the sharp lawnmower blades kept in perpetual motion by his father to keep for themselves a portion of the tribute collected, forming a thick pad of wet grass as delicate and finely wrought as the feather cloaks of the Hawaiian kings which he could disturb with his small fat fingers or pat gently together, all the while having no fear of the razor-like teeth of the blades that he knew were powerless to hurt him so long as the contraption lay enthralled in sleep.

As he walked behind his father that morning, he saw the knuckles of tree roots appear and then surface-dive into the brown dirt, tasted the bitter sweat that ran over his lip, watched the blue overalls moving in front of him and heard the duet of lawn mower and cicadas in the rustling green trees. It was this morning that he found the white cocoon that lay on the kitchen window sill until one day he came home to find a punctured sheath and a damp moth hanging onto the curtains.

All that afternoon he had thought about whether he would kill and keep the moth or whether he would release it into the dark night which had already begun to grow black with creeping softness, punctured by the visual peeps of the lightning bugs and the drone of crickets. Yet we would be ill-advised to dwell on the outcome of this reflection, need not linger needlessly over the desperate fluttering struggle of the thing to escape the wet fumes he was spraying at its head which pasted to the side of the sink its wings barely dry from their natal dampness until with a panic-stricken pull it would wrench itself free and begin its crippled progress up, out, anywhere at all to escape the poison that surrounded it and which poured from the hole under his finger gone white with pressure and the tension of waiting for the terrible struggle to stop so that he need watch it no longer.

Perhaps he carried the dried creature into his first-grade classroom between two layers of paper towels; perhaps he admired it a while. What is certain is that some years later he found, in the bottom of a drawer, the crushed and wingless torso of a very large moth still smelling in the deepest part of its fur of a faint smell that could very well have been insect poison. And though it was in the winter when he found this and barely midday and the sun was shining into the top layer of the snow it was in the process of icing hard, he could think only of the warm summer night which crystallized into the darker forms of trees, bushes and garbage cans and around in which hung the soft smells of earth, slightly sour milk, and the far-off music that was seeping from the open window across the quiet street but which seemed to be all around them, to be oozing from under the rocks and from the rough bark of the trees against which they leaned, breathless from running. For surely only this could explain the remembrance of gulping into their lungs and stuffing into their ears a part of the night, of being themselves bits of the evening, concentrated clots in its blackness caused by uneven mixing, the dark stars of the earth created to serve as a counter-balance to the light ones of the sky. And all around in this night was the smell of poison.

As he walks by the end of the glass case he catches the sharp smells of the soaps pressed into the shapes of flowers, golf balls, and round-sided fish with perfectly circular mouths which blow bubbles back across their rudimentary fins and symmetrically-arranged scales that stick to the body like watery tics so filled with the fishes' pastel blood that they show none of the legs that would identify them as insects, odors that notwithstanding their initial sharpness to the nose are blunted and softened by the floral perfumes that permeate them, as if in a curious combination of opposites. The combination of the soap's intrinsically soapy smell and its perfume is like the tactile sensations it offers: an unyielding block that nonetheless, when wet, suddenly is mediated by a slippery and almost soft outer skin resisting our attempt to grab the solid bar and hold it tight. **Question:** Why should this scum be? **Answer:** Clearly it was created by a nature working on the principle followed by mothers who give their children sugar with unpleasant medicine: we are more likely to get at the hard truth in life if it is coated with a frivolous and somehow ridiculously slippery skin.

Across the aisle are tables piled with tin boxes opened to reveal the lumpy breads and cakes within that are coated with irregular patches of silver-white. Upon close inspection, these are seen to be nothing but those parts of the crinkled cellophane which catch the light and become opaque, appearing nonetheless to coat the dough with cold hard patches of inedible frosting that would cut the soft insides of the mouth if bitten into too suddenly and be themselves coated with thick red blood.

Behind this table are shelves of smaller cans stacked precariously in medium-sized towers that appear to derive their sole support from the equally teetery piles around them. The cans bear identical labels but have been arranged with no thought to uniformity. Rather than the same picture of hearts of palm or artichokes being stacked monotonously one above the next, the plane they offer to the eye catches the circles of the labels spinning in a wild stroboscopic skew down the stack,.so that the viewer must re-create the entire design from the scrambled parts as if re-constituting a hand-held puzzle. Below them on the bottom shelf is a single row of small cans, each topped with a soft plastic cylinder filled with brown snail shells rising from the solid metal of the can like a trail of bubbles that are cut off by the shelf and which must, by rights, either dissolve into it and become a part of its fibers or form patches of smashed shell and air on its bottom surface. **Note:** The latter will seem the more probable to most of us who have suddenly been seized by revulsion as we gripped the edge of a restaurant table before sitting down and discovered upon investigation a slimy gray blob of chewing gum clinging like a leech to the under-surface. The under-surfaces of things, be they shelves or desks, seem to be preordained as the parking lot of the squashed and discarded detritus of the world; all we see is the Potemkin-village series of upper surfaces presenting to us an artificially positive view of the world.

There is a woman standing behind a desk offering pieces of cheese impaled on red toothpicks to those who show an interest in her. He does show interest, and receives in exchange the slightly tangy bitterness of the cube that changes slowly under his tongue from sharp-edged and cool to soft and slimy, then breaks apart into pieces that catch between his teeth and slide down his throat, carrying the flame of their taste with them but leaving behind some of the secondary heat of near-bitterness it generated which causes his cheeks to tighten slightly into his teeth. Even the toothpick tastes faintly of the cheese's insides. He reverses the toothpick and puts the other end in his mouth. Now he tastes only the dye, which may or may not be mixed with salt from the woman's fingers. Its end begins to shred into slivers, but with some energetic sucking he manages at last to collect the bits of wood and picks them gently from the end of his tongue with his fingertips. He wipes the froth of bubbles and wood into his pants front. The result is a circlet of dark through which light slivers are strewn, like the photographic negative of a fried egg whose hardened yolk has been chopped up with a sharp object and then dispersed throughout the white.

Conjecture: Perhaps this imaginary scrambling was the result of the arrival of a member of the palace guard who had burst in the door on instructions to rid the land of every newborn chicken and immediately began hacking at the egg with his saber, this despite the fact that the animal was quite dead, if indeed it had ever lived. His excuse for this feverish over-reaction might well have been that he had been driven temporarily insane by worry for his life in the event that the prophecy should come true that out of this land will rise a chicken which will lead a revolution against the king, for the king's decree was that all those soldiers who were entrusted with the job of preventing its success would, in the event of their own failure, be plucked naked of body hair and roasted on spits for the last meal of the king and his retinue, who would commit mass suicide afterwards by opening their aged veins.

What happened then?: The king and queen would hear scratching through the gratings of the Moorish windows, then clawings and peckings, and finally the roosters' cries that once banished the ghouls to their graves and now would be summoning them back. The crowing signified the opening of the maws of death and the disgorging of the fearful vengeance-obsessed ghosts of all the slaughtered chickens of the land, which would re-assemble themselves from their fertilizer heaps and the bodies of the humans who had eaten them, organizing into the ranks of airborne fighters whose far-away but insistent cries would have told the cringing king that he could hope for nothing more from life but a quick and relatively painless death, that his own period of suzerainty was over and that of the oppressed was at hand.

Suite: The following morning the creatures will screech their raucous victory cry from the turrets of the palace, otherwise silent but for the quiet rustle of blood down the corridors. Yet this edifice will resist their entry; they will peck in vain against the barred windows and the Cyclopean walls that compose it; the castle will remain the unpuncturable mausoleum of the human suicides whose bodies are draped over couches and propped against tables within until finally, dispirited and fatigued, the resurrected bodies of all these vengeful chickens will simply give up and return dispirited to their graves, this time for good.

Question: Who will have been the victors in the end, the humans or the chickens? **Answer:** We cannot say, any more than we can decide for certain how those who took their own lives within the painted walls of the palace spent the few minutes between the last sips of the purple wine with which they wiled away their last minutes and their deaths. Did these doomed people suddenly engage in a wide-scale if somewhat half-hearted orgy in the hope of collapsing the minutes remaining into a more intense moment in which time was forgotten? Or did they sit with eyes screwed shut and arms wrapped around their knees in an equally final futile attempt to grasp the fleeting essence of the current of time in which they had bathed all their lives? First one, then the other? Neither of these?

Reflection: The admitted necessity and rationality of an unpleasant course of action rarely makes for a pleasant state of mind in the creature who has elected to undertake it. But what does any of it matter? As we hold the bucking crab over the pot of boiling water, we do not think about its pain, for the creature will end soon in red death and distended eyes, in stiffness and silence. And why should we pay any more attention than this to the actions of humans who suddenly grasp that their death will come within a comprehensible period of time, wiping from the earth their hopes, their wishes, and their fears? Yet let us not sweep away all human emotions merely because they have a common end in darkness. We should rather concentrate on the light that precedes it, should focus our attention on the sunrise and not the sunset, on the happy and not the sad. Let us forget our troubles in the joy of wine, in dancing, and in wild sports! Let us make of our lives one great fête! Let us close up our prince's palace against the sickness that ravages the land and stage one great masquerade in its vari-colored, jewel-like rooms. Let us admit no talk of the plague, no unpleasant words of any sort. We will rejoice! We will make merry! We will banish the world outside! **Concession:** Unfortunately our forevers do not last longer than our lives, and we too are doomed, doomed as utterly and irrevocably as the soft honey bees which we, as heartless children, crushed between clean stones in the garden in order to scrape from the cool rounded rock the sweet-tasting insides which lingered long on the tongue and whose mangled and empty corpses we buried in tiny graves under the clover. **Parenthetical:** Sometimes we were not as careful and merely threw the limp scraps into the dusty depressions the raindrops had made at the bottom of the sliding board which would coat their damp body cavities with the thin cover of gray that served as their shroud.

Behind the woman and on another set of shelves are cans of tiger's milk or bamboo shoots, tall glass jars filled with twisted pink flesh or colored green with the glow of pickles, and squat ones filled with the caviar that presses black and grainy against the inside of the glass like a growth of smallpox wistfully surveying the outside world that it will be unable to infect as long as it remains captive within. **Question:** What would be the harm in freeing these poor unfortunate gherkins from their solitary and airless cells, in popping the metal tops off torture chambers built so that the prisoners cannot sit down and are thrown together with a crowd of other unfortunates which bear no greater likeness to them than that they are of the same species and which, were they to meet in their natural habitats of the water or the grassy hillock of some untended field, would certainly have nothing to do with one another? Yet here they are, squashed one into the next with the intermediary of only a thin layer of juice wrung from their insides and some celery seeds.

Suggestion: If a meeting must be arranged between these things, why should they not be given the opportunity to make contact as civilized creatures ought? For they are not naturally unfriendly and would be only too glad of the opportunity to make one another's acquaintances under less strained conditions than those in which they now find themselves. They would probably be more than happy to befriend a trickle of tiger's milk as long as it refrains from curdling in their presence or shake the hand of a tender young bamboo shoot which would undoubtedly be so deficient in social graces that it would trip over its thin legs in its haste to carry out the ritual of some plantlike greeting. **Alternately:** Perhaps such a shoot would make no effort at all to be polite and would merely extend a cold and limp appendage, even going so far as to assume an air of superiority, if it was being introduced to one of the wizened smoked clams, because of its clearly greater height. Such, after all, is the blindness of youth that it thinks great physical size is equivalent to wisdom or value. All of us know that this is laughably far from the truth. Furthermore, as classical scholars will tell us, it is the tallest stalks of wheat whose heads are lopped soonest from their shoulders.

The alcove that shelters all these things is for the moment empty except for the young man who, having just disposed of the toothpick, has nothing to do with his hands and is stroking the side of a can as he stands by a shelf and watching the back of the woman with the cheese. For lack of a better target, she is offering a piece to a child of six or seven who stuffs the whole thing in his mouth, neglecting to remove the toothpick. A moment later he produces the beginnings of what promises to be a lusty yell that is stifled by the sharp right arm of the woman shooting out of its lair behind the table and attaching an iron grip to the child's lower arm. So suddenly has this happened that the child, his eyes closed as he fills his lungs preparatory to the howl, is evidently startled and produces in his shock a fat hiccup and then sudden silence. This apparently makes the woman suspect that he has swallowed not only the partly-chewed cheese cube but the toothpick as well, whereupon she produces a perfect storm of flutterings, solicitous chirpings and useless shushes.

The young man does not want to stand here any longer tracing the accordion ridges beneath the paper skin of these cans and watching this spectacle which is outlined against the background of hurrying people. He curves around the pickled pigs' feet display and moves out again into the main stream. Turning down the aisle nearest him, he moves past the wig counter where rows of white-faced busts sprout carrot-tops or curly masses of blond and whose pale salesgirl reveals herself as the sole human among all of these unthinking heads only by a tiny stifled yawn and a flick of one of her dainty fingers to rearrange the scalpless pigtails that are laid out on the counter like eels at the fish market. These make no reaction to the girl's idle prods and, inasmuch as they are like the fish they resemble, seem to corroborate the words of the famous modern thinker: death out of life destiny makes.

Thus: Anyone who has had any contact with these fibrous twists that seem to blanch pale and then regain their normal hue as the eye follows them down the spectrum of colors on the counter knows that in their present quiescent state they can have only the destiny of becoming part of the sprayed and piled excrescence on the head of a fifty-year-old who grips her husband's arm in a paroxysm of joy as they step down the marble stairs into the ballroom at their first embassy ball. **Further details:** They have finally managed to do it, the woman for whom this means far more than her unexpressive face hardened by years of scowls can show. It means months of servility, years of toadying, so that they too might be among those who dance until the stars have begun to wink out in the soft heavens, might be among those who glide noiselessly in satin and patent leather shoes about the shiny marble floor, whirling their billowing dresses about the sturdy legs of their handsome escorts as they turn to the strains of the waltz that drifts upwards to the glowing chandeliers and mingles with the rich painting on the ceilings from which smiling cherubs perched on the edges of clouds look down upon the champagne growing flat in the delicate thin glasses, the near-exhausted musicians who play slower now and less in tune, the occasional couple who still twirl wearily in each others' arms, and the woman and her husband who sit at a side table, limp but with peace in their hearts, for the woman has been spoken to by a Duchess and her husband has been greeted by a Prince.

Finale: We should not think this evening is over, dissolved into a paste of flat wine and sweat. Let us look in as the weary couple gathers their patched cloaks from the coat room and hurry us from the door so that no one might notice the contrast between the finery underneath and the rags in which they lead their ordinary lives; let us look in as they rattle home in their old Chevy, as they climb weary-limbed up the narrow flight of rickety wooden stairs to the door of their flat, as they collapse in the frayed armchairs that are, save for the table and the bed, the room's sole furnishings. Yet here, abruptly, there is a sudden motion of terror as the woman's hands fly to her head, as she realizes in horror that her suspicion is correct, that somewhere in the cloakroom or on the street her hair has fallen off, that she is totally bald. Then her husband's weary movements, his tired smile, his shake of the head as he seems to realize that games can no longer be played, that the truth must be spoken, his soft intonation: "But my dear, it was totally artificial," the woman's bare head buried in her hands, her sobs dying off into the quiet dawn.

As he passes, he sees from the corner of his eye the scalps hung on the wall from hooks, not varying smoothly in a rainbow of colors like the swathes on the counter, but moving in a step-function of hues as if designed by a tipsy mathematician. There has been no effort to let the yellow change to red, the red to brown or the brown to black, which for all the abruptness of transition would at least have provided us with some sort of rational progression along the spectrum of colors. Instead, the yellow turns sudden jet black and then blushes to red, which grays in immediate age and rejuvenates just as completely to a lush brown that, hanging closest to the aisle, throws up into the air single hairs in a greeting to those people who hurry along trailing a wake of rapidly-moving air, a salutation which goes unseen and unappreciated and which quickly damps down to stillness again and leaves no sign of its ever having been made except the slight fuzziness of the not completely re-integrated hairs on the otherwise shiny surface of the wig.

For some reason, he feels more uncomfortable with this merchandise display than with the soap, the food, or the false eyelashes. It may be the salesgirl's stillness and the fine line of her eyebrows penciled in an inch above the shaved ghosts of their predecessors that seem to have leaped from her eyes in startled curves at something monstrous that she saw; it may be because no one is seated before her counter now nor anyone looking in the mirrors that line the counter like a Mercator projection of a many-faceted diamond, or it may be the strange glow from the row of small rounded lights around the rack on which are hung these strange-smelling cold hanks of hair; it may be that he does not like the tiny puffs of toupées crawling like giant arachnids on the otherwise bald craniums of fatter plastic busts, or it may be merely that he has grown tired of loitering here and sees nothing more to interest him. **Concession:** There are so few times when we can be sure about what it is that he is thinking or feeling that sometimes we are led to wonder if there is not something wrong with our monitoring equipment. At other times, we are convinced that it is not the fault of our pick-up machines but of our presupposition that every motion is supported by internal dialogue, that everything can be analyzed into reasons conscious or unconscious.

Perhaps this is not so; perhaps there are times in our lives when we simply float, our moorings with the world cut and our own production of words and stories silenced so that suddenly the air is full of words not our own that normally are too faint to be noticed, like background radiation that provides the aural snow on a Geiger counter, the world full of data that, had things been other than they are, we could have had a connection with, the air about us heavy with scenarios we could have been a part of but in fact, as if only by chance, are not, until suddenly something rouses us and touches us, a word or a phrase that fingers the all but dead nerve within us in a way that no other words have done simply because they speak to the trivial particularities of our own tiny corner of the world, reeling us down from our drifting among the clouds like great bloated balloons that are finally anchored to the ground, making us once again solid and placing us as finite creatures once again within the world.

He is stopped now before the piles of boxes in which the smooth sheets of tan writing paper seem to have absorbed the color of the box around their edges, for these edges are tinged with the same blue as the cardboard. **Thought:** Is it possible that this sort of reaction of object to object, this transference of spirit from one thing to another, is going on in less visually evident ways all about us? Can it be that our bodies are slowly turning to cloth from contact with our garments? Or, more likely, that we prevent this from happening by our habit of changing materials, which keeps our poor epidermisses so busy trying to rid themselves of the effects of yesterday's cotton that they barely have time to begin to absorb today's linen and will be defeated here too by the nylon of the day after? Are not the wrinkles and toughness in the skin of the old really the result of this terrific strain imposed by flitting about from object to object, never touching anything long enough to allow the sponges on our skins to fill themselves with the essence of that with which they are in contact before they are ripped away and wrung dry again in order to start on something else?

Substantiating evidence: It stands to reason, as there are some things in this world that are clearly natural absorbers and some that are naturally absorbed: objects bifurcate neatly into those whose skins age and become brittle and those that do not. Glass, plastic, and rocks do not change; humans, iron, and wood are examples of things that apparently long to turn themselves into another sort of object. **Q:** What can cause the insatiable desire of things to be something other than they are, to suck the nature of others into their own bodies and become nothing but a second-rate copy of the incorruptible? **A in the form of a Q:** Is not their own wretchedness, their conviction that they must alter themselves in order to become acceptable in the eyes of the world the cause of this futile search for smoothness and health taking them ever further from their goal?

He feels a sudden patch of air-conditioned coolness. As it breaks against him, he pulls his coat a bit closer, then lets it go loose again as subsequent seconds prove that this was no herald of a coming ice age but a mere fluke, a mistaken prophet or one come so early that centuries will have to elapse before its predictions are corroborated, its veracity proven. He stretches out a finger and ruffles the edges of the stationary lying exposed in its paperbound coffin, naked save for a belt of clear cellophane that seems to strap it in and prevent post-mortem cramps from turning it into origami flowers. He tickles the cut end of this ream, gathers slightly more than half with his finger, and jerks it upwards so that the sheets phlipp down flat gain in a stream that was for a moment a motion-picture blur, a pleasant tannish half-existence through which, he might even have believed, he could have stuck any of his fingers without damage either to himself or the blur. **Commentary:** No damage, certainly, not at least in any conventional sense of physical damage.

But damage, of course, can occur to the spirit as well. Who can doubt that someone who had thought to have found a kind of half-world in which solid things give way to beautiful miasmas, a world in which a person who is but a cloud himself can have no fear of being ill-supported by equally filmy furniture and floors, and found it destroyed by a finger that poked inquisitively into its center since it is but a creation of sight and not of any of the other senses would in fact suffer the most acute remorse and disappointment? **Concession:** Of course many of us would have been able to say beforehand that this would be the result, for we have learned that of all the senses, touch is the most destructive and brutal because it is the most direct. To take into our hands the fragile things that make up the world is to invite tragedy and heartbreak, for we are liable to crush them without meaning to or even being aware of it.

Other results: Worse still would be the self-hatred and remorse that must follow such an act of such unintentional destruction on our part: we are liable to decide that we are great clumsy creatures too graceless to live side by side with such beautiful thinnesses as those we have smashed. In fact, we must merely learn how to co-exist with them, learn how to keep them on the perimeters of our perception and not force them into the hot glare of its center where the wax of their wings will melt and cause them to smash on the rocks of our bodies. **Lesson:** So much heartache on our part would be avoided if we were able to figure out at the beginning how close we can bring ourselves to the various elements of our world. The noblest efforts of our greatest philosophers have been attempts to draw this ideal map with man in the center and the things animate and inanimate of our world spread out around him at varying ideal distances. This explains the fascination the stars and planets have always held for us, for even from the beginning of science we must have had a presentiment that some day we would be able to make drawings of the heavenly bodies in relation to the earth, find the distance of each part of the universe to our own blob of dirt and rock. The similarity between microcosm and macrocosm is inescapable and the fascination of moral philosophers with the heavenly realm completely comprehensible. **Furthermore:** Man, we might well say, is the wandering planet, the creature whose distances to other things he must himself decide. The pleasure of the philosopher in that natural system where this question is already answered, where all is completely decided and immobile, is the affinity all of us have felt for the simple, the concrete, and the unlettered, for the love of the sturdy country lass and the friendship of the ruddy country lad, for that pure and simple grief we experience over the graves of friends that lie now in the clay under the gnarled apple trees dropping the pink tears of their petals onto the cold slabs below.

Near his probing finger are cardboard boxes of plastic pen cylinders, some of whose cartridge tips have rid themselves of the wax that had stopped their mouths and are bleeding bits of blue blood onto their container so that anyone who comes by later looking for clues will be able to tell at a glance the nobility of the victims and see how they met their untimely ends, though much about the nature of the wounds would likely not be evident. Due to the closeness of their confinement, a small dribble is about all any of them can manage with no possibility of writing any words—unless, of course, some well-meaning bystander catches the look in one of their eyes and is able to deduce that he is meant to take the pen into his fingers. At this juncture, he will not, as he had undoubtedly thought, write his name or several tempus fugits or now is the times but would instead find himself trying to hold with all his strength a mightily bucking suddenly-come-to-life creature that would pull his hand to the side of the box and force him to write out "we we..." or "Rache" before it finally collapses into shudders subsiding into stillness, leaving the person with nothing but a sense of puzzlement and a certainty that the childishly vulgar connotations he has for the first message cannot possibly be what the energetic thing had meant to convey nor a vague interest in the girl Rachel whose face had filled the dying thing's last thoughts.

Commentary: The blindness of the unknowing is so much sadder than that of the physically sightless, even if the latter kind of disability has been incurred by the attempt to save a golden-haired child who leaned from the top floor of a burning building and fluttered her delicate hands in panic-stricken appeals for help [the swaying ladder, the screams of the reinforcement fire engines, the flames curving out against the night sky not in the energetic and momentary flits of fireplace flames but in the leonine ripples of the larger and more powerful wall of fire, the screams of the trapped, the collapse of the top floor]. Life is filled with unpleasantnesses, and sometimes the most unpleasant thing of all is to have to cope with those events that arouse our intellectual disgust at their trite construction or bad execution but which also, for better or worse, evoke our sympathy.

Above these bundled pens rises the one writing implement which must have sold its comrades into slavery in exchange for its own safety and the advancement of its position. To its head, after all, has been affixed a towering ostrich plume of the same bright purple as the robe that girds its slim body so tightly it ends up being as smooth and shiny as the pen's own skin. Around its waist has been clasped a thin girdle of gold-colored metal and on its feet has been slipped a single delicate shoe that poises its point on a ball bearing of the same gold encircling its body, which in turn is affixed to a pedestal of marble held off the shelf by four small carved feet of metal. The pampered creature leans back in an attitude of inflexible hauteur, the cross-currents of the room ruffling the individual furry fingers of its headdress in the shy admiration of a powerful being for an especially well-formed specimen of a weaker one.

Theoretically possible scenario: The blue and green fellows it has betrayed will be carried to their eventual deaths while the upright pen, by virtue of its new-bought gaudiness, will remain untouched and unhurt here on its throne, seeing as time passes many new generations of simpler pens such as it once was come and go. **Note:** It will have either to refuse to see them being carried in by the cartonload and carried out one by one, or convince itself that it did right in buying its own life and safety in return for the lives of its fellows. Had it not done so, some other less deserving pen would have been willing to play the traitor, and it would itself have died as wretched a death as its fellows. The world is cruel, it must reflect, but there are ways to beat it at its own game, even if doing so involves some mental acrobatics bordering on mendacity to convince one's self one is doing as one ought.

In another box nearby lie handfuls of sleeping erasers that give off tiny surface fragments as the release of tension arrives in their restless dreams of eradicating whole pages of the symphony-in-progress of the wizened genius who uses pencil instead of the ink that spotted his earlier works with the meandering tracks of diminutive fingerprints and with an occasional palm-printed half moon too faint to obliterate the notes but which did nothing for the general neatness of the score, or of reducing to blankness the entire pile of ageing love letters of our long-dead sweetheart tied with purple ribbon and placed with a now dry and scentless rose in the drawer of a dresser

Reflection: Were they not so heavily drugged by their captors, any one of them could be counted on to erase up to sixty pages an hour of important graphite traces, and just one boxful could destroy the world's pencilled riches in less than a year. **Yet:** We cannot figure out why it is that there has never been reported any case of the terrible destruction that such an unleashed eraser would make, for certainly there are some lying around in the drawers of long-dead children, unused and falling apart into dry fragments and old enough to have outlived the effects of the drug. Why are these not about on the streets, carrying on their destruction and wreaking the havoc they were brought up to cause? Why, for that matter, have not the unused erasers of forgotten pencils sitting quietly in pencil cans or lost under sofas wrenched themselves free from the metal clips that bound them? **Self-doubt:** Is it possible that we have been wrong all these years in supposing that erasers are sleeping volcanoes? Is it possible that they present no threat to us at all, being totally debilitated not by our chemicals but instead by our cool climate which is so different from that of the sweltering jungle in which they were born and from which, at least spiritually the descendants of the rubber tree's most saleable product, they were taken in their prime, ripped from the bosom of their mother who cooed to them the raucous but soothing cries of the gaudily-colored parrot, who sang to them in the night the peeps of the tree frogs and the rustlings of the lions swishing between the ferns, whose all-seeing glowing eye of sun diminished at night to a cooler white moon to which her awakened infants could look for reassurance?

Worse: Is it possible that we have wasted hundreds of liters of this soporific chemical and hours of our worry time? Perhaps these cubes of tan and pink rubber can only come alive with the sharp heat of a vigorous rubbing and not spontaneously at all. Perhaps that power which had seemed controlled by us is harnessed instead by nature, and it is not we who render our world safe but some other beneficent force over which we have no control. **Conclusion:** May we bow our heads a moment in admission of our own frailty and of the power of the unknown.

At eye level several feet off is an arrangement of clear plastic paperweights in which half-opened flowers and small translucent sea shells are trapped. The blossoms disclose a pearl of air nestled in their petals which they offer shyly, the smaller inner petals still seeing to hide beneath it. Perhaps the partly-furled flower is pressing against the mass of clear hardness that impedes its progress towards full bloom, straining and sweating small drops of liquid which are re-absorbed immediately into the petals since they cannot permeate the plastic that surrounds them, moisture which will ultimately rot the flower within its confines like a prisoner who dies of leprosy in his chains, turning the flower purple and brown and then withering it to a thin dry film that leaves a rose-shaped hole in the center of the paperweight.

Reflection: This state of tension for the rose, struggling and straining against an implacable foe, is probably no more unpleasant than the state of the plastic that surrounds it. Initially, when the plastic found itself suddenly surrounding a beautiful young rose, it was unable to contain its surprise and delight that it should have been chosen as the one worthy of protecting and displaying this piece of beauty. Yet its delight will not have lasted long. Eventually it will begin to feel the physical discomfort of this hard opaque tumor in its otherwise crystal-clear body, begin to dislike sitting down for any long periods of time because of the pain of the position. And presently it will be unable to forget even for a minute of its waking life (which grows longer each week: it develops insomnia) the incredibly unpleasant sensation that, it decides, can be compared only to having swallowed a basketball that its body keeps trying to squeeze to the bursting point within.

Still it does not curse the rose inside it, does not chafe at the long hours of the exhibitions it must now give to expose the flower to the eager public that would otherwise be beating its door down at all hours and robbing it of even the last small amount of sleep it manages to get, does not complain of the way its ribs are beginning to stick out under its glassy skin or of the bags that are starting to form under its haggard eyes. For it respects this rose more than it can say, is conscious that all its life it has longed to be near such an object of great beauty compared with which it is nothing, is conscious of the duty of every creature to grow what flowers it can and, if it is not gifted with an especially green thumb, to support those so endowed and protect their products.

Yet soon its whisper will grow hoarse and its voice strident with the repetition of the rationalizations it mouths to itself each morning as it curses the dawn for having broken its fragile fitful slumber. Those justifications now sound hollow in its own ears and have become positively unbearable to its wife, whose life it has so changed by the public appearances that take it far from home for many days on end. Now it goes completely naked, so that as many as possible may see the beauty within it, and it has virtually stopped eating for fear that the digesting food will obscure or befoul the rose.

It will be sitting quietly one evening for a few well-earned and all-too-rare moments of relaxation, simply letting the cool of nightfall flow around its curves when the first real thoughts of rebellion come creeping up to its head and buzz around inside for a moment before it manages to beat them away like a swarm of annoying cranial mosquitoes. But ideas come back, and before the night is out it will have thought long and hard with growing resentment about the thing in its belly that seems to take its sacrifices for granted, that seems to regard all this suffering as incurred by way of giving the thing its due. Before the morning comes (for it will stay awake all this long night), its hatred of the thing it had once vowed to serve so faithfully will have coalesced into a lump as hard as the thing itself, and its conviction will be strong that no matter how much greater than itself the thing that it respects is, the object of its respect cannot demand of it the abandonment of its happiness and goals. It will be convinced that perfection and greatness are intellectual values which, when they call for more than intellectual support, should be rejected by those weaker than they, and that nothing is worth the sacrifice of its own dignity.

Having realized this, it will welcome the dawn for the first time in many months, for it will know that the hour of its deliverance is at hand. It will creep up to its bedroom where it will stand looking for a last tender moment at its wife who is curled under the covers like a baby animal by its mother, though it will shed no tear from its sleep-bleared eyes, being now past the point where it can feel anything at all. It will walk softly down the stairs, being careful to step only on the parts where they do not creak, and force its stiff legs to carry it to the kitchen where it will find the butcher knife behind the hard-boiled egg cutter and the salad forks. Then the walk out the back door and onto the moss that dampens the soles of its bare feet and the grass that draws wet whip-strokes on its insteps until it reaches the copse of birches by the pond. There it will plunge the knife into its abdomen, cutting from it the tumor and turning onto the grass and sand the bloody mess from which its life's liquids ooze. As it teeters and falls, it will be overcome not only by the pain that paints the world around it searing yellow but with a sudden exhaustion of the body that dulls its consciousness of the blood spurting rhythmically from its gaping stomach cavity, an exhaustion through which float its last thoughts of its shattered life, of its inability to devote itself as perhaps it should have done to this flower.

Just before it dies, its brow will soften and the thick creases its gasping mouth and terrified eyes have chiseled into its forehead will disappear, its lips will close in a sort of smile, and its eyes will lose their look of fear. When the sun is high and its wife finally traces the footprints to the blood-bespattered ground, she will see the body lying there, its hands reaching towards the dirt-encrusted and fly-covered visceral mass in what may be a gesture of renewed love or of regret for its own ruined life. Yet she cannot know which, nor perhaps did it itself understand the meaning of the feeling that overwhelmed it as it sank in final sleep and death and moved its emptied body as close to the clotted lump as it could before it limpened and became motionless.

Not all the paperweights have flowers and sea shells inside of them. Some are swirled with a sort of marbled twist of what looks like gossamer but which is less solid even than this, being only the wraiths of the colors that have traced their paths on the inside surfaces of the glass and have left these vague spirits behind to mark their progress. **Human analogy:** We all leave behind this sort of marker as we move through life, or at least those of us that are strong-willed and ambitious. **Further:** The twisting trails are not one solid color but a mixture of several variations. **Lesson:** This is the case with us humans as well, with us whose effect on those around us is not constant but rather a succession of mixings of our own basic color with those of the ones with whom we interact and whose pigments may well not only overpower or change ours for the moment but also effect a more permanent alteration on our color dispensers in the direction of the stronger shade. **Note:** There are some people who operate under the notion that the point of the apparatus is constancy, that the person who can achieve a solid color the earliest in life is the best person and that the aim of the remainder of life should be to keep one's track as pure as possible. They are wrong.

At the end of the counter is a line-up of chalky-white plastic busts of composers whose famous profiles make all but unnecessary the names molded into their bases. Though one or two of their number is available for sale with the pianos several floors up, the greatest part of the collection is here, perhaps because one use to which they might be put is that of a paperweight. However they are a good deal lighter than the glass globes with which they rub shoulders. We cannot expect the weight of their thoughts or the power of their prestige to subdue papers blown with any degree of force by a ruffling wind; it is folly to think that filmy white thoughts (for such are what chalky busts must have) can do anything to keep down more substantial correspondence which, set in motion by the cool autumn wind that whispers through the screens on the window and bathes the room with the smells of burning and dry leaves that crackle softly in the yard, would as likely as not simply upset insubstantial portrait busts such as these that had the temerity to act as if they were able to subdue them.

Reflection: This is cruel of the wind and the paper, that could without any damage to themselves just as easily have left the thin-skinned and ghostly pale busts under the illusion that they were doing some good. It would have cost the paper nothing to sit still a while. So what if the bust thinks that it is because of its own inherent strength that those under it are so calm? Sacrifice of self is virtuous, and even more virtuous is the course dictated to the paper in this particular situation. For what it would be overthrowing, were it to take the more hot-blooded course and simply upset this plastic shell, would be not merely some molded synthetic blob but rather a shrine to a great man. And shrines to the dead are a very good idea.

Justification: Support of composers and their like during their lifetimes is always a risky business because one never knows which of them is going to turn out to be a great master, and the terrible possibility exists that we will be conned into supporting someone who is merely good or possibly even mediocre. After these people have been dead for a good long while and we have had a chance to assess their works, however there is less probability that we will honor the wrong sort of person. **Reflection:** As a great writer once said, memory is the most valid form of life. By this we can only suppose that he meant it is best to wait until people are dead before we make any positive judgements or award any sort of honors, and the only way to do this is to be respectful to things like busts of the people or pieces of their printed music and their graves. **Note:** Some of us are anxious to get a government grant in support of the arts to erect a Tomb of the Unknown Composer in some suitable spot. Not only would this show our regard for those whose works are more well-known than the whereabouts of their bodies, but it would give a grand goal to the numerous musical societies across the country, who could devote their efforts to beautification of the tomb and to designing flower arrangements in musical shapes such a violins or trumpets, as well as to laying flowers on the graves of any local musicians.

Suggestion: Such societies might well look into the possibility of having the new meeting room of the local public library named after the composer of their choice, and they might devote several meetings to deciding on the proper color scheme, decoration, and wording for the plaque that they would surely want to erect on the spot to remind all those who passed of the noble purpose of their musical society and of the great name that graces the hall in which they are nibbling their sugar cookies and sipping at their watery cups of tea.

He looks up, and sees the escalator over the top of the boxes of the lined paper and the piles of octagonal pencils that lie beside them. Reaching forward, he replaces on the counter the small statue with which he has been playing, that, he had soon discovered, had in its base a hole for sharpening pencils.

In this process, the painted protrusions are chopped from pencil ends, and the wooden hide that has only just begun to turn the neutral gray which indicates that it is nearly healed and once again out of pain, protection for the end of the tender black nerve in its center that is just about tortured back to the level of its wooden sheath where its torment will at last procure for it peace and protection, is skinned away and once more made susceptible to all those inhumanly painful contacts with paper. **NB:** It would only be able to endure these contacts again by the subterfuge of telling itself that soon it would be worn down again and be as protected as when it was young and surrounded entirely by its wood. **Reconsideration:** Were it to allow itself to be honest, this lie would crumble to the ground like the small ebony particles of the graphite that the torturer blows from the silver blade in the sharpener. For the graphite knows well that its life is nothing but a succession of sharpenings and dullings, of painful episodes, a series of preludes to the dance of death which, if it allowed itself to be conscious of them rather than letting them merely slip by unremarked like the sound of the cicadas' screams in the darkening summer afternoon which go unnoticed to all but him who suddenly opens an invisible door in his mind and is abruptly aware of the song of bitter woe that makes the air jagged with its piercing power, would render the pencil quite as dispirited as those who cringe in the corner of the condemned hold on the eve before their execution or as paranoid, hypersensitive, and hallucination-prone as those who insist on seeing in every inanimate thing the ghost or token of a living being that feels and reacts as would the thing it resembles.

Standing still and looking up, he notes the rows of ridges on the escalator steps that slide smoothly from their source like the colored stripes on the toothpaste that, he discovered one morning to his ten-year-old dismay, were the product of the notches on the choker through which the paste had to pass and not a quality of the substance itself which had gushed white and unappetizing from the ragged slit in the belly of the tube. About a foot up they slowly reveal the jagged edge of their teeth and become steps which seem unplacated by the soothing hum of the machinery, for not until they reach the top do they feel safe enough to re-cover these fangs and slide them back into the works which run metal fingers over their skins and teeth as they recede.

Surprisingly enough, those people who dot the stairs and who disappear upwards as they gesticulate or talk do not seem afraid of these incisors that are bared so close to their vulnerable ankles. In fact, except for an occasional nip at an unruly or clumsy child, the stairs do not inflict any injuries at all. **Conjecture:** It may be that riding this escalator is like standing on an alligator's head: as long as the position on top can be maintained, there is no cause of worry—another case of our civilizations's clever use of the hitherto unchained power of nature to provide that safe energy it needs to stay strong and healthy and free.

Alternate theory: The whole thing may simply be stuffed and hence quite harmless, the life-work of a certain taxidermist whose every waking moment was spent in installing the levers and motors that would make the jaws move as if powered by the animal and who got to know every individual line on every one of the animals' skins so that finally the conviction grew on the man that his own brain had taken on the pattern of these ridges and that he himself was becoming one of the creatures in his great machine. **Note:** It is lucky that the contraption was almost completed when he was found that night in his workroom, out of his head with pain and liquor and laughing like a hyena, for the worktable and the knife he clasped in his hand were covered with the blood that formed a pool on the floor where under a table were later found two squashed and jellylike blobs that might have been his eyes, thrown away with a shrug by an unconcerned and unperceptive janitor; out of his own eye sockets stared not the soft brown orbs of human eyes but two horrible glassy yellow pupils just like those that glinted in rows from the corner of the half-lit room where sat the motionless creatures in the machine.

Hearsay: It is said that when the man came to his senses the next morning he began screaming and, though he made no effort to stop the doctors and nurses from plucking the horrible marbles from his wounded face, has not stopped vociferating since. **Fact:** If a curious visitor to a certain asylum ventures down a particular darkened corridor that contains at its end a single half-lit cell, he or she will hear from behind the locked and padded door the hoarse wheezing sounds of a person trying to shriek through vocal chords ripped to shreds by overuse, a sound that will at first interest the visitor and then fill him or her with feelings of horror so vague but so insistent that he or she will snatch from that door the hand that was all but ready to knock in inquiry and scurry to the lighted hallway. **Result of visit:** From that day forth, the person will never be able to wash from memory either this sound or what seemed the grotesquely twisted smile of the thin nurse who looked at the visitor from behind her desk in the suddenly deserted main lobby, nor her unblinking eyes that seemed to have slit to the thinness of a leopard's.

Result of madness: The engineers will have chosen more stable sorts than the poor mad taxidermist to finish the machine—men who, unlike him, were not aware that the end of our life is darkness and despair, for though we are more than a little bit attached to our belief that we are the dearest and most intelligent of God's creatures, we should seriously consider the possibility that we are but unfortunate accidents in nature's evolutionary chain, one of those truncated branches containing dinosaurs and the like that geneticists are fond of adding onto odd and bare-looking spots of trees of descent, one of the freaks conceived one night when our racial father was in a particularly lascivious mood and had for the first time gotten up the nerve to ask our racial mother to engage in some of the more outré pleasures known to the ancients and she, being a bit tipsy herself and more adventurous at heart than she felt proper to let on, had giggled a quick and only slightly shocked giggle and smiled a crooked smile of acquiescence.

He pulls regretful fingers from the piles of envelope packages in which are bound prim rows of smooth folded paper artworks, those sorts of envelopes that stick shut not with a lick from our moist and pulpy tongues but merely by our pressing together the two flaps that now hang one above the other. These are dry lips here, pale, bloodless, and paper-thin, as if the sun and a wordless terror had leeched from them the color that, in a moment, will return all in a rush as the strained and contracted blood vessels open with a weary shudder. **More on lips:** These are not, however, cruel lips about to issue an order for flogging or torture, nor are they especially attractive or kind ones. Instead they are emotionally androgynous lips that, by their parallel position and seeming lack of any connection of upper to lower, express simultaneously everything and nothing, show sympathy to the weak and admiration of the strong, condemnation of the guilty and a promise of exoneration to the wrongfully accused—and so magical is their ability to be all these things that even if the same suppliant were to come to them at two different times in opposite circumstances and receive from the paper idol two opposite messages, the person would attribute this alteration to a change in the envelope and not to himself, would leave even more convinced of the thing's powers and of his own dumb luck in having been born under the protection of so understanding a deity and giving no thought at all to the sculptor who made such a marvelous statue that produces these wondrous results as a factor of its design alone.

Lesson: Men are blind sorts, refusing to acknowledge the contributions of the other people who have made the world they live in, moving in a perpetual cloud of the belief that no one has inhabited the earth before them and that they alone have shaped the universe. They are unable to see that the smallest thing in this world is the culmination of a lengthy process of development and of the most concentrated thought which stands supporting the timbers of the present like the back walls of a house that, though invisible from the façade, are nonetheless vital to the structure's existence. Thus they make plans for what they see as monumental changes that will re-organize the world, and do not realize that the commonplace things they understand so quickly and against whose bland background the projected influence of their own work seems monumental is itself a construction of a huge number of similar monumental changes which have been eroded by time from the mountains their creators envisioned to mere unimposing wrinkles. Nor are they aware that their own contribution will never induce in their intellectual heirs the same compulsion as it did in them, never appear the same to generations that follow precisely because it has been accepted, digested, and taken for granted.

Query: What, upon realizing the intrinsic impossibility of passing on our vision in anything approaching its full power, should we do? Should those in whose minds the mountains are growing simply cease their labors when they reflect that to their great-grandchildren their work will be not the huge craggy rocks they envision towering over the waves but a mere pile of sand among other piles, when they think of the queer contrast between the total dedication of their beings to what they hope to produce and the merely relative stature of the product of that complete immersion once it is done? Why should they aim for the sky when each level becomes the ground upon which the next generation grows? Should they despair when they have begun to understand that the viewpoint which filled them totally is only one chip in the mosaic of life?

Possible solutions: It seems likely that at times they would be incapable of ever admitting the debilitating power of this paradox in any but a purely intellectual fashion and could not be affected by it, would reassure themselves that they do what they do because they must, and are not concerned with what will happen to their works, would respond that the world impels them to what they do, crying out for liberation or justification or vindication that only they can provide. At other times they wonder if this must not be faced as a real issue and be allowed to impose its consequences, as they have always prided themselves on being open-minded and willing to consider all contingencies. Then, they must think sometimes that perhaps the answer is somewhere in the middle, in that mythical place where the more tiresome of our savants believe all unfound answers to take refuge. Or it may be that they are simply cowards who, though unable to block their minds to the consideration of such issues, are not going to let them influence their lives in any way.

The package of envelopes before him on the shelf is crushed on one of the upper corners, each piece of paper having the same squashes and creases as the one in front and in back of it like a line of kick dancers that retract and extend and now have crumpled in unison to the cues of the music. Yet, because of a sudden and protracted silence during which not even the scrapes of the musicians putting away their bows and reeds or the stifled giggles of those who are indulging in a bit of mirth are heard, they are now unable to release this position, being as they are constrained by their contracts to wait until they hear the proper cues from the musicians before moving. Alternately, it may be that the lack of any attempt toward getting out of this position is due only to a common cramp of all the individual envelopes simultaneously.

NB: The first explanation is amenable to expansion into a more general lament about how we poor creatures are nothing but hired dancers on the stage of life, bound by the contract of our birth to performing our lives away in front of a shadowy and vaguely-seen audience whose reactions, whether positive or negative, cannot affect the fact that we must dance, and furthermore must do so in a rigidly-controlled manner to the sounds produced by an equally unseen set of musicians whose instruments sing the songs of human joy and misery.

He steps onto the bottom stair of the escalator, behind a girl whose tight shorts are barely able to contain her massive and pulpy thighs that quiver as she breathes and are covered with the texturing of shallow criss-crossed lines like ceremonial scars, and in front of an old man with carefully wetted and brushed hair that makes his red protruding ears the more evident. The old man seems to have gotten it into his head that one of the younger generation has been rude to him by cutting in front on the moving staircase and is thus showing his annoyance by glaring at the back of the young man's blue jacket with as much venom as his slightly out-of-focus eyes can muster and by muttering and snorting to himself. This goes unnoticed by the young man notes that this almost completely enclosed oblique shaft between two sound-damped floors is alive with noises produced by the people in it which bounce off the walls, only to be re-absorbed into the aural torpor of the floor above them.

About midway, there is a break in the wall through which he can see the contrary downward motion of the other elevator and of the people on it who are separated from him and those around him by a sheet of Plexiglas and do not turn to watch the people moving upward. **Rhetorical query:** Is it not our archetypal nightmare to find ourselves on such a conveyance moving slowly but unstoppably away from the woman for whom we have been searching since we were children together in our kingdom by the sea, to whom we begin to gesticulate and cry out? Of course, she cannot see us since she is turned towards the other wall and seems to study with an inexplicable intensity a wretched chow dog held in the arms of a stony-faced nanny to whom clings a child sticky with peppermint that opens its mouth in what must be a wail, but which cannot be heard for the clear barrier between the stairs and remains imprinted on the mind as a wordless cry of misery made the more moving and potent for concentration in one sense rather than two. For this wail cannot penetrate the barrier any more than can one's own inarticulate cries of recognition and discovery, and the face moves slowly past the portal and downward and is gone, leaving in its wake only a succession of totally ordinary faces that stare straight ahead as still as masks. **Note:** Usually in such cases the dream coordinator is more alive to the symbolism of such things than to permit the male to be moving upwards to salvation while the adored woman moves just as swiftly downwards to damnation, for this goes against all of our deeply-ingrained cultural presuppositions.

As the escalator brings him up towards the level of the next floor, it offers to him the opening space that seems the vaster and more lofty because he cannot yet see the floor or the people on it and is still several feet below its level. As he rises, air full of dampness, mulch, and plants sweeps across his face and fills his lungs, and tables of African violets come into view. Over them hover arc lamps as well as a thin man who purses his lips and pinches brown leaves from the plants with flicks of his perfectly manicured fingers and sympathetic clenches of the fist on his free hand.

The fragile pink and purple blossoms of these violets look out of place against the lush hairy leaves, as if someone has slipped by their table one day and, looking guiltily from under his fedora to make sure he was not observed, had pulled a brown paper sack from the insides of his voluminous overcoat and sprinkled onto the plants an assortment of the sugar frosting roses from his daughter's birthday cake, the paper poppies bought on the street for a good cause, decaying near-transparent yellow cloth daisies from his wife's Easter bonnet of five years ago and even, surprisingly enough, a rosette of the Legion of Honor.

Alternative: Perhaps the plants had become so lonely and begun to feel so barren that they had embarked one night on a search and seizure mission which had resulted in the appearance in their bosoms the next morning of a slew of small delicate flowers already dropping their soft thin lifelines to the crown of their new mothers, having either a very short memory from which all images of their former protectors had been expunged or a gift for simply making the most of whatever situation presented itself. This does not eliminate the possibility that should there come sweeping down an irate squadron of the plants that only a short time before had been contented mothers and were now childless (think of the tears and lamentations at finding their breasts bare and cold that terrible morning when they awoke to find the results of the violets' robbery—but the tears are now shed and the plants have nothing in their roots but a desire for revenge, a wish to tear stem from stem those that had stolen their progeny from them), the delicate and guileless flowers would simply break these new-made ties and allow themselves to be carried away again without a murmur.

Note: There is some question as to whether, should this occur, such sorts of vengeance-ridden flora could rid themselves of the poison of their thoughts sufficiently enough to leave any room for the milk of maternal love to flow in their veins again, whether indeed this liquid would not have long since curdled and been ejected from their bloodstreams to make room for the stronger liquor which is so fiery that by the time the plants get themselves prepared to act, it will have eaten away most of the inner lining of the tubes. It would seem that a raid of vengeance would leave all of them worse off than they had been before: the flower without a plant competent to care for it, both plants either childless or in no condition to pay a child any attention.

The flowering Christmas cacti nearby have been deceived by their keepers, for it is not even winter, much less Christmas—at least not outside where the sky is dark from the clouds of warm summer rain and where the time is not close to any sort of joyous birth. From the ends of their hairy green segments drip feathery red pendants that do not become heavy enough to fall until, somewhat paradoxically, they are dried and shriveled, caked with the dust of their unshed pollen. Each plant is elevated on a tall pedestal that lets its fronds hang free over the side of the pot and down the sides of the pole, so that the whole arrangement seems like a forest of heads on pikes whose executioners have done up their locks, in the manner of the hairdressers to Egyptian princesses, into a thousand braids which drip the blood that the necks, their muscles still tightened in spasms of terror, are not able to shed.

Behind the Christmas cacti, baskets of ferns hung from poles descend into view, and soon he sees a line of the plants across the top of the more colorful half of his horizontally-bisected vision field. The baskets look like a set of rattan cages from the tops of which are crawling the huge green spiders that had been imprisoned within, insects that brace their furry legs against the outsides of the reed covering in their attempts to pull from the constraints their dark and pendulous bodies. **Note:** Some philosophers argue that this escape is foolhardy, for while the creatures lived within the basket their bodies were supported, the delicacy of their legs was universally admired, and they were fed and watered regularly. **Objection:** But on the other hand these advantages were clearly not enough, for after all did not this life corrupt their youthful potential, soften their bodies and reduce their ambitions to nothing but desire for physical pleasure?

Commentary: Surely this sort of pampered existence is the most debilitating and terrible there is, for it plays on the strong bodily wants of the young and leads them to do things they will later regret. There is more than a good possibility that, try as they may to hoist themselves from their baskets of leisure, their thin legs will be too frail to pull them from the embrace of the hempen net into which they were once so glad to sink and they will fall back exhausted into its embrace, quivering impotently in the strain of great effort. And, having once admitted this, it seems necessary to question the point in their ever having realized that they must make an effort to escape their dissipated state and cease their debauchery—for the realization has brought them nothing but heartache and muscle strain and the remorse of knowing that once when they were young they made a wrong choice that has laid waste to their lives.

Implication: Would it not have been far better for them to have lived out their time in unquestioning enjoyment of these bodily pleasures and die a happy and peaceful death? Would it not have been better never to have tried to escape at all? For even making the unlikely assumption that these insects could have overcome the effects of long years of inactivity with mere willpower or the strainings of their frail feelers, there is still to be considered the situation which they would have to face in the outside world where competition with the younger and not so dissipated arachnids would be necessary. In this case, they might very well find that their newly-acquired resolution and high-flown principles are really of very little practical use at all. They might find that being well-meaning is not a saleable quality and that indeed they are so buffeted about by those who have never known the temptation to which they succumbed and which thus pay so little attention to them and provide them even less sympathy that they would soon lose all of the firmness of purpose they had developed and long once again for the haven of their sloth and the protection of their inactivity.

Conclusion: If they are able to drag themselves back to these baskets from this disastrous encounter with the world, they will in any case not have much longer to live, for their hearts as well as their strength will be broken and they will hope only that their poor battered souls will soon leave their equally bruised bodies. If, as is most likely, they are quite unable to find their way back to the haven they so recently spurned, they will probably die as they stand or as they push their way blindly through the crowd that cannot understand their groans and would feel nothing but derision for their pot-bellies and tattered garments.

By now he is almost at the top of the escalator; he sees the fluffy clouds of water vapor that puff from the atomizer another attendant is holding at arm's length over the display of terraria whose plastic upper halves have been removed and are lying on an empty part of the shelf, clear half-round shells, some of which do not sit straight on the ones below them in the pile, making more precarious the perch of the ones above them. He can make out the shapes and colors of the tiny rocks in front of which grow miniature plants and diminutive china frogs, and it is possible to imagine the myriad of tiny drops that are at this moment being strewn onto the microscopic flowers of the moss and the fingernail-sized ground covers.

These plastic Lilliputian showcases that are so amusing when presented alone on a dining room table or on top of a stand by the front windows seem somehow ridiculous when seen here. After all, what was so appealing about them was their air of having come from another world than that which spawns us gross and bumbling humans, and of having been only momentarily abandoned by the miniature fauna hiding in tiny nearby bushes that would soon come prancing out to put on a show for the gargantuan eyes that are pressed against the glass. When he sees them now in decapitated rows in the process of being looked after by someone his own size, he is faintly disgusted and does not even try to bend his head to see the rainbow through this white cloud of drops that is fluffing and preening itself before one of the lamps which cranes its neck over this table, a cloud that settles and then re-inflates as the attendant plunges and releases the handle of the bottle.

He steps off the end of the escalator onto the floor level and skirts the edges of the plant display, hesitating a moment before the rows of pots growing swamp grass that are lined up behind the glass partition. He raises a hesitant finger to the partition as if trying to confirm his suspicion that the drops that have steamed up the glass and then cut through that steam with their downward trails are on the other side. His finger brushes the smooth warm surface and leaves a small smear of grease, blurring the drop behind it on the other side that has joined with another and is now heavy enough to cut one great swath, snowballing as it goes with the accumulating weight of the drops it ingests by collision. These drops are probably doing nothing more than sitting around waiting for their own evaporation, so it is a good thing that something came along that was able to use their pointless lives for some meaningful purpose.

Warning: We would be well-advised not to conclude that those people who can answer the question of what they are going to do tomorrow or next week or next year are more worthy of adulation than the rest of us. To be sure, those who go out with the intention of saving the world are the ones who are going to do it if anybody does, and those of us who live from day to day just may not seem too important to this sort of folk. But our mistake has been in thinking that there is some particular reason why the world ought to be saved, in feeling guilty at taking the time that the more energetic spend thinking about what is going to happen come next year or ten years to look what is going on around us now. Time is going to keep on ticking away without our having a thing to do with it; nobody needs us to go out and push the hands of the clock around the dial. So there's no reason why we can't just sit back and let time flow all around us, carrying us along like sticks on a stream's surface that just lie there waterlogged.

Reminiscences: Some of the old men talk about those places in the river of time where if you're not careful you can get caught on the outside of a corkscrew that will spin you around in the same place forever and ever—or get caught on the inside where you'll be sucked straight down and never come up again. Or those places where it gets wider and the patches where it speeds up and the banks go by so fast you barely have time to see a blur before you're past, and others where it slows down so that a person floating on the surface hardly knows he's moving. Sometimes these folks even talk about the underwater caves that they all seemed to know about, where you drifted along without a thought in your head and how you knew it could never end and how if you ever thought of the river rushing by above you it was just for a moment and without regret, drowned in peaceful azure and drifting on the almost-imperceptible currents.

He moves past the corner of the cloth department on the other side of the plants. With his head turned towards the racks from which the free ends of cloth bolts drip in multi-colored confusion, he almost runs into a stiff-armed mannequin who blocks his path with a forefinger extended in a perpetual *j'accuse* of some fellow model. He sees its frozen grin out of the corner of his eye just in time to avoid toppling with it in a tangled heap that would have caused him some embarrassment and possibly not a little pain.

They are in the process of removing one of the line of humanoids that poise dainty legs and curved feet on the long counter in the back; apparently this figure is to be its replacement. Strange that they are doing so during store hours; usually this kind of housekeeping doesn't go until people are gone and lights out. But after all it is getting on to closing time. Time? He uncovers his watch and watches the second hand creep up from the six to the twelve at which point he focusses the two shadowy hands he has kept in a mental blur and discovers that it is ten of six.

Uncertainty: Others of us, upon seeing this same scene, might well have wondered why the workmen are replacing one pink plastic model with another. Why is one pose preferable to another? we might ask; why one false front over another equally false? Are we not all ourselves but changeable mannequins whose preference of one moment or mood over the next is as futile and absurd as this switch-off of falsehoods? Is not our existence a tissue of lies as thin and delicate and carefully wrought as that cloth that covers the stiffened limbs of these statues? Is not our pose of morality, of thinking one mask better than another, merely the substitution of one lie for another? Are we not all guilty of this absurdity of preference when in truth we can never escape our cage of inherent equality in which nothing is better than anything else?

Reassurance: Let us not draw our conclusions too quickly, let not the disgust that wells from our stomach and leaves as its high-water mark the bitter taste in our mouth that no amount of wine can wash away overcome our more circumspect and less emotional reflections—even after admitting that these figures frozen in meaningless surprise or amusement or sophisticated blandness have an essential likeness to us who resemble them in all but length of time that each pose is held, all is not lost. There still remains beauty, that goddess who in her own way is as mercifully blind as her sister justice, for beauty neither understands nor cares to know about morality. To her, it is enough that things aspire to the state of her name. We *can* get by in this world of moral uncertainty and ethical indifference. We have only to let beauty be our guide, let it be her dear preferences that mold our lives. **Application:** There is admittedly no inherent reason to prefer one of our poses to another or to change one statue for another here in this department store, except that it pleases our eye better than another. And yet this is reason enough to choose it, reason as solid and incontrovertible as those moral ones we once thought so necessary to existence. **Note:** Yet we should not get the idea that simply because we have found a new standard of choice that has risen like a phoenix from the ashes of the old, we are freed from the task of deliberating or of thinking before making our pick. Beauty is as demanding and as hard a mistress as was truth, as hard a taskmaster and as implacable a foe as the goddess who ruled us before. We are not free to choose on the basis of nothing more solid than our feeling or conviction; we must if anything learn to dedicate ourselves the more firmly to our cause and to her whom we serve.

Development: The choice of the most beautiful involves long and arduous selection, involves a complex analysis of our intellectual and emotional reactions, a serious comparative study of the ramifications of this moment on our future. For let us not be misled into forgetting that there is beauty which can be discovered, and that need not be immediately evident. There is the beauty of effects as well as appearance, the beauty which, let us not blush or hesitate to say it plainly, can only be called moral beauty, the beauty of fitting well and properly into the larger whole of which we are all parts. And finally, in addition to the lengthy selection and analysis processes, there is an extra added period of hard and scientific thought in which we re-check our figurings and make sure that we have not made mistakes in our scholarship and our manner of presentation.

Concession: There are those who have criticized our process and methods, have accused us of overcarefulness and even pedantry, have had the gall to turn the old age that brings wisdom into the ugly, evil epithet of "superannuated," have vilified us for our long and self-sacrificing service by mocking what they call blind devotion to an ideal that is served only because of its constancy and the large amount of an ancillary and equally unchanging clerical work that surrounds it. This is not so. We are not the self-made eunuchs who, out of an inability to stay away from that which their hasty action one impetuous night in the throes of their grief deprived them of the ability to possess, find themselves going out voluntarily and seeking the positions as keepers of harems that those who were gelded by others are forced against their desires to assume. This said—and, we hope, conceded—the fact remains that we must have figures, numbers, calculations on which to catch as we slide down the cliff of the offhand towards the yawning abyss of the transitory. It is only upon these that we will be able to base our salvation, if indeed salvation is to be our fate rather than dishonorable death and oblivion.

He stands for a minute by the end-of-bolt clearance table watching the two workmen on the counter in the process of upending the mannequin that is to be removed and handing it to the two below them on the floor who will pall-bear it away to a drawer somewhere or to a mausoleum-like storage room. There it will stand in a corner, completely naked but for the white and dust-laden sheet that drapes it in symbol of the purity of death from which it will all too soon be snatched before being re-clothed in order to enter another life in Lingerie or Sleepwear, or be taken joint from plastic joint and be re-distributed throughout the store, the lower part of its body modeling pantyhose in Ladies Undergarments, each of its arms stretching a white evening glove to its full lovely length in Gloves and Handbags, growing disembodied from a clear plastic stand, and the remainder of its torso gracing a pink and white patterned wheelchair in Disabled Accessories. It is worthy of reflection that the new mannequin that is to take the place of the old seems quite unaware of what has been necessary to the improvement of its own position, seeming instead intent on getting its molded eyebrow at just the right angle to express the surprise it evidently feels at something being amiss with the invisible whatever-it-is it cups in its left hand.

The mobility of the men on the counter seems strange in contrast with the stillness of these smooth and self-assured models that do not deign to change their expressions to note the presence of moving versions of themselves or even to acknowledge the demise and removal of one of their fellows. They must find such matters uninteresting, these beautiful beings in contrast to whom living humans seem gauche and boorish, these beings who never sweat, never urinate, and never let a burp escape their perfectly even and milk-white teeth or their red lips that never twist into curses and are never wet with a stray salty tear of grief. **Plea:** Let us not castigate them for their lack of feeling, for this is as silly and wrong-headed as criticizing a native of the tropics for not wearing the clothes that we inhabitants of colder climes must assume. Our vestments, like our convictions that grief is powerful, moving, and ennobling, are but compensations for something we lack. If there exists another who does not need either our fur coats or our feeling for tragedy to protect him from the cold or the pains of loss, let us not put him from our midst, let us rather welcome him as one who was born under a luckier star, one who cannot be expected to understand the tides of interior seas that leave us alternately flooded with bitter brine and drying mercilessly under the white heat of desolation. If these creatures are less human for all that, let us praise their inhumanity just as sincerely as we attack the inhumanity of those who are constructed like us; let us not recoil in horror but rather take them into our bosoms and give them what love we can.

Note: We must not be misled into thinking that these things can reciprocate this feeling any more than they can initiate it. These actions must not be for their satisfaction, but for ours. At the same time, we must remain eternally on the alert, for these things to which we have given so much and which by human standards are bound to us by almost unbreakable ties of gratitude are as likely to strangle us with icy, hollow fingers through which no blood runs as they are to grasp our hands in friendship or pat us on the back; all such actions are equally acceptable movements in the world they perceive through their painted blue eyes.

Lesson: If we admit them into our society, we must be careful never to let ourselves be exposed to them in a vulnerable position, must be sure that we keep their amorality in mind at all times. Sometimes in our darker moods we are forced to admit that we are in a very strange position with regard to these things and indeed even a tragic one, for though we are drawn to them by unrequited love of their unchangeable vinyl bodies, it is for this same reason that we must protect ourselves against them and in so protecting ourselves re-affirm our humanity and vulnerability as well as acknowledging the great gulf that separates our nature from theirs, a chasm which no degree of physical proximity or integration into our society can ever bridge.

Further: We cannot simply throw these things into jails or put them behind bars in zoos so that we can visit them on Sundays with our sticky-fingered children in tow. To do this would be to give up all pretense at looking on these things as equals with whom we can have the normal day-to-day contact that gives us the fragile but nonetheless real feeling of being within sight of the goals we would so like to attain and thus of this metamorphosis being, if not within our present powers, at least within the realms of not-so-distant possibility. We must live with them in a state of dangerous and delicate balance that at any moment may be destroyed by our own creeping consciousness of the futility and sadness of having always hanging before our eyes the golden apples which, if plucked, change instantly to rotted pulp and, if nurtured too well, take over our gardens and turn us from our homes.

There seems to be something amiss with the figure the men are lifting down, for they are pawing and fingering it when it should be already in the arms of the men waiting underneath. Perhaps it is broken and the men are being careful not to let it fall into pieces or crack further: it may be its removal is not as pointless as he had thought. The workmen have hunched over it and all he sees is the uniform dirty blue of their jeans. Perhaps if he were a different sort than he is, he would feel a wave of pity and protectiveness for this specimen of pure and unsullied plastic womanhood which is being pawed and even mauled by these fat men with their two day's growth of beard, would break himself from the lassitude of his momentary hesitation there in the aisle and leap onto the pattern counter, yelling threats and vows of revenge and being as undeterred by the well-manicured hands of the women resting there that he must in his haste and indignation regretfully trample on as by the hands of those few shoppers in the area which would fly to their mouths in expressions of distress, shock, admiration, and sympathetic pain before reaching out to his pants legs. With one gigantic lunge he would spring over the aisle and grab the cowardly workmen who had at first been struck dumb and motionless by his shouts and then begun to scramble onto the floor, dropping as they moved the body they had defiled but which he would catch in mid-air and lay tenderly on the counter before taking off after the hoodlums who despite their size would be making good time towards Gift Wrapping and on whom he would not actually lay hands until well into Boys' Wear.

He conquers a momentary and fleeting wish to reproduce the pointing gesture of this thing he has run into and turns to the left in the direction of its point to find the bathroom for which he has come into this store the location of which he knows even without the unintentional aid of this misplaced model. Green plastic plants stretch plastic wings to him from beds of gravel in planter boxes along the sides of the lounge; their glossy leaves curling and crisping in mimicry of the real plants they reproduce. Their roots, if they have any roots besides the stiff single plastic and metal stem that is anchored in the crushed rock, must stick straight outwards as if a head of hair on a person who has just received a severe electric shock. **Reflection:** Surely there must be roots. The time is past when we can continue to assume that we have the right to re-make the world in our own image, to construct an artificial universe in which is preserved only the parts of the real world that we humans have found interesting or unusual or beautiful and from which are missing those parts which to us have become abhorrent or have simply gone unnoticed. We cannot commit the aesthetically chauvinistic act of reconstructing from our own point of view; we must also preserve those parts of the world we dislike and are neutral to. If we do not, we will be cheating ourselves and our children of the chance of acquiring the humility attendant on discovering that people are merely one species among many, scraps of skin and bones buffeted relentlessly by the unceasing winds and liable at any moment to be tossed head over heels in helpless circles.

Still on roots: These roots must at least be in keeping with the rest of the construction of the thing and be bunches of hard wire that are not afraid of the bruising power of the gravel around them. There is no point in producing things too fragile for their environment, just as there are some places in this world where it is simply ridiculous to ask the beautiful to thrive among people who will never understand it. **Example:** There are some people who will never understand the tragic beauty of the transient, the ephemeral, and the soon-to-die, who are without comprehension that the most entrancing sort of woman is she whose fragile milky translucence and slight tinge of ice-blue around the temples betray the interior ravages of the illness which will soon separate from her diseased body the delicate and butterfly-like soul that was too good for the dirt and filth of this earth. Nor could they possibly grasp the fact that our attraction for the soap bubble is based on its shifting spectrum of colors that flow and melt one into another, changing and varying and never staying and fixed, like a rainbow melted by the sun from its unyielding hardness and rigidity into a liquid pool and on the fact that it is held together by the most fragile of bonds that can at any moment loose its hold and change the thin-skinned bladder into two or three rather heavy drops of soap that are good for little more than washing one's hands or elbows, on the fact that it teeters perennially on the brink of the abyss of non-being and may at any moment disappear from before our eyes.

Another example: Nor can they ever hope to understand that the extensive use we moderns make of glass in all our buildings is not due to such quotidian and Philistine considerations as light distribution or view of the exterior landscape but rather the elusive but nonetheless real pleasure we take in having constantly before our eyes these panels of things that are present to our sense of touch but not, most of the time, to our sense of smell. Like the reverse phenomenon of ghosts which are frequently amenable to being seen but never to being felt, they excite our sense of the half-existent, of the other worlds beyond our comprehension in which live and work creatures far different than we or anything of which we have ever conceived. **Conclusion:** It is not the permanent after which we lust but rather after that state that is as changeable as the soap bubble and as ungraspable as beauty itself, the state we call happiness.

A wall clock above the planters that stand on tubular metal legs hums a blank hum as it jerks forward two minutes' worth of its face and then is still again, hanging above vinyl chairs set between the artificial flowers. In the chairs sit people whose legs he must skirt as he walks down the corridor. Suddenly he is at the door of the men's room, pushing his shoulder against its metal stubbornness that releases suddenly as the copper-colored handle turns in his hand. On the other side of the door is an empty ante-room that is painted a uniform army gray off which shine dull reflections of the low-hung fluorescent lights and of the red from the lighted sign over a door in the opposite wall.

The whole empty and extremely resonant room with its hard floor that magnifies his footsteps seems as eerie as the antechamber to the purification room of an ancient temple. **Anthropology:** The function of the counterpart of this inner room in the temples of old was as a suicide chamber for the use of those who felt they had offended the gods and could buy absolution only by their deaths. There is precious little of such sort of conviction running around these days, not to mention especially few chances here in the toilets since there are simply no weapons for suicide available, unless, that is, some inventive soul figures out a way to choke himself in the curve of the sink pipes or to braid toilet paper to a strength sufficient to render a hanging from the lightbulb feasible or to use the liquid soap to develop his bubble-blowing technique to that point at which he is able to enclose himself in a huge iridescent prison in which he will smother.

He crosses the room to the accompaniment of his own shoes which clatter all around him first at normal pace then in dramatic echoes broken by several seconds of empty silence, then faster in a run that brings him to the door, which he opens with a push to reveal a more brightly painted cubicle than that through which he has just passed. Even though originally it was off-white, it is by now considerably more off than it was originally, what with the chips peeling from the corners to reveal yellow plastic and a fine lacy pattern of black fingerprints around the sink. It is less brightly lit than the entrance chamber, being illuminated only by a single bulb that nestles in the remains of an old-fashioned socket like an egg in a small and mangled nest from which the bird that laid it had run twittering in terror as it took the first look at what it was that had cost it such sweating and effort.

The tiled floor is festooned with strips of toilet paper that squirm seductively against the ceramic squares and with wads of dry paper towels that overflow from the brimming trash can underneath the sink, as if paper blossoms and grasses were all that this cold hard floor was capable of producing even with the liberal amounts of water that have evidently been added to it at various times and which have left thin whitish deposits between the cracks of the tiles.

The shiny black lipstick of the plastic toilets seats has been applied to their pale horizontal mouths frozen in perpetual ovals of interest. On the surface of the water within, waterlogged cigars and cigarette butts floating in leisurely swirls distribute as they move unraveled handfuls of their insides like a Mayan dancer engaged in a death waltz, systematically cutting out organs in mid-step and flinging them away into the crowd beneath the dancer's platform so that they strew blood on the expectant spectators who are open-mouthed not from surprise—these sorts of things happen every year and the old-timers can remember when the consciences of the people were so strict that once a month was not too often for the spectacle—but because they were promised eternal life if they managed to catch on their tongue a drop of blood from the entrail that was sweeping low over their heads and was due to land any minute with a soft squash against the face of some especially fortunate fellow.

He closes the metal door with a hasty flip of the wrist and turns away to the urinal, which contains no cigarettes. This may be explained by realizing that this particular mouth seems a good deal less energetic in the expression of its feelings than its two fellow maws in the stalls: its jaw hangs open in dull incomprehension rather than showing the beaming and extroverted expressions that grace both the sink and the toilet, and this of course would be less attractive to hot-blooded sorts like cigarettes. Its throat, moreover, has been gagged by a huge blue plastic epiglottis riddled with what must be holes made by a shotgun and further blocked by two great white pills that slowly dissolve into the gullet. **Note:** No one likes a thing so hypochondriacal as to have taken to injecting a perpetual stream of medicine into itself by means of slow-melting pills as big as golf balls.

He pushes the handle that sticks like an absurdly large electrode from that small exposed part of the thing's skull. This action precipitates a cataract of water rushing down the sides of the urinal, washing away drops of yellow that hang onto the porcelain and gurgling into a writhing white froth which disappears nearly as quickly as it has appeared down the holes beneath it.

He has stepped back a foot or so in order not to be in the way of any bits of water that might try to use this time as an opportunity to escape from their servitude in the dark and partly rusty pipes and their immanent re-incarceration in what is, if not the bowels of the earth, at least its pancreas or gall could do anything with the parts of the body except the arm and things like that and where the heart is because that's where we used to pledge allegiance when we were little and I had blond curly hair and pink ruffled dresses that you always used to try to get dirty because yours were always so plain and simple and you used to say I flounced my skirts and primped my bow whenever I went past you but of course how ridiculous you were, we all were and how strange it seems to us now that we're grown women and the best of friends that we ever quarreled Helen what are you doing with that knife Helen stay away from me Helen Helen] and between which this short interval of light and open air is enough to make every weary prisoner stamp his enchained ankles sore from such a long and close acquaintance with metal shackles and kiss the earth and the flowers in gratitude and sing a great chorus of praise and thanksgiving to the Being who had made him and allowed him his moments of respite and more to the point is enough to make goodly amounts of splatters from which he does not entirely escape.

The gurgling has subsided now to low growls. He pulls his zipper in a sort of ending glissando made less effective than it might have been by the fact that it catches in the front of his underpants about halfway up and he is required to spend a minute unhooking these tiny sharp teeth from the prey in which they leave their prints. The second half of the glissandus interruptus is a flat and uninteresting buzz, which is only what is to be expected, for the effectiveness of this sound lies in the conjunction of the first half with the second, the necessary though aurally uninteresting acceleration which culminates in a grand swooping finale that can best be reproduced by the person who is willing to incur great costs in the pursuit of the perfect sound by ripping lengthwise a bolt of silk.

He rounds the edge of the half-wall separating the two receptacles and stands a moment surveying the sink. It is not quite as bad as it might be; one might well be apt to form a bad initial impression from the great quantities of water puddles on its back and sides and from the thin tomahawk-head-like pieces of soap with sharp white edges that have been produced by wearing away what were once prim and useless rectangles with blunt sides and which now are pasted in various skewed positions against the enamel as if in a sudden pacifistic resolution that they not be used for any sort of murderous purposes.

He twirls one of the x-shaped ceramic knobs that are like crucifixes cut from white dough and baked into puffy cookies and receives in return a healthy spurt of water that, though advertised as hot, neither is nor becomes so during the few seconds he has the patience to wait and to twiddle his fingers back and forth under the stream. He thrusts both his wrists under it and pulls them out quickly, allowing the more fast-moving drops to flow from his wrists down his hands and off the ends of his fingers and reversing the directions of the slower-moving ones as he reaches up to the paper towel dispenser and coaxes it into producing a folded brown monosyllable that opens with a shake. Mere seconds later it lies crushed at the base of the trash can and he is out the door.

He looks at the three check-cashing windows on the side of the corridor behind which sit three women who have placed their folded hands on the counter before them and seem like sculpted busts, silent and serene. Suddenly the one in the middle (the bleached blond with the string of beads) blinks her heavily mascared eyelashes and the one on her right scratches the Formica counter with a meditative forefinger, at which point a positive flurry of activity breaks out, what with the fingering of pearls from the teller who was hitherto motionless and a primping behind a suddenly-produced compact mirror by the scratcher and a clearing of the throat from the one with the beads.

The people sunk in the armchairs on the opposite wall do not remain unaffected by this crescendo from silence. They shuffle their feet and produce handkerchiefs which they press to their noses or foreheads, open pocketbooks, and jingle keys in pockets until there is in this room what seems a perfect cacophony of sounds in which voices play no role whatsoever.

He may well feel as if he is running a gauntlet down this short aisle between people whose weapons are sounds and who, not needing the added strength of their eye contact to reinforce their already formidable power, look away casually at other things and seem not to be aware of his existence at all as the object of their assault. **Meditation:** If sounds are in fact weapons, it may be his fate to be wounded by a well-aimed click of two quarters in the pocket of a well-to-do old gentleman in a pink lounger, to die from the scrape of a fat lady's chair, or to be paralyzed by the hissing squeak of a nylon stocking against a well-formed and flexing leg and to fall in a pile of writhing limbs here on this floor, each groan that is forced from his lips but cutting the more deeply into the lesions that by now criss-cross his body, and each sound of his shoes or the buttons on his pants or shirt against the floor making new razor cuts on the exposed areas of his arms and legs, the cries of unabashed pleasure from his tormentors attacking his vitals, ripping apart his organs that feel as if they are turned into giant rodents implanted into his innards while under the influence of a sedative which has just begun to wear off, leaving the creatures kicking and clawing in a fury of suffocation to which the only two possible ends are death or immediate freedom by the most direct methods available. Is he thus to be defeated by forces in which he had not seen the potential for danger and against which he had not thought to guard himself?

Response: Surely this cannot be. The world is not so skewed and deranged a place that it kills those who have made their reputations as the greatest swordsmen of their generation with an infected pin prick incurred while sewing a button on their jacket, that it allows mountain climbers to meet their deaths not on the icy and rocky slopes of Everest or even on the olive-covered hills that cling to the lower parts of Olympus but by tripping over the hillock in their backyard erected around the tomato plants, or that it smiles benignly as race car drivers are reduced to masses of bloody pulp by drunken farmers in pick-up trucks who slam into the side of their cars while they are stopped at the traffic light at the corner by the grocery store.

Another explanation for this sudden crescendo might be that, after the near-silence of the toilets, any amount of clearly-defined background noise is liable to seem extremely loud. There is no question but that sound travels well in this rectangular room painted yellow with a lighter ceiling hovering over it like a solid and sharply-defined cloud layer, or that it bounces easily from the plaster walls and engages in a bit of fancy footwork and an occasional pas de deux with a chair leg before it returns to ear level the stronger for its travels. **Useful information:** Sounds are like the characters in a dream who are protected from harm by the gift of being able to pass through solid things without hinderance or interruption. Thus, though they are not necessarily cowards, they taste a thousand times what for three-dimensional beings in a worldly existence would be death before their actual destruction with a flick of the sleeper's eyes that exposes them to the morning mists creeping through the open windows into the bedroom and roiling the thin white curtains at the foot of the bed so that they billow out over toes and settle for a moment on the blanket, deflating slowly before being sucked back by the outgoing tide and plastering themselves in gauzy supplication against the screen only to be repulsed by the heartless wind that forces them away and back in a ceaseless cycle, an existence which to this dream figure's airy tongue has as little savor as does distilled water or an overcooked gruel to the more substantial palate of the human whose sleep has produced the so-ephemeral beings of their fantasies.

He stands once again by the edge of the cloth displays. The mannequin is gone from the aisle, there is a blank space in the lineup on the far counter against the wall, and the workmen are gone. **Interlude:** Where is she who so effectively pointed him on? Where is the vision of loveliness at whose feet the entire world of mannequins would have knelt? Where is she to whom his earlier show of indifference must surely have been but mime and acting undertaken to arouse her interest in him and been founded on the certainty that she would be his when he returned from that place to which she had sent him, a bit uncertain as to what it was that he was supposed to bring back as proof of having accomplished his mission? **Note:** Such things are usually reasonable requests. There is, for example, little possibility that in this case his return gift would be the Koh-I-noor or several silver roses wet with drops of Persian attar or a chip of the unbreakable glass mountain, or even one of two unhatched eggs that sit rotting in a nest overhanging the Grand Canyon far out on the end of a tiny thin branch that arches halfway across the gorge in a display of unself-conscious virtuosity. A more suitable trophy would be something more in the line of the innermost square of toilet tissue or the wad of hair that is caught in the elbow joint of the sink's pipes or the filament from the light bulb. **NB:** This last he would be the most hesitant to obtain, for he would be loth to smash the bulb since doing so would involve plunging the room into blackness. Thus, he might consider bringing her instead of that for which he was sent the identical vitals of another bulb. After all, if a switch of a deer's lungs and liver for those of a human princess can fool as crafty a sort as a magician queen, it is unlikely that a filament from a light bulb, the twin of those in all other bulbs, is going to be seen by a considerably less astute creature to be not precisely the one she had sent him for.

Further reflection: Indeed, there is something of a moral sanction for this cheating in addition to his desire to win the princess at all costs. He wishes to save her from her wicked stepfather who is using her to kill off all the princes of neighboring lands by forcing her to ask of those who come to pay her suit all sorts of impossible things while force-feeding her the nourishment that in her grief at being the instrument of such destruction she would not of her own volition eat, food which keeps her beauty at that high level which attracts the young princes and inspires them to such superhuman attempts, despite the fact that their efforts are never sufficient to avert the death that is the price of failure. At least, it blinds them to the piles of bones of their noble predecessors that are heaped in grisly profusion around her throne and over which the palace vultures huddle and flap with whooshes of their great wings and clatters as the dry bones re-arrange themselves under the added and unsteady weight.

Suite: Soon this situation must change, for the wicked king whose nefarious plans feed daily the pile of bones will himself fall victim to the fate he had constructed for others: so successful will his efforts be to fuel the fire of his stepdaughter's beauty that soon he will feel himself being drawn under its spell, feel within himself the glow of lust he had thought long extinguished by the oncoming tide of old age. **Thus:** One night there will be a banquet when the vultures will be making a good deal of noise ripping flesh off bones and flapping their wings around with more than their usual vigor. To take his mind off them, as well as to impress his guests with his absolute suzerainty over all the things in his kingdom, the king will order the salami on the table to dance for him. Even a half-drunken monarch cannot fail to be impressed by such strong phallic symbolism and so at the end of the dance during which the meat peels off its outer skin, exposing the spongy red and whitish marble within, he will be so aroused that he bends his stepdaughter back over the silver casserole of cow's tongue in red wine and, paying not a bit of attention to her screams of pain as the dish upends under her weight and douses her back with a stream of near-boiling alcohol, takes her then and there. His guests will be too well-bred to show any surprise and will continue calmly eating their vichyssoise, though some of the less self-disciplined of them will sneak an occasional peek at the goings-on out of the corner of an eye.

Lesser monarchs might have become the victims of a mutiny at this point while engaged in an action that would leave them little inclined or able to defend themselves against the upraised daggers suddenly produced from the voluminous cloaks of their rebellious courtiers. But the power of this one has been unchallenged to this point and his subjects are not in the habit of thinking of him as deposable. He is known far and wide as a generally kind-hearted man and a good ruler who, by judicious use of the natural gifts of his sulky and ill-liked stepdaughter, has managed to insure the security of his country by eliminating the next generation of rulers from the surrounding lands who otherwise would have attacked his tiny but rich country and sold its subjects into slavery.

At the end of his labors, at any rate, the king will fall back onto the floor, exhausted with the arduousness of his ardorous labor to which he had for so long been unaccustomed; the princess, who rather enjoyed the sensation in her crotch if not that down her back, will stagger a little and sit down in the middle of the relish try to think things over. The king, overcome by a remorse he could well do without, will soon be horror-struck at the thought of what he has done. Suddenly he will hoist himself up by the tablecloth, spilling in the process the few remaining cups and upending the cream pitcher which urges onto the edge of the table a stream of thick whiteness that separates, in verticalizing, into slow meditative drops that create on the marble tiles a rich glistening and vibrating pool quivering in time to the rhythm of the new drops that break its surface and, snatching the carving knife from the sideboard, neatly decapitates himself and falls at the princess' feet, the eyes in his severed head as glassy and staring as the artificial yellow ones set into the slippers with which she is shod that are made from the hollowed bodies of white doves.

The princess will lean down and pull the head up by its hair and, holding it so that she does not add the king's blood to her already well-stained gown, deposit it daintily on a silver tray recently vacated by a ham that in all the confusion and goings-on has slid off in a slurp of grease into a corner where it is quietly collecting the dust curls left by indolent maids. She will re-seat herself and, humming a careless sort of tune, display a hitherto hidden talent as she expertly carves up the face and scalp and passes the plate to the person on her right who, a perfect guest, accepts with pleasure a choice section of the forehead; when the platter reaches her again all that will be left are the lips which she will transfer to her own plate and after rendering them bite-sized, chew thoughtfully and swallow with evident enjoyment.

Objection: It is all very well for writers and their like to concern themselves with personal development, but we are interested in more weighty matters and cannot be sidetracked with consideration of the individual when what we want is a comprehension of the general. We wish, in short, to know the political implications of all this. **Wish fulfilled:** The guests all went home after thanking the princess for a simply wonderful evening and the next day she let it be known that the king had fallen into a cistern and broken his neck and that she was assuming control of the government. Among her first actions were a public belly dance on the palace lawn wearing only the veil of the temple which was followed by a proclamation that all of the bones of the dead princes were to be made into corset stays for her old age, and by the addition to her domestic staff of a retinue of brawny wrestlers whose function was to provide her with certain services of an athletic nature.

Happily ever after: The wise precautions of her stepfather preserved the peace and harmony within her little kingdom. It is said, though we have no evidence that this was indeed the cause of the widespread destruction that we note at this level in the excavation of the capital city, that when she was an old woman the princess began to realize that a new crop of princes was growing up in the countries around her and that her government was in the same situation as that for which the old king had found a solution. This realization must have been the cause of the sudden appearance of a beautiful child by the side of the ageing and wrinkled monarch who, so the palace news sources let it be known, was the immaculately conceived issue of the queen herself, brought into the world the night before as a result of an hour-long gestation period inside the ruler's all but completely withered womb.

The queen proclaimed that all the noble scions of the surrounding countries were more than welcome to try for her daughter's hand, the test being a two-fold examination of which the first was the standard sort of bringing back a far-fetched and utterly useless token lodged in an unreachable place, and the second a private consultation with the queen during which, it was rumored, she made certain tests of physical competence whose failure produced instant death from her headsman as a reward. We are forced to conclude that this section of the world must produce exceptionally weak and flaccid princes or those who require youth in a partner to call forth a show of their manhood, for none ever came alive from the queen's chamber and the pile of bones around her throne grew as high as it had when she was a girl.

Further: As the princess aged, she apparently became somewhat unbalanced. Occasionally she was seen in the wee hours of the morning doing some sort of dance to the disassembled skeletons in the throne room which gleamed chalky white and smooth in the pale moonlight streaming through the windows, using the vultures which sat quietly on her shoulders to carry away the veils which she peeled from her sagging teats and wrinkled haunches. Apparently the old woman regained her sanity and her moral sense the night before she died, which was not long after the servants had begun to pass among themselves the information that the young princess was, as of the preceding week, no longer a girl but a young lady, at which news the queen had seemed to go completely mad and begun to rant and rave before abruptly stopping and going to her room to write what she said was her will.

The next day, she called a meeting of all her retainers where she made it known, as the tears rolled down her cheeks, that she had led a dissolute life and could not face having to pass on to her beloved daughter the legacy of death and debauchery that had plagued her and her line of succession which, she was resolved, must end with her own death. To this end, she was planning a magnificent deed whose effects would be remembered long after all else about her or her fate had been forgotten and that tonight, after consultation with her ghostly advisor, she would make her plan known.

And make it known she did, for though at midnight the courtiers and staff had decided that the old woman had merely been talking and really didn't have any more plan than they did and had all gone to bed, they were awakened around three o'clock by the crackling of flames and the acrid smell of smoke that swirled around them and by the hoarse crackling cry of the old queen who ran staggering through the halls carrying the charred body of her daughter, of which only one lily-white hand remained unburnt, laughing a hideous laugh that grew louder as she neared the throne room which was by now a swirling inferno, into which she was seen to plunge. It is said that her hysterical cackling continued several seconds after she entered the room and then suddenly changed to screams that were scarcely more spine-chilling than her laughter and then a few seconds later fell absolutely silent and all that was audible from this room was the crackling of the flames and the rifle-like reports as the bones expanded and burst.

Wrap-up: It seems that the other inhabitants of the palace escaped from the blaze; we have found nothing amid the rubble but the nearly intact corpse of an infant which had been preserved by being covered with a pile of wet laundry and by dying of suffocation rather than immolation. Its little mouth was set in an expression of dreamy pleasure undisturbed by the noises that must have surrounded it that night which, though they were undoubtedly enough to wake the dead, were not enough to rouse a child sleeping just several seconds this side of the grave.

Lesson: We, the living, move in a continual haze that clouds our senses and blinds us to the world which, after we have clasped the thin and icy hand of death in a grip of welcome and been ushered into his kingdom, is revealed from the other side to have been marvelously colored and designed with hues that our living senses were incapable of perceiving. At this point we may conclude that death brings greater perception and not lesser, that only when we are enfolded in the soft dark wings of the dark goddess will we ever be granted the gifts of sight, sound, touch, smell, and taste that were withheld from us before. Only then, we might say, will we be sensitive to the sounds in the night that we will hear coming from the world which we have left, and we will be like the insomniac to whom the ringing of the telephone at midnight in the darkened house next door seems impossibly loud, a sound so shrill and piercing that he feels that those asleep must be brought bounding immediately from their beds in sudden awareness, their hearts beating wildly against their breasts in consciousness of this cacophony, but which apparently does not disturb their slumbers for it continues to ring and there is nothing he can do, absolutely nothing to make these deaf ones in the adjoining abode rise and simply answer it.

Query: What good does it do us to be suddenly aware of colors and sounds that go unseen and unheard by the living if, though the glass through which we see them is not darker but more transparent than any substance in the world of mortals, it is not the less impenetrable for all that? Of what use is greater perception if we are unable to use it to guide the footsteps of our living children and surviving friends around the pitfalls they cannot see and help them avail themselves of opportunities that remain invisible to them? Why, in short, should we acquire a gift that is no use either for ourselves or others?

Response: The answer is evident: we are made aware of all we missed while living so that we may the better and the more sympathetically watch the never-ending drama of mankind from the sidelines, where there is no possibility of personal feelings or human position interfering with our appreciation of the beauty and sadness of their condition. For while we are caught within the shells of the body we are incapable, no matter how hard we try, of ever obtaining a totally disinterested sort of outlook on the world in which we live and upon which we have effects. It is this fact of a personal perspective which is inescapable during life that makes us unaware of all that becomes obvious to us upon our deaths, when we lose what has limited our vision to only 180 of the 360° of our head and our other senses to the very small and well-defined areas of our bodies.

Development: It was once said by someone who ought to have known better that the philosopher spends all his life in preparation for death. We insist, by contrast, that it is artists about whom this must be said, though we would do well to understand this within its specific philosophical context and not get the idea that these beings are "half in love with an easeful death" or "lads who are in love with the grave," for their death-wish is not one for rest or respite from the toils of the world like that of the vast majority of people but rather a rational one which longs for total fulfillment of their artistic nature. (And oh, the tiresome nature of living among those who cannot possibly understand this craving for death, the pain of being misunderstood by the very people that form by their actions the center and core of our life of observation, by those people to whom we have devoted ourselves completely!)

Objection: There are those who try to make us believe that we do not love those whom we observe, do not and cannot ever feel such an emotion for the people we observe so clinically, that rather than warmth we are actually apt to feel disdain for people who are not like us.

Pained response: How can this be? How can we devote our lives to someone we do not love? How can we accept the burdensome existence of our caste if not because we believe in the supremacy of something we do over what others do? How could we bear the insults and gibes of those who cannot understand that we are gifted with third eyes which discern what they can never hope to see were it not that we love something better than ourselves?

Yet it is unlikely that we will convince anyone of this. Therefore let us drop the pose and simply admit that it is not people we love, not those despicable creatures who mock our work and dare to criticize us. It is art we love, that great power that re-aligns and makes interesting the inherently uninteresting and unworthy world and the boring people that inhabit it. It is that sublimely beautiful goddess "whose tread we seek to hear on the stair" that gives hope and encouragement enough to keep us going against the dragons that open their dark and slavering jaws and would swallow us whole were it not for this powerful deity whose hem we clutch in our sweating hands. It is art to whom we have dedicated ourselves, not to the poor fools whom we can consider as nothing more than puppets which, neutral in themselves, become worthy of interest only when they are made a part of our synthesis. Let us acknowledge where our sympathies lie, now that the truth has come out. We have no particular reason to hurt those normal ones around us, those who are not marked on the forehead with the mark of the artist. But on the other hand neither have we any particular reason to spare their feelings, for the spectacle of their grief and hurt at realizing that someone they had always taken for their comrade and friend is in actuality their superior is as worthy of clinical observation as any other state.

He hears something that he had not sensed on his last trip through the cloth department and cocks an ear as he fingers the last inches of a piece of satin. It is the sound of insistent but soft voices that shape perfect rounded foothills and shallow valleys instead of the more jagged constructions of quotidian speech. They seep softly through the row of cloth bolts on the opposite wall, taking on a sort of undefinable graininess or sponginess that seems to mottle quiet sounds with a pattern of lights and darks as if the noises were formed, like the pictures of the televisions that produce them, of tiny dark dots and the white of spaces between that diminish and fill in as the intensity of the picture is increased and the dots grow fatter and more sprawling. These many whispers are talking in a unison chorus, the effect of which is that it suddenly seems very loud. **Analogy:** A stone lodged in the corner of our shoe remains unfelt until we become abruptly aware of a sharp pain that seems the more severe for its being preceded by what was felt as a neutral period.

Then, as he lets the last of the satin slip from his fingers, he becomes aware of something he has not noticed before, of some sort of interference or impediment to this flow, a cross-current filling in the valleys of the stronger voice with hills of its own: a television turned to a competing station. He can imagine these banks of flickering screens all turned to a talk show in which dozens of hosts gesticulate in multiple surprise or rearrange their coiffures with their myriad of arms or fondle dozens of tubes of toothpaste and cans of deodorant before offering them confidently from the screens in a show of unbelievable precision. All except, of course, the one lone dissenting voice, the interloper, the destroyer of the pattern, the out-of-step dancer, the fly in the ointment that advertises a competing product, that smiles and laughs while the others are quiet, that flashes up news of casualties of wars going on somewhere in the world while the others show an episode in the adventures of a talking baby whale. This lone voice returns for every piece of fact one of fiction and for every one of their pleasant dreams a nightmare; its images flicker by madly in silent-film jerkiness when the others show the liquid movements of a dancer, a daisy undulating in the breeze in colors ranging from gray to pale yellow to near-orange of which only the dark center remains constant from screen to screen; late at night, it may well glare the unmollified stare of a test pattern when the others twist madly in the scarcely containable gyrations of joy of a woman who has just won a hundred dollars and a washer.

The rows and columns of moving pictures that, save for this one out-of-place flicker, move in perfect concert, probably produce the effect of a person looking into an evening dress of black sequin scales that reflect the viewer's every movement a hundredfold, each tiny concave mirror seeming to have captured within itself a homunculus inspired by its resemblance to the looker-on to move precisely as he does himself. **Query:** Will this one iconoclast be hiding its face in the corner of the arrangement or will it be in the center where all can see it? For it seems that this is one of the most profound problems facing our society, the question of whether those who disagree with its fundamental tenets should make their disagreements as loud and as public as possible so as to enlist behind them the crowd support that they feel necessary in overcoming the official disapproval of their projects, or whether we have a system solid enough that we can allow malcontents to air their complaints more openly and have them considered on their own merits. We cannot stop to consider this weighty matter to the extent that its importance demands, for if we were to do so, there is no guarantee that we would ever return to the subject at hand, given the fact of our notoriously bad memories and our willingness to be taken off on another tangent joined to the curve of thought. **Weakening:** Still, we would be willing to take the time to develop a defense of the method of associative thinking of which this very passage is an example to offer anyone who seriously questioned its validity, through an analogy with a game that involves covering of a sheet of paper with rows and columns of dots which are then connected with lines, each of which must grow from the end point of another line.

The analogy: The strategy of the game is to avoid constructing boxes, for the one who is forced to close a square is penalized. The results of this defensive sort of play are, first, that for most of the game the board looks totally unstructured to an uninitiated person who would see here and there only an inadvertently completed square, and second, that a perfect flurry of square-filling commences in the last minute or two of the play. It is not until then that the intricate but seemingly disjointed strategy gains its point, not until then that the pattern of the game becomes beautifully clear. What had earlier seemed mere free-association of lines to lines is now seen to be serving a very specific purpose, and to have been bounded by the sheet of paper which had all the time provided the limit on the patterns and yet made irrelevant the choice of particular order in which it was filled, as long as this choice was made among a number of alternatives that were of equal strategic value.

Defensive aside: That a theory for serious thought be modeled on the pattern of a child's game might distress some of our more self-righteous acquaintances, but we must keep in mind that there is no part of the world from which we cannot learn, that be something never so humble it can influence and affect the loftiest of men. We may, if we so choose, regard the world as a great classroom that we never leave and which provides opportunities for nearly unlimited education for all.

He walks up the aisle past the knees of the end mannequin, past the display of threads shining smooth and silky on their spools that blotch the counter with families of related colors, and moves around the corner to the televisions, radios, stereos, and slide projectors that cram the counters and walls. The out-of-place voice comes from the guts of an amplifier several feet away that grins in perverse enjoyment of its situation, showing the green and glowing teeth of the dial from between which a hair-thin red tongue pokes its vertical tip in spiteful glee. It is a radio; there is not one of the televisions that has the nerve to buck the combined force of the others.

As he watches them, they abruptly go blank and show their varicolored but uniformly bland faces in complete non-expressions, as if they were robbers or foreign terrorists who had abruptly pulled stockings over their faces preparatory to producing submachine guns and splattering the other equipment with a rain of bullets that would smash through their metal shells and bury among thin delicate and finely-wrought innards or exit through their backs and flatten against the concrete wall behind or on the tile floor under the counters, bullets that would cause human victims to feel the pounding of hot blood in their heads and the salt taste of their blood and the liquids their gnashing teeth have ripped from the inside of their cheeks and cause their murderers to grasp as nearly as they will ever be able to a certain indefinable duality, the dyad of the totally controlled element and that which is totally free that live together in the animal that is man, cause them to see simultaneously the being who is killed and the being who is dying (respective representations of these two factors), cause them to see this fundamental truth of existence in this situation somehow more strongly than in any other fragile equilibrium of these two forces.

Explanation: We see this truth for some reason the clearer and have our brains the more firmly imprinted with its message when our hands are wet with another's blood, when the gun hangs heavy and hot from our fingers and sends upward a tiny thin trickling of white vapors, or when the knife clatters to the floor, throwing outwards a trail of droplets that splatter around it. Only when we see the contortions of pain of another's face are we able to grasp the enormity of the being that we are, only when we hear the groans from a bleeding throat or the futile scratchings of fingernails against the barricaded door of the burning house that we are able to understand that of which we are made.

Concession: Of course, there are those who commit such crimes for nothing more than personal gain or personal advantage, but I believe that they are few within our ranks. There can be no doubt that, except for those who would kill for money or revenge and thus in the proper sense cannot be called robbers and murderers at all, every crime is committed in the quest for truth. That the smallest and most inexpensive shoplifted toy train is the first step in a search for a level of comprehension of the human condition that only a few ever attain should give us pause to think, for it may well indicate that the talents of childhood reach fruition in only a very limited number of cases, that the environment we provide our progeny actually stifles creativity and produces uniformly uninteresting and unproductive adults.

He casts a last glance at the screens jabbering away in front of him and is soon in front of an elevator, having passed from this part of the field that, apparently sown long ago with the bloody helmets and shattered weapons of the army which had fought here so valiantly, had brought forth these metallic offspring of televisions and radios. He passes the area in front of the elevators where nothing is for sale and that, it is clear, has neither history nor interesting sub-surface deposits and thus cannot suddenly bring forth a bush laden with guinea pigs grown from the single moldering corpse of a child's pet whose funeral had involved a shoebox casket lined with the leaves of the weeping willow and with tufts of cotton pulled by childish hands from behind the bottles of iodine and underneath the thin metal eyebrow tweezers with serpent-like heads. Nor can it produce a low-lying ground cover that puts forth miniature kitchen utensils of all descriptions gleaming from under its thick green leaves and peeping from behind its blossoms, cover which had taken root from the old pancake turner the baby used to drag along in its travels and had abandoned one day in the yard while under the influence of its rather too-close perusal of a rose that had also caught the fancy of a passing bumble bee not about to countenance this sort of blatant claim-jumping that had told the child so in the most direct terms it knew.

He sees watch chains disappearing into pockets and women's belts of silvered or gold-colored links girding sagging waists, sees jeweled chains encircling the wrinkled wrists of painted matrons and braided fetters of human hair encircling the skulls of teenaged girls. Were he not immune to such low humor, it might occur to him to reflect that man is born free and yet everywhere he is in chains. But this is not humor that can be classified on a standard scale of height, is rather the sort of joke likely to be told by a demi-intellectual eager to please the uncomprehending matrons of the Saturday afternoon garden and poetry club in exchange for his weekly ration of tea and cakes and society and be met with the half-hearted titters of the unamused which he will attempt to increase by explanations that will bring the women's well-padded bottoms to the edges of their lawn chairs and elicit periodic head bobbings.

When he is finished, there will be silence but for the asthmatic breathing of the eldest member. Finally after several more painfully protracted seconds, one of the younger and more spry of them will lean back in her chair with a sigh of comprehension and raise a bony finger for attention. Girls, she will rasp with her eyes alight with the triumph of understanding, girls, it's politics—it's just politics. And at that the other women will sigh a uniform sigh of relief and will loosen their tensed bodies and look at one another with a knowing gleam in their eyes that strengthens as it is shared, will look at their savior with gratitude and at the demi-intellectual with a gaze that bespeaks commonality of interests and ends. At this point, in all likelihood, they will all find it necessary to raise from their laps their delicate eggshell china tea cups and to moisten their reddened lips with some of the brown syrup inside and to nibble a corner from off the cucumber sandwiches the maid has just handed around before they trust themselves to talk. When the silence is broken by one of the more adventurous of their number who is jealous of the enlightener, still collapsed in her chair in what she hopes is interpreted as a clear statement that some feats cannot simply be followed by sandwiches and tea but is more likely to be read by several of these bitter old women who are always looking for signs of infirmity in peers as a slight sunstroke brought on by overwork and who glitters her hard eyes fiercely at the one who has had the temerity to try and top her act, the women begin to chatter volubly, absorbed in their conversation. This is dotted with periodic exclamations of "politics, yes politics" that produce on that section of the lawn in which the words were uttered a momentary silence, broken by the sound of pendant earrings clicking as heads are shaken meditatively and that bring a smile to the lips of the one who, even if she never utters another word in this club, will be enshrined forever in all memories as a quick thinker and a woman of wisdom, a smile that alternates with a recurring scowl produced by her conviction that she hears Rose Marie Underwood and Alice Ann Thomas talking about tea cozies and their grandchildren rather than her recent coup. Nonetheless, she is unable to keep the threads of conversation straight now that a slight breeze has begun to drive away a bit of the heat and is mingling with the sounds and the sultry smell of the wisteria vines hanging purple and full in the arbor.

Another motif recurring among the people crammed beside him in the elevator: rings. There are rings on the fingers of the women and hanging from their thin ears, and fatter and heavier ones on the fingers of the businessmen around him. A plastic ring hangs from a pink plug that seems to have been thrust as a muzzle into the near-formless lips of a baby that is drooling globs of spit onto its mother's shoulder. There is a thicker metal ring on the end of the umbrella poking its insistent ribs into his side, which at the moment is hooked through the rather cruelly-taloned finger of a woman who, when looked in the face in a quick aside designed to seem as if it is really a general tour of the elevator that happened to stop for an instant on her head or a glance at the control panel that for some reason was compelled to take a detour, is seen to be startlingly plain in spite of all the blobs of color that dot the ends of her fingers and her eyes and mouth.

There are rings formed by the raised and lighted rims of the buttons, and rings on the sandals of the large pair of feet he sees exposed in the corner through a separation in the forest of legs, but to which he can attribute no particular body. For halfway up the gap closes, and there is no top that should belong to these tan jeans with the grass stains on the knees and these rather pale feet that seem to be constructed in sharply-defined sections held together by some sort of fleshly gravity until, when he looks again, there is a shine off one of the straps and it is clear that these brown swatches are not the sole of the sandal seen through a gap in the foot, but instead convex pieces that straddle the instep and the toes.

Reflection: Surely this informal lower half with the sandals cannot, mermaid or centaur-style, be topped with a totally unrelated upper half such as the wide-lapelled torso he sees below a prissily mustached face that hovers in the same corner as these pants, for this is one of those huge elevators in which a single line of sight may cut through several persons, with the well-filled blouse of the redhead who stares moodily up into the corner of the ceiling and chews a single dainty fingernail.

Reasoning: Even if the creature was born this way, like a person with horsehair on its lower parts, laws of nature would discourage its living in this half-man, half-beast state and would induce it to commit suicide, ripping from its waist the belt that looks as if it is an accessory that could be shed with ease but whose removal in fact flays the creature alive. In doing so it spatters itself with the juices that will gush from the opened ends of the interior canals that abut on this tactile epidermis, the powerful tug that is made the more insistent by the pain that is now beginning to craze it and drive from its mind all memories of why it was it wanted to die in so terrible a fashion, the belt loosing itself an inch at a time until there is around its waist a great wide band from which the lymph dribbles and spurts. Finally it holds in its weakening hand the alligator band that halfway through its width turns into frayed rope, marking in this boundary the line of demarcation between the well-dressed upper part and the slovenly nether regions stained with the marks of the outdoors and of manual work which could not be allowed to co-exist and which had done so thus far only because of the creature's cowardice and propensity to procrastination.

Further, there are rings (or at least half rings) under the eyes of the rather pained-looking woman by his side, great folds of purplish skin that seem quite at home with the other red blotches of pimples on her cheeks and the livid explosions of veins that he sees as he looks down at her foreshortened legs glistening with the shine of the heavy stockings. These cannot hide the marvelous colors of her legs beneath their thick tannish-brown blur echoing in blurred twin the bluish snakes that writhe down the backs of her hands and seem to disappear into the skin at the knuckles. There are rings between the sections of the pocketbook strap that he glimpses to the side of the minister's black coat, which moves just then and covers it with more of the black, and with a pair of hairy hands folded across each other that appear unnaturally pale against their contrasting background and against the black hair that coats them down their backs and extends onto the fingers' second joints. The hands seem to have been disembodied with a sharp slash of the black silk and left stranded and exposed so that it appears only chance that they hang with the fingers sideways, locking into one another as they must if they are attached to arms, and the result of chance as well the fact that they are located at this particular place near the bottom center of the coat rather than blooming from the slight bulge that must be the right kneecap or growing like fleshy wings from the center of the black-clad back.

Were it not for the exceedingly efficient ventilation system, he reflects, the elevator would certainly be stuffy. Prevailing smells would certainly be wet wool and perhaps the less widespread but unquestionably more penetrating bitterness of baby's vomit, of which a small patch has just appeared on the towel draped on the shoulder of the woman next to him. She quietly folds it up and stuffs it into the side pocket of a voluminous purple pocketbook from which she extracts a plug that she pops into the child's mouth.

Question: Why is it that the circular motif predominates in the decoration scheme for this strange collection of humans packed into this slowly descending chamber? **Answer:** We humans are impelled to decorate ourselves with symbols of our eschatology: we wish to have near to us at all times a solid representation of our faith in our eventual rebirth. We have all of us drunk for too long the dregs of human servitude not to be convinced that so much misery cannot properly be visited upon any single creature forever; some day we will enjoy the ambrosial flavor of the freedom that belongs only to those unregulated by the stifling conventions we have constructed around us that imprison us more firmly and more surely than any bars we could forge.

Explanation: There is not one of us but believes that we will one day return in, let us say, the flowers that float in the wind-rippled waters, the yellow crowns that are their souls open to the warm rays of the sun that sends to them orange-striped insects clutching petals with their thin black legs and opening their shelly plates to the golden heat, exposing their vulnerable and downy backs; the creatures fly away as the sun begins to fade and the night breezes come and the petals themselves close in soft protection against the white glare of the moon that would chill their insides with its implacable gaze and turn them frigid within, were it to look upon what was meant only to drink in the soft and more loving gaze of the golden sun. Alternately, we may return in the gnarled trunks of aged trees that reach their legs skywards, their heads being buried in the ground in cool communion with the dark earth and the worms. Or, we may become the wild boars who grunt their contentment with their every breath, or the flying squirrels that have only to spread their diminutive feet to become living gliders upon the balmy spring breezes.

Alternate explanation: Perhaps it is not this at all that impels us to bedeck ourselves with these simple closed curves, but instead a desire to become a different sort of creature than we are, to be instead of the heavy and opaque beings we are a more vulnerable and fragile being that, unlike a donut or a flour strainer, are not essentially a solid thing incidentally pierced in one or more places, but rather the definer of this emptiness, the hoop that calls attention to the non-being of what is within it and yet is itself thick enough that to it accrues whatever advantages are part and parcel of being something rather than nothing. Were we to approximate this thing that is barely more than air, we would be less than we are and in some sense thereby made the greater, for in cases like these, delicacy is its own defense and though heftiness defends one against attackers, it also attracts the eyes of enemies in the first place.

Lesson: The world does not like the excessively good or the excessively beautiful or the excessively talented, as I reflected one wintry night last year when, the wind howling around the shutters and the snow making its quiet piles higher around my door, I looked down and saw a swarm of ants that had nested within the bark of a log that was just beginning to catch on fire. **The incident:** The ants streamed from their cozy home in terror of the conflagration that was threatening to cook them all and which indeed had already rendered black curls those outside members of the hoard which had been unlucky enough to miss their step on the treacherous bark layers and had fallen headlong into the roaring inferno below. At this point, I considered briefly whether I should become the messiah of these creatures, preaching salvation to them in the best approximation I could make of insect voices, though I feared that my knowledge of such languages was limited to a reasonable approximation of cricket chirps. I realized, however, that it would be wrong to make salvation available only to those ants which, by virtue of a superior education, had learned to understand cricket speech, that it would be better that none of them be saved than that a few reach salvation by unfair earthly advantages.

Suite: Even as I thought this, a vision rose to my eyes of a dream-like scene in which there was at first nothing visible but a curtain of raindrops that, unlike many romantic conceptions of a dream rain, did not appear as a mist or a gray fog but which stood out stark and clear in my mind, each ruthless glistening drop evident against the background. Gradually, I became aware of an interloper in this vision of steel-gray, a thing that resolved itself into a human body and then, as its face was framed in a hole in the curtain of rain, into myself. The rain, I muttered to myself, I have seen me dead in it.

The meaning becomes clear: In a flash I understood what I was to do with these small dark animals. I ran to the kitchen where I filled a bucket as quickly as I could with the water that burst with a rusty shudder from the spigot. Leaving the stream gushing to drown the sound of what I was to do, I ran headlong into the living room, dripping gouts of water from the bucket I clutched to my chest with both my hands. With a great heave, I doused the log and everything on it. As the wave swept over the wood, it caught in its path all of the insects, drowning most of them instantly and washing those it did not drown onto the crackling flames, which took perhaps several seconds longer than they might have under less damp circumstances to dry out the bodies and evaporate the pustules of water on which they rode before burning them.

I stood watching the pool of drowned ants quickly diminishing against the hot bricks, heard the slight hiss of the steam as the edges receded, uncovering the dots of hard blackness that, as the water level fell from the top of their bodies down to their lower parts, became less glossy and shiny and more like knots of dark thread swept from a seamstress' lap into the fire. I heard the rush of water from the spigot in the next room and the roar of the wind as it charged around the corner of my chimney—and I understood the teaching of the dream and of my action.

Lesson: I comprehended that here it was not a conflict of death and life that was at issue, but death by fire versus a death by water. I saw that there was no way that I could ever become to these things what would in effect be nothing more than a noumenal God, a deity so far removed in nature and intelligence from the creatures in His power that it would be better for their mental health not ever to know of His existence than to reveal Himself as this inaccessible creature whose decrees seemed to come from nowhere and be headed in no discernible direction. I realized too that I could not intrude myself upon their civilization and rock its foundations to the extent it would have to be shaken in order to accomplish this action of a *deus ex machina* of saving their lives. I knew then as I stood there feeling the heat draw together the skin on my cheeks and forehead, purse my lips and warm my eyebrows and still clutching the bucket foolishly in my right hand, that these creatures must for their own good die in the conflagration and that my only function was to decide and carry out the manner in which this was to take place. In this case, all that mattered was that they perish through the liquid element and not the fiery one, that their deaths be suitable ends to their lives. Since these were not impetuous creatures but cold-blooded and hard-working ones, it was most fitting that they should die by drowning in cold water rather than consumption by flame. **Note:** We Moderns tend not to emphasize enough the importance of a fitting end, seeming to feel that if the beginning and middle have been beyond reproach the end will take care of itself. But this is wrong; we must know how to finish something as well as how to present and develop it.

There are without a doubt many more such trails of symbols among those in the elevator that would repay close perusal, but sometimes our search for the truth must bow to mundane considerations such as the fact that such studies would have to be done on thin air: there is a dearth of subjects now, seeing as how the elevator has eased itself to a stop a good twenty seconds ago and opened its doors, permitting a general exodus that has now completely vacated the contraption but for a woman who stands at its open doorway and stares dazedly into the crack between the shaft and the elevator, stares down into the darkness from which the clank of chains can be heard and the flicker of glowing lights can be seen. She seems to come to herself in a second or two and, rearranging her steel-gray bun with a free hand and an authoritative pat, lifts her sensible black shoes over the low sill and is gone, clutching her pocketbook a good several seconds before the doors clank shut on the empty and lighted chamber and the whir of its machinery is heard pushing it upwards again, the sound rising in pitch to accompany the light that ascends the column of numbers on the wall where no one is and which no one can see.

He turns the corner between elevator and front entrance and soon finds himself outside the department store, where he pauses a moment under the awning to check for rain. The noise of water comes from puddles sloshing under the wheels of the cars that move in jagged columns down the street, and the few hurrying rather than plodding footsteps are the solitary clicks or splats of isolated people who have been so intent on avoiding the puddles on the sidewalk that they have failed to realize that the rain has stopped.

In a moment, therefore, he is around the corner and walking down a side street, which seems only a crack in the tall buildings on either side of him, created by the powerful hand of a vengeance-set god. He looks up, almost colliding with a particularly fat raindrop that crashes to the pavement at his feet. The starkness of the right-angle fissure is broken by air conditioning units sticking from every window like buttons on a huge switchboard. He is so intent on them that he misses the glass-fronted shop on his left and he is past with no consciousness of it at all save a vague blur created by its sign saying “Antiques” that sticks out above his head.

Inside, the tables full of *objets d'art* become slightly darker as his shadow passes over them, deepening the soft color of the ivory elephant and making its small beady eye glow brighter in contrast. In his shadow, the dark insides of the filigreed metal box seem momentarily so deep as to make it appear that it is no ordinary box at all, but the stage-prop cover for a trap door that leads through the surface of the table and down into the black space under it, enclosed by the frilled red cloth. Back in the recesses of the shop, by contrast, a grandfather clock ticks ponderously and is not affected by his passing, no more than are the polished Louis XV chairs that flank it or the marble tables that extend delicate legs down to the floor like fawns sticking hesitant front hooves down onto the shining surface of a small woodland pond.

All these riches, even without the additional darkening of his shadow, are caught in the half-lucent limbo of a cloudy evening and hidden on this dark street behind a glass that even at its most accessible moments reflects back the exterior world instead of disclosing what lies within to those passers-by insufficiently interested to stop a moment and destroy the reflected façade by pressing their faces against the warm pane and wiping out the glare with the shadow of their hands. The light inside is not so dim but that, had he done so and with a few seconds of adjustment for his eyes, he would have been able to make out the burnished gold on the corners of the picture frames, the oriental silks whose turquoise folds seem almost to writhe in suppressed passion against the cooler and more subdued pattern of shepherds and shepherdesses repeating itself in greens and pinks up the pale back of the couch, and the thick pile of the rug that leaves off its pattern long enough to cushion the feet of the furniture before taking it up again on their other side.

His shoes skirt small pools of water and slip slightly sideways on his feet as he steps onto the street to escape a sunken section of the concrete glistening with the rain. He steps over the river that flows straight and dark along the trough formed by the curved asphalt and the concrete barriers that crumble a bit every few yards, exposing their pebbly innards to the air. Towards the end of the street, this edge becomes pale and loses its blemishes as if finally having pulled itself together and being able to continue without breaking down or wringing from its nearly dry body a few more gulping tears. There are small drops of water sticking to the rough and broken surfaces, nestling in holes in the concrete as if playing at being small stones of especially clear quartz or kin to the more opaque pebbles that are anchored beside them.

He hears the footsteps of someone behind him, and has begun to hear the people walking across on the larger street up ahead. He is soon at the corner and among them, leaving the dark street to whomever had entered it after him.

The people are fewer here on this sidewalk than on its parallel thoroughfare and the stores smaller and abruptly seedier and cheaper. Many of the people are black. Men strut along in shoes that add several inches of glowing yellow or red leather to their height, wearing loose pants that swish past their ankles and flop up and down at the slight hitch-and-dip that is inserted into the middle of each step as if the walker were waging a perpetual battle with the forces of the underworld that manage in the weakest point of each stride to pull him down; these demons apparently never succeed well enough that they cannot be defeated on the stronger upswing.

Precept: An upright man cannot be overcome by evil except when unable to resist with the force of his own body motion, that is, when asleep. **Discussion:** Whether this is to be interpreted to mean moral sleep or the more biologically necessary physical sleep is not decidable on the basis of the evidence alone, and in any case must be turned over to a licensed philosopher to figure out. **A layman's opinion:** It is the more dangerous of the two alternatives that is meant. We simply cannot believe that all these years of literature about the night and the velvety blackness have been allegorical only and did not really concern that portion of our lives in which we lie with hearts beating so loudly we are sure the people in the next room must hear them and take the sound for an intruder at their door, our bodies covered as best we can with the thin sheets that cannot possibly protect us from anything at all and are liable in any case soon to fall from us as a result of the shudders running through our limbs and our clammy hands.

Suite: We are unable to accept that the crackles and pops in the woodwork are not the sounds of the flames of hell or that it is not the noise of the lost souls that screams around our windows but merely the wind. We cannot accept that the sweet music we hear wafting from the corners of our dream world bearing up our bed and supporting us on cushions of moving sound are not the seductions of the evil angels played upon harps made from the bones of the damned and strung with their sinews, seductions that enter our bodies and possess them with deceptive and honey-sweet tones which are attractive only because the sleeper hears them from afar, hears only the unending line of their melody prepared from the distilled and sickly-sweet liquor of rue and not the coarse texture of the notes which are the echoes of human sighs and of false promises woven so well that we discern only the rich tapestry of sound and not the thick and nubby filaments from which it was made. We are not convinced, finally, that these dream images are but the happenings of the day transformed by a half-dormant mind alive to all of the symbolism that the fully alert brain is unwilling or unable to decipher and interpret, and not the actual perceptions of another world as real as our waking one.

In the hair of many of the men stick the ends of combs parked in the midst of that to which they minister. Perhaps this is meant as an assertion of the idea that beauty or order must not be understood to be self-generating, but instead as the result of the expenditure of more than a fair amount of blood, toil, tears, and sweat, with the final product displayed along with the thing that made it that way.

Problems with such a project if carried out on a grand scale: It will be difficult to trace and display an entire causal sequence if that sequence is of essential causes. Here the comb that ordered the hair is being displayed. But what of the plastics factory that produced the comb, the store that sold it, and the mint that produced the money with which it was purchased? The factory could not have continued functioning were it not for the janitor, the company that made the janitor's broom, the bus that brought the janitor to work, and so on. Should we display the bus with the comb? Or does the bus belong more properly to another object entirely? Does the bus perhaps belong to the crutches of the little boy whose bicycle overturned in a pothole partly created by the passage of the bus's wheels? If we attempt to trace the genealogy of more than just a few objects, in short order we will be involved in an ungodly labeling tangle.

Worse: The situation becomes yet more complicated when we consider the argument that the opposite of a given state is logically necessary to it, for without its opposite a state would not be what it is, and thus is a cause of its being that should be displayed with it. This argument would seem to have us going out painting moustaches on the Mona Lisa, adding a plaster-of-Paris pot belly of middle age to the youthful torso of the Apollo Belvedere and thalidomide arms to the Venus de Milo as well as strewing diamonds or robins eggs in mud puddles, propping tubular metal sculpture against the windswept and decrepit porches of the abandoned General Stores in ghost towns, and restructuring precisely half of the mauled faces of those pawed by lions or disfigured by gasworks explosions.

Related interpretation: Or is this comb merely suggesting that the mechanism that is used to put something the way it is can be exposed along with the result of no loss of beauty or grace? This is such an obviously correct notion that there have been a number of its proponents recently who, overwhelmed by its truth, have latched onto it as if it were a revelation from the muse herself. The result is that they have lost sight of the fact that there is no more inherent reason for baring the machinery under the doll's plastic skin than there is in leaving her decently covered; there is no point in dropping sly hints or thinly-disguised self-references if one has not some larger justification for doing so other than the childish desire to shock that has led all of us at some point in our formative years to exhibit to someone with whom we were piqued a pink tongue loaded with and all but obscured by a mouthful of partly chewed food.

This always produced in our viewer such gratifyingly shrill cries of rage and disgust that we felt quite justified and did not reflect until later that the effect of such an exhibition was two-sided. It appalled with the simple sight of the lumpy and salivated mash that was the food, and at the same time enraged with the exhibition of the unpleasant and actually revolting machines that, working away inside the unseen darkness of our bodies, makes it more pleasant exterior possible. **Warning:** There is little point in engaging in these sorts of shock tactics for the sake of the initial gasp of surprise and outrage at seeing all that which goes into the making of something we are unable to think of in any state other than complete and fully mature.

The girls hanging onto the arms of these men are not so uniformly attired as are the men. Some have swaddled their thin legs in long tight dresses that bear the marks of wear identifying them as blue jeans which have been slashed up the seams and converted from two thin tubes to one much larger one through the addition of two great triangles of material, one front and one back. The effect of this transformation is a curious sort of visual effect in which the eye flickers between seeing a skirt that is merely oddly discolored and the flat projection of the dead pants that hangs on the garment like a ghost around the scene of its violent end and through which one is forced to look in order to see the present garment.

Some wear halters and shorts cut off at the bottom of the buttocks, and teeter along on the shoes that imprison their feet in perpetual frozen arches down the fronts of huge blocks of cork and wood as if they had bought on some traveling medicine man's advice a contraption designed to calcify the bones of the feet into new and interesting solid shapes. As the salesman would have been quick to point out, the contraption would serve double duty: after the feet were petrified in the shape desired, they would not be able to be used for walking or locomotion without support by a special shoe, and what better or more fashionable footwear could there be but the presses on which the hardening had taken place?

Results: One morning they would finally get up the courage to unstrap the contraptions and put pressure on their naked feet, full of pins and needles from disuse, that would send them crumpling to the floor at their first step. Finally they would be able to pull themselves up onto the bed by the sheer strength of their arm muscles that raised them hand over hand up the twisted covers trailing on the floor. At this point they might well discover that the process was as effective as its advertiser had claimed and that they had acquired as a result about four inches in height so long as they were able to get used to walking on their toes. Alternately, they could try to walk normally; the problem here would be that now only the heel and ball of the foot would touch the ground, the arch being nearly semi-circular and the toes sticking up at an angle of at least 30°.

Second thoughts: The other possibility is that they would come to their senses a bit sooner than this and remove the presses when the process was half completed. Yet the result would be little short of disastrous, for when they finally put all of their weight on the disfigured appendages, there would be an initial moment in which the feeling of solidity was stronger than the feeling of fragility, as when stepping cautiously out onto half-frozen ice on a wintertime pond. But as in the case of this ice, there would come from the feet distant pops and crackles as if the edges were tessellating or pulling away from reeds, and then the noises and vibrations would increase in strength and frequency. The rather alarming feeling would localize in the arch and all of a sudden the foot would shudder and crackle and begin to bow downwards in a curve that would break with the noise of the snapping of many small bones whereupon they would find the foot flat on the floor and already beginning to bruise and turn blue from the shattered innards.

The stores along this street apparently assume that the most effective way to advertise their merchandise is to display as much of it as possible: mountains of vari-colored objects rise in the windows by his side, obscuring completely that which is behind them except for a thin clear space at the top in which the hanging fluorescent lights are to be seen. In the jewelry stores, rows of bracelets and rhinestone rings begin at chest level and arch upwards, watched over by small pink-faced dolls with billowing white skirts and veils and eyelashes as long as the legs of fat black spiders.

The dolls stand against open watch boxes or are propped against the paper-covered steps up to the backs of the showcases on which the goods are crammed. Perhaps they are meant to instill the wedding spirit in those couples who stop in front of the window, the sailors and their girls who lean against each other chewing gum and looking in the window, the thin men whose tattoos peek from a pale strip of white upper arm showing underneath a sleeve rolled into a wrinkled donut, a strip of flesh that is usually protected against the sun which has turned their wiry lower arms brown. The arms ripple slightly with the tight muscles under the skin as the men shift their arms to a different position on their girls' backs, moving across the sleeveless knit blouses from which stick two fattening upper arms and a neck nearly covered with the bottom of a rounded mass of teased and sprayed hair that is sometimes blond, sometimes brown.

Some of the goods in the clothing and jewelry stores are displayed on mannequins or their plastic parts, disembodied hands modeling rings or torsoes wearing bathing suits that look as if they might be used to clone whole new plastic people who could simply step into the clothes that are hung beside them. **A difficulty:** The production process might fail to take the genetic cue it ought from these rounded, tan, and unwrinkled fingers and instead of completing the bodies in a comparable fashion, attach to the arm a horribly wrinkled body, the body of a crone about to die whose thin breasts hang to her waist and whose white hair flies wild and unkempt about her puckered face, or to this smooth and athletic male torso the extremities of an underdeveloped twelve-year-old which would hang thin and short beside the bulging plastic pectorals.

Questions: When the time came for these misfits to die, for these plastic freaks to pass from the earth, would these parts that are in their prime be content to trade their public position here in this sunlit window in a cut-rate clothing store for the silence of the grave? Would they be content to leave their easy lives here in the window for a moldering bed in the earth in the company of the attached limbs or bodies of the world-weary and world-worn? Would they leave this endless pageant that passes by in dejected and dispirited or aggressively flamboyant parade before them for the cool embrace of a box lined with white satin, a material they would have scorned as effete in the days in which they modeled blue denim, gray cotton twill, and surplus army khakis? **To be kept in mind:** Their headless selves cannot retain the past and are incapable of looking into the future and thus have neither recollections of the dark storeroom from which they were taken nor presentiments of the trash bin in which they will be thrown, and thus are quite sure they have been here forever and will stay here as long.

Answer to all questions: We cannot conceive of their being willing to rest in the earth with those parts of their bodies more ready to die than they. We cannot but believe that they would make every effort possible to get themselves caught between the lid and the box as it was being screwed down in the hope that the severely myopic undertaker's helpers would attribute the rickety lid to mere warping and continue to the bitter end their job of joining casket top to casket bottom. In doing so, they would inevitably sever the limb that would fall to the floor and rest a moment before trying to creep unseen out of the door, or hide until night under a nearby casket when its escape would be more safe, trying to accomplish the whole trip on the palm and fingers of the hand and not on the flat of the arm so that any blood or stray embalming fluid would have to drip down the length of the appendage before reaching the floor and dry into a red crust on the skin instead of splattering the floor in tell-tale tracks.

Another possibility: The mismatched younger body parts might have tried earlier to effect their escape and smeared the jointure of the fair young skin and the wrinkled and horrible epidermis to which they were attached with the small pieces of greasy meat they had snatched from the dog's dish in passing as they were being carried from the basket to the slab by the careless assistants who had simply slung the rather light and not completely stiff corpse over their shoulders. The smell of this meat would soon draw the stiff and frozen white rats that live in the icy corners of the room-sized refrigerators at morgues and which move with jerky twitchings of their legs as if each motion were an overcoming of inertia or of muscles nearly immobilized by the cold which causes their skin to crackle and their fur to tinkle with small icicles that have formed between the hairs and drip off the ends of their stiff whispers and their frosted eyelashes. The rats would come stealthily forward and, their white teeth flashing with ice crystals in the pale moon that streams in the unshuttered window, begin to chew on the flesh line. If all goes well, this will result in the eventual severing of the alien limb.

It seems only natural that as soon as the arm finds itself free, in one way or another, it would go straight to those for whom this complicated escape was effected (a psychological certainty used to law-enforcement advantage by detectives everywhere) and so would make haste to return to this seedy section of town—if indeed it still inhabits the same city in which it spent its hot and happy childhood among the clothes for sale gradually bleaching lighter in the direct afternoon sun, if it has not by the body to which it found itself one day suddenly and without warning attached been transported to some far-off and completely unknown town from which it would have to begin a long and arduous homeward journey—to return to those among whom it had grown up and from whom it had been separated for so long and which, happy as they would be to see it outside the window after all these long years, would be unable to leave their perches to let it in.

As for the arm, it would press itself against the pane, its strength rapidly ebbing, trying in the anguish of its blocked and thwarted desire to get as close as it could to those for whom it has undergone so much: with a last gathering of its forces it forms itself into a fist and pounds at the glass, at first feebly then with a crescendo of power and strength, so that abruptly the glass shivers and shatters inward, showering the clothes with a sharp rain of glistening razor blades. The arm will fall stiffly onto a pile of blue jeans and, with one last convulsive grasp of its fingers, gather into its fist a clump of the material and then be still, so that when the owner comes clattering down the stairs in his nightgown waving a shotgun with which he means to frighten off the young ruffians who have smashed his window and interrupted his sleep, there is no noise of juvenile footsteps pounding off into the night with air popping through the armfuls of clothes that are unwinding out behind them. Indeed, there is no noise of anything at all, though in the shattered window is a plastic model arm that the scamps must have used as a club which the man picks out with a helpless shrug and carries indoors to hold for the police in the morning, wheezing up the stairs to bed, shaking his head and leaving his idiot son outside as a guard against looters.

Future developments: But the poor man's sleep will be disturbed more times than just this once, for during the colder winters of the succeeding decades he will sometimes in the middle of the night be awakened by a sound of scratching and pounding at his shop windows downstairs and will burst through the door at the bottom of the stairs to see only the blackness and a whitish glow bobbing about the outside of his window that cannot be other than a reflection from the street lamps across the road that disappears into the night at the sound of his footsteps. Finally, after the fifth or sixth time this happens, he again puts on guard duty his son, who is by this time nearly into middle age himself, though none the less idiotic. This son will be found the next morning in a heap on the street, strangled even through the piles of thick scarves with which he has been bundled and the window above him smashed. There will be no trace of finger marks or of any garotting string around his neck and nothing has been taken from the window, though the man's hands are clasped together in fists as if he had tried to grab at something that had slipped from his grasp.

Note: This is all in the realm of speculation.

In the window before which he stands, the display is liberally sprinkled with huge price tags hissing black dollar signs at passers-by. Most of these pedestrians do not ever take their eyes from the sidewalk before them, littered with papers and crumpled wrappers only a little less intermittent around the base of an overflowing trash basket which hangs from a pole and gushes its contents like a misplaced autumnal cornucopia placed here in public view.

On the sidewalks are small white trails of pigeon droppings that have been broken from what was undoubtedly coherent form into a white paste by the force of their fall. Above him fly the culprits, or their cousins or grandfathers, and on the sidewalk in front strut the more adventurous birds that walk jerkily and stiffly and bobble the heads that are set with red eyes connecting to their bodies with what seems a chain-mail hood and neck-guard of feathers that undulates as the head swings to and fro. The smoothness of this jointure is broken at the base where there is a line of separation from the body, the point of attack by an observant foe which would have only to slip the sword under this flap and jiggle it a bit to be rewarded with a gush of blood. **Note:** It might receive as well a bit of a shock if, as the bird rolled over in its death agony, the headdress fell off to reveal the mole that, in the costume of the bird, had lived for the past two years in the hope of some day attracting the beautiful white female pigeon who flew so gracefully and dropped such lovely pure white droppings and had once, with a coy look in her eye, even dropped in his direction as she soared overhead a soft white breast feather, though the treacherous wind had caught it and wafted it over to his rival who had plucked it from its fall with his beak and strutted about showing, to all those who would look, the puff of white down from her he called his lady dove and only the poor dejected mole in pigeon's clothing had seen the gleam in her eye that was directed at him.

The young man skirts the extended feet and legs of an old man who lies nearly full-length out into the stream of those going by. Many people do not hesitate simply to step over his legs rather than going around him. The most arresting part of the man is neither his bearded face nor his black pants and threadbare suit coat, but the thin strip of flesh exposed between the end of the frayed pants cuff and the wrinkled sock of which the elastic in the top is broken, sticking out in short white strokes like straw. The band of exposed leg is as white as the belly of a long-dead fish and is blotched with a few stray spots that seem to have paled along with the skin and are like ghosts of even the lightest and most indistinct freckles.

The young man's downward glance enables him to miss the small pile of dog droppings that have been deposited precisely in the center of the sidewalk beside the sign telling all dog owners that pets are to be curbed: the owner is obviously something of a scoundrel and the dog something of a wry humorist.

Suddenly he looks up again. Had he not done so, he might have missed the knot of sailors and lonesome-looking men with battered suitcases that are milling around the entrance to the bus station and have walked through them and ended up not on the bus to his home town but instead sitting in one of the threadbare seats of the nearly empty theater next door, or in its cousin down the street watching pornographic movies.

Still, we are not to take this as some sort of pivotal point in his life, not to believe that everything in the near future and perhaps the longer term as well is going to be affected by the length of time that he looks or does not look at this unhealthy leg. He is practical enough that, even were the bus trip to have been driven clean out of his head by the cinematic contortions of these fleshy forms in front of which he might find himself sitting, upon emerging blinking into the light and realizing that his bus had left twenty minutes before, he would hardly have been so embarrassed that he would slink back into the station, retrieve his suitcase from the locker, and disappear into the crowd, never to be seen again by anyone in the vicinity of the bus station, un able to go near the scene of his great shame and afraid to use any other form of public transportation in order to leave this city for fear that his exploit has been spread among those in the business who store up such amusing incidents to tell their fellow-workers

He would, for example, have no fear that when he appeared at the airline counter the girl manning the reservation machine would at first smile a professionally uncommitted smile which would broaden a bit as she recognized him, begin to tap her finger lightly on the counter top in suppressed amusement and would soon have to hold up a warning finger and turn around to stifle a fit of giggles badly concealed as a cough. As he would patiently explain his needs, she would continue to be incapacitated with laughter at close intervals so that when looking up from the fifth or sixth such outburst, she would be overcome with regret that her customer had left her, and lean over the counter with a frantic glance down each end of the aisle in hopes of seeing him. In this position, she would again dissolve into giggles that she now made no effort to conceal, and only when her friend from the rival airline next door came over to get her for lunch would she be reasonably in control of herself, all except for an occasional hiccup which would bring again to her lips a faint smile.

Nor would he be afraid of the reactions of a cab driver who, one would think, would be only too glad to suffer a bit by squelching his urge to laugh in return for the large sum he would certainly have been promised for the three-hour trip, who would betray this unwritten contract after the first ten miles with the repeated glances in his rear-view mirror that would assure him of his passenger's identity so that he would turn on the radio at loud volume to cover the sound of his guffaws and give him at least the nominal excuse of absorption in the music for his continual and rhythmic shaking. Nor would the young man be willing to show up at either place in a false beard or a pair of hornrims carrying a thick volume which he would open conspicuously as he approached and from which he would murmur phrases which would have to consist primarily of expressions in all conceivable tones of voice and emotions of the assertion that time flies and the not so grammatically complete situation that of many, one.

Even if he were to miss his bus (and there are any number of reasons besides the skin flicks why he might do so), he would simply resign himself to waiting another three or four hours on the hard chairs in the waiting rooms, finishing the book he is in the middle of, and simply arriving at his parents' empty house three hours later than he had planned. There is no one to wait there for him, and the house has been vacant for three days. Indeed, no living thing is there but a few wilted flowers and possibly a cricket or two that has gotten in through the air ducts or from the cellar.

He looks up at the painted red profiles identified by the huge letters underneath as topless dancers that are the sole ornaments on the boards over the window areas of the building next to the bus station's overhanging portico. The slight coolness of the rain is gone and the effects of the air conditioning of the department store have worn off. Now it is simply a rather muggy and warm evening with the streets beginning to show the first traces of dusk on the little pools that dot them and on the pockmarked tops of the sidewalks that have barely begun to return again to tan from the brown they have assumed under the rain.

As he seeks the protection of the overhang that is now redundant in its absence, he shrugs himself out of his jacket and, letting it fall from one arm, sweeps it around with the other arm on which it is still hung in an arc that would be much greater in size were it not for the presence of a possibly unsavory character who is planted right in the projected path and who might object to suddenly getting an outflung coat arm across his mouth.

He is able to get the thing slung over his shoulder and its collar hooked into his extended finger before he is at the door. Yet his good timing is all for naught, for he has to wait until a large woman maneuvers herself through the doorway. This is a rather long and complicated operation, what with her two suitcases and a hatbox. He waits, his back against a planter built into the brick wall of tiles and filled now not with living greenery or even with artificial plants, but with a thickening layer of trash and cigarette butts and the crumpled tissue paper receipts of bus tickets that, wet from the rain and their nether ends soaking up the discolored water that stands an inch deep over and around and under this soggy mass and turns the carbon paper numbers around the letters to spread-out and even more indistinct blurs, the water still bubbling an occasional small bubble of absorption for the benefit of those who are willing to wait around to see it, a tiny parcel of fetid air that flutters to the surface and pops after several seconds' wait under the slimy surface layer, as if delaying its entrance into the air to make the most dramatic gesture possible.

Suddenly the doorway is clear, and he tugs at the handle that produces just a slight swaying in the glass and then seems to give up in his hands, swinging outwards with a groan and disgorging as an afterthought an old man who shuffles through and seems to find it natural that the door has opened at his mere presence and is being held ajar by a young man with a blue coat slung over his shoulder. The man looks neither right nor left and continues his path straight to the curb without hitting anyone, crossing the street in a clear space that has opened among the cars and taxicabs.

Apparently this miracle has occurred for the man alone, for when a pair of thin middle-aged women clinging to one another as if each were the other's piece of driftwood in a strong current try to take advantage of an event that appears comparable in importance to the parting of the Red Sea, they are nearly run down by a blue Chevrolet that seems to come out of nowhere and are sent scurrying back to the curb hanging onto one another so tightly that the sweater of the slightly more feeble and gray-haired of them ends up twisted around her waist, the pearl-white row of buttons curving across her flat breasts and down her side like the scars from a particularly bloody and potentially life-saving operation.

But he cannot stand here any longer craning his neck after the vanished old man, since there are three other men behind him, waiting to get in. They make further delay unadvisable if not impossible, for they look like the sort who do not readily tolerate the continued presence of someone else in a doorway they wish to use. So use it they all do, with the young man leading the way. They enter the waiting room in a quartet that disbands immediately afterwards into an unequal separation of three and one as if, like all show business professionals, they had buried any personal grudges for the length of the public contract, but, now that they are through their act, feel more than free to let personal feelings come to the surface.

He stands for a moment looking over the bus station from his vantage point by the machine that, with the inducement of two quarters or five dimes, can be coaxed into shooting onto the floor a package of blue folded plastic. With the addition of the breath of life—which in this case cannot be started by spanking or shaking the thing but must actually be applied mouth to mouth—this becomes a rather plump pillow, of which a living cousin is shown in the bowed display window above the coin slot. The popcorn machine beside it, with its bottom parts made of opaque metal and its head of glass, exposes the yellowed curds of its brain that are flying madly through the air, sprayed from a rotating tube within. Before it stands a small child twiddling a pair of black plastic Mickey

Mouse ears attached to a thin cap that he cracks between his sticky hands. The child gazes open-mouthed as if in wonder that his own coin—or that of the bored and hot-looking woman who is bent over beside him, picking on the stitching unraveling from the front of her worn and run-down loafers—can incite to such activity the huge machine that stands before him. As the twirling tubes begin to slow down in exhaustion and the bin of warm fluff begins to empty itself into a cardboard carton, the child readies his hands by the plastic sliding door. When the carton plops down behind this, he wrenches open the door and seizes the cardboard, nearly bending the top of the box from its square shape into a thin slit and littering the floor with the contents. Reaching in a hand, he begins to transfer a fistful of them to his mouth.

The mother has been involved with her footwear and is paying no attention to the child; the young man in blue leaning against the nearby pillow dispenser has turned around and is gazing at the lines of people wilting before the ticket counter with their suitcases at their feet. Some of them are standing behind these heavy blocks that hide from his gaze the bases of their legs that seem inordinately delicate in contrast. It is as if they are swaying statues set into heavy sockets without which they could not be guaranteed to balance themselves and remain erect against the buffeting forces of the occasional and infrequent breaths of air that blow through this room, perhaps when the two doors on opposite sides of the room are opened simultaneously. The air, at any rate, cannot cool even the sweat-stained shirts of the men who stand in this line or the blouses and dresses of the women streaked dark down the sides, and thus would seem to present no threat to the stability of any statue of any weight at all, regardless of the thinness of its legs or the seeming precariousness of its position.

The line stretches all the way across the free part of the room and blocks access to the dingy cafeteria as well as to the bookstall outside, whose protective canvas overhangs several revolving metal racks bristling with brightly colored paperbacks, like especially fat hyacinth plants brought to full bloom in the hothouse and transferred here, where they are sold blossom by individual blossom. Those who need to get by this barricade of lined-up people, either to get to one of the bus doors or to these wonderfully inviting shops, must look for a weak spot and elbow their way through. Doing so produces a scraping noise as a suitcase is pulled reluctantly sideways or a sort of gate in the line that swings open, a person who steps back to let them through before moving back to his or her place to close the gap.

Sometimes when the line is moving slowly and when all the others who are a part of it look appreciably more determined than (say) the little old lady hugging the overnight bag to her flattened bosom or the inoffensive and mousy-looking man who, though the day is hot, wears a jacket and a long- sleeve shirt and has not taken off the halyard necktie that closes his collar against his perspiring neck, this gateway will be used all the way from back by the rows of molded plastic chairs up to the counter, this same victim continuing to step aside as the line moves forward like the patch of flesh all but torn from the side of a python that flaps in and out as it slithers along in the dust.

He pushes himself from the top of the pillow machine and walks towards the closest of these rows of molded chairs that bend slightly under the body's weight. He selects an empty one between a tired-looking black man whose gnarled hands are clasped on the silver knob of an expensive walking stick which looks even more out of place than it might otherwise do for being so well-polished and without any nicks or gouges, and a white woman whose acetate-clad leg he must step over to reach the chair. The leg is withdrawn immediately and held as close under her chair as possible without her drawing it into her lap. The woman raises her head with its hair frozen in a mass of swirls and spirals as if she had had reproduced in her coiffure the stylized curves of a wave from a Japanese print, sniffing in what seems contempt for this seedy bus station in which she is forced to wait, contempt for these malleable chairs in which she is forced to sit, and not least of all for these two men, one young, one old, between whom she is forced to arrange her shapely legs ending in ten shiny red nails and her arms that abut in the same way as if, without the nail to soften the blow of flesh meeting unmediated air at the ends of her ten extremities, these so-disparate substances would be unable to co-exist without open warfare.

Conjecture: The result of such conflict between flesh and air would be to produce a horribly disfigured set of extremities. There would be long thin inroads made in the fingers by the air and equally long nodules the flesh has reached out against its enemy which would continue to form, branching off and branching again, until the ends of the fingers and toes could not really be said to exist as discrete entities at all.

The young man has barely settled himself with a sigh when the woman pops from her own seat as if the two of them were corks bobbing in a bowl of water in which the depression of one meant the immediate elevation of the other.

She teeters for a moment on her thin high heels, getting her balance and, having arranged her pocketbook in her left fist and her umbrella in her right, taps away, her undeniably attractive buttocks shifting underneath the tight shiny sheath of her pants and the tails of her matching jacket that cover them halfway down. The old man does not lift his head to follow her and the young man wonders if perhaps his neighbor is asleep, for the wrinkles of his cheek and forehead are so deep that no one can say whether the older man's eyes are open or closed.

Attached to each chair is an individual television set that flickers into life when quarters are inserted into its top; if the lighter tinkle of dimes or nickels is sounded in their ears they sleep on, undisturbed. Another child, this one on the other side of the now-vacant seat, sits raptly before what has in foreshortening become a slit of moving gray that can be unfolded to reveal the people on it only by sitting in the child's chair. The young man notes this blurred ribbon in which no one thing can be distinguished from any other, where all things animate and inanimate are reduced to the common denominator of shades of gray in a translation that is sufficiently removed from any language he knows that he is not distracted from contemplation of the shapes by their similarity to those of human beings or other recognizable everyday objects.

The child seems interested as well, though he cannot possibly understand what the nasal newscaster's voice is talking of—which, if the young man is not confusing this with the sounds of another television from behind him, is a revolution in the southern hemisphere. Perhaps the close attention the child is paying is due not to the subject matter but to the novelty of having for the first time a private television set which performs for his satisfaction alone. Perhaps too it is the strangeness of having bought, by the twenty-five cents his mother has put in the machine, the right to dissolve this man in a business suit who looks earnestly at the camera into the dust of the O K Corral and then into the emoting visage of the blonde who throws herself into the arms of a gentleman not her husband. Perhaps too it is the ability to bring grainy life forth from this dark and glassy eye for no other reason than that he wants to and with no other justification than that he is able to do so that makes him sit so straight, his legs with their soiled white socks sticking out in front of him and exposing the pale young skin between its limp top and the bottom of the pants that have been pulled up around his waist by his having been plopped in the chair by his mother with not a great deal of ceremony, his hands folded quietly in his lap and his eyes straight ahead on the screen.

The young man looks down the row of seats with their individual black plastic television cases stuck on metal poles that curve familiarly around them, and at the rows of the people in them who are seated back to back as if on segments of a centipede that, instead of thin and vulnerable tubes of living tissue for legs, have metal bars ending in plastic feet. Clearly this great insect is taking no chances of collapsing under its burden of back-to-back Siamese twins. The chairs curve in a gentle arc and so he is able to see those around him without craning his neck in an unseemly fashion or giving himself a muscle strain. This is fortunate, since otherwise his field of vision would be limited to this child's head with spiky blond hair and the upper torso of the sullen mother, who is occupying her time popping her gum in timid little taps as if to reassure herself that all is well. She stares ahead with a determined look at—at what?

Ah—her husband, who is walking towards her, stuffing a ticket envelope into the pocket of his tight blue jeans and chewing a companion wad of gum, as if these were the recognition signals for two people from whom the voyage might drive the memory of less important remembered characteristics. The man makes for the empty chair and sits down, popping a bass ostinato to the woman's tenor tremolo, silencing the click of the metal plates on the bottom of his pointed boots that scrape the floor now and then as he moves his legs around in what must be involuntary jerks of muscles not yet aware that they are no longer moving in the dance of walking. In doing so, he cuts off the young man's view of the tired old women, of the old men, and of the young couples with silent children sitting in these chairs who stare down at their laps or watch the televisions before them with the slightly drooping heads necessary to aligning their eyes with the screens.

The young man sees a white T-shirt and a tan arm ending in knobby fingers that are engaged in poking the wad of gum held clenched between front teeth to see if it has been chewed tough enough to throw away or whether more time in the torture machine is necessary before the wad can be loosed from its saliva fetters and released into a trash can, or more likely, onto the bottom of the seat where it can grow hard and tough in the air, calcifying in the patterns that the teeth incised into it. Certainly, at any rate, it will never again be the soft and dry a stick of gum it once was, untouched and safe in its aluminum foil and marked only with the slight cross-patch pattern of the machine that made it.

He looks at his watch and gets to his feet, rising on his toes and interrupting his progress forward so that he does not crash into a woman who is running past him with her suitcase and who sees only those in front of her whom she dodges, having no time to waste on those on her side. He has timed himself perfectly and the downward weight of his arch pulls him forward into the wake of disturbed air she has left behind her.

He jingles the keys and change in his pocket as he stands before the row of gray metal lockers. Finally he manages to grab hold of the harmless thick plastic handle of the single key's teeth and so to extract it with no damage either to his fingers or to the delicate white gullet of his pocket that opens between the coarser tan checked lips of the cloth. At the moment, its mouth is set in a sneer, since his hand has just withdrawn from it. The pocket's lips are not quite as soft and spongy as human ones, and so do not fold back quite so quickly as human lips to a neutral position. In their more pleasant moments, the edges of his pocket have been known to smile, and even when they are merely closed, their expression could not be called offensive except perhaps by hypersensitive types who would be liable to find something insulting in every rustle of the trees they didn't like the sound of, every formation of pebbles in a stream that happened to spell out something of questionable taste in Braille, and in every lapping of the water against the edge of a dock or a pier or a diving float that happens to approximate something of questionable taste in Morse code.

In a moment the key is lodged to its hilt in the lock; the door is loaded to the muzzle and awaits only a twist to swing open and let into the dark depths of its insides the rays of light which are not quite so bright and glorious as the sun but which are sufficient to aid in the liberation of this prisoner that has here languished so long in solitude and cause paroxysms of tearful relief at its sudden and unexpected freedom. This is all to the good, for this suitcase may well be as ill-tempered as the dragon which lives in a similar manner in the dark recesses of another cave and which, it is rumored, possesses as the most valuable of its treasure hoard a helmet forged by the gods that changes the wearer at his will from whatever emotional state he or she is in at that point to its opposite, making the happy out of the sad, the melancholy out of the giggling, the shy out of the bold.

Comparative mythology: There are legends about a similar helmet of this sort which was able to turn the wearer into the form of another animal. Yet no one can doubt that the switch from one emotion to another within one human body is far more cataclysmic than any alteration of mere corporeal bodies could possibly be. No one, that is, who has encountered the enraged alcoholic who stands over his cowering wife brandishing his belt and shouting curses and snatches of drunken ditties so loudly that the neighbors in the next four flats groan in their sleep and cover their heads the more firmly with the pillows, and then later see him clean and brushed and well-dressed with his wife on his arm (she hangs on somewhat gingerly, to be sure, and it is odd that on such a fine spring day she is wearing long sleeves and dark stockings and a high collar) and pushing a rosy-faced child along in a carriage simply bristling with bows and lace trim.

Warming to the subject: Nor can anyone doubt this who has seen the look of religious light and conviction that shines in the preacher's eyes as he speaks of God so softly that those in the back rows must still their braided palm fans and lean forward, whose words become so sweet and heavenly at this point that even those who are hard of hearing and who have not really understood what the man is saying are able to hear in the music of the soft murmur of his voice the low strumming of the harps of the angels, no one who has heard this man as he talks of the fires of hell that gape before the damned and heard the crackle of his saliva in the corners of his mouth that bubbles out and froths over in his excitement and felt the old wooden pews vibrate with the screaming insistence of his voice that has begun to be so hoarse that once again the slightly deaf have trouble deciphering his words despite the great volume, who has heard the sharply enunciated words of doom that are spat from the man's lips like bullets and chopped off sharply by his teeth, his eyes nearly popping from their sockets and his hands clenched on the sides of the pulpit so that his knuckles are turned white from the strain and the huge shuddering breaths he must draw through his dark flaring nostrils so as to sustain this abrupt motionlessness and its wild intensity after the wild emotionality of the previous minutes, no one can doubt it who has heard all this and happens to be visiting the local house of ill repute the next day and, hearing strange gurgling noises and cries of pain coming from the next room, looks curiously and possibly with a bit of alarm through the crack in the wall at the scene of this selfsame preacher on his hands and knees being beaten across his hairy buttocks already criss-crossed with thick red welts by a woman naked save for the pointed boots with which she periodically kicks him in the groin. **Note, on good authority:** She is bored with her work and rests one fleshy hand on her lumpy hips while she beats with the other, and looks down with a face much the worse for years of exposure to misfortune and ill-usage and made ugly by its utter and absolute vacuity, its lack of any expression whatsoever. This is certainly the reason for the unpleasantness of the face of the poor man of God which twists itself into fantastic contortions at every lash and from whose mouth escape groans of the most blood-curdling sort, as well as the snorts for breath from the nose from which had so recently sounded sniffs dedicated to the work of the Deity and now used to punctuate the work of Satan. No one who has seen both these extremes can doubt the vastness of the difference between two states of human character that makes every conceivable difference of form between any two physical shapes as of nothing at all, make a snake and an armadillo practically identical twins and the lion and the mouse blood brothers in comparison. **Final observation:** We humans have gotten too used to looking for similarities between a string of pictures and once having found these forgetting any differences in the characters of the beings portrayed, as if all of life were one great psychological test in which we are only given credit for a single type of very specific responses and reactions to stimuli.

As he slides the suitcase from the opened locker, the rounded metal feet scrape against the metal bottom, signaling to the little overnight bag in the cubicle below with which it had managed to establish verbal contact during its two hours of imprisonment that she too will soon be rescued from the dark by her owner, an aging deposed countess who, the suitcase had learned during the course of the conversation, was fond of carrying her pet boa constrictor with her wherever she went that was at this moment lying nearly smothered between the negligées and the stockings in the overnight bag. For all her talk, the woman clearly does not care enough about the creature to read up on how to treat it properly and has affected the habit of carrying it around with her to begin with only after reading one story too many about dowager princesses and eccentric bishops whose demented company she had been distressingly eager to join.

Further details: The countess was traveling to the seashore where she hoped with the aid of all her bottles of make-up and the moonlit nights on the beach to get herself married to some handsome but foolish young man whom she would seduce by the Hungarian accent she had copied from a famous family of hopelessly inept movie actresses and with tales of the Revolution she had read in her history books. She would trust to the inherent wooly-headedness and stupidity of her companion not to question the dates of her story or draw any conclusions, for of course, the Revolution (whichever it was) happened a good ten years before her birth.

The door slams shut with an empty thud. This is unsurprising, as it is only thin metal: there is no need to erect a Fort Knox to protect the contents that quarter lockers in bus stations are likely to contain. Such, of course, may be precisely the reasoning of a clever thief who is storing in this very room inside a battered cardboard grip printed with a pattern of red plaid a priceless silver cow creamer stolen from the cupboard of a country house right out from under the nose of the staunch defender of the Law that the Baronet had set to guard it, or a handful of the parts of a diamond necklace torn to pieces in a fit of rage by a jealous young aristocrat upon finding—or suspecting, which is enough for these hot-blooded sorts—that his mistress had been unfaithful and left strewn in the embraces of the dust curls under the bed from which they were torn by a watchful housemaid undeserving of the confidence the family had reposed in her. **Commentary:** If indeed these wretched suitcases contain something of great value such as these, then it appears to be an illustration of the fact that natural value and worth do not automatically rise to the position of honor they rightfully deserve, but are rather all too frequently hidden from the public eye by things of merely second or even third and fourth rate that happen by some quirk to have been placed around and over them.

Explanation through Q and A. Q: Why is this bus station a perfect hiding place for such treasures? **A:** Because we do not expect to find anything of great merit or particularly outstanding among all this tiredness and ordinariness, if we may use these words to express the effect of no effect at all that these rows of lockers make, lockers that are identical but for a greater number of dents or scratches in one than another, and these public telephones that look just like all public telephones and these multiplicities of everything that look so much like their neighbors to all but the most alert eye that we do not even bother to look for valuables in the most exposed places, much less think of ferreting around in more obscure hiding spots.

Further: Even if some talent scout should be sent here just on an outside chance, there is little possibility that he would be able to see through the sides of a cheap suitcase to find the precious stones it by some fluke encloses, little possibility that he would be able to hear through all this muffling the sound of the things singing their hearts out in your old favorite melodies or see beyond even this thin metal door to the thing that just has gotta dance, hoofing its way not to the stardom it deserves but to the cold stares of the locker walls and the silence of the crumpled and empty packages of chewing gum in the corner.

Moral: Just one thin layer of cotton cloth suffices to cut the shine of silver from the eyes of the world; just the slightest and cheapest of cardboard boxes is enough to hide from those who would appreciate the glowing white fire of the diamond, just a coat of common mud is enough to hide the prettiest face that God ever made, just the talk of one youthful indiscretion was all it took to stain forever the honor and virtue of the best and most pure woman that ever walked the earth, just the vicious gossip of a dark-haired low-down slut was all the proof those people wanted to drag my darling down with them into the gutter and dirt where she died.

True fact: I have passed through the entire spectrum of emotions and now I have no feeling left, nothing remaining with which to manufacture an emotion that, by its position at the end of my life, may be regarded as its summation. I am no longer capable of thinking, of feeling, of wanting anything but death, which I seek not as a great release from my suffering but because the grim reaper is the only being I am capable of meeting now without flinching. I ask only a prolongation of the neutrality I have found which can happen only in death; I know that were I to live, my body would overcome me and I would once again start on the pointless treadmill of human existence, that wheel in which our changes of spiritual state are both the cause and the results of our continuing to run, in which what seems to be one completed cycle links with and is seen to be only the beginning of the next. To escape this I must hold the cool hand of the skeleton who carries the scythe, must have the aid of that Fate who cuts the string of life out of mercy and out of annoyance at the creaking sound of her sister's wheel that would spin it forever if it were not stopped with the jerk of her hand that is as sudden and as productive of peace as the abrupt opening of the scaffold's trap door.

He picks up the suitcase and turns the corner. His seat has been taken by a substantial woman whose thighs bulge from beneath her shorts and over the curved sides of the seat, and whose breasts sag from her bowed upper body like two of her young being sheltered against the cold. She appears unaware that he has so recently sat here, appears not to feel the small bit of his body heat that must have clung to the plastic for at least long enough for her to arrive and trap it again beneath her ample buttocks. Were she to leave and her successor to arrive soon thereafter, this person might be in a position to entrap both the remnants of her heat and the bit of warmth of her predecessor that she had nurtured and kept whole, so that, if each of the successors of this third person were to arrive soon and save this built-up accumulated warmth before it dissipates into the air, eventually with enough care and speed of succession on the part of these people, the warmth might be fanned up into heat sufficient to produce a flame, a flame that will burst in joyous release from the bonds of coolness and inactivity which had held it in thrall so long.

Moral: This shows the two choices open to us: we may let the embers of our predecessor's intellect grow cold and gray, or we may help them live with concentrated fanning and bellows-wielding in the hope that eventually they will put forth fire, a blaze that is the product of many people's labor and which signifies the inestimably great results that can spring from the uniting of a number of contributions into one great whole that is infinitely more than the sum of its parts, for it possesses not only the accumulated strength of the people who produced it but radiates as well the spiritual glow that is made by a number of human beings working together in love and harmony for one end that is above and beyond the needs of any particular individuals.

There are people standing around the sides of this waiting room staring with ill-disguised desire at the seats which, since his absence, have all been filled by new arrivals who have thickened the layers of standees clinging to the wall like beetles along the edges of a pond. **Hopeful thought**: Undoubtedly the rapidity with which one of these people will detach himself from the wall to fill a seat just vacated is evidence of some latent consciousness of the necessity to warm the seat that others have incubated, to carry on in as unbroken a chain as possible the progression of people who have sat here.

If this is so, perhaps we have been too quick to assume that the woman who buries her chin in the pad of her hand and lets her lids slip halfway shut in a drowsy blindness has no understanding of why it is that she is sitting here. Perhaps she does not really want to be here at all, but does so out of duty, and would be immensely more comfortable standing in a corner. Perhaps this somnolence hides an internal struggle of the greatest dimensions, a struggle of duty versus the animal instincts, a struggle of the imperative to inaction here in this spot against the corporeal will to movement that would urge her off her perch and into a wild and abandoned dance in the middle of the floor.

A realization: Is it not, however, certain that this very night when the fluorescent lamps over the book stall are out and the lights in the center grow bluer by contrast with the gloom that enshrouds parts of the walls, when the station is deserted except for an old man who has slipped in and is asleep in the corner by the dollar changer as yet unnoticed by the sleepy policeman who stares woodenly ahead at the baggage counter glowing bright even though it is absolutely deserted, when the station is silent but for the sound of an overhead fan and the clinking of glasses by the lone waitress in the cafeteria who takes desultory swipes at the counter with a damp dishcloth and scratches her ear, when the only person in these chairs will be a young woman whose head is nestled against the uninviting top of the dead television set attached out in front of her—is it not certain that at this point all the other seats will have become stone cold and will show nothing to mark the fact that once those who sat in them had hoped for great things to come of their actions and that now these vacant things are dead and gone and all their hopes come to naught?

Warning: We should not be so foolish as to think of the possibility of anyone's coming here for the express purpose of sitting in these chairs so as to keep alive the dying dreams of another person; we should not be so naive and so trusting in human beings' willingness to make sacrifices for others that we envision vows of sleepy housewives, their hair in curlers and their feet in bunny slippers or thin husbands with tousled hair with their pajamas awry who would volunteer to spend even as much as a half-hour every other night warming these places until the next person showed up.

Concluding questions: Must not the knowledge that the station will not always be this crowded discourage those who envision the period of slack during which these chairs will not be sat upon by anybody at all? Must this not chill those who realize that by their efforts they are not making progress towards any sort of great goal but are only keeping alive a life, which is to say only perpetuating a deception, only making one more step along a dead-end road, only one more move in the chess game whose pieces melt like the guilty spirits of the dead into the thin air of the morning and upon which, as a result, no one can ever complete a game?

Answer: Yes. We no longer have time for any of the foolish and unqualified make-doism that has afflicted mankind during some of the less perceptive ages of his development. We can no longer delude ourselves with the sort of philosophical nonsense that placated our ancestors, that philosophy expressed succinctly if not too subtly in the assertion of the well-known philosopher who was for so long the rage of all the European capitals: "It's not whether you win or lose, but how you play the game." This bit of silliness has fooled us for too long into thinking that there is no particular reason to object to playing a game in which it is not even theoretically possible to win, a game in which each hand we play, no matter how utterly smashing it seems at the time, is doomed to the same ultimate result, to wit: failure. It is about time we replaced our attitude of acceptance of things we cannot change with a few howls of righteous indignation expressing our displeasure at finding ourselves in this situation.

Clarification: It is not as if we hope for some sort of change or reparation to be the effect of this end to cheerfulness, for we are too firm a believer in the truth of our conclusions even to consider the possibility of respite at this point. It is simply ourselves we will satisfy with this overdue rebellion, simply ourselves to whom we will be doing honor by the resolution to participate no longer in the process of living. We have no desire to try to convert those rosy-cheeked sorts who still foolishly believe in an ultimately happy ending. Our rebellion need not be public at all: there is no particular reason to litter the streets with our inert bodies or to chain ourselves to the prime minister's carriage wheel, for this would be to engage in publicity stunts of questionable taste. Ours is a more private struggle, a war of conscience and intellect, a war that must be entered at the warrior's free will and cannot be spread by mass conversions.

A manifesto: Those who wish to join us will know instinctively what it is they must do without our having had to make asses of ourselves in all sorts of public exhibitions. We will clog up the flow of life, but we shall not do it by shutting up the factories or by closing down the workhouses. We will not obtain our goals by bringing the trains to a halt or by stopping the ships. Rather we will accomplish our aims by simply neutralizing ourselves as sentient beings. By rendering ourselves perfect conductors of the electricity of living we shall, paradoxically, thereby impede its flow. For this current looks for nodes around which it can gather to shoot off sparks, looks for tangles and twists in which it can linger and establish a beachhead.

Resolution: We will cleanse ourselves, rid our muscles of kinks, straighten our backs and dare that which flows smooth through us to find a chink or an overlooked impediment that it can use as an excuse to becoming sluggish and using us for a temporary storage place, making batteries of us. We will render our insides so glassy that our esophagus will no longer need to engage in peristalsis, for the food along with the current will be unable to help itself from simply sliding down the tube into our equally smooth stomach. **Note:** Unfortunately, we will not live long after we have taken up this philosophy, for the food will slide out of the other end with just as much speed as that with which it slid in. This, however, is a minor concern: death cannot but be a trifle to those of us who have managed, for hours or for a short time, to make ourselves perfect conductors for the life flow.

He fumbles in his pocket and extracts the crumpled tissue paper of his ticket across which march the even, capital letters of his destination made blurry to the point of illegibility by being the last layer of a three-carbon pad, the letters beginning to seep into the paper around them as if soon they would abandon all pretensions to the stiffness or discipline of meaningful markings and become totally liquid. He tightens his grip on his suitcase and moves forward to door number 12 where the bus driver stands with his hat pushed back on his head, brandishing a holepunch from which perfect round tears drop onto the floor.

He is forced to wait a moment behind a thin woman with half a dozen bags of varying sizes and degrees of lumpiness that she is continually bringing closer with her hands or nudging inwards with her nervous feet as if they were chicks that, without constant attention and reprimands, would wander off and become squashed in a swinging door or lodge under a vending machine. **Conjecture:** It seems that she would be compelled to move from place to place in a very strange way, picking up as many of the bags as she could pile on to her frail arms and run forward some distance ahead where she dumps them and then runs back for a second load that she would carry further on than the other—for not even a woman like this would fail to see the obvious labor-saving advantages in doing this rather than dropping them all at the same spot and shouldering the first ones again—and so on, like a kind of machine with caterpillar treads that moves slowly forwards while a small exposed gear in its middle is grinding busily in the opposite direction.

The woman snatches the layer of paper hanging from the fingers of the driver and, folding it with a sharp crease and a rustle, lodges it firmly in the recesses of her pocketbook before closing the bag and stooping to gather the first load. As he watches, a miracle occurs, surely not less in importance or power to amaze than some of those Biblical ones where in a small amount of food is made to go a long way towards satisfying the wants of fifty thousand or the more modern sorts of miracles in which twenty-five persons are reported to have successfully crammed into a telephone booth. The woman does not stop at three bags, at four bags, or five. As he watches and as the driver chews his gum with what may be extra vigor due to excitement at what he is seeing (or on the other hand may be merely a last healthy mastication to make sure the gray lump is indeed quite tasteless before spitting it into the Kleenex he will draw in a tortured wreck from his pocket), the woman hooks the sixth and last bag with her remaining free finger and swings it in an arc, catches it neatly on the top and with a deep breath and a push-off of the toe of her pointed shoe, sails through the open door out onto the loading platform. He offers the square of paper to the driver and when it is handed back there are two holes neatly snipped in it, vacant eyes that stare at him from the page.

Yet he cannot stand here all day holding up the middle-aged man behind him who jiggles his too-large hat as he snorts and does a snuffling dance of suppressed annoyance. The young man has heard the noises behind him and understood their import, and thus it is strange that he seems to change his mind about shoving the wadded ticket into the pocket and pulls it out again to fold carefully in sections, a diminutive bundle which he holds between thumb and finger of his left hand while extracting a wallet from a back pocket, which must, it seems, be unsnapped and fished around in for a good ten seconds before it can receive as precious a bundle as the ticket receipt.

Finally a hole is dug in the piles of other papers that fatten the bovine sides of the wallet to porcine proportions and the folded tissue paper is lodged safely within. He reaches down to scoop up the suitcase with his curved hand and, feeling the jolt in his arm as the slack is taken up and the handle firmly lodged in the wrinkles of his palm, heaves it several inches off the floor and walks out the door.

The driver pauses a moment before punching the next ticket to search for his snow-white handkerchief, which he unfurls with a shake. Soon it is wet-colored with the sweat from his forehead which, along with the rest of his face, is turned towards the floor and not towards the ticket which the man in the hat holds at arm's length and shakes in rustling undulations.

The late afternoon air and the smells of wet concrete and gasoline seem, perhaps merely by association with his visual images of the cement, more brown and earthy than the gray smells of inside the building. He takes several deep breaths, but loses the veiled pleasantness of the smell he is searching for with his energetic inhalation. He stands a moment to allow the air to puff its scent into his nostrils by sniffling gently. But this smell, this feeling of being surrounded in a thin curtain that can at any moment be torn aside, must either be available only as a gratuitous gift to those who are not looking for it or be only a first impression that he will not be able to recapture except after another period of confinement in the bus station.

He stands on the steps of the bus, in the shadow of the awning that falls on the sidewalk below and onto the fronts of the busses. The shadow is the emissary of the approaching night sent to accustom all those here with its slight darkness to the deeper black which will soon be upon them. His shoes scrape against the rubber matting between whose ribbings nestle the small stones and sand they have received from other shoes as the fruit of previous shakedowns, though what this matting could want with them is really quite beyond our comprehension. **Suggestion:** Perhaps the mat is tired of living so right-angled and stiff a life and enjoys the rounded feel of these smooth stones along the valleys between its bones. Perhaps it even forgets itself to the extent of thinking of these things as part of itself, of imagining that finally it is losing some of its inability to bend and relax and is beginning a process that will transform it into a flowing river of curved rubber into which the shoes of those that tread on it will sink, a perfectly shapeless blob that will be able to hold no shape whatsoever, much less that of the sharp ridges like those that now scrape along the soles of his shoes.

He stands for a moment at the top of the step by the trash can. All that remains within is a piece of chewing gum that has stuck to the side and has not escaped the graying of cigarette ash dusting all the rest of the interior surfaces. He grasps the round vertical railing that flattens before making a curve at right angles where it attaches to the divider between the stairs and the first seats, and then imitates the pattern himself, flattening his body by bringing the suitcase behind it as he turns the corner into the aisle.

He sees the heads and shoulders of people that have fallen back into the padded headrests, leaning forward and turning to him the animated profiles from which their neighbors are able to decipher words, people staring vaguely out of the windows that show nothing more interesting than the windows of the neighboring bus which, were they not tinted green, would show people looking vaguely out at his bus who will soon be on their way in an altogether different direction and whose contact for this one brief moment at this station with these others is prevented by nothing more substantial nor less effective than the opacity of the windows. **Reflection and lament. Reflection:** It seems a shame that we cannot more easily strip this world bare of its extraneous films, its colorings that blind us to so much that we should see. **Lament:** If only we could live in palaces of glass set on mountains of crystal and, for our food, pluck translucent fruits from trees wrought of ice! Could we but clothe ourselves in cellophane and drink nothing but water, gin, and clear soups! Could we but sleep on a nest of soap bubbles and keep as pets only those delicate and exposed creatures known as glass catfish; could we eat meat bleached to colorlessness on bones made of Lucite and ourselves be rendered as clear and pure of soul as those things around us would be of body!

He stops before two empty seats, one of which is set upright; the pad at its top bears the marks of its last occupant's head. The other seat is pushed back into reclining position so that the pair of them together looks as if they were jaws that had been petrified in mid-sentence by the exodus of their previous passengers with whose weight the seats spring into action, chattering madly about nothing at all. With no passengers, evidently, they are condemned to silence, as if the privilege of speech were the reward for their service as chairs, as if this scissoring back and forth—odd given the admitted discomfort to the riders whose bone structures might be bit loosened as they were jerked backwards and forwards—were only possible when triggered off by the weight of a person.

Yet the seat does nothing but accept his presence, produces no violent reaction at all to the weight of his body. For this sort of thing we must refer to television cartoons in which otherwise inanimate things become motile by virtue of a draftsman's genius and the viewer's persistence of vision and where the characters seem to be able to accept with extraordinary aplomb a series of ridiculous situations. The first of these would have given any real person pause, and the second and third would have confirmed his suspicion that he had been transported unawares to some sort of nearly congruent world whose main divergence form the earth he was born on is that in this other world the untowards has become the commonplace, the outré has turned into the quotidian, and the unexpected has lost its negative prefix. **An idea:** The farcical in the world can be broken into small enough chunks or administered in miniature enough doses that it is like an eye-popping color that loses its power to amaze and astound by distribution throughout a mosaic and is noticeable only as a faint sheen if it is remarked at all. Perhaps, in a similar manner, we can distribute the ridiculous through life so that not only do we find its presence acceptable but even grow to feel it necessary for our well-being, like certain trace elements whose applications are made tolerable by their very infrequency and their minuscule proportions, but which are absolutely essential to our continued good health. **Related question:** Is truth stranger than fiction? **Answer:** No. The world is simple, safe, and sanitary, and it is only the wild imaginings of bored brains that impart to it mystery or humor or interest. Indeed, none but the dullest of those blockheads who have never surrendered their minds to the wiles of a novel of adventure or romance that casts from us for a few brief hours the shackles with which the ordinary world usually binds us so firmly and substitutes for this cold and unfriendly existence the warm caresses of a tropical breeze over the white sails of a schooner or the soft stirrings of the air on the dark rocks overhanging the falls with its pool of cool blue waters at its foot (a pool as deep and dark as the cataract is high and frothy white), none but the most unimaginative of mortals who have never gasped in ecstasy as they felt themselves floating away over the treetops to the end of the rainbow upon the wings of literature, wings that are like those of the princesses enchanted into swans during the daytime and permitted to return to their human state at night in that their strength is restricted to those times when the sun of imagination shines bright and bring them bumping to the ground with their precious cargo at the arrival of the darkness of the everyday and unromantic, the black of the soul in which all is asleep, none but those who are so devoid of higher yearnings that never in their youths did they feel the desire to play at pirate with a stick found by the wayside serving for a gleaming sword and a battered coat rescued from the scrap pile playing the part of the velvet garment they did not have, none but those with the heart and mind of a stone can truthfully hold this outrageous opinion, can honestly be so ungrateful to forgotten sources of pleasure or so unfeeling that they have never tasted the sparkling and refreshing issue of these fountains that they would attempt to assert that fiction is less strange than truth. The world itself is utterly neutral; we alone give it its color.

Two teenaged boys are swaggering up the aisle, their smudged white T-shirts making their sallow skin glow an unpleasant yellow to which the acne pimples that speckle their cheeks provide a vivid red contrast. In the moment when their mouths open in speech, they reveal the silver rows of the braces on their teeth, though their lips close in instant self-consciousness at the end of each sentence. Yet all that is left of them when they are past are the faint wisps of the cloud of words that followed them down the aisle and which is only beginning to penetrate his consciousness.

He relaxes the neck muscles that he had tensed to watch the passage of the two boys, exhales himself into a curve congruent to that of the chair back, and closes his eyes. For a moment or two, he watches the yellow blurs forming behind his eyelids that gradually begin to drift across the blackness and then evaporate like patches of fog illuminated in the night by the headlights of a lone car that are suddenly gone, the white wall that surrounded the vehicle having been abruptly breached, and listens.

The noise of the two boys that had begun again in the back loses the prominence it had gained by having absorbed his attention for an instant, and fades back to its deserved level. This is still somewhat above the intensity of the thin high-pitched giggles that must come from the two ten-year-old girls of whose blond heads he has seen only the well-brushed tops, bobbing behind the backs of the seats in front of them like spherical fishing floats that poke above the gentle blue waves of an inlet, but softer than the conversation of the two middle-aged women who are two or three rows behind him and whose bluish hair is lacquered into immobility.

Hair: Their hairs are wrought into a delicate cage of the finest silver threads that block an over-arching network covering the less dense layer of scattered shafts, pillars that support a solid roof like the sparse and towering tropical trunks holding high above the damp floor of the rain forest the solid mass of the lianas and creeping plants blocking the sun's passage to the dark underparts. **Development:** It is a hair style within which one could imagine the bright streaks of the ruby-red wings and turquoise breasts of tiny birds that could fly around these supporting follicles and not become entrapped in their curls. Yet they would be stopped at the surface, unable to pass through the thicker weaving of hairs there or the tiny and barely audible grunts of the miniature warthogs that would be able to make their homes among the spongy pads of these undoubtedly dandruff-laden scalps in nests lined with plucked hairs. **Fact to consider:** Probably any old lady who has gone to the trouble and expense of having her hair silvered would be unwilling to put up with the constant pin-pricks of the hairs being plucked from her head or the undoubtedly annoying feeling on her scalp of the warm breath of pigs of whatever size.

He has seen these two heads and the tailored tweed suits the women wear before he sat down, as well as the brown paper bags that they clench between their black oxfords. The bags must be the source of the crackling noise that has begun as an undercurrent about the middle of their last sentence that, if he is served correctly by a memory made increasingly drowsy for no other reason than that he is sitting still for the first time all day, was concerned with the utter unsuitability of Mabel's young man and the necessity of conveying to dear Harriet the information, obtained just today, that would certainly result in Bob's taking a firmer stand than he had had the courage for before, and absolutely forbidding the wedding. He supposes, at any rate, that it is a wedding that is going to be forbidden, for the object of the verb is left unspoken, though it seems to be the only thing that fits. The object of the verb floats behind his eyes on a tide that bathes him in a thick sweet liquid lapping rhythmically against the sentence, as if setting it vibrating in this manner were an acceptable alternative to actually making the word-bridge so that its interior tremors could be communicated to all its parts.

Suddenly he is brought fully awake again, though his eyes remain closed and the slight jump he has made does not re-tighten his muscles for more than a few seconds. The sound that has disturbed him resolves itself as it fades away into the concrete noise of a slap which, since there is no resultant wail of a pained child or horrified gasp of a woman whose hand flies to her cheek to finger the hot palm print that is reddening into a fiery blotch, must be merely a rather emphatic punctuation carried out on a knee during the conversation of the two women. This conversation seems to have turned in mid-stream on the pivot of the sharp ejaculation and is now concerned with the impossibility of getting well-cleaned shrimp in the supermarkets. Or it may be that some strange association of ideas unintelligible to someone who was not around for the crucial changeover has accomplished the swift alteration. Or, finally, it may be that this subject is only an inserted digression or an amplification whose true place will be revealed when it is finished and we see to what part of the original talk flow the speaker returns.

The crackling stops and he wonders vaguely what it is that they have been searching for in their bags. They can still keep up an animated conversation which, we can be certain, would have been interrupted by wheezes and coughs had they been bent over as they looked. He wonders what it was so little related to their conversation that the process of searching for it could span two such divergent topics and stop suddenly without either an expression of regret at not having found it or cries of satisfaction at the more positive outcome or even a change in the intonation which continues no less strident than before.

Now that they are stopped, the sounds of this crackling disassociate themselves from the area around these women's feet to which an ear fooled by the visual association had assigned them and switch over to the other side of the aisle. They raise themselves several feet as they do, reaching lap level. This, he reflects consulting his memory, must place them in the folds of the dress that covers all too much of the lovely legs that, right at the moment, are being given a respite from their enviable job of supporting the tanned torso of the beautiful girl who, when last seen, had been edging the point of a nail file under the perfectly-shaped ends of one of her shining fingers. She has evidently given up this project for the undoubtedly no less gracefully performed one of searching in a paper sack for something she wants.

But what? Silence, then a soft squashing sound and a ladylike slurp, which alternate in this pattern for several seconds more until he suddenly smells the pear that she is eating and realizes that the bag sound has been the high-pitched thin noise of a small lunch sack and not the more ominous rumble of a lower and coarser shopping bag. This additional sound has been the signal for the cessation of another sound to which he had paid but perfunctory attention, a sound which by the pattern of its repetition and the leisurely hills and shallow valleys of its pitch movement can only be hymns sung by the old man who has been humming softly to himself as he rocks back and forth in his seat with his leathery hands clasped on his knees, and who may have stopped from the desire to taste in his own mouth not the salty bath of saliva or the close hot air of the bus, but instead the sweet liquid gold of the fruit that is running now in the girls's throat, after the gratification of which desire his words of praise for the Lord would ring out the more sincerely.

Alternate explanation: Or it may be that even as this young woman sinks her perfect white teeth into the fruit, the old man's mouth stops its mumbling and his jaws separate not in the expression of a bodily wish for food, but in a momentary paralysis of spiritual horror, since what he would see before him would not be merely this girl enjoying her late lunch but a second Eve who, instead of plucking an apple from the boughs of a tree, pulls its cousin the pear from a sack of dried wood pulp that is pasteurized and processed by modern machinery and who, not of having to be enticed by a wily serpent, acts out her momentous role in seemingly unforced willingness and even eagerness. If this is really a repetition of that story of yore, then the analogy forces us to believe that her decorous demeanor and modest costume are the closest we are able to come in these permissive times to a state of blessed innocence of her body, a kind of nudity which she will soon cover in the shame of the knowledge that will flood her soul and the souls of her descendants.

Note: The girl must be a hermaphrodite or have an invisible consort if she is part of a great and terrible tableau that involves both the matriarch and patriarch of a great line of mankind who are to be stamped forever upon their foreheads with the sign of her transgression and bowed eternally with the weight of his sin: the seat beside her is quite empty save for another bag entirely too small to contain anything that could possibly impregnate her.

One possible result: The old man would be overwhelmed by the desire to haul himself to his spindly legs and, supporting himself on the extended arms of the seats, lunge towards the girl with the intention of wrenching from her delicately curved hand the fruit upon which so much depends. If he moves quickly even now, he may be able to withhold it from contact with the soft interior of her mouth; he may still be able to preserve the skin of the pear from the rupture on which depends the fate of so many unborn and unthought-of, the pear that by its ripeness would render foul and fetid the fruit of the girl's womb and those of her wretched daughters.

Considerations: What if the old man's palsied hand had missed its target and fallen instead on the girl's exposed neck upon which stands a drop or two of glistening sweat that has grown from a tiny subcutaneous spring right under the collarbone against which it is nestled, rather than being caught after tracing a glistening trail down her trachea. What if the old man were to overbalance and by his clumsiness send himself sprawling across her lap? **Note:** The drop of sweat seems more like a solid thing plucked by pale fingers from the depths of a jewel box and applied here against the neck with the full knowledge that unusual as its positioning might be, it would nonetheless look absolutely perfect.

Probable consequences: Would not then her screams of terror or her gasps of surprise (not to mention the gurgles of a second or two of choking in the event of the former possibility) result in even the more lethargic of those nearby passengers jumping to their feet in an effort to apprehend this fiend in human form who had suddenly risen from his seat and attacked a girl who was doing nothing more than eating a piece of fruit drawn from a paper bag? Would not his arms be pinioned and he be marched off to jail, where an attempt at explaining the utmost urgency of preventing this terrible deed would get him neither a sympathetic hearing nor better treatment but only a straitjacket and a padded cell? **Further:** Would not his whole life be shattered if he were punished for an attack like this, even one that had been motivated by nothing of lesser importance than the fate of mankind and which, had it gone as projected, would have resulted in no bodily injury more serious than a few hours of mild hunger on the girl's part and perhaps a slight discomfort caused by her inability to remove from her fingers the stickiness of the dried patina of the juice that had flowed from the pear as it was knocked from her fingers onto the floor?

Perhaps all these possible consequences would have crossed the man's mind (if this explanation is the correct one, then something of the sort must have occurred to him, for he has been silent for several seconds and the girl is by now well beyond the first bite) and led him to fall back, silent, into his seat rather than doing his duty. Why, he might have reasoned, should he face the chance of incurring the reproaches that would land upon him if he himself were to fall upon the girl merely for the sake of altering the course of a history he will not live to see made? Nor could he be sure that he would be doing the morally right thing by preventing what we mortals are able to see only as tragedy, but which might in the infinite eye of the Creator be conceived as the necessary if regrettable result of man's free will or as the beginning of a sequence of events that will culminate in something that legitimizes everything, wiping from the record all the darkness and misery and discouragement that went before. **Admission:** Whether the low singing that starts again at this moment is a litany of praise to something we cannot comprehend, or whether the old man has seen nothing beyond the back of the seat in front of him and heard nothing other than his own wheezy breath and thus has simply been using this period of silence to wet his lips enough to make continuing comfortable, we cannot say.

He has heard the rustle and the clomping of several more pairs of shoes coming up the aisle, and the people they carried have settled themselves somewhere not too far in back of him. Without visual help, he is at a loss to make sense of all the new noises that are seeping hazily to his brain and those few sounds that are loud and distinct enough that identification would ordinarily be very easy do not last long enough to let him confirm a conjecture that must remain in the soft state of the hypothetical and is not permitted to assume the solidity of fact. He can, to be sure, make guesses at the crinkle of plastic bags, the scratch of a fingernail against a leg clad in a nylon stocking, or the soft silky rustle of hair being brushed (this one must be very close indeed to be audible), but regarding more complex things like the pop of a rubber pacifier as it is pulled from the tense mouth of a determinedly-sucking infant or the clicking against each other of thick and colorful costume jewelry beads or the metallic loosening of a spring as someone puts his seat back, he can make no guess at all.

Nor, in fact, does he try, thinking of nothing much except the warmth of this plastic seat cover against his head and the heaviness in his arms and legs and perhaps the sticky hotness that has only in the last minute or two changed from being uncomfortable but ignorable to being a positive good. There is something right about the way his hair sticks together and to the seat, something right about the moisture on his forehead, something right about this motionlessness in the middle of all these sounds which are not really as loud as they once seemed and are not really very audible at all, are more like a thick murmur that bathes his veins so that they seem totally to fill the skin that encloses him, to fill as full as a sausage the arms and legs that lie helter-skelter about him and of which he must surely have some sort of extra-sensory perception, some sort of consciousness that communicates not through the vulgar mediums of flesh and bone but through the upper regions of the azure skies above the winds that roil slowly below the thick white masses of clouds undulating so slowly that one must stare at them for ever so deliciously long before any motion at all can be detected. This must be so, for he has no connection with these limbs that are here beside him, no veins that join him to them, nothing but warmth and a misty dampness.

He awakens with a jolt. The bus is out of the city and on a road through a woods, and the people around him are either asleep or talking only softly. There seems to be something about the droning sound of the wheels of the bus that discourages as well as muffles competing noise. Perhaps people hesitate to break the sweet monotone that says all things to all people with its neutral blur through which one can hear the screams of the terrified, mothers singing softly to their children in the early hours of warm summer nights, explosions of rage that give way to hysterical laughter, and voices of calm surety into which are soon injected notes of unsteadiness shattering their complacency into pieces that eventually fit together again to form the rising inflection of an insistent and unanswered question. There is, in this noise of the bus's tires, everything from the clatter of pots and pans in a sweltering tenement and the tinkle of silver bells on the sides of a Victorian sleigh; there are the quiet footfalls of the restless one in the sleeping house; there are the running steps of a girl hurrying down a country lane; all these things are submerged within the sound, waiting only for someone to cut them from the uniform blur.

The bus must slow for some reason, for the noise falls in both pitch and intensity and then rises slowly again to its original level. There is something disappointing in the realization that all these things are produced only by a machine that, by nothing more prosaic than the workings of some metal cogs, makes the noise from which one who wishes can disentangle so much, the realization that all this is produced by parts that take up a finite amount of space and that run on gasoline and grease. The effect is much the same as when we turn around to uncramp our shoulders and brush the popcorn off our lap after a particularly absorbing movie and catch a glimpse of the lighted projection booth in which stands a little man with a week's beard and a cigarette hanging from the corner of his mouth who is poking stubby fingers at the machine to get it ready to rewind.

The shock is not so much that we did not know perfectly well beforehand how these things worked, but that we had not thought about it in any but intellectual terms, as anything but as theoretical truths. **Observation:** And yet there are some people who do not realize how horrible this sort of revelation is, some who have not yet realized that we must refuse en masse to look for causes beyond those we already have, to tear aside the black veil that shrouds in mystery the visage of one who is perfectly acceptable to us from the nose down but whose flesh, were we to throw caution and discretion to the winds and rip from the face the shroud which had been intended to stay until the mildewy hands of death plucked it from his brow, would be revealed as a loathsome mass of hills and discolorations that bear but the slightest resemblance to a human face, the remnants of a man's forehead, nose and chin that seem human only by the two reproachful dark eyes staring from mangled sockets with infinite sadness and overflowing with pity for those who have started back in horror, their hands over their own faces so that their eyes might not behold this terrifying wreckage of what had once been a person.

Moral: Let us be content with the beauty of what has been given us already and preserve a healthy respect for that which we are not to know. The danger is that we will be like the too-impatient farmer who slaughtered the goose that produced a daily egg of the purest and most solid gold in order to uncover the wondrous mechanism so that it might be made to produce at twice, thrice, or even four times its usual rate and found, instead of a gleaming womb or blood of liquid metal, only the normal soft organs of those fowls which produce eggs of white filled with nothing nearer to gold than the yellow yolk. We too are in danger of killing the geese that laid our golden eggs; it is best for us to accept the world as a gratuitous gift of Nature or God or Beauty that looks after our wants and gives us only what is good for us, only what we should know.

Personal Observation: Though the well-known tale of the Goose that Lay the Golden Eggs is usually explained as having as its point a moral lesson regarding the farmer's greed, I have always wondered why no one has ever explored the other fruitful avenue of interpretation that must grow out of noticing the fact that the goose under question seems to have differentiated itself from its less special fellows by nothing but its will power. For how else can we explain the combination of its physical unremarkableness and its extraordinary productivity?

Nor can our analysis stop here: the vein of unmined material is rich and it is our fortune to be among the first of its excavators so that on our shoulders fall the weight of making the categories that will influence coming generations. We must account for the meaning of the premature death of this bird which, had the products of its fecundity not taken the metallic course they did, might have lived a good deal longer to breathe the mountain air and drink the water of the farmyard pond, and examine the emotional state that led the farmer to take such drastic measures against a creature which had never done him anything but good, if we may for a moment adopt without question the somewhat questionable notion that wealth is good. **Aside:** This is a philosophy that led one of the last of its defenders to make a famous speech in which he expressed the opinion, so extraordinary to us moderns, that he would even be willing to face the agonies of crucifixion if only his execution were carried out on a cross of gold.

We must sacrifice the intellectual pleasures of a full exposition of the reasoning process to the demands of time which the circumstances have made so pressing and insistent. To wit: the most important element of the grand drama that unfolds within the deceptively small framework of this story through its beguilingly simply language is the motivation of the farmer, resulting in his precipitous act of aggression against a creature that seemed no different from his other geese in any way but concerning what it produced. Indeed, as he found to his intense chagrin, it actually *was* no different from his other geese.

Aspects of the goose: The goose, it is clear, must be regarded as merely a common fowl that had, by virtue of its own initiative, managed to make itself into something greater than its fellows. Undoubtedly it longed to escape the small chicken yard with the fence that kept out the spectators who might, if news of its ability were to spread through the gossip of the goose girl, come and provide the adulation that it so badly wanted. At this point it was receiving as praise only the satisfied grunts of the farmer as his filthy fingers poked into the warm nest and found the hard treasure they sought and the horrible threats that fell from his slavering and dirt-caked lips that menaced terrible punishments if another such egg were not there on the morrow. Clearly it longed to display its talent to some audience more appreciative than the other geese which pecked at it or the rats that skulked in the shadows or the eternal rain and mud that kept the animals huddled under the rotting roof of the shelter.

It is unfortunate that the goose had spent all its time perfecting its art (burying the original misshapen gold nuggets and the half-metal eggs of the middle stages) and not enough time exploring the social situation in which it found itself. So lost was it in its fantasies of throngs of admiring spectators that it failed to realize that people will only worship in this manner that which they accept to be far above and beyond them, and will never venerate one of their own kind who has not the trappings they have come to associate with greatness. It requires a star of Bethlehem to make kings sink to their royal knees before a rude manger filled with straw and a child that looks no different from other children except for the slight glow around His childish cranium and the look of wisdom in His piercing eyes. Nothing less will suffice to overcome the rigid barriers of situation: thus the goose, which is no God but simply a talented bird, is bound to remain unappreciated by the farmer. Were the farmer to see the creature on display in a traveling road-side show, by contrast, he would be as impressed as the rest of the crowd and would as little dare to ruffle the slightest feather on the goose's queenly tail as he would, upon being granted a royal audience, to goose the queen on her ruffle, but who treats as he wishes something that he regards as nothing more than a piece of his property that has displayed a hitherto hidden use.

Conclusion: The farmer is only acting like most men in demanding that those things that he is required to treat differently than their fellows be clearly marked in a manner he understands. The goose is clearly at fault for having developed its talent without at the same time making provisions for being accepted at its proper valuation by making sure that it was clearly labeled. In fact, it would have been better not ever to have raised itself above its commonplaceness if it could not guarantee that its produce would be recognized and treated as the noble achievement it was.

Final indictment of the goose: Its death at the knotted hands of the farmer will bring to an end a life whose proceeds only provided the means for its master to go on a series of incredible drunken binges and, further, deprived the villagers of some edible eggs. We must sympathize with the rage and disappointment of the farmer upon beholding the bloody intestines of an animal whose insides he had expected to blind by their glare and glitter. He had every reason in the world to expect of this animal production of its wondrous fruits by the normally accepted principles of mechanics and not by some unfamiliar and mysterious method, had no cause whatever to suspect that what he held in his hands was no simple physical oddity but an example of supreme greatness of spirit and discipline.

Final defense of the farmer: As for the greed of the farmer which most exegetes of this tale make so much of, let us state our firm belief that our colleagues have been making too much out of it. Greed is one of the unfortunate but not unbearable characteristics of the human animal, and certainly its presence is not of great enough importance to justify the formulation of such a lengthy parable whose only purpose is to condemn it.

Final Moral: The social order has been constructed for a purpose; following it rigorously may make the difference between life and death. **Note:** In the literature of these people is another fable that continues on where this one leaves off, changing a number of the more important qualities of the characters so as to tell an essentially different tale. The farmer is unsuccessful in hiding the bloody knife (or his equally bloody apron, or some other piece of incriminating evidence) from the prying eyes of the goose girl (or his neighbor) and just enough has leaked out to the local magistrate about the extraordinary creature that had been slaughtered by the farmer that the air of secrecy and mystery surrounding the story had served the function of the star of Bethlehem. That is, the judge had the situation presented to him in such stealthy whispers that the story quite lost its air of the commonplace and took on that of the miraculous. The result was that the farmer was accused and convicted of murdering a miracle and hanged.

Interpretation: The tragedy in this story is that the stupid farmer was so dulled by years of routine reaction to unchanging social signs that he failed to recognize greatness when it was presented to him and, in his ignorance, destroyed with his blindness both that which he did not understand and himself. The moral is clearly that we must be alert to the innate value of whatever appears to us, regardless of its outwards trappings.

The air conditioning has been on since the bus left the station, and the mugginess and closeness of the atmosphere has been replaced by a coolness that is devoid of smell. The sweat on his forehead has dried to a patina that feels as if it would crack if he were to raise his eyebrows in surprise. Above the top of the seat before him rises the tousled blond wisps of what is evidently a wig, for no real hair possesses this perfect sort of shine and that smug sort of curl. **Speculation:** Perhaps it is a wig that has begun to slip off its scalp as the woman has sagged lower and lower in her seat in drowsy unconsciousness. Perhaps it will even eventually pop off her head and fall into her lap so that, dreaming of the tigers that creep up to her hands and feet as she lies helplessly trussed by the evil traders who have sold her as a concubine to the local chief and breathe on her with their hot breaths that reek of blood and the dark smell of extinguished life, she will shudder as the synthetic hair brushes her twitching hands and wake up screaming. She will then be faced with the double embarrassment of having to explain away the disturbance she has caused and dealing with a scalp from which grows not the luxuriant tufts of this store-bought hair or even the wispy frizz of her own poor locks, but tiny flattened sausage rolls of hair that are pinned crossways with long brown hairpins.

He stretches forward a finger that strokes the plastic stretched over the seat back. When the finger is finished, it falls to the ashtray where it hooks over the edge of the receptacle. It feels within not the smooth coolness it had expected but the gritty crunch of the ash that must have been hidden in the very bottom. He holds the finger before his eyes for several lazy seconds and then blows on the gray smudge that disperses and settles quickly and wafts to his nostrils the faint odor of burn and cigarettes.

He looks across the aisle at the seats opposite him, which are filled with the two young girls collapsed inwards onto each other in sleep, their arms clasped tightly about each other as if to shelter themselves from some great and unnamed danger that would take fright at what would seem to be a pair of Siamese twins, never before having beheld such a double monster, or for assurance that they would not be eaten by a creature from the deep that, though not given to the sorts of cowardice displayed by its fellow fright, would simply be unable to ingest such a bulky package and leave them unharmed.

Note: The plan seems more effective than it really is at preventing these two innocent things from dying at an untimely age, for even were their lives prolonged a few minutes by this stratagem and they were spared by a creature that had stopped the bus and, reaching a great paw through a broken window, was about to make its meal or had managed to cram its loathsome front parts into the doorway and was craning and twisting its neck about as best it could under the cramped conditions in an attempt to discover which of those before it was the juiciest and most tender, it would not be able to stave off the encounter for long once the bus was empty, perhaps lying on its side in a ditch with half its seats ripped out and the suitcases and pocketbooks and even a stray shoe or two belonging to those who had been snatched from within scattered about, carrying in one of its empty seats nothing but a child's doll that sat primly in the corner smiling its empty smile as if nothing were amiss and on the seat itself several drops of pale pink blood and a clump of long blond curls pulled out by the roots. For once these two were alone in the mêlée they could not fail to be so overcome with terror that, unable to move their stiff limbs or unpry their clenched hands from each other's arms and not being calm enough of mind to reason that rescuers would soon be at hand and that an overturned bus must be rather conspicuous to travelers-by who might take it into their heads to stop if for no other reason than to be on hand when the rescue squad started carrying out the bodies, they would expire from shock and fear of what is to come, would die together with a sharp intake of breath, their eyes glazing simultaneously and their limbs growing even stiffer than they are already made by their terror.

He looks down and discovers that his feet are resting on the metal bar that hangs below the level of the seat before him. It is the tension resulting from this position that is pulling at the backs of his legs and not an insistent midget that wants something of him and has been waiting until he awoke and the world lost that heavy stillness it has when we have slept too long when we did not really need sleep. He lifts his feet carefully one by one and places them gently on the floor as if he were afraid to break them with too rough a treatment. Certainly he has no concerns about waking the man hunched in the corner beside him who must have climbed over him when he was asleep. The man's pulpy buttocks fill his thin pants shiny from wear around the knees, and protrude over the line of separation of the seats. His white socks are bunched around the tops of his scuffed brown shoes, and even his ankles look puffed up and overweight. His upper body heaves as he breathes, thought the actual noise of these breaths is inaudible against the hissing of the air conditioning that is blowing up through a line of square ducts at the base of the windows. Suddenly the odor the man produces becomes evident; until this point the man has been a kind of visual curiosity which, not perceived by any other sense but sight, might be believed to be a mirage or an evil spirit left over from the young man's dreams. Yet once the young man convinces himself that the things he sees and smells and the warmth that he feels beside him are all tied together into one creature, it is as if the rest of the world is re-focussed as well. Still, there remains the feeling that the alignment of the lens is not quite perfect, or if it is, that it has gotten that way too soon for him to be able to accept it, like the feeling of getting new eyeglasses through which all things are quite sharp and precise but against which one wants to squint as if against a great glare.

It is beginning to grow dark outside, and the windows have begun to reflect the inside glows and shines off the smooth inner surfaces, crystallizing into barriers between the inside and the outside where before there was nothing. It is as if the cold air that is sweeping up and across the surfaces from the ducts is making them opaque, spraying them with some sort of chemical that hardens them and is gradually sealing the bus into a long impenetrable tube. The darkness outside is moving in, warm and damp; for those inside the bus it seems to be dispensed in puffs of inky clouds from ventilators under bushes that are mixed by the air into a uniform and lighter shade of gray.

The bus passes by woods that have begun to lose their daytime green and to assume the more drab colors of the evening. It passes open fields planted with soybeans in short black ruffles that show above them the darkness of the warm evening in which float the smells of pigs, manure, and pine trees in the night and perhaps also the sharp odor of a skunk that those inside the vehicle, at any rate, know nothing of. He is barely able to make out the silhouettes of the farm houses far back in the fields, beside which rise the round corn silos, yoked two and two, huge cages of wire mesh as tall as the houses themselves that now contain nothing but the sweet odor of the earth wet by the rain but which will never enclose the exotic birds that their aviary-like shape would lead one to foretell; the shrill cries of multi-colored tropical parrots will never float over these flat brown fields. All they will ever hear are the raucous caws of black crows that will drop one by one from great clouds of flapping wings that break apart completely into single birds as they hover lower and then separate to scatter over the field; all these cages will ever contain are the hard cobs of the feed corn whose kernels can be broken off with a twist of the hand and need not be cut or ripped with the teeth, made brittle and hard by dryness and kept that way by the sun that comes in the middle of the summer, burning and browning.

Occasionally there is an ice cream stand or a gas station on the outskirts of the towns of a dozen houses growing from the sides of the road through which the bus passes, and a flash of light and perhaps a glimpse of teenagers leaning on their cars, laughing and talking, or of automobiles lined up by gasoline pumps where all is silent and only the single attendant moves or crouches by the rear of the car. Then this too is gone, and the only breaks of the blackness are the pairs of burning eyes that come at them from the other side of the road and blind him temporarily. Even if he were willing to lean over the fat man beside him who sleeps on and clear away the glare by pressing his face against the cool glass, leaving the small greasy mark of his nose, he would be unable to make out, during that brief period when they are opposite his window, the dark shape of the car that powers these lights and so he is unable to say for sure that they are not merely four lights connected together with wire or string that float above the ground, created in a moment of pity by an unknown goddess in order to break up the darkness of the night for the poor humans who travel through it in buses.

Occasionally too there is a billboard standing by the side of the road against a clump of trees, lit up brightly by the bulbs that hang head down over its top so that the glowing rectangle breaks through the glare on the windows and is clearly visible to those within the bus. Their pinks and purples and blues blare from the silence of the night into the cool bus with its undercurrent of wheel noises and the soft voices of a few people talking. Around the bottoms of these signs, held above the ground by creosoted poles, are tall pointed bushes whose tops brush the signs' bottoms and below which are progressively smaller shrubs as if the billboard, by arranging a family around its skirts in this manner for the photographer, had hoped to buy visual evidence that it is not a sign but a malformed tree, that it is no interloper here by the forest but something that belongs in these clumps of woods foiled in its plans by the photographer who was indignant that he had been expected to be a party to such dissimulation and who had turned on his lights and hastened away on some pretext or another, telling the billboard not to move under any circumstances. Surely it would not want to be caught in the ignominious position of bending over to admonish the smallest shrub that wanted its mother and brothers and not this gaudy billboard and these other strange trees or of smacking one of the older bushes that was making snide comments and which had thus been frozen forever—for the photographer never came back, of course—in this attitude of sickly smiles and unnatural stiffness under the lights for all those to mock. **Note:** We cannot imagine the billboard suddenly relinquishing its pretensions and simply walking away, perhaps taking the time to shoo the shrubs in the general direction of the woods where they would find their parents or some suitable substitute.

By now, even the gray ghosts of farm houses are invisible. They are not, as they might be elsewhere, set on hills, alone and stark so that they could be seen as ebony cutouts against the lighter sky. Indeed, there are no hills at all; the landscape is perfectly flat, sandy and dark. Occasionally he can make out tiny plots of graves surrounded by rusting iron fences that spring suddenly into view by the side of the road, illuminated by the headlights of the bus as it sweeps around a curve. The graveyards are black again an instant later, and all that is left in the mind is an afterimage of pale curved-top stones overgrown with vines and surrounded by the sandy fields out of which this enclosed plot sticks undisturbed.

Abruptly he is aware that the light over his head is turned on and is pointing at him, making a watery circle on his lap. He reaches up his arm and extends his finger to flick it off, but is still an inch away and when he tries to stretch the muscles in his finger, it arches backwards instead of becoming longer and he is forced to raise himself for a moment, touching the ridged button at the top of his arc and then falling back down onto the seat. Things are appreciably darker now that the light is off, and the images that separated him from the outside are fainter. Only a few other people have their lights on and the only other illumination is from the lights in the aisle that shine bleary through the thin cloud of cigarette smoke that he cannot smell, hovering near the ceiling.

He thinks briefly of going to the bathroom to wash the stickiness of his sweat from his hands and face, of rocking back and forth with the bus as he tries to make his way down the aisle, having to hang onto the loops of plastic that protrude from the sides of the seats, of looking down upon all the tired men and women who slump silently in corners or stare out of the windows or at the seats before them, thinks of the tiny bathroom which would have its window painted over in chipped whitewash and a sink smudged black with fingerprints and a floor gritty with sand and dirt, whereupon he turns again to the window.

By not going to the back of the bus, however, he misses seeing the pair of old men who are sitting by the bathroom door. All four of their half-closed eyes are watery and yellow, as if the tobacco they chew had discolored not only their teeth but the other white spots in their face as well. Their moist red tear ducts drop small blobs of mucus that, not wiped away, have hardened into crusts along the inside of the bridges of their bulbous noses. One of their noses is sunburnt and splotched with stray freckles that seem to be a different and wilder species than the small tame pores and freckles that spot the wrinkled ridges of the accompanying thin face; the other nose is a thick dark one that shines even in the small amount of light coming from the aisle, shines with the sweat and grease that is not quite so noticeable on the white man's bony features. Four lips work in slow pulping motions, silent but for the squishing sound of saliva being forced from the plugs held between their teeth; four hands hang in pairs between their legs, wrinkled knuckles clasped beside the worn denim of their work pants. Their backs are curved forward so that their elbows are focussed on the floor, eyes that are cloudy as if from boiling and which are shot through with the red veins that seems to have popped in the great heat which has done no more harm to the vision than to slow it a bit and made necessary long periods of squinting adjustment as if to allow the image to penetrate the murky depths.

He listens to the ticking of his watch and tries to synchronize it with the patterns of the headlights sweeping by in what is not a steady if widely-spaced stream, but their progress until that moment when they rush on below eye level is so slow that it cannot be meshed with the rapid clicks of the time machine. He leans back in his seat, being careful to keep away from the protruding parts of the fat man beside him, and closes his eyes again. The dark world shakes and he feels himself bouncing slightly as the bus goes over rough parts on the road, the springs in his seat jumping under him. He opens his eyes with a jerk as his neighbor begins to move, and watches the rolls of fat around his waist re-arrange, form slightly new hills and valleys and then subside again as he settles and goes back to sleep.

The lighted houses are becoming more closely strung; it is evident that the bus is about to enter a settlement of some size. These larger towns are formed in small knots around a single main street which in this case is the highway, larger and more well-traveled than in some of these country towns through which threads a dusty street where old men sit in chairs outside of the stores to absorb the afternoon sun, an asphalt knife that cuts the settlement in half and across which run only those children who are without fear of the cars. The bus turns a curve and he sees a bridge on the other side of the woods, arching high over a river, and a cluster of houses at its base. As the bus mounts the bridge the town recedes below, its lighted streets and its white church steeple taking on for an instant the appearance of a toy village, different than when they are seen from the ground and are ordinary small houses clustered around a small store and a little church. Now they are transformed into a lit-up model train town; in this instant it seems he can scoop into his hands these dwellings that contain diminutive people, as free as dolls of the hopes and fears, the disappointments and joys of normal-sized creatures.

This feeling is as fragile as a dandelion globe plucked from a meadow on a summer day whose feathery perfection we try to fix in our minds before it ruptures, though it begins to float away almost immediately as if broken by the force of our gaze: the window divider blots out the town and the bus curves up to the top of the bridge and down the other side, its interior lit for an instant with the eerie white light of the mercury arc lamps reflecting blurrily on the water which is too far under them to be able to make out clearly the ripples of the wind or the tide on which the images must be reflected sharply even if they are twisted and repeated in wrinkled translations. The lights continue for a few yards beyond the end of the bridge, where his hands lose their paleness and take on again a shadowy cast.

There are fewer trees by the side of the road now and the low blackness stretches out on both sides into what might as well be the end of the earth, that point at which the solid dirt stops and the pitch blackness begins, into which those who are walking along with no premonition of the fate that awaits them may fall. This is no matter to those in the bus, for they must stay on this dark track and are in no danger of suddenly derailing and careening down the center of one of these fields towards the precipice, nor could they hear the cries of terror or fear of those who were so unlucky as to fall over. They are held safe within this machine and hear only the sounds which they make themselves and the noises of the bus; it is nothing to them what happens beyond the darkness. The terrors that lurk in the woods pose for them no treats, nor do they fear having to see the sun rise over this horrible gorge, exposing all of the grisly truths that the false cloak of the night had hidden from their gazes.

The houses begin to be thicker again, no longer country farm buildings but one-story family houses. There are cross streets that are not dirt roads, and lights over the street. There is a steady stream of cars coming in the opposite direction and the bus has slowed up to jolt across the railroad tracks by the antique store that glows green through the bus's windows. Streets branch out in every direction, with outlying stores and laundries that are closed for the night. He can see the lights of a larger shopping area; it would seem that the bus's headlights would be drawn to this larger and primeval fire with so great a strength that no one would be able to control their impatience or keep them away. But this machine is more powerful than its eyes, and with a wrench it turns a sharp corner by the gas station and starts down a dark side street, the headlights casting one quick gleam of despair at the buildings with which they had been denied contact as the bus whips around the angle.

On both sides of the street are huge oil storage drums, great metal curves that reflect in dull gray the lights over them. Ahead of them is the shine of the river, quiet and slimy with scum. The road does not go straight into this thick water: there is not, in this quiet summer night, a splash and a great stream of bubbles that roils the surface and finally stops except for an occasional tiny pop that might as well come from a crab wallowing deeper into the mud as from the recently dead bodies of the passengers that float still and cold behind the windows, their skins beginning to wrinkle and tighten from the cold water and their hair floating out around their heads in a nimbus. By the water a small building comes into view from behind an oil drum; only the white-painted sides are visible in the night, the lights illuminating it set below the roof.

The bus pulls up abruptly before the building's almost deserted platform, and turns off its motor. The abrupt silence is broken by people scraping their feet and standing up, and by others beginning to make the pleasantries of safe arrival. He can hear the voices of the two middle-aged women on the single bench outside the station, though he cannot make out what they are saying. He thinks he hears the slam of the screen door that leads to the inside through which he can see several men in short sleeve shirts who are leaning on the counter with their heads together, but when he looks he cannot see anyone who has come in or out.

He steps into a break in the line of people, turning at the same moment to slide his suitcase over the rubber rope that holds it in. It snaps back with a vibration that starts down its length and is not damped until several yards away, through several metal brackets. He had prepared his arm for a much heavier burden than the suitcase, and his tensed muscles loosen in relief as the weight falls on them. There are a few people standing before their seats with their necks curved against the top as his had been when he stood to get his suitcase, like plants grown so large that they slither against the greenhouse roof and attempt to hide their malformation by putting out even greener leaves and blossoming in greater profusion than ever before.

He moves along haltingly behind a thin man wearing wire-rimmed glasses whose flared blue jeans bear the horizontal creases of newness that have not been pressed out by an iron or by his ride and which end some inches above the tops of his dirty black shoes. He steps on something and jerks his foot away. It turns out to be nothing more odious or odorous than a paper cup which he has squashed flat so that the wax chips away from the white creases he has made down its red-striped sides. The line of people, which had been shuffling along at a fairly constant rate, stops, probably for some man who has gallantly let a woman out in front of him and discovers too late that not only does she need someone to lift down her suitcase but that she is the sort who offers his services to her seatmate and the two old women across the aisle as well, or [though this is a question that could certainly be answered merely by looking over the shoulder of the short man in front of him instead of at the top of his suitcase and the floor] it may be that an arthritic old man is poising a stiff leg over the abyss of the first step and looking around importantly to encourage all those who were thinking of other things or looking anxiously into the station for the relatives and friends they do not see to look at him, to appreciate his pain and his perseverance and courage in actually descending these stairs himself without the aid of a cane or a pair of stronger and younger hands under his wasted armpits.

They are nearly at the front of the bus and he can hear the talk behind him that has swelled louder and the sounds of heavy things bumping their corners and edges on the floor that grow fainter as he moves forward. He smells the warm night air that is rushing into the cool bus, bringing with it the sharp twinge of the oil and the water and the sound of whispered and gentle lappings against the pilings as if it were a cat nuzzling up against the columns it had taken for human legs and a faint burst of music that is coming from the bar barely visible around the corner of the station.

As he steps off the bottom stair, he hesitates for a moment in the cross-current of bland coolness and the odorous warmth, then turns and begins to walk.

He passes a bar and sees within the large plastic clock that simultaneously tells the time, advertises beer, and blinks. Behind it is a line of brightly-lit bar stools nearly all filled with people and the round plastic-topped tables with tubular metal legs where an occasional woman in slacks sips a drink and looks through the large plate glass windows and into the night. He crosses the street and starts across the short concrete bridge, not bothering to stay on the sidewalk. He hesitates for a moment in the middle of the bridge and, walking to the rail, looks at the river that twists and curls in the colors of oil patches illuminated by the feeble lights over him, occasionally being disturbed by the motions of a fish fluttering its gills and fins under the surface.

There is a solid line of stores closing around both sides of the street with lights that are more closely spaced than on the other side of the river, and parking lots and side streets.

Once, the bridge had been a wooden and metal drawspan. Under it still hang the giant cogwheels and cranks of the machinery that were never taken away and now sag unused and rusted like pendulous genitals brushing the water that is overgrown with weeds and algae, too shallow to allow passage by anything more than a rowboat.

There is a warehouse up against the water on his left, unused and ivy-covered, and a short and dusty drugstore wedged between the drugstore and the road. It is closed for the night, but its windows are filled with fading advertisements and boxes of candy so uniformly dingy that from the outside it seems as if it might very well be that the man who ran it had simply locked the door on its dark inside and dirty corners one winter day twenty years ago and walked away, or that inside the store sleeps an enchanted maiden and her retinue who, as they sat at the counter in their bobby socks and saddle shoes drinking malted milks and talking of their boyfriends, were touched into slumber by the good fairy who was attempting to soften the fate of the head cheerleader who in mid-sip had pricked her finger on the safety pin she was playing with and, victim of the wicked fairy's malevolent plans, had fallen to the floor in a swoon to the consternation of her friends who were soon themselves slumped around the bases of the stools so that when the girl awoke to the kiss of the handsome football captain, she would not be frightened at finding herself in a dark and deserted store.

On the other side of the street rises the back end of the dilapidated hotel down which crawl fragile latticed fire escapes that stop a moment at every floor to see if they are being followed and then change their direction as if to confuse and befuddle pursuers. There are lights in some of the windows, stacked up the red brick wall in columns so high that he must lean back to see to the top. Some of the windows are open and he can make out curtains that puff out of them and then are blown back. He cannot hear any sounds except the soft swish of the water and the music from the bar at the other end of the bridge and somewhere the faraway sound of a car starting and pulling away. No, the music is not from the other side of the water but from in front of him, from the street that curves between the tall stores facing inwards like the noses of pigs around a slop-trough, but of which he can also see the backs on the other side of the hotel that are dark and uneven and shadowy, for the lights are not as strong on the side streets that cross between him and the stores, and some of them are broken.

There is no one in sight and no sound of any footsteps, and he starts up the deserted street. Behind the windows are mannequins wearing brightly-colored dresses, rows of empty shoes, and displays of candy in which a cardboard figure powered by a battery swings its arm back and forth and offers its wares to the emptiness. Above the lights, the sky is dark blue-black and starry, but it is difficult to reconcile this soft beauty with the harshness of the street level.

In those few stores that do not have blocked-up windows, like the five and ten with its huge chipped plastic sign from which several of the letters have been removed so that naked light bulbs gleam through the holes, the nightlights are on; the depth of the building seems a corridor of glowing emptiness receding into the darkness. Above the street level are the shadowy top floors of these buildings that are never noticed by anyone and do not need to cover their brown stones with plastic sheaths, in whose cracks and eaves roost pigeons that strut on the empty asphalt before him, their windows blanked out with Venetian blinds from behind some of which faint light seeps.

He realizes that the music that he has heard is coming from loudspeakers set up over the doors of a shop displaying electric guitars and drum sets. It bounces off the fronts of these buildings and echoes off the pavement. The run-down stores patched up and covered over with purple and pink plastic and filled with these inexpensive wares that during the daytime draw the women in curlers and the middle-aged indigents who amble down the sidewalk and watch those who pass them have now, in this cold white light, the air of fatigue that must come to every ageing woman who in the evening sits before her mirror and suddenly wants to scrub from her wrinkled cheeks the paint that, she had hoped, would cover over the traces of the years and who, when she raises a hesitant finger to her forehead that comes away tan with make-up, drops her head to her arms and begins to weep so softly that no one can hear her.

But it is not up to these buildings alone to suddenly renounce the folly of their charade. They cannot, one evening, allow to drop from their cheeks the multi-colored scales and patches and send from their windows the bright-colored dresses and the cheap gadgets and snuff out the lights that glare so tinnily on them and be revealed as the morning sun rises for the gaunt and decrepit constructions they are. It is not up to them to take part or not in the dissimulation, for they are dependent on the people who are not here and to whose invisible spirits it must be that the lifeless things in these windows offer themselves. It cannot, at any rate, be to this young man walking up the center of the white-lit street carrying a suitcase and a blue jacket that these buildings offer their plastic wares and their music, for the moving things will continue their motions when he is gone, the chipped-face mannequins will smile at the empty street, and the painted metal airplane ride outside of the drugstore that rocks back and forth when it is fed a dime will be no less ready to start its gyrations for the fact that there is nothing before it but a few pigeons that peck aimlessly at the sidewalk. He turns down a dark side street where the neon sign of a furniture store glows green and flickers as if in response to a breath of the warm black air and starts towards home.

II

The Luncheon

THERE ARE YELLOW FLOWERS atop the paddle-shaped cacti, tiny cupped blossoms that look so innocent and fresh that no one would ever dare to demand their business hanging like ticks on the smooth curves of these plants or their justification in perching here so saucily as if they were not aware that they looked out of place, nor to demand why they are so shameless as to be yellow and fragile instead of making at least minimal attempts at accommodating themselves to their surroundings by turning as hard and fleshy as the plants that support them and onto which they have attached their parasitic suckers—or at least having suffused themselves with a touch of emerald so that they are not to eyes such as his, which are several feet away, the most obvious part about the plants that grow here at the foot of the wild cherry trees.

The blossoms are perfectly formed but somehow suggest disease. **How so?:** When the rose petals that drop onto the hard crushed stone of his parents' driveway press their velvet layers down onto the sharp-edged pebbles, the result is dark wet bruises on scraps of softness, creases and blotches of near-translucence through which he can blurrily see the bushes from which the petals fell when he holds the soft flakes to his eyes. Of course, the cactus flowers have not been injured by trampling or crushing; it is the rain-streaked bark of the cherry tree that has suggested this sickness to him and against which background the petals seem to be equally maimed, or perhaps the fact that, amid the wet grass the tree and the drops of water that fall occasionally from down the shining chutes of the leaves and against the matted blades of grass and the rough tree trunk, these blooms look more breakable and weak than they would if they grew on thin reedy stems around rocks in Alpine meadows that stretch multi-hued down the sides of the mountains and through the grasses and flowers of which we can run headlong until we collapse breathless in a helpless heap.

The leaves of the plants are polka-dotted with tufts of thin white spines that are like the clumps of gray hair on the face of an elderly bearded lady who sits slumped on a stool in a carnival sideshow, oblivious to those curious few who grope their way along the passageway that, despite the row of naked light bulbs over the exhibits, seems dark to these who come in blinking against the glare of the outdoors sun which in the afternoon makes the air so close that the bearded lady begins to grunt and gasp as she breathes. **Note:** Her sharp chin does not raise itself off her wrinkled chest ridged with her protruding breast bone, nor do her withered breasts caught and supported by the cloth cut so brief as to expose the patches of hair on her body heave with especial force. Her arms that end in the unnecessarily bony hands and knuckles do not stir from her lap, not even when the small boy darts from beside his father's dusty overalls and, stooping under the rope, runs up and tugs at her skirt before wheeling in terror at his own courage and running back to the man who stands grinning, his arms folded against his chest. The flat and fleshy paddles are attached to the dirt by a thin round base so that the whole plant has about it the same air of stretched probability that surrounds a ship in a bottle whose neck is too small even to admit a little finger without it growing white from lack of blood so that the glass feels as if it is constricting rhythmically around the flesh, and yet which has seemingly swallowed this entire schooner rigging and all, for the plant too has been thrust into the air from its home in the ground and is grown fat and a good deal wider than its small jointure with the earth. **Note:** Unlike the ship, the bottle of air into which this plant has been thrust is not free from danger such as the threat of being lopped off by the whirring blades of the lawnmower in a perfect knife-clean cut that oozes clear sticky sap, or of being impaled on the sharp stick of a small child which crouches above it and drives the twig with all its might into the middle of the pulp—unless it is the possibly chimerical one of injury by flying dust particles or the considerably more possible but almost as improbable fate of being shaken violently by an annoyed human so that the impact shatters the masts and spars which are no thicker than matchsticks and toothpicks, crushing them so that the painstakingly-strung rigging is reduced to a twisted tangle of thread and string.

Further consideration: If what crushes the cactus are the black pads of an animal's feet separated by thick dark hairs or the hand and arm of an unwary human, the cactus can leave in return for the injury some of these harmless-looking spines that lodge invisibly in the skin and twist with the bite of tiny gnats if accidentally touched and which must, in order to effect their removal, be held sideways to the light so that the blunt noses of the tweezers do not snap at empty air or so that the needle's point burrows in at the thing's base and does not draw needless drops of red blood at points on the white skin that would form an erratic circle around the area but do not approach it.

Fantasy: They would, perhaps, form a magic circle across which the captive spine cannot escape except in the middle of the night when its jailers are snoring at the gates and their gleaming swords have dropped onto the ground, and all that is audible from the surrounding field is the fading chirp of crickets and the swishing of the wet stems as they brush against one another in the suddenly cool wind. In a desperately calculated sacrifice, it breaks its stalk off at the skin level and leaves it behind in the hopes of the skin remaining sufficiently irritated that the person would not suspect its prisoner's escape and crawls across the greasy epidermis, diminished by its amputation as well as quite bent under the weight of its misfortunes, which are heavy since the cactus used these spines that grew in clumps from its shiny green sides as the intermediaries in the expression of its wrath without giving much attention to what would happen to them once they were sunk in someone's skin. **Reflection:** What eventually must be answered is what extent our existence is purely linear and what extent it can double back on itself and be twisted into any number of strange shapes for the sake of bringing into contact two points separated by feet and even yards of the line of time. For should we consider that once these spines would have given anything in order to serve that which had plucked them from the rain and winds and given them a dry place against its breast. Now this intense gratitude has evaporated into sullen bitterness that they should be asked to do something which, to be sure, is far from pleasant, but which they would have once been only too happy to perform. At this point, we realize that it is not sufficient merely to throw up our hands in helpless resignation and mutter as we shake our heads some homily about time that not only heals all wounds but which reduces the greatest edifices of feeling to rubble, that destroys the towering emotional mountains of hate, of love, of gratitude and of fear nearly as absolutely as if a magician had waved a wand and changed them instantly into four grains of yellowed dust.

Further: It does us no good to shade our eyes and survey the distance between the present and the past, gleaming white in the afternoon sun, for the impassability of that distance is one of our own postulates. We are like those who justify the immobility of the rug under their feet on the basis that there is a great weight holding it down. In fact, the time line can be knotted as easily as we do our shoelaces, though some of us have never learned the correct method of doing even this. This is because we ignored the smiling teacher who sat splay-legged on a chair too small for her with her skirt stretched tight between her thighs and demonstrated on a piece of cardboard shaped like a lopsided peanut the correct method of teasing and twisting those limp strings that were threaded through holes punched in the thing so that they ceased being graceless and spineless caterpillars and metamorphosed in a matter of seconds into butterflies unfortunately as constrained in their movements as those creatures that little boys pin live to their walls, skewering them through their thoraxes so that they flutter and struggle as they die.

Confession: We ignored the woman who demonstrated this miraculous change to the roomful of little ones clutching identical shoes whose fingers twisted the laces into knots during the untangling of which the teacher's well-manicured fingernails cracked and her practiced grin seemed to grow a bit tighter and more strained. Some of her pupils, ourselves among them, preferred to watch something more interesting than this little charade, staring out the window at the flag undulating and twisting at the top of its shaft and trying to count the stars from where they sat, though no sooner had they fixed a dot of white firmly with their gaze than it was ripped from under their eyes and they lost their place in the row, their eyes growing bleary with the effort and they beginning to blink in irritation, looking down again finally to see the teacher standing before them and rhapsodizing about the perfect symmetry of the bow they had tied so quickly and neatly, and seeing behind her the blushing little redhead who bent over her own shoe where there was tied an identical and equally perfect bow.

Half of the cherry tree above these cactus flowers is brown and dry, the branches of the dead part still covered with leaves that crackle when the living leaves beside them rustle, their slick green surfaces slipping off each other in the breeze. It is as if the tree were once a prince held in thrall by an evil sorcerer, his fair limbs having been turned to the tree boughs that are now damp with the afternoon shower and speckled in tiny white dots that can on closer inspection be resolved into the soft silken covers of insects' egg clusters spun in cracks in the bark. **Note:** This curse was effective only during the daytime: when the sky turned ebony and the moonbeams painted the yard in their white glow that seems so liquid it must collect in pools on the pale leaves and drop in shining streams onto the grass below, the tree began to heave and sway and twist and, as the moon pushed from behind the dark clouds that have obscured it and shone full, there stood below by this small clapboard house a handsome prince.

Unimportant the way the prince spent his nights; unimportant the dewy-cheeked maidens, the glasses of wine as red as the throats of hummingbirds, the sapphire lake across which floated purple gondolas lit with golden globes. All that matters is the fact that one night he must have been careless of the time and, running blindly through the trees of the elementary school playground, tripping over deserted plastic shovels and a mislaid roller skate and through the nearby woods on his way to the yard that he must reach before the cock crowed lest he lose forever the ability to experience these few brief hours as a human, he had stepped in a misplaced bear trap that he had finally wrenched open, though not without a great deal of blood loss and a pain so intense that, fatigued as he was, he nearly fainted on the spot.

The Prince's skin was more tender than that of ordinary mortals and his body far more fragile, and so before nightfall half of the tree had turned brown and withered. And when again the moon shone, it illuminated not a prince poised to run off to the enchanted ball that awaited him but a sweaty boy with a withered arm and leg who was huddled miserably upon the ground weeping tears that, it is said, grew each night into the soft golden flowers of the dandelion plants that dot the base of the tree and that show in their growth cycle the duality of the tears that were wept partly as warm drops of remembered pleasure as delicate and glowing as the lamps that lit the gliding boats and partly in gray sorrow at the accident that had crippled his limbs and condemned him to nights exiled from his enchanted land on the wet grass.

Further: It is likely that the possibility of being hauled away by the local police, alerted by the inhabitants of one of the nearby houses who had heard moaning and become suspicious, as well as simple wretchedness at having to behold himself in this maimed condition, were the considerations that led him to abjure his period of freedom now become so hateful and beg that his transformation be complete and never-changing. Surely this is as good an explanation as any for the fact that if the family across the street comes in late from a movie or a night of bowling, they see not the shaking shoulders of a sobbing boy but merely an old half-dead cherry tree rustling and crackling in the breeze and the brown line of the broken and rusted rake that hangs on it from a nail.

Beyond the strip of crabgrass that frequent cutting has turned slightly brown, as if to harmonize it with the patches of exposed dirt that dot it, lies the small back yard of the old lady's house. It is uneven, hilly with piles of sand dug from holes and left exposed to become green with small weeds and with the low bush-like plants with stems whose insides are so spongy that their crisp outer shells can be crushed between thumb and finger, cracked in vertical slashes so that they cannot support the plant which bows immediately to the ground, the air already rushing in to dry the frothy pith that has been exposed in the destruction. Over them crawls the leafy net of vines covering all the ground surface save for a few newly filled-in holes where molder the rinds of cantaloupes from yesterday's breakfast just beginning to become soft and lose their juice into the sand, or the considerably older coffee grounds and bruised cabbage leaves that are nearly absorbed and are now hardly more than a faint richness in the otherwise infertile soil. There is even the mark left by the yellowed water of last night's washing, a swath of smoothness produced by the liquid slopping from the white enamel pan. **Second thought:** This could not have survived the rain that has pocked and wet everything; it must be merely a glare of the sunlight on the sand.

On the side of this overgrown plot is a huge crawling rosebush covered with hundreds of faded pink blossoms that seems to sweep up the side of the gray garage and anchor the building to the ground. The boards are nearly obscured by the plant, but enough of them is visible on the sides and top to see that they are splintered and rotten. The roof shingles have begun to come apart in pieces and there is one hole where they have caved in, the loose pieces of wood on the sides of the cavity suspended over the abscess by nothing more substantial in some cases than the pressure of a single sliver that is liable to give way at any moment and send hurtling to the dirt floor below the hapless piece of cedarwood that has at last come to the end of the line, to that point at which it is no longer fit for service and will be carted away to the incinerator rather than being put out to rot quietly in a mulch pile in return for the years of faithful service it has provided not only the beech leaves which fell upon them and thus were saved from the unpleasantness of a considerably longer tumble with a commensurately stronger impact but also the bugs that were only too glad to find a warm dry place between them to molt and lay eggs and raise their families.

The vines and the new thick green shoots of the roses have begun to cover the crumbling hole in the roof and to reach bold arms down into the garage as if eventually to lay larcenous hands on the pile of broken boards, the rake missing several metal teeth, or the yellow garbage can, the only thing under the low roof that is not brown or gray. **Alternate explanation:** Perhaps these plant shoots wish for some unexplained reason of their own to scoop up great piles of the thin and dusty sand that has been turned damp and darker under the hole, handfuls that will trickle over their pale leaves, leaving as they fall a dusty residue on the plants' ends like the ghosts of elbow-length evening gloves.

On shelves sit the thin-sided strawberry boxes that could crumble at a touch and leave only the thicker rims with their brown metal staples, as well as flower-pots as brittle as the bones of the woman who put them there a decade ago and has not moved them since. Thinner shoots of tall weeds push through cracks in the boards of the back wall, not content to stay out in the air under the sun and soak up the smells of the decaying vegetables the neighbors throw over the back fence knowing that the old woman never goes back there, not interested in the soft buzzings of the wasps and honey bees attracted by the pink juice of the watermelon rinds: the shoots have given up all this in their quest for what they thought was the more preferable society of the droppings and possessions of mankind in an old run-down garage filled with cobwebs and hiding places for shiny coal-black crickets. **Lesson:** This is so often the case, that the dispossessed and the inexperienced in the ways of the world are induced by some fast-talking hustler to give all their money for what turns out to be a life more wretched than the one they had left; it is only when the poor duped one finally awakens and realizes that it has been living in squalor and poverty and that it has not even the means to return to the place it has left that it will understand what has happened.

The tree that shades the small rickety garage drops occasional bits of accumulated water onto the roof and the ground around it, small built-up portions saved from the downpour of an hour earlier in the small cups and valleys along the branches and leaves, and dispersed now under the misapprehension understandable in a plant with a memory as feeble as that of the tree that this is the time of drought for which the water has been saved. **Note:** Possibly even some of us with initially better mental equipment would be thrown off track by the contrast between the ferocity of the rain and what seems now to be an almost unearthly calm and an intolerable dryness, and would be induced as well to make the mistake that this green tree is making. When we consider that, if not dispensed, the water pockets will soon be dried up anyway, the tree's actions even begins to make good sense, for there is no point in trying to put an overly-sophisticated theory into practice with low-level technology. There would, for example, be no point in the desiccating weeds clutching their brown and crisping throats come the next dry spell and cursing the foolishness of this tree if it could not have kept its bits of water to that time in any case, though perhaps such curses would at least serve the purpose of diverting the attention of the dry plants from their own wretched condition.

The screening on the house's porch is rusted and has formed fuzzy coatings that have thickened the wires so the gnats which once found passage easy would now have a hard time getting through the holes. The screens do not lie flat as they should, but hump and bend as if afflicted with an advanced case of boils that has left behind the pocked indentations of its earlier stages as well as the current extrusions. The paint on the wood slats that serve as the frame is chipping off in brittle white curls. Behind the curls, the gray squares they have exposed, as if the chips were the doors of an Advent calendar opened before their proper time so that there is visible behind them not the picture of the toy drum or the lighted candle they would have revealed had they been left to develop to maturity, but instead the unorganized gray of the particles that have not yet begun to clump together into squares of colors or even to differentiate themselves, an amorphous and homogeneous mess that gives visible clue that they would soon have coalesced into the cheery decoration they can never become now that they have been exposed to the air before their time, like a chicken's egg which is broken on the side of the frying pan and found to contain a half-developed fetus that can never be glued back together again and bear fruit, even if the yolk had not been congealed by the hot grease of the pan that turns it white and hard.

By the two brick steps leading to the small porch is a flat stone beside which sag damp violets, some of which have even bowed their purple heads onto the rock as if so dispirited that they would welcome the death that will be theirs with one swift tread of a firmly-planted shoe and have laid their necks on the block so that the harbinger of death need not go out of its way to bring them peace. **Alternate explanation:** It may be that they are bowed not under the weight of their own cares or even under the weight of the raindrops caught between their petals, but are instead engaged in a set of deep-breathing exercises that calls for them to limber up their stems by twisting and turning in every conceivable direction and to bend nearly to the ground. If they were to be injured in the process of carrying out their harmless recreation, so much the more senseless would their fate seem, and so much the more would we have cause to rend our tunics and beat our breasts in anguish.

Ah, memory: Under this rock he had once found a salamander that had wriggled between his fingers, turning and twisting on the pivot of two fleshy pads until he had let it go under the house and it had flashed from sight, its moist clear skin becoming covered with the dust that it raised as it vanished. In replacing the stone, he had destroyed the elaborate holes dug by the termites and had probably even crushed under some of the bumps of the rock's undersurface insects moving jerkily along the dark earth, pulping their white wings in which he could see all the colors of the lighted world they shunned so that if ever the stone were lifted again they would no longer be iridescent and beautiful but instead would be covered with the dulling sheen of dried blood or whatever it is that flows in the veins of these creatures.

He turns the car's motor off and attempts to pocket the keys. The cloth of his pants must be curled and twisted, for his fingers refuse to slide in and so, holding the cool flat pieces of metal in his right hand, he opens the door and twists himself out, standing for a moment by the cherry tree. Finally he is successful in forcing his pocket to accept the metal wafers and does equally well in straightening the shirttail that has pulled from his pants during the short trip. As he walks by the tree, he reaches out a hand and rips from the branch a dead leaf that he immediately lets fall, disappointed in the helpless acquiescence that is unlike the soft resistance provided by living leaves, the straining and then the plump pop as the stem looses itself from its socket. The air smells not of brown earth or of damp plants but of settled dust and disturbed mold. He kicks from the patches of sand the gouts of dark wet dirt that, in spite of the hardness and ferocity of the rain, is not more than a quarter of an inch thick, exposing the hard-packed under-layer into which no liquid has penetrated. It is a layer as coherent and as tightly-knit as the lid of a vast treasure chest that lies only millimeters below the surface of the earth, and waits only for someone to lean casually on a spade or to scuff his toes to be discovered. **Reflection:** What is this earth of ours but a great treasure chest stocked with that for which so many long? What are we but the poor unconscious ones who walk above and through this storehouse never dreaming of that which lies below, unconscious both of the riches and the skeletons who have made this earth their grave, the remains of those who knew too much of where and what these treasures were and who paid for this knowledge and their attempts to attain them with their lives?

Concession: Still, we would be wrong to imagine some swarthy pirate chief standing astride the hole and kicking sand over it with a disdainful boot, or better, urinating over the corpses that are draped in impossible angles over the lid of the chest. We must instead adjust the analogy so that it is the treasure itself that kills the two diggers, for it is a well-known fact that the author as subject is dead and that we are no longer the masters or mistresses of our own actions. Many gallant and brave men have died in their attempt to hold or acquire these riches and are killed by the object of their exertions rather than by their own motions; these actions are but the mechanism of a death to which they have sentenced themselves long before by their commitment to the treasure. **Technical note:** To establish this correspondence, however, we cannot simply insert a long and drawn-out tale of acquisition and concurrent degeneration. To preserve any semblance of believability, we must keep the time blocks in relatively constant order. We cannot freeze the sand and the sea and the gulls in their tracks while the two hapless ones who, we know, are going to end up dead because of the box they are in the process of uncovering clamber out of the hole with their pockets stuffed with doubloons and with strings of precious stones twisted round their necks and wrists and hop the next ship to the city where they spend themselves into ruin and stagger back, broken men, to fall into the hole and gasp their last breaths before the sands cover them with a landslide and the waters suddenly come to life with a crash and sweep over the top, obliterating all traces of any activity and leaving only a smooth swath of wet sand through which occasional bubbles force themselves, making small holes that soon ooze back together again. We should not, for instance, try to express this death at the hands of the treasure by saying that the two diggers, eager for one last look at the jewels and gold that they would be leaving for a while, opened the trunk only to be attacked by the sharp teeth of the coins and the razor edges of the necklaces and by the daggers that chomped and carved and bit and tore until all that was left were the two skeletons, picked smooth and clean. Nor would we want to postulate an elaborate firing mechanism built into the chest itself that shot them through the hearts. Perhaps it is best merely to throw ourselves on the mercy of those we are trying to convince, admitting that we are unable to find any way to redeem this story, to bring it into alignment with the point we are using it to express. If we frankly and quietly make it known that we have simply made a mistake or have lost our way, others will forgive us. There is, after all, more than one way to gain the sympathy of those whom we are addressing, and frankness can usually be counted on to disarm any objections and eliminate any annoyance produced by our faults.

He scrapes the grit off his shoes onto the edges of the bricks, nearly falling backwards with one particularly vigorous swipe. When he has finished the pawing at the air necessary to prevent his fall, he takes a deep breath and tugs at the handle of the screen door that opens several inches and then stops with a jerk. **Note:** This is probably not due to an unexpected hardness in the air, or to the invisible hand of some giant that has impeded his progress. Either of these may well be the case, but it is worth pointing out that there is also a string loop into which a metal hook is inserted and which he nudges with a finger crooked around the edge of the door still quivering slightly from the impact, a finger into which the sharp point of the vertical hook end digs with special force as if having laid in wait for prey such as this at the edge of its trap not as elaborately and delicately spun as a web, but instead only a single loop of string that, for all its plainness, is not less effective than its more beautiful and complex cousin in attracting the animal's dinner. He pulls the teeth from this creature simply by closing the door a mite so that both the loop and the hook go slack and disengage easily from one another.

His shoes slip slightly on the wetness of the painted porch floor and leave a thin scum of dirty water in their wake that rearranges and coalesces into lines of brownish beads. There are worn places in the paint, tracks made by the rockers of the two chairs that are pulled together by the wall as if deep in conversation about the weather and everyone's health, or as if plotting to gather their energies next Sunday afternoon, when the old woman sits down with her braided palm-leaf fan planning on a peaceful time of quiet rocking and of watching the cars and children go by on the little street that runs by the house through her eyes bleared with age and cataracts, and hurl her from her perch through the screening, which would pull loose from the rusting staples in the frame at the impact and pop out along with her hurtling body.

Beside the further rocker is a trash can whose lid is too large for it and hangs over the edges, a can with a semi-circular wire handle that has been forced up and over the outsized top and that presses inward on the rounded ridge, distending it slightly out of its perfectly shaped arch so that the whole resembles a child trying on its father's cap and having to hold it tight with both hands lest it fall over its eyes and engulf it in a warm smell of sweat, burning leaves, and wool. The can is ridged in vertical accordion folds that do not show the dents and nicks usually afflicting trash cans which have become old enough that they shine no longer with the brash metallic gleam of youth but have, like this can, taken on the more subdued hues of maturity. **Analogy:** The juxtaposition of these contradictory qualities of being unblemished and yet undeniably old give the trash can the look possessed by certain women who, having spent their lives under the brims of lacy white hats or within houses furnished with couches upholstered in Russian leather and with Oriental lamps that support great fringed shades dripping rows of scarlet and ebony fringe, arrive at maturity as fresh-faced as when they were first introduced to society and yet exude an elusive odor of immanent decay, as if at any moment the years they had so carefully staved off would suddenly and without warning transform their smooth cheeks into the wrinkled pouches of a fisherwoman and their plump chins into the dry protrusions of a beggar hag, and whom one invariably wants to expose to the elements or to smack across their ruby-red lips or otherwise shock with an abrupt pain so that the quantum jump from this hermaphrodite of age to a legitimately old person might take place immediately and relieve us of that anxiety and uncertainty during which we wait, scarcely daring to breathe, for the inevitable end of this attempt to combine two parts of nature that are incompatible, to hide deterioration with an outer façade of youth and freshness. **Note:** This is a façade which must crumble under the pressure of the rottenness within, just as surely as did the false Moorish front an architect of the last century is said to have added to the West Portal of one of our better-known cathedrals, a façade which crashed the day after its completion into a pile of multi-colored rubble as if the spirits of the thirteenth century enshrined within the vault had combined to push this heathenous excretion from them and which, in its fall, killed the chief architect and his two assistants as they stood below admiring their garish handiwork.

There is a shade pulled part of the way down over the window in the door. Through the dusty pane he sees the stitching she has put in a horizontal rip and the transparent several inches of window below the shade's lower edge that show the legs of a table and chairs and the bit of light that is coming onto the floor of the next room where the base of a door and several inches of reddish carpet are visible. The door is ajar and, scraping his feet on the top folds of the rug that is gathered outside it, he pushes its edge and walks in.

The house smells not only of the mustiness which indicates the presence of aged things left to themselves without disturbance for a long period of time, but also of a newer sort of odor that almost fits in with this more stable smell as if it had been processed by someone able to take the freshness from objects and age them immediately, though not so well that there does not still linger about them a taste of the youth that could not be completely hidden or destroyed and that makes them uneasy partners for the more gradually mellowed air; the faded green linoleum on the floor shines slightly in the light that filters through the dusty frilled curtains and enters through the venetian blinds stacked like so many open eyelids in front of the window.

He leans for a moment against the doorjamb of the small living room. Given that it is summer, the large oil heater is not running. On top of the vents is a large doily with a pot of artificial flowers, blue plastic ones that seem to have been attached carelessly and without thought or coherence to the brown stems that have the tortured and twisted look of knotted branches, not as a result of having endured the wind and the rain through many seasonal cycles, but as a result of the infinitely easier method of acquiring deformities of having been molded that way in the factory, though in all fairness, we should be aware that the state of boiling liquidity and the inevitable claustrophobia of being pressed between great blocks of metal could not possibly have been pleasant either. **Lesson:** The technological revolution in which so many of our more prominent citizens have placed such faith is not going to be a cessation of pain and hardship but merely a re-arrangement of it, a squeezing into one small time period of all the woe and Weltschmerz that formerly took much longer to work themselves out. Nor should we curse the despair that must overwhelm us when we discover that our hopes for a better world are vain, since people need some sorrow to realize the full depths of emotion that they are capable of reaching, to know, as well as the glorious summits of joy, the dark and dreamy trenches of mourning.

Development: Surely we cannot believe that we have really lived until we have felt the heart-wrenching anguish of death, that we have really known pleasure until we have been seared with the red-hot iron of pain, that we can really savor peace until it follows a period of violent and sleepless turbulence. Man lives by contrasts, and only fully tastes one state when he has lingering in his mind a recent memory of its opposite. The pity is that we are endowed with such feeble imaginations that these things must actually happen to us personally for them to sink in to the extent necessary to affect us; visualization of these things on others or even on ourselves is insufficient. We have such feeble memories, moreover, that even if they do happen to us, they must occur within a short period of time before their opposite, else they fade to pale ghosts of themselves that cannot influence us, serving only to fill our minds with disembodied images and words whose tongues are silent or whose letters cannot escape the surface of the page where trace meaningless designs of curls and angles.

The blue flowers contrast with the bright red foil that crinkles around the pot and reaches upwards with rough tongues of fire as cold as the dark insides of the dormant furnace, and thus do not bring down upon themselves liquid brown and blue drops that would sizzle as they made contact. The strangely artificial color of the plastic blossoms is no fit companion for the hearty and frank red of the foil, unless we see this red as the color of the skin when blood vessels break and suffuse us with a scarlet flush so deep and hot that finally the liquid bursts from the pores in hundreds of tiny fountain streams oozing onto the bedclothes or the carpet as the person drops with weariness that comes suddenly upon him.

Notes on red: Most of us have more healthy associations with this color, red holly berries nestling against the smooth green leaves and the gently-falling snow, the fragile colored glass balls that shine among the fragrant needles of the Christmas tree, the red candles in glasses that glow on the picnic table and out into the summer night as people sit quietly savoring the taste of the scarlet pulp of the watermelon and watching among the dark shadows of the tree trunks the tiny yellow glows of lightning bugs that blur into long fuzzy trails when they rest their eyes on some point far back in the soft blackness, the flame-colored leaves that cover the maple and birch trees in the autumn and which, from the bubble of a helicopter that hovers over the valley floor, seem to have been painted up the hillsides in great wide swaths that alternate, and are mingled, with blotches of bright yellow and patches of evergreens seeming to rush towards those above it and to surround them with welcoming arms and the soft bosoms of its foothills as the aircraft dips and swerves.

The doily under the pot is made of white circles of webbing that push out from a larger round center like buds of yeast. The lace would not be so appealing if ever these young sprouts managed to exceed their small area and, having covered the upper surface of the heater, begin to flow over its edge onto the floor, and would become an actual menace if it tries to entangle the feet of those who come in the room. **Lesson:** That which is acceptable and even decorative in small amounts more often than not can become odious in larger doses. Our life is but a process of trying to achieve the correct balance in ourselves, in others, and in the world, in trying to equalize each and every one of the pan balances out of which we can see ourselves to be constructed if we are but willing to engage in the same sort of reconstruction that produced the complicated figures of mythological heroes from a handful of disorganized dots in the sky. We need only see every case of symmetry in the human body as the basis of another such construction until, like the fancies of some of the Flemish masters who constructed series of human faces out of vegetables and plants of the season which the figure was meant to personify, we too can draw ourselves and the world as a skillful compilation of balances, of meat scales, of the tiny molded weights used in measuring gold, of patterns formed with the string of the tightrope, of the delicate mechanisms of hydraulic equalizers. In addition to producing a creative work of great magnitude, we prove our point. And what can be greater than this marriage of philosophy and art? What union can possibly be imagined as more fruitful and more beneficial to mankind, not to mention productive of progeny that are stronger and more beautiful than the offspring of any other couple?

The wallpaper in the corner behind the furnace is more brittle than that in the rest of the room. In several places it has separated from the plaster and is bulging in flat bubbles from it or from the earlier layer of paper that has been only partly scraped from the walls, though the darker paper is more successful at hiding this than is the light paper covering of the ceiling in whose corners hang broken cobwebs. The base of the light fixture is of white-painted metal from which hangs a dusty glass globe like a cloudy-clear egg that a frog has nearly forced from its straining insides. What would step or crawl from an egg laid by this ceiling is impossible to say, and perhaps the result would be dependent on the nature of the absent parent. Surely this affects whether it be a perfect miniature replica of the house itself that is revealed on the carpet among the shattered remains of the shell, or whether the result would be a run-down shack of which the ceiling would undoubtedly refuse to reveal the paternity and from which the fluids and blood might well not even be permitted to dry before it was hustled off to be drowned in the toilet or thrown into the back yard where dogs and the neighborhood boys could be counted on to destroy it within an hour, or whether there might not even emerge a tiny mansion, of which the surrounding furniture would become immediately solicitous and which they would begin to pet and spoil even before it had gotten its balance and, though of course the shutters on its windows would be closed tightly for several weeks to come, had already begun to hold up its upper floors alertly as if it were at least taking some notice of what was going on around it.

There are two tufts of unraveling thread on the front of the arms of the chair that is directly below the light, places where years ago hung tassels he can remember from his early childhood, trailing brown bobbles that even then were beginning to come apart by themselves and that he was never allowed to finger because she was afraid that the thin threads would be broken between his childish fingers, that he would pluck these ageing fruits from the musty boughs that bore them rather than leaving them to rot and drop from their own exhaustion onto the dark red rug, undoubtedly a more appropriate a resting place for these cloth tassels than a grassy sward or even the weeds and crabgrass outside the little house that are now wet with the rain. **Note:** The rain will encourage the growth of the centers of the plants into thin stalks that blossom out into small feathery coxcombs of seeds that, in sufficient numbers and when properly dampened with the dew, cast over the lawn a whitish haze that breaks up with the morning sun.

The cushion, back, and lower arms of the chair are plump, overstuffed with the dusty cotton batting that was shoved inside so long ago and fattened as if to make the more diminutive by contrast the woman who sits alone at night under the light with the page of a newspaper over which she traces a bony finger with the Venetian blinds closing the outside darkness from her and who whispers the words at which she squints through watery eyes magnified behind startlingly black eyeglasses. **Further:** There are other parts of her that are plump like the chair: her feet that swell within the heat until the ankles no longer show the sharp side bones, so soft and smooth and distended have they become; the last inches of her fingers that, with the joints enlarged above the thickness of the bones between them and with the fingernails that have become yellow and hard and wide, they look as if, one night as she slept, the muse's son in a golden toga twined with the yellow creepers of the vineyards had crept across the squeaky wooden floor and touched to his young lips the tips of her fingers that had swollen and expanded in the soft warmth and sweetness of his breath and the dampness of his tongue purple with grapes, or as if her nocturnal visitor had been a balding scientist with an evil glimmer behind his glittering pince-nez who had managed to sneak both himself and a canister of gas into the room illuminated only by a single ray of moonlight that fell on her disheveled white hairs and had grabbed, with a suppressed cackle, the wrinkled hand lying on the yellowed sheet, pressing to each of the fingers in turn the outlet of a cylinder that had bloated their ends.

Note: We imagine he would have gotten quite a shock when, instead of her hands being elevated by the lightness of the fingers or at least bent at the wrist and arched slightly with the hand trailing behind the raised fingers, they simply fell back to the covers, larger but not lighter than before. **Lessons:** It is quite certain that nothing short of forcing the entire body full of the gas would lift such a person as this old woman from the ground, and perhaps it was only her sigh and her efforts at changing her position that saved her from this fate and scared the fat man with his apparatus, his teeth gnashing in helpless rage at the failure of his plans, from beside the thick walnut bed. For now she is sure to be even more clumsy than before; all the man had wanted was to add some delicacy and lightness to her life, a goal towards the fulfillment of which he had lugged his cylinder and his rubber-soled shoes through the world. Apparently the man, noble though his intentions be, has simply not learned that there are some people who cannot and will never be able to understand the fragile and delicate and beautiful. Even when it is suddenly put into the ends of their own fingers or when their feet abruptly begin to move in the patterns of marvelously complex dance steps, they cannot comprehend the enormity of the gift they have just acquired and force their heavy and dense brains to produce elaborate medical explanations dealing with age and arthritis or, in cases of extreme talent, St. Vitus's dance, which they attempt to cure as if it were something to fight and defeat rather than to develop.

This would be the case with the old woman, for though she weighs less now than she did last year, this is not due to any untowards lightness and flightiness of her hands, which still hang thick and heavy at the sides of her thin dress, but rather to the steady diminution of her flesh that sometimes occurs with the very old and cannot be stopped by any amount of nourishment added through the mouth. **Suggestion**: It might be corrected by food applied directly to the thinning places—strapping a ham roll to an arm, a tin of biscuits to an upper leg, a chocolate cake to the crown of the head and sticks of gum to each of the toes. To be sure, this would do nothing for the interior of the body and might actually be deleterious to the skin, causing mold and rotting if the foodstuffs were not changed with reasonable frequency or if the person could not get used to spending much of his time in a refrigerator or in the cool corners of the cellar.

It is not only the far ends of her body to which the thickness that once plumped her hips and breasts and buttocks appears to have migrated. Apparently some of the blobs of thickness found the trip outwards more rigorous than they had thought and had decided to drop by the wayside at such halfway points as the elbows and knees, which were neither so desolate nor so far away as the hands, advantages that clearly to some of them made up for their having to admit to their grandchildren that they had lost their resolution and accepted a settlement place where the land was not quite so rich and people not quite so free. The joints are rough and, though not swollen like the ankles and hands and not red like the corresponding parts on farmwomen such as she once had been, are coarser and larger than one would be led to expect by examining the arms and legs beyond them in which the outlines of both sets of bones are clearly visible and between which the skin sags like the seemingly solid layer of green between two low hills that dips slightly into the valley, as if a landslide down one of the outside surfaces of the slopes falling into another dip of this smooth blanket would cause a sudden tightening and elimination of the slack between the ridges, making a plateau where only minutes before there had been a valley.

The springs supporting her when she sits here are hidden above a gauzy bottom cover that has become so thin and pale that if someone were to poke a finger in its direction it would probably dissolve into the air like a spider's web that, miraculously preserved from mutilation by an auspicious position in an untouched corner of the barn, has remained intact throughout several winters, a web that has lost the strength that once would have let it sway in the breeze without rupturing and simply falls apart as soon as it is touched by the first edge of moving air that surrounds and trails our bodies so that our eager outstretched index fingers are not even permitted to approach it before it is indistinguishable from the air around it. **Note:** This total privacy of the web also led to the early demise of the creature that built it. For, too proud to admit that it had chosen its location unwisely, it curled up and died of starvation some weeks after its birth. **Lesson:** This illustrates the sad case in which some of those who were not born for themselves but for that which they produce to leave behind them are utterly unwilling to damage the webs they have so lovingly constructed by using them for practical purposes. And so they die, having no means by which to keep themselves alive and being unwilling to spend their lives turning out misplaced webs merely so that they can fill their bellies with the blood of the gnats and flies that would blunder into them, were they to devote their time to constructing webs over the pig trough or across the spreading fronds of a fern so that they become white with the seed pearls of the early morning dew.

When seen from below, the feet of the chair that stick from beneath this gauzy cloth seem absurdly heavy and sturdy like the lower parts of ostriches standing in two of those elephant's foot cigar and tobacco canisters of which our grandparents were so fond, though they do not seem out of place when seen from the front or sides as extensions of the heavy arms and back and of this thick covering cloth, nubby with a pattern of knots. The designers of this furniture could not possibly have been able to foresee that someone would be willing to court a nasty crick in the neck to crawl around on the rugs of an old lady's living room, picking up the particles of dirt and dust that she cannot see with her near-sighted eyes and that she cannot feel through the thick rough soles of her black shoes nor through the somewhat more slippery but equally durable soles of the bedroom slippers, and thus cannot be blamed for the strangeness of this one view.

The lamp by which she reads is topped with a frothy white silk shade overhanging the chair and caught in the sun shining through the open Venetian blinds. He can see within it the pale outlines of the metal hoops that hold it taut, make out the dark lines around the top and bottom that the layers of beige frills cannot cover and the curving interior supports between them that fade and become more murky the further they move from the cloth. Its stem is in shadow and is partly hidden by the back of the table at the end of which it stands, and thus the shade seems to be suspended above the cushion by invisible hands as if it were the crown about to be lowered onto the head of the monarch who should be sitting below it but who had overslept and is this moment frantically stuffing his shirt into his pants and pinning his medals on in such a haphazard fashion that his valets are forced to wrestle him to the ground to subdue him enough to make dressing him possible, rather than sitting regally upon the cushion of this chair waiting for the headdress that will officially add to his already bulging territorial pouch yet another country. **NB:** We must take it for granted that the mighty ruler of such an empire would have a head that is swelled sufficiently enough to allow the lampshade to rest comfortably on his hair line instead of slipping down to his neck as it would surely do with anyone of a hat size less than XXXL.

He has seen lampshades from which the clear and crinkly plastic in which they are wrapped at birth have never been removed and which, as time went on, has become more and more yellow and brittle-looking as the cellophane started to crack and come off in chips that, when they finally fall, reveal the bright hue of the material underneath that had been shrouded and obscured in the shiny folds behind which all colors taken on a neutrality and seem less intense than they really are. This shade, however, is nude and as a result of this fact and of poor housecleaning, has become grayish with dust. When the room is dark, the lamp throws a disc of light on the ceiling that folds over onto the wall in the corner where the chair sits. In this semi-circular light patch is illuminated the top of a heavy gold-colored frame protruding enough to cast on the picture it displays a shadow that is ragged because of an excess of ornateness made odder for the fact that the print within is a sentimental farm scene of peasants, an old woman feeding her chicks before a country lane.

Reflection: In this setting the picture is stronger and more worthy of study than its small portion of artistic merit would entitle it to alone, gaining its interest not from qualities that would be apparent were it removed to the cold walls of a picture gallery and exposed to the scrutiny of strangers but instead from its place in this particular room above the old woman's armchair: it is only here that it becomes apparent that the country lane winding off into the distance is little-traveled, that the back of the old woman is bent not from a necessity of the work she is engaged in but from some other cause, and that there is something that has been strong enough to inspire this untalented painter to hide the woman's face behind the rim of her cap as if aware that his skill was insufficient to capture what must lurk there. It is only here, among these objects in the room, that we can feel gratitude that the fingers of the farmer woman have been painted all together in a blob of tan so that we need not look on them one by one and see the wrinkled skin and the callouses that must protrude from their ends like the sticking pads on the tips of frogs' fingers, only here in the middle of this room that we can appreciate the shamelessly sentimental thatched roof and the daffodils that grow beside the path which provide relief by pleasurable contrast.

He pushes himself from the doorjamb with a sideways undulation of his back and stumbles for a few steps before righting himself again and walking towards the window. He reaches down as he passes and brushes the arm of the sofa that is smooth and shiny with wear, feels his fingers trail from the surface of the cloth down the curved side of the arm and off into thin air which seems cool as the layer of his sweat dries with the sweep but which returns almost immediately to the stuffy warmth of before. He leans against the roll-top desk and stares out of the window at the white-painted sides of the house next door and at the sweet pea vines that hoist themselves up onto the cracks between the boards by the thin green tendrils that, when they are unwound from the flower stems to which they have attached themselves, become tight fleshy springs that bounce after being pulled at from either end and, with their cores removed, are reminiscent of the tightly-wound curls of generations of women gone by, evocative of fashions and leisure time beneath the magnolias and bearing little if any trace of the deadly-serious purpose that impelled them to apply their vise-like grip to these posts, that induced them to raise themselves and the plants they served above the level of the ground that is populated with heaven knows how many dangers, with any number of animals and people who would be glad to snip the fragile green stalks from which grow the rows of flowers. **Reflection:** But so it so frequently is, that our creations are displayed by those who follow us outside of the context of the stresses and strains that produced them, are regarded with the core around which they were built removed, and are thus understood differently than their creators understood them. And so? Different is not worse, except when it is.

The purple flowers seem to shimmer against their background of green leaves and thin flattened runners, not contrasting enough in color to be visible as discrete purple units like the few blossom clusters that stick up and are silhouetted against the house but instead are like gradations of the rich green as if bruises that are just beginning to form, still so faint and amorphous that their outlines cannot be drawn, so pale that the darkening spot cannot be sharply differentiated from the skin around it, so undefined that we must blink our eyes rapidly as if hoping thereby to clear from our pupils the miasma that we know must be obscuring the clarity of our vision. **Confession**: We are unable to believe that there can be any part of the world in which the boundaries and differences between things are really and truly not to be found no matter how hard we look, for it is our natural human propensity to look for and insist on what we persist in calling with a note of praise in our voices "clarity" and "cogency" which of course is nothing more than a method of expressing the fact that we are drawn to such qualities and that they please us.

Note: Some people claim that this propensity must be unlearned if we are ever to attain that state of consciousness higher than the merely corporeal and attain, if not the highest rungs (for those are reserved for the few very special and very holy men of whom not more than three or four appear in a generation), then at least one that is a good deal higher than the poor ground level on which most of us condemn ourselves to live. **Suite:** If we are ever to learn anything of worth, we must be ready to cast off the ropes that have moored us for so long to the divisive conceptual delineations enshrined in our books, must learn that clarity is only one state of existence among many and far from the best, must learn to accept that living in a haze is quite possible if we only develop certain habits such as wearing padded clothes so as to guard against bumps and getting over our embarrassment at colliding with other people. This, though potentially painful and once considered the chief disadvantage of such clouds, is nothing in comparison with the advantages derived from the pleasure of self-induced melancholy that some people have found themselves able to sustain for unbelievably long periods of time, and indeed this disadvantage may be seen to be a positive good since this constant knocking into other people is a perfect way of making friends and breaking down the barriers that separate us. **Conclusion:** When we are all equally lost, we come to appreciate each other to a greater extent.

Some of the flowers are faded and limp on their stems, as if sucked dry of their color by the rain that drew their essence like hot water pulling insistently upon the fragrances of tea leaves steeping in a pot, as if the raindrops had begun to color deeper and deeper purple, dropping onto the ground and staining the neutral brown with gouts of violet as they fell and broke and had gradually become clearer as the supply of dye within the petals was exhausted. It is as if whatever starch that had kept them upright had been dissolved as well, for now they hang soft on the green cups that once supported them erect and firm. **Warning:** We should not read too much into the flaccidity of these flowers, should not draw unwise conclusions from what seems to be utter and complete lack of spunk: they are only so soft and helpless because they wish thereby to hide the firm green swords that are growing within, wish to hide from the jealous world the symbol of fertility and power that is building on the soft ruins of the flower's old age. **Explanation:** Too often we are misled by the inoffensive looks and subdued demeanor of the aged, do not even bother to look for anything in the chest x-rays but the dark blots of tuberculosis, do not even pause long enough to wonder why there seems to be the outline of another bone structure, smaller but heftier and younger within the brittle skeletons that support their wrinkled flesh; we are so conditioned to regarding the old as harmless that we do not even consider the possibility that if we but part the petals of the flower we will find within it the seed pod, immature as yet but bearing within itself the small fuzzy beginnings of what will later pop from the dry and curling halves of the pod like two rusted metal springs magically grown as the fruit of an otherwise normal green plant, seeds that spring from their moorings onto the ground which, it is hoped, will receive them with soft muddy embraces and not stiff-arm them with a rocky bosom and stony lips, hard brown near-spheres bearing little relation to the soft green lumps that once grew in the spot from which now they escape with such speed, little relation except that intangible and totally mysterious one of maturity to youth.

The people next door have driven into the ground a crooked line of gray stakes that perhaps were intended to stop the motion of the vines but which of course do nothing of the kind, the tendrils pushing themselves between and curling around their bases as if the plant were an octopus held on the tongue of a great gap-toothed animal that is unaware of that creature's almost unbelievable ability to push itself through the smallest of crevices and thus which will be surprised when it feels coming through its clenched teeth the tentacles that clamp with their suckers as they move to ensure that they cannot be dislodged either by frantic paws or by convulsive swallowing motions. **Note:** One may be sure that the slimy creature will have flattened its slippery head and squeezed it through the teeth and found itself free, or almost so, for it will have before it only the fleshy folds that form the lips of the unfortunate creature which had hoped to eat an octopus for its dinner and instead has had to feel the unpleasant thing squirt from between its teeth and has been so revolted by the sensation that even when the thing finally issued from its mouth, it had no desire whatever to pluck the horrible jelly from its face and replace it on the tongue.

The plant has twined itself around these guardian stakes as if attempting to seduce them and lull them into a state of inattention during which time the plant would gather its forces and make a break for freedom, leaving behind as a memento for the stakes of which they had become fond one strand of its climbing tendril wrapped around their bonnie waists. There are some who might want the plant to reconsider its decision to leave, for they hold that freedom without love is valueless and that with it any state of existence is free, any jail cell is as good as a palace and any life the equal of a king's. If, they say, the relation of jailor and prisoner has ripened over the years into a feeling deeper and warmer than friendship, then it is against the laws of the court of love to betray that relationship for the sake of any other goal.

To be considered: Those who hold this opinion have clearly never been possessed by any great emotions or seized with any great desires. If they had been, they would have realized that beside the longing for heroism, for freedom or for self-sacrifice, that feeling of love or affection for another human is quite paltry and decidedly second-rate and of course, quite unable ever to take precedence as a goal over these truly noble things. **Note:** We do hope that it would not be necessary for the plants to splinter or otherwise harm these stakes in their attempt at freedom, but if these things must come to pass, we must bear them without becoming excessively upset, for at least we can be sure that the stakes were destroyed in a good cause.

The entire spreading plant, being the climber it is, adheres in a concave sweep to the side of the building and to the ground rather than, as it might do, puffing out into a great quarter-sphere with all of its vines on end like the hairs of a person charged with static electricity. It is as clinging and bedraggled as the coiffures of those men who tame their very curly hair with grease that plasters it stiffly and straight to the curvature of the skull and gives us the sense that the careful preparation can be made to come to naught and the hairs be made to spring back despite their oiliness merely by delivering an energetic rap to the head with a ringed knuckle. It goes without saying that no vibrations could possibly work such a loosening on this tangle of sweet pea vines, if for no other reason than that we are unable to imagine this sort of athleticism from a plant whose vines have flat wings running along the sides of the center core, as if a wire had been glued lengthwise between two pieces of tickertape so that they end up looking like a chlorophyll-producing version of the chalky cartilage that we pull laden with sweet white meat from the second joint of a crab's claw, the thin damp structure that extends downwards from the claw mechanism and of which the thin leaves on the sides dry quickly in the air to the brittleness of paper and can be torn away from the center with little effort, though when we have done this they lose whatever bony qualities they gained from their association with the claw and work themselves into tight curls like thin shavings of milk-white wood by the sides of our plates.

He is draped over the curving front of the desk and can feel the horizontal ridges between the slats through his shirt and the metal forms of the door-pulls against his thighs. The top of the desk is not pushed completely shut and the interior must be faintly illuminated with a strip of weak light across the bottom as well so that the piles of postcards cramming a row of the pigeonholes within do not sit in complete darkness and their old-fashioned painted scenes that all seem to melt into a soft brown haze do not grow old isolated from the sun which lit the workshops of those who created the fantasy world they portray. Not only are many of the things they picture no longer extant, but it can only have been by a freak of nature that any trees anywhere ever resembled the fuzzy green swaths that represent them on the cards here, or that those who came in their large black cars to admire them were as pasty-faced as the tiny pink blobs that peer out, from white-highlighted windows, at the dots of bright red and yellow in the green grass. Further, it can only have been with the aid of the generously-plied brushes of a paint crew intent on enhancing reality to the level of illusion that any world could ever have looked as misty-bright as do these country roads, these mountains, these boardwalks and beaches with their red and blue umbrellas tilting against the uniform brownness, these houses of famous people over which hover cameo portraits of their illustrious and long-dead owners recognizable only by the almost caricature-like accentuation of their distinctive features and by the ribbon bearing their name that floats beneath their truncated necks as if it were this cord that had struck their heads from the rest of their bodies and not the brush of the painter.

The cards are piled with their pictures facing up and their stamps in a column, so that the brown ink writing of each card is in contact with the picture of the card below it, as if such physical separation of sentiments and thoughts were necessary to make these greetings from dead acquaintances a series of discrete individual emotions instead of an amorphous and uniform mass of commonplaces. Some of their one-cent stamps have been canceled with great dark discs that radiate half-round ripples from their top and bottom and some are imprisoned only by wavy bars so light that it seems they are not meant to prevent the escape of the stamp from the card or as if they were applied by lazy jailers who were sure that the glue which pastes them flat on their backs against the paper would never dry and yellow to the point where the further deterrent of the bars would be necessary to prevent their separation. Some of the stamps have been cancelled only across their bottoms or on a single corner or on one of their sides so that were they ever to be able to dissolve the glue they would still be held in a bond that no amount of struggling could break, held by one appendage like a small animal that wrenches or flaps itself around the trap that holds fast to a single leg or wing. **Similarities:** As among those animals, there may be a stamp or two of such great strength of resolution that it is willing to chew off the captive portion of its anatomy rather than die at the hands of some grubby-fingered nephew or grandchild who, happening on a cache of what it regards as inestimable philatelic gems, proceeds to mangle them in its efforts to remove them from the cardboard, prefers to twist its free corners so that it can begin to saw through the shoulder or face or hair of its green portrait bust with the perforations that old age has rendered somewhat less sharp and leave riveted to the paper the scrap with the newly-cut edge ragged with tiny white filaments that are lighter than the yellow ones which soaked up a bit of the coloring of the card beneath them.

The cards in the upper two pigeonholes of the desk become progressively glossier and more modern towards the tops of their piles, the denomination of their stamps increasing gradually in a step function, lingering longer on some values than on others but always shifting to the next higher number when they change. **Lesson:** There is no direction for people to move in but forwards on the inescapable line of time, no way whatever to go back. With concentration, however, it is sometimes possible to prolong the joy of the present so that it almost seems as if we have stopped the sands in the hourglass, so that we are able to blind ourselves to the march of events that continues without our knowledge and perception until that point when we awake to the far-off tramp of its rapidly disappearing feet . The vague images of memory can never, after all, satisfy us, cannot ever recall to us that which is gone, are incapable of doing anything but seducing us with their mysterious and vaguely sweet taste that lingers in our mouth but which is incapable of ever nourishing us any more than the clouds of pink spun sugar that melt instantly to several tiny crystals on our tongues and make us miserable with the sticky residue on our fingers. In another pigeonhole are pens piled in such profusion that they fill the space completely and extrude only their rounded points, some of which are tiny dark round dots of surprise edged with silver lips protruding from elongated skulls which recede backwards until their smooth lavender or green skin is covered in shadow and the two eyes that must be peering from the darkness are invisible. The cheaper plastic pens have no way of retracting their gold-colored tongues into their bodies; here and there one sticks out saucily, its insulting or flirtatious effect somewhat dulled by the traces of blue smearing them that resemble nothing so much as the remnants of a recently-chewed slice of blueberry pie; the unsharpened pencils present a single, perfectly round eye with a tiny dark pupil. Below the pencils and pens stands a small metal world globe embraced by a plastic curve that seems to make a comment by grasping the earth with only two disdainful protrusions, being careful not to sully itself by contact with something unclean and taking an extra precaution by keeping the two points of contact inside of the two frozen regions where life is held under a spell of enchanted immobility by the huge white ice mountains and the packed snow that covers them like an albino soil.

The flat writing surface of the desk is covered with neat piles of yellowed paper that are filled to varying extents with a spidery blue handwriting, notes that she has at some point written to herself and then stowed away in the desk to be used later as scrap paper. She might well be praised for having saved the white parts of these notes from intimacy with the vegetables in the garbage can that would otherwise have bled onto their pristine surfaces their variously colored juices so that the cards would end up a mass of off-greens and reds and nondescript colors that would blotch and crisscross. Perhaps it is not so good as it seems at first glance that these carefully saved pieces of paper of varying sizes are not simply gathered from the desk and thrown in the trash, for they are probably tired of having been handled only by brittle fingers that took care not to wrinkle them as they were stowed neatly away. **Explanation:** Most of us harbor within us the unconscious desire for brutality, the desire to experience life at its most raw and elemental, and by no stretch of the imagination could it be said that a life passed within the faintly dusty interior of the old desk in this small living room is terribly jolting, unless the nerves of the paper are so fine that they become riled up over the vibrations of the radio on Sunday morning that blares out the sermon at volume which is just the right level for her ears to catch without straining or over the soft scratching sound that is produced when she dusts the table tops with the decades-old turkey wing whose bones show through the worn feathers, its broken end long since dried of moisture or marrow and so knobby and flattened on the side she scrapes along the surfaces that it merely draws a few thin lines in the dust with its protruding parts and leaves the remainder of the layer undisturbed. Or perhaps they are contented with the sound of the old lady's slippers shuffling by, the sound of whispering as she reads to herself, squinting at the magazine, the popping of the oil heater as it re-adjusts itself and the hissing of the wind into the cracks.

The heat from his body warms the wood against which he leans and a small bit of the warmth may be conducted through the thick front of the lower drawer, a small fuzzy parcel that is strong enough to bathe the things within with a fleeting breath of heat before it disperses into the close and already warm air. Perhaps the thin pair of rimless eyeglasses within would thrill to the unconscious animal recognition of this patch as being of vaguely human temperature and not merely a bit of air slightly warmed by the sun, would shiver a tiny frisson of remembrance for the days when they perched daily upon their old woman's long thin nose, when their thin sidepieces contacted her skin and curved around the backs of her ears and their rounded ends came close to touching her elongated lobes, completing the curve that begins in the center with contact at the nose and then branches out sideways in identical shapes.

We should probably, in any case, find fault with whomever or whatever is deemed to be the initiating force in these eyeglasses, for even given the limitations created by the material, there is a myriad of ways that the glass and metal could have been put to better use, or at least to a more spectacular one. The gold could have been beaten as flat as foil and smoothed—or rather wrinkled—to the shape of the old woman's face, so that from the cotton collars of her housedresses would rise a gray-colored neck surmounted by a visage that gleams with golden cheeks and lips as shiny as the silent mouths of the states of gilded saints glowing from inside clouds of thick sweet incense, a face as unrelated to that which supports it as a tulip blossom to its green stem or a lollipop to the pasty white stick that dissolves into layers of paper if left in the mouth after the hard candy that surrounded it has been melted away into liquid and is now only a thick sweetness on the tongue.

Alternately: As a variation upon this beaten-gold technique, we might possibly ask that the precious metal not be left shiny but instead be etched with pictures or be pierced with holes and cut designs that would alternate the flesh tones with the gilded covering. This would provide, at least within a sculptural context, a rendition of the blotches and the disease that attack our bodies when we are dead, and might even prevent this in the old woman by virtue of having simulated the state during life. For certainly nature is not so cruel that it would inflict upon a person the same punishment twice over, and perhaps we humans can with this false representation fool those beings that check upon the health and sickness of each creature so as to make the punishments and rewards come out evenly. **Note:** This trick seems assured of success by the fact that these pain policemen are evidently not very careful about their reports and must even go so far as to falsify or invent data when they are tired and have no desire to go on to finish their rounds, for it is clear that the burdens of pain and suffering in the world are far from equal.

Another variation: The glass lenses could be attached to the cheeks of the mask so that they would play the part of the discs of rouge on the cheeks of women who go to costume balls in the guise of dancing dolls. **Concession:** The weight of the glass might cause the thin foil to shred and tear. Nor would plans to place the lenses one on the forehead like a cyclopean eye and the other upon the tip of the chin like an extremely large drop of spittle frozen in mid-fall be any less liable to wound the fragile gold skin. **Yet another variation:** The glass might be crushed to tiny beads that can be strewn across the mask like tears glittering on the cheeks or precious stones that, by some fluke of nature, have been deposited at birth in the golden flesh of this woman's face and had remained unsuspected until now in old age when the skin is shrinking and the fatty layers that once obscured them are disappearing.

Complications: It might be best not to consider this last particular design too seriously, however, for the cupidity of mankind is such that were certain individuals to suspect the presence of jewels within other people's bodies, they would feel no compunctions about, say, taking a butcher knife and ripping open the flesh of their sleeping bedfellow's arms upon which they saw the beginnings of bumps, which as likely as not would turn out to be nothing more than pimples or goose flesh. In addition, they would certainly discourage mastectomies by women who had become aware of lumps in their breasts, pushing them to risk their deaths from cancer for the possibility (no matter how small) of these lumps being infant sapphires or immature rubies.

Another tack: There are probably hundreds of ways we can work these materials other than by beating the metal thin. The mind boggles at the delicate tracery it imagines drawn from this quantity of gold, at the artistry that could be expended on a great spider's web of wire arching across the old woman's face like the guard of a fencer in the center of which would lurk a great arachnid with a pendulous body made of a translucent drop of glass supported by golden legs from which sprout tiny golden hairs. Or, we could abandon altogether the imitation of nature and simply draw out the metal into abstract designs, inserting within the maze of metal the razor-edged shards of the shattered glass that would provide both decorative accents and assurance that no one would hurt or even threaten the wearer.

The glasses have been folded carefully and have lain undisturbed for several months, having been touched last when they were lifted to let her place, in one of the flat boxes upon which they rest, the birthday or Christmas cards she keeps, aware of the money that has been spent upon them. There are small screws in their angles. Save for the perfect groove down the center of these screws, they are as smooth and unblemished as only those screws can be that have never been attacked by someone wielding a screwdriver of not precisely the right size that gouges from the edges of the groove tiny fan-shaped digs sheer on the side to which the twisted burr adheres. The threads of these screws are locked securely in the dark embrace of the perfectly-interlocking rings that clasp them, alternating bands that are not loose or crooked as are the comparable parts on the glasses of someone whose movements were more energetic. On the lenses are faint ghosts of fingerprints that were not wiped off; and around the screw that pierces the edge of the glass a thin black crust of dried grease to which the dust has adhered.

These so-carefully folded eyeglasses are not alone on their perch on top of the thin flat boxes of greeting cards. Beside them is a razor, its long thick blade jackknifed into its plastic pod and grown fuzzy with rust. Were it suddenly to be flipped out, the person whom it had threatened would reel in horror at beholding not a silky-smooth metal tongue but one half-rotted and coated with the bristling offshoots of brown mold, a horror occasioned not only by repugnance at the thing itself but also by the terrible and suddenly-revealed divergence between the expected and the actual, between the pristine images of the shining sharp metal that had filled his brain and the malignant and distorted reality that is suddenly substituted in its place.

Reflection: Though the shock is greater when this disgusting sickness is shown to us suddenly on top of our fantasies, it is at least short-lived, for such an intense and unexpected disgust cannot but burn itself out quickly, exhaust itself through its very strength. In this respect, it is unlike that disgust which comes more slowly upon man, growing from a source at the very well of being and seeping into our body only a few soft drops at a time until the point when we are slightly aware of the heaviness and sponginess of our arms and our stomachs and then more so and begin to wring our hands and twist our arms in helpless attempts to rid our tissues of this debilitating hot liquid and find ourselves unable to eject from ourselves even one sticky drop, unable to draw from a puncture anything but blood that falls thick and red upon the floor. For we realize then that this terrible disgust and revulsion has pervaded our entire being, that we are unable to shake its curse from us or to empty our stomachs of the nausea that weighs down every part of our being.

Application: This is a feeling that creeps up and takes possession of us so quietly that we are unaware of its presence and are unable to fight it, a feeling that suddenly seizes the last part of us and claims us for its own as we hold in our arms trembling with desire the milk-white beauty with the plump red lips and the pale pink blush in her cheeks whom we have so long coveted. Looking deep into the limped pools of her eyes, we read within her soul the evil and sickness of the world, see the disease and the insanity of all mankind twisting in garish dances within, writhing shadows and serpentine limbs knotting in bloody pantomimes of their own horrific natures. And in our fright and anger at what seems the trick the devil has played upon us of attempting to capture our soul by seducing us wearing a body that bespeaks freshness and naivete, we let drop the witch-woman we had held and flee in terror and sickness, our eyes forever to be tormented with the image of the moving figures we had seen within the shell of this virginity and our brains forever to be filled with loathing.

What happened then?: We do not see the blood that spurts from her skull as it cracks against the hard ground, nor the swarm of dark imps that ride upon the crest of the scarlet wave, paddling and splashing each other with the liquid as if they were wading in the ocean, black malignant spirits whose tiny gnarled bodies are spattered red and are soon indistinguishable from the flow and must sink into the ground along with the liquid, for there remains nothing upon the earth the next day but a dried brown crust and a patch were a few grains of sand have been stuck fast together. **Reflection:** It may be that this final mélange of the human and the diabolical would, if we were to see it, teach us something about the basal compatibility of the two, teach us that they are not, as we had thought, opposites that cannot co-exist in one being except as warring elements. Perhaps if we were able to accept this, we could be capable of living with this truth and of not being overwhelmed with disgust when we see a particularly blatant example of the marriage of these two forces and would then simply take for granted the presence of a bit of the satanic in all of us and not drop a perfectly innocent woman who with her human part probably loved us dearly and cause her death for no better reason than our own naivete concerning the way of the world, our own inability to accept the fact that there is a part of each of us over which we have no control.

Note: This notion grows and matures along with our own selves like the young of a certain black beetle inserted by the parent under the skin in tropical regions and hatch within after several months, being then required to burrow back up through the skin in search of air where more often than not they are plucked by the ready brown fingers of those whose bodies they have used and conveyed to their mouths where, it is said, they have a pleasant crunchy taste not unlike that of baked poultry skin.

Impossible feelings: It is a shame that this rusting razor is not ivory- or ebony-handled, for then we might be able to indulge in a bit of nostalgia for the days we never knew, to reflect a bit upon the transience of all things and on the fact that the solid houses and objects with which we surround ourselves, hoping to feel in the body we know to be mortal the permanence and immortality of the brick and steel in which we live, to be able to transfer the eternal life we fancy these things to represent to our own brains as a substitute for the fearsome frailty of men with which we are obsessed. Yet even these solid things are not as long-lived as we had thought, and our efforts to calm our fears by having before our eyes our great buildings and machines are failures as colossal as the attempts of our distant forebears to induce longevity by eating the testicles of sheep that had been killed in the light of the full moon by a naked virgin.

Self-evidence: It is unlikely we can have these feelings upon beholding a razor that is obviously not more than forty years old and rather flimsy as well; we are unable to reach the same depths of profundity with an ungainly instrument that was dull to begin with and that probably left the face of him it shaved rougher than before he started, an instrument that folds into two thin plastic sides held at the ends by rusting pegs that are hardened brown around their heads, encrusted with a mixture from their own bodies crumbling apart and being consumed by the air that leaves this weak residue in place of solid firmness. **Sad to note:** The plastic sides, unlike their most obvious visual analogue the seed pod, are not the cradle of life but the walls of a tomb, being like the trees that are used not to build a house that will be the scene of the trials and joys of a family's life, but a coffin and buried in the ground.

Explanation: We do not have the same sympathy for the demise of that which was intended and made to be transitory and ephemeral, made of those cheap materials that were meant merely to serve their purpose and be discarded; we see in our mind's eye those fellow humans who decided the lifetime of their products and cannot feel tragedy or sadness that something which was intended and produced by men has come to pass, cannot feel that lovely sense of melancholy, of being caught in the ever-moving stream of a force larger than ourselves that we get upon seeing the rusted pail sitting by the dry well nearly overgrown with honeysuckle and green vines, or the picturesque ruins of now-vanished civilizations.

Contrast: Sometimes when we see the broken and now-useless things that have been thrown in a small woods or a badly-mown grassy field rather than being folded carefully and put in the bottom drawer of a desk or, in the case of larger things, put decently out of sight or taken to the garbage dump, when we see sticking from the weeds in a lot that adjoins a housing development or an apartment complex a crippled tubular aluminum chair with a ripped oilcloth seat and back from whose wounds the excelsior or metal is unwinding, or a child's metal truck bashed in in the middle and left to lose its red paint to the roots of the brown grass clumps in which it has found its final rest, we are seized with a sort of melancholy.

This feeling is qualitatively different from that one we get from the deep rich browns of wet earth and the ageing smells of wood and the crackling noise of autumn leaves. **Explanation, after Schiller**: The smells of rotting leather and musty books and the belongings of the aged genteel inspire sadness in us because we see in these things our own fate, are able to see our future in the pasts of those who have gone before us. We are drawn to these things and derive pleasures from feeling the faint warning winds of our own dissolution because we are none of us ever sure that the façades we mount of youth and energy and competence are really any more than lies sustained by a fortune that acts in our favor because it is bemused at the deception.

We know at heart that we are no firmer or more secure than these things which have dissolved into weakness, these things whose solid parts are gone and whose soft bodies are now brittle and incapable of motion. We long at the bottom of our hearts to grow old instantly and quietly and nobly so that we may silence the voice within us that calls us a deceiver, so that we may cease our useless turning upon the treadmill of life and sink at last into helpless honesty that will clean our souls and minds of the falsehoods they had sustained throughout their active lives.

His fingers have found an edge along which they have been running until the newness of the sensation is lost and the motion is mere repetition, is mere continued dogged stimulation of a soft area no longer sensitive, mere blunted bludgeoning. He looks down and discovers that he has been touching the flange of a shell beginning to crackle away along its edge, its pouting lip no longer blushing with soft flamingo pink preserved under its glassy surface but spotted with the soft light brown that attacks and finally covers dried museum flowers which those few families who venture into the long and silent galleries where botanical beauties are lit by flickering fluorescent lights can see them arranged in their various grouped postures like the dancers in the final tableau of a ballet of the last century, each blossom delicately curved towards or away from its bouquet mates. Each and every one of the flowers is turned a uniform light brown, as if there were something in the faded lights causing this strange uniformity that, unlike a common chartreuse or vermillion hue, might not be immediately recognized as unnatural by eyes used to seeing the world in the gray monochrome of the television and movie screen. The echoing footsteps would die away and come to rest in another set of rooms in front of the cases where birds' eggs are offered on wire like hollow lollipops in neat protruding arrangements on the backboards of shallow showcases before the visitors realize that the transition from one wing of the building to the other seems to have brought with it the power of their eyes to see the blues and grays and red-browns that should have colored the flowers.

His fingers wander around to the other side of the shell and pull a flake of the brown skin adhering to the nearly smooth surface. Such flakes of skin are usually carefully scrubbed from the shells sold to summer visitors of beaches, as if we would be offended at seeing upon the hard surface we are accustomed to think of as the essence of the shell the drying remains of a skin that betrays the fact that what is perched upon our mantelpiece or set on our kitchen table was once an integral part of a creature that after its fashion ate, breathed, and excreted its wastes. **Commentary:** Probably those who market these curiosities have gauged our desires and revulsions correctly, for we show a remarkable propensity to ask from life not the full flow of all its manifold experiences but instead a special sort of condensation after the fact, a polished husk that is rid of all evidence of difficulties and pains. We tend to put labels of time or place upon these shells that are extracted from the flow of life and once having done so, forget our initial scruples about the act of extraction, adopting the conviction that we have captured in these tagged things the entire existence whose dates adorn their labels. We forget that the correspondences to which we have become so attached so quickly are utterly false, and are no longer aware that what we have forgotten is far greater than what we have remembered.

A smaller, fatter shell is pressed into the base at the side of the larger one, its concave face set upwards and its ridges outwards so that it looks like a curiously mittened hand outstretched in supplication for alms. The whole creation is a souvenir of a nearby ocean resort, a keepsake bought to remind the old woman of a happy day fifty years ago whose aura had for a time probably surrounded the object like the mist that hovers over the great black rocks down at the breakwater, dark sharp masses between which live horseshoe crabs and the yellow strings of the conch egg cases that dry in the sun so that when each individual sausage slice is slit, out pours a mixture of sand and perfectly-formed shells not much larger than the rough grains of sand. Yet this mist of memory has by now surely quite dried from the shell arrangement, dispersed by the heat of the furnace through the cool nights of many autumns and winters so that now it is only an object that takes up space and has been here so long she has forgotten it.

As he withdraws, he brushes against the plastic flowers growing from the blue glass vase that teeters on its too-small base and would have fallen save for his extended hand that prevents it from doing so, setting the vase upright again and taking for a moment between thumb and finger one of the dusty green leaves that spread out just enough to cover its broken mouth. In the blue depths of the bottle's sides swim the shadowy wire stems of the flowers. When he drops his arm to his side, he can still feel the tingle of the trail that the tip of one of the plastic leaves has traced across his skin, a leaf that barely touched him and seems by its very lightness to have made more of an impression than those more aggressive in their advances. It is as if, like those insects that one hardly notices, so lightly do they land and so quickly do they fly away but which have on their way managed to inject beneath the surface a poison that festers longer than the juices of more clumsy annoyances like the mosquito, it has affected the inner layers that will continue to feel the transitory contact even if the bitten one scratches fiercely at the skin in an attempt to eliminate the sensation by burying it beneath a stronger one.

Consideration: Perhaps all skin contacts affect those layers under the epidermis to a greater or lesser extent, causing reverberations that sink deeper into the body the more strongly it has been stimulated. Perhaps it is the thumping of those echoes that we feel deep within our chest cavities and not the palpitations of a regularly contracting muscle, the heart, which is not the instigator of movement but instead the sounding drum upon which the effects of the outside world are worked out. Perhaps we are a good deal more dependent upon our contacts with other things and other people than we had hitherto been aware, we confident ones who postulated the ridiculous concept of an organ that beats continuously for seventy or eighty years, resting only between contractions.

Practical application: The proper cure of heart attack that stops this thumping in the chest is clearly thus not to pump the victims full of drugs but to tickle them with feathers, to draw wet threads across their cheeks, to bounce rubber balls upon their chest and to prick the soles of their feet lightly with pins, all in the hope that one or more of the stimuli will turn out to be of that sort which makes such a deep impression upon the subcutaneous layers. **Concession:** It must be admitted, however, that the state of our knowledge about such matters is not so great that most of our therapy could avoid being trial and error, as we cannot yet say precisely what it is that affects the skin more deeply or less. **Conclusion:** Clearly we need more research towards discovering that sensation the experience of which, say, once a day, will guarantee the strength and continuity of the heart forever.

The best researchers will be those who have spent their lives feeling and touching interesting or amusing things around them, who have taken the time to sit dreamily before the crackling fire trying to find the precise distance at which their outstretched fingers begin to shrivel and each pad seems to separate into drought-baked flakes divided by cracks in the skin, which search involves gradually damping a reverberation that carries the hands into the cool nearness and back into the singe area, who have sat for minutes at a time lightly running their fingers over the blue veins in the backs of their hands, feeling increasing smoothness as the sweat on the fingers evaporates and then the returning friction of new-produced moisture and finally the numbness when the fingers seem to be contacting a hard stream of tepid air without any texture at all. Suddenly their mind manages to point out to their fingers that this feeling can be stopped by a simple cessation of their own movement, and they are as surprised and momentarily upset as when, in the middle of a nightmare while the instrument of torture draws nearer, we realize that it is within our own power to destroy this horrible tableau with a wrenching open of our eyes, realize that our salvation can be achieved ourselves and is dependent on no one else. The sudden reversal of power leaves us momentarily breathless, staring into the dark with our hearts thumping, or those who know the joys or probing at a dried piece of skin on their lips until it is soft with their tongue's spit and then pulling at the flap with the teeth until they feel it barely pass the point at which it begins to cover the live pink polyp of the lip and biting it off sharply next to the skin.

Musing: What will the magic feel turn out to be? Will it be the burning feeling of a blob of oven cleaner foam slowly breaking up into a scum on our arm? The bubbled cascade of aerated water descending from a faucet into the palm of our hand? The vaguely revolting feeling of tracing our fingers in the jellied softness that has formed on the bottom of a cake of soap sitting overnight against the flat ceramic sink top? We cannot know for sure, though we can be certain that we have not yet found it yet, for our short lives are bounded in all but a very few cases by the pitiful line of a century. **Optimism:** No one of us who has any conception of the attempt to reduce the bewildering complexity of the world to the no less bewildering intricacies of art, philosophy, or science can believe that some perverse celestial power has arbitrarily doomed us to the inferiority of producing works that are less than they might be for no other reason but that their creators cannot live long enough to mature beyond the life span of the ordinary person. If we are capable of wanting a longer life, we must also have reached the level of development necessary to finding the means to achieving that goal; it is only a matter now of seeking.

Lying on the daybed in the back bedroom, he listens to the sounds of the old woman dressing and talking to herself in her bedroom which are louder and closer now than they had been in the kitchen or the living room, shutting his eyes and breathing out as if to release the air that is keeping him from sinking as deeply as he wants into the faded bedspread and the thin blankets. Yet even had this been a useful measure for lightening himself, he would not have sunk any lower, for he would be stopped by the understructure of the bed and by the lumpy mattress that does not give way any further.

The windows are closed and he can feel a bar of sun across the white underbelly of his arm. At first he had been unaware of it, but by now it has sharpened its edges and is biting into his flesh. The light enters through the panes of glass that are exposed beneath the half-descended Venetian blind, and though the light must twist and deflect slightly when it hits the tiny knotted imperfections in these old pieces of glass, he cannot feel any darker or lighter spots, blotches where the skin is looser or tighter with lesser or greater heat.

Suddenly he becomes aware of a gap in the sunline that divides his arm into light and dark, a hole in the side of the stripe. Until now, his mind must have been filling in like a blind spot the small piece of coolness that intrudes into the heat. Somehow, like blinking his eye or moving its point of focus ever so slightly, he has managed abruptly to perceive it. The chunk is probably bitten from the sunbeam by a leaf of one of the African violets beneath the window, a fuzzy green spade whose whiskery protrusions are turned gold by the light which makes tiny shadowy dots at the bottoms of the deep pores lying under this layer of thin fur illuminated from the side. He can smell the potting soil burning under the heat of the sun, and may be able to hear the faint sound of the sand particles that have adhered to the plant, drying gray, and now are loosening their grips to fall one by one back onto the dirt, or the crackling of the drops of water still imprisoned between the wire cells of the screen outside popping as they evaporate. On second thought, at least this latter sound must be his imagination, for it is so soft, even when heard next to the ear, that it seems impossible for it to have penetrated the window and be heard amid the louder sounds of the sides of the house losing the soft wetness their exposed surfaces have taken on and becoming once again gray and hard, shrinking back again to the state from which the rain had rescued them for a few short hours by fattening them so that the cracked boards become solid again.

Mixed in with the earthy smell of the violets is the slight odor of warm chocolate from the box of candy in the open drawer of the flower table which the strong sunlight warms. Like all her candy, this must be many months old, left to break out in white blotches while earlier boxes with higher precedence were eaten. Perhaps the sun has melted the chocolates inside, so that when the box is opened and the sheet of waxed paper is gently eased aside, it will reveal not a road of humped cobblestones but flat bricks between which grow fluted paper weeds. If so, the chocolates must have begun to sag into the cavities of their soft centers and to swoon against the infirm sides of their brown paper cuts so that the liquid trapped within their sugary confines begins to ooze slowly out from a spot where the chocolate wall is pulled thin and spread its viscous vermillion in a thick layer over the sticky surface.

It is a heavy smell, this odor of heated chocolate, but it is not evenly dispersed throughout the room. When he breathes, he is able to capture it only occasionally. Sometimes his nostrils catch the smell of the wax fruit instead, pushed behind a photograph on the dresser, visually unsuccessful imitations of nature from which chips of yellow and red have been taken by outstretched sharp edges of tables and the rims of bowls as if, like the chickens in a barnyard that will sometimes peck to death a new bird or one which has transgressed the unwritten laws of chickendom, these poor brittle blobs have been punished for their audacity in masquerading as the true article by the objects of a world interested in preserving some minimal level of honesty.

Reflection: Alternately, it may well have been the initial carelessness of just one human fingernail that took the first chip from the banana and revealed to the world the fact that it had under its yellow skin not the soft sweet pulp of the real fruit that separates lengthwise into three sections whose inside edges are hairy with stringy ties but only this hard white wax in which the teeth would make a set of shallow impressions surrounded by an opaque white edge where the wax is riddled with minuscule cracks. The smooth insides of these painted waxen fruits are half-translucent like skim milk and do not, unlike the fruits they mimic, thicken in the middle and enclose the tiny dark seeds which were meant to create the next generation. **Analogy:** They are like those people who have themselves sterilized from the desire to devote themselves to pleasure without fear of unwanted procreative side effects: they have had cut from themselves the core of their being, and have acquired the pastiness of countenance that eventually results from all such dead-end and wasted lives, the near-transparency of a pearl that is pierced through the center for a necklace and deprived of its core of a grain of sand or a fragment of a shell that caused it to come to be.

The color of the fruits' insides is like the horrible whiteness that forms around a wound in the tongue that is so much more frightful than a similar encirclement in red would be, for the lighter color seems no part of us, an alien encrustation that sets off the wounded area and in so doing appears to deny that it will ever belong to us again, ever be reintegrated into the smoothness of our body. **Development:** We seek out what resembles us. It is, for example, the natural affinity for those things the color of our own thick red insides that determines what we eat. Tomatoes, for example. No one can believe that it is for their strange flavor or the consistency of their disgusting soft innards that we ingest tomatoes, that were there not some compensation for putting into our stomachs this pulp veined with tiny yellow lines as if all its vessels were gorged with an excess of lymph, we would even think of consenting to do so. In fact, it is the redness of the fruit that draws us. In addition, we are drawn to foods that approximate the shapes of our organs: egg-plant the heart, grapes the eyes, peas our gallstones and so on. So too for the flesh of the dumb beasts which we, like the primitive tribesmen of whom we make fun who eat the hearts of lions in hopes of instilling courage within their tremulous breasts, consume in hopes of being as untroubled by the problems of existence as these creatures which we ingest.

When he turns his head closer to the pillow, the odor of the waxen fruit is gone. All he can smell is the smooth dustiness of the gray silk cover with what he imagines to be the slight odors of the dye that paints upon it in light purple a Roman fountain. He feels on his cheek the rough frills of the thin yellowing lace that is sewn to its edge, convinced for a moment that this is cooler than the other pieces of cloth around him. If so, it is only because he has just touched it, and not because it is colored in the yellowish-white that we associate with fragile autumn afternoons rather than in the green of the bedspread or the brown of his shirt. As he rolls his face over, it becomes warmer and he feels the thin line of air along the edge where his flesh separates from the cloth that is a mixture of the heat of his advancing cheek and the coolness of that cloth which has not yet been touched.

The bed and the pillow are merely concentrated caches of the half-musty smell that is inescapable everywhere in this small house. Everything here is permeated to a greater or lesser extent with the smell, as if the whole building and all its furniture were but a huge extermination jar for some one particular person with specific allergies who one day would be frog-marched across the back porch and into the house where he would be locked among what would seem at first sight like the possessions of an old woman, but which would in fact be a stage-set constructed to bring on his death. The prisoner would soon realize that the windows that seal out the fresh air are as poisonous to him as is the telephone that the fiends have left connected, knowing full well that contact with it will mean his death. Indeed, he will soon understand that there is no way out, no way to escape this smell, and will opt for a quick death by flinging himself upon the sofa and clutching to himself the dusty cushions that will have to be ripped to shreds in order to remove them from the vise-like grip of his corpse.

Aside: Of course, there would be no harm in finding an old lady who could live in the house until it is needed as a death chamber. She would only have to be ejected for a day or two, or at the outside a week if the victim tried to wait things out by balancing himself on his tiptoes in the center of the room so as to be as far away as possible from the solid things around him that contain the smell. The woman, not suffering from the particular allergies that the poor hunted wretch is known to be afflicted with, would be perfectly safe among these surroundings, and her presence would guarantee that the odors would not dissipate out of a window that might be broken by the delinquent boys in the neighborhood were the house to remain uninhabited.

It is likely that judicial officers with enough taste to plan the decor of this death-trap so artistically (including, for example, the thermometer hanging in the living room attached to the gold-colored metal plate that is painted with the name and address of a now-defunct funeral home in the town that shows the sense of humor of the most clever of the inquisitors, a man subtle enough to be able to find amusing the idea of this gentle warning concerning the temperature of their clients' afterlife administered by the proprietors of the mortuary) would have taken the bit of extra time necessary to re-program the mind of the old woman they finally put in as the unconscious guardian of the house of extinction. Certainly they would have put within her brain the conviction that she knew the histories of these pieces of furniture and the contents of her drawers: for example, that the rocking chair alone had been saved from the terrible blaze that had incinerated her farmhouse that fearsome night when the lightning was crackling across the sky and the thunder shaking the foundations and left her homeless and helpless, her husband's bone disease having become so painful that three years before on an August afternoon he had gone into the barn with a shotgun and not come out alive.

Further: Certainly she would believe too that the heater had broken one winter five years before and had not been fixed for a week, that sometimes when it was cold the pipes froze and when they finally thawed the faucet coughed and then suddenly regurgitated a yellow-colored stream that eventually cleared like the colorless juices marking that point in nausea where there is nothing solid left within the sufferer's stomach and indicating that soon the heavings will subside. All this she would certainly believe, all this she would think to be her own memories gained from the seventy-five years of her life and not the brain-traces etched with sharp needles in a sparkling white laboratory.

The spread has wrinkled across the back of his neck in turning, and he feels the layer of cotton batting between the two pieces of cloth that has coagulated like clotted cream into thick blotches barely connected by a few fibers likely to break at any time and set them free from each other. It is only the sewing around the patterns that anchors the stuffing sufficiently to prevent it traveling to one side or another. The threads pierce and then are pulled out from these squashed tufts of cotton that must in the process of flattening have become shiny and dense, almost hard-looking and matted like the center layer of a strip of fluffy cotton cut with scissors and thus pressed together by the blades, that appears on both sides of the edge to be a piece of paper miraculously not present an inch farther along where the fibers are pulled apart to search for it.

It is as if this worn quilt is diseased within, its innards having separated from the normal smooth configuration and having begun to re-congeal in different patterns that nonetheless do not seem to have caused its death. **Reflection:** If only we humans were so lucky as to be blessed with an equal ability that our organs too might pull gradually apart and rearrange themselves without our being the worse for wear. We might go confidently into battle, sure that all the guns aiming directly at the place where our heart is expected to be would, even if they were to hit their mark exactly, only carry off a chunk of our colon and half our appendix, and a head wound that might hitherto have been expected to be fatal would only give us a rather severe stomachache for a few days. **Note:** Nothing being without its disadvantages, we should of course have to be careful of blisters on our heels that might have terrible consequences for our small intestines and scrapes on the thigh which might seriously impair our breathing capability.

He curves his fingers and touches the quilt as if to smooth out these lumps, but they are too hard-packed to come apart with mere gentle rubbing through a layer of cloth. He would have to pick out the threads and, laying aside the cloth covering, pull apart the cotton into a great fuzzy heap of individual fibers, which would then have to be pressed again into a smooth tight piece of batting so as not to make from the quilt a great bloated pillow that sinks to nothingness when something is put on top. **Remark:** Such a major refurbishing effort would seem almost an attempt not at producing a thicker and warmer quilt (which would be more easily bought) but rather at proving a point by showing that a second youth is possible for absolutely anything given enough hard work and concentration. Unfortunately, like the quilt which will never again be quite as soft as it was that day it was finished, we can never cover or hide either the wrinkles of our body or the experiences imprinted on our brain.

Question: Why choose the quilt as the recipient of this attempted process of transformation? Why not, for example, the window screens? Each and every one of their wavy metal threads could be scraped with knives, and, when clean, be painted silver again with a tiny camel's hair brush. **Concession:** To be sure, not even assiduous cleaning would be able to cut from their surface all the rust, and the wires would be thin and brittle and not so perfectly tubular as they were before. **Note:** Were we to undertake the process of cutting out all the aged parts on ourselves, we would continue paring until our bodies are a heap of bloody cuts of meat and our souls, like the elusive center of the onion that turns out to have escaped our grasp, disappeared.

Further: Alternately, why not rejuvenate the little green-painted table that once held three plants until they turned brown and crackly, and their pot-bound roots, still clinging with the stiffness of death to the soil they encircled and from which they were unable to wrest enough nutrients to live, were thrown out all in one coherent pot-shaped lump? It is a table from which the chipping paint could be stripped by heavy applications of the thick chemical syrup that burns us if allowed to touch our hands, applications from under which would rise green bubbles so that the surface would come to resemble the skin of the mad scientist whose nefarious plans finally catch him in his own net as he drinks the poison he takes for lemonade and he begins suddenly clutching at his dissolving throat with his instantly-gnarled hands from which the skin is bubbling and peeling.

Technical note: It might take a while for the moisture to penetrate these thick layers of paint of which the green is only the uppermost and liquify the brittle covering that is chipping from those cracks rotted by water overflowed from the bases of the flowers that, once dead, had been unable to hold any of the moisture percolating past their stiff and lifeless roots. **Further:** Finally, this process could have been tried on the pane of glass through which runs the shining curve of a crack like a slightly drunken line of silver mercury in a thermometer that always registers 110. To be restored to its youthful state, it could be remelted and molded again. **Problems:** Some of the contents are bound to be lost in the great heat, and unless we are satisfied with a full-sized pane so brittle and thin that it could be broken by a moth taking a nose dive in an attempt to attain the lighted interior that, with its barely-extant brain, it assumes to be preferable to the warm and open night air through which come the soft cries of the crickets and the far-off crunch of a car's tires on a driveway and the rhythmic swish of a lawn sprinkler, we would have to make do with a re-cast piece of glass perhaps two-thirds as large as the others that would be held in place by the contents of several cans of putty extending three inches on all sides between the wooden supports and the glass. **Resemblances:** The result would look like the half-sized thumbnail of a man who had closed a car door on his hand at an early age that glitters small and hard from the middle of the flesh surrounding it. **Note:** We have no reason to think that beneath such a truncated fingernail cavities are the hiding places for the secret messages of kings who, instead of tattooing on shaven heads, have chosen to bury in the soft and agonizingly sensitive skin of the ends of fingers.

He feels the halting wet progress of the drop of sweat that seems to have oozed from the skin somewhere around the bridge of his nose and is trailing across his cheek. It slows at the curve of his jawbone as if wondering whether to drop straight down or try and hang onto the nearly horizontal surface long enough to get directly to the fold of cloth touching his neck. He feels it trembling with the vibrations of his mouth, which he has opened to breathe. Then it is gone and he hears the soft plop of the water hitting and spreading out on the cloth. For a moment the end of the trail that it has left across his skin is cooler and he can make out the shape of the path against his cheek. Then it evaporates and he feels another drop beginning in the folds around the corner of his mouth.

He sits up abruptly, opening his eyes in the middle of his motion and shutting them again immediately. His elbows are resting on his knees, and his fingers are pressing the skin of his forehead up into the folds curved into the shape of ripples caused by the ends of his hands that approximate their pattern less and less closely the further and higher up they go, and at his hairline are almost flat. Behind his eyelids, fading into a purple negative, is the pattern of the open window roughened on the bottom edge by the leaves of the plants outstretched to the sunlight and of the server with its dull gold-framed picture of a young man in uniform, a young man whose lower jaw has disappeared into the white glare which is now all that remains of the photograph in the dim after-image in his mind.

His eyelids flutter and then open again with a convulsive effort. He sees first the stained upper legs of his pants and his arms, which seem to be supporting his head like the columns that hold up the painted ceilings of eighteenth-century palaces. His face seems absurdly large in comparison, since for this analogy to hold he would have had to have opened the top of an empty doll's house and have rested his face in the open rectangle of the walls of a room in hopes of scaring to death upon their return the creatures who live here—for, instead of finding only the clouds and cherubs they had left above them, they would be greeted with a great human too terrifyingly three-dimensional even to be the ghastly joke of the perverted but genius-touched painter who did their ceiling.

He sees a blur of brown and blue, and then the disordered heap of her hairnets piled on the white cloth like a handful of spiders' webs collected to stanch the bleeding cuts of a hemophiliac, the tablecloth wrinkling a bit around the bowl of fruit and dropping over the edge in the front like a sheet of snow loosening itself from the rock layer underneath that will soon begin to slide and end up in a shattered white jigsaw puzzle on the ground. From the next room he hears the gentle sigh of the bed and then the sounds of shoe heels on the wooden floor: she is dressed and is walking into the kitchen. Evidently she has not heard him come in, but if he makes an entrance from the living room he will have to explain, loudly and distinctly and slowly, where he has been.

He pushes himself to his feet and, retracing his steps, is sitting in the kitchen rocking chair before her bedroom door opens slowly with a creak. Over her head he sees the relative darkness of the room and the top of the huge oak frame in which are mounted the pictures of her mother and father, oval patches of gray, minuscule in relation to the great squares of black matting and carved wood around them and tilted inwards towards each other from lack of contact with any bonding material. From where he sits, they seem like two crossed eyes looking down disapprovingly from an otherwise featureless face darkened with choler or apoplexy.

Now she is silhouetted in the doorway. Most of her white hairs are confined under the net she wears on the top of her head, but those at the sides puff out from the sides against the background of the dark-painted door and the shadowy room. As she walks towards him, the air currents stir them lightly so that they seem like clusters of pale insects' legs still twitching and waving from the shock of having been torn so brutally from their bodies, or like the long feelers of the white and pale yellow crickets that can occasionally be seen among the clusters of shining black ones uncovered in dustbins and under trash cans. Soon they have exchanged her words of greeting and his own louder ones of response, with the soft squeaks their shoes make against the linoleum as the boards below the plastic give way slightly and the sound of his lips pulling apart and kissing the air in the neighborhood of her wrinkled cheek.

The skin on her arms is like the skin on the cold chicken necks he used to tie with crab line and a weight and throw from the gray and splintery pier not far away from this town. The skin was yellow and loose and could be pinched into great fatty fingerfuls, cool folds of sterile soft flesh that bore no discernable relation to the bone and meat below them save that the skin happened to be attached to them by the shredded veils of its underlayers that looked like damp strings of rubber cement. And if there were any meat on these bits of bait when the afternoon was done, they would be cut loose and thrown in a low arc to the gulls that would break out of their great arcs and follow them until they sank into the gray and salty water.

When he pulls his hands away from her arms, the skin follows the direction of pull and retains the pattern for a moment before moving back slowly to near-alignment with the wrinkles that spread out and fan down her arm from the back of her hand. Her legs seem to be molting, covered with the bagging translucent skin of her stockings that she has not yet been able to cast off. If she is shedding, it must be that she has soaked her legs in water that makes them malleable and soft and fall in folds rather than peeling from her in brittle chips and hanging in tatters. She must at some point have climbed upon the cracking plastic that covers the counter and into the big old sink pockmarked with the nicks of pots and pans with an agility that one would not have expected of her and, with water running down the side dyed rust-colored from the rest that has collected from years of constant dripping, climbed in and sat with her legs tucked beneath her.

Note: There is not room enough in the sink to stretch out her legs in the water that rises around her, staining her dress dark a constant several inches above the surface of the liquid as if to warn her upper parts that the flood was rising and that not even her coy pose with her hands folded in her lap could hope to save her if she were not willing to turn the water off. The threat of death in the sink would be more empty than such threats usually are, since she would not in any case be covered more than to her waist: by then the water would be trembling at the surface of the sink, ready with just a few more drops to gush over the curved front edge onto the floor and flood the counter and the bottom of the scrubbing cleanser and the soap dish.

Alternately: She could lift a withered leg over the toilet and then shove it down the gullet so as to get it wet all over, though this would necessitate an even greater rubberyness of body than in the sink. The toilet, moreover, makes a sudden angle about a foot down which she would have to navigate if she wanted to dampen more than the bottom part of her leg. **Note:** The most obvious choice, namely the bathtub, is ruled out by her antipathy to any form of overall bodily cleaning but sponge baths administered with a brownish washrag smelling of iron and mold.

The scum of milk that he removes from the bottom of the pan is thick and soft under his spoon edge like anaemic algae deposited in the depths of the boiling whiteness. When he is done scraping it all in one direction he begins in another and draws the spoon sideways, feeling it catch on the thin hills left between the bare furrows he has cut, hearing the dull scratching of metal against metal alternating with blips of silence that are made less audibly different than they might be by the bubbling that produces the thinner white scum falling to pieces on the surface between the hills appearing and disappearing around the throat of the spoon.

He pulls the spoon from the pan. Some of the soft deposit is left on its edge. He touches it lightly with an outstretched finger that quickly pulls back for a moment and then hesitatingly returns. This deposit is burned light brown on one edge like the side of the seaweed when the clumps of slimy green hair are wrenched from an anchor, revealed to be caked hardness in which tiny shells are entrapped and through which occasionally winds the clear white line from an unlucky fisherman's rod like the strand of a plant that suffered the malnutrition and oblique sunlight that makes of kitchen greenery thin white tentacles without leaves, climbing up the curtains and twisting onto the drapery rods.

He drops the spoon once again into the pan and swishes it back and forth. The lima beans are roiling the surface, forced up by the bubbles. As they rise and fall, they make an arc across the surface. Their curved sides look like bubbles turned green by a poison slipped in when he was not paying attention that instead of bursting and spraying him with their fetid insides simply sink again, perhaps diminishing in size as they fall until when they reach the bottom they are the size of those tiny unbelievably perfect pearls produced in the first stages of boiling, as if in a closing of the cycle of birth and death.

As the spoon moves back and forth it gouges ruts into the softening sides of the beans. Though this does not slow its motion, he can feel the jolts that are as dead and as soft as the thud of the stray bird that plunges into our windshield as we drive along the dark country road and causes us a moment of pity or the effort of murmuring a few words of annoyance but which otherwise does not affect us, so small the creature is and so unimportant in comparison to the throbbing metal machine in which we have encased ourselves. He would undoubtedly be surprised if, instead of simply falling brokenly aside to nurse their wounds as he expects them to, these beans were suddenly to be propelled from their juices and to fly up to his face and arms where they would attach themselves and begin sucking at his body like great green leeches until they are as bloated as balloons and he as thin as a stick figure. He would be even more shocked were the things to be in an altruistic mood so that instead of sucking his blood through the holes their tiny rapacious mouths have broken in his skin, they reverse themselves and force into his body their small portion of green pulp, plugging the hole with the minuscule plant bud within them that will sprout leaves outward from the pale green mound revealed when the shell, emptied of its contents, falls off like the fragile brown casing of a cicada hung from a single hooked feeler on the rough bark of a pine tree.

He turns the fire down with his free hand and, bending, watches the blue tear-drops that enclose the yellow genies within, like magic haloes that burn all those who dare approach, that sink into the tiny holes as if, like the earth spirits which can be awakened and brought up only long enough to mumble two or three sleepy words from their yawning mouths, their audience is over and they are retreating into the dirty black bowels of the stove.

The spoon leaves a milky trail across the vaguely white enamel surface around the gas vents. Perhaps the intense heat has at last been too strong for the paint, and it is returning once again to its liquid form, beginning in this bumpy rounded pool that protrudes from the surface like decorative scars. Soon, the enamel surface having liquified, the whole appliance will stand dark and denuded like a plucked chicken in a pool of white feathers spreading on the floor at its feet, or like a less chalky puddle at the feet of a child which has been imperfectly toilet trained and which does not know whether to cry out for adult help or to confine its misery to a trembling of the upper lip so as to delay its punishment for as long as possible.

He wheels a quarter turn and grabs the horizontal handle of the refrigerator. It pulls an inch towards him before his arm absorbs the jolt of having come to the end of its tether. He hears the rubber insulation breaking its contact with the surface of the chamber with a sound that is like the rupture of the spit curtain that stretches between the lips of a mouth opening to speak and abruptly he is assaulted with the cloud of coolness that puffs outwards from the open box. The light bulb remains off for a second and then, taking a hint from the daylight or perhaps being revived by the warmth of the outer air, suddenly flickers on and illuminates the glass shelves. They are filled with food enclosed in jars and cans, kept carefully one from another as if some terrible explosion would take place were a bit of unsheathed vegetable or meat ever to touch the shelves or the metal insides of the refrigerator. **Second thought:** This cannot possibly be the case, since the shelves and the sides are even now liberally polka-dotted with hardened pink and yellow spots that may have started out as heartier colors but which have been blanched by constant exposure to the dark like the blind and pasty-looking fish one finds swimming in the icy pools of subterranean caverns.

A half-cut lemon lies, like a captive bug in a collecting bottle, on the bottom of a glass already beginning to frost over with condensation from the warm air which clouds the sharply-defined wheel of its sections into a yellow blur in which he can nonetheless still make out the tan of the seed that has been exposed on the surface like a vein of diamonds laid bare between the layers of the rocks on the side of a new-cut mine shaft. The jars and cans stand stiff and straight like the pillars of a ruined and roofless temple which have been subjected to the ravages of the passing soldiers who, instead of taking the potshots that have so disfigured others of the great monuments of civilization, wielded brushes dipped in garish colors so that their mute white solemnity is buried under huge and brightly-painted pictures of lush red tomatoes, chartreuse string beans and fiery yellow corn kernels. This uniformity of columnar shape among the jars is broken by the half-full bag of bread on the bottom shelf, placed between the catsup and the jar in which float two dill pickles, and by the box of candy on the middle rack.

The two slices on the end of the loaf have fallen forwards into the space between the last slice and the twist of the bag, like time-lapse photography of the motion of a single piece. When he reaches out for the butter dish, his hand brushes the bag, which is stiffer and more crackly than unrefrigerated plastic; his fingers close on the cold glass tray and cover. When he withdraws his hand, the parts of his fingers that have touched the chilled glass feel as if they have been burned and numbed. Only when he lays them flat against the smooth white metal of the door do they begin to lose their curious shocked feeling and return to a neutral state.

He hangs for a moment on the door, feeling the air that puffs from the refrigerator becoming warmer and watching the clouds of vapor that are becoming thinner. Even when he shuts the door, there is a moment when the last bit of this coolness lingers, and then he is surrounded once again by the hot air of the room. He hears the plop of the applesauce from the old woman's spoon and her voice: the neighbor's cat, the boy who cuts the lawn, the garbage men, and the pauses that he fills with appropriate comments.

The metal key from the bottom of the canned meat tin digs into the quick of his index finger and he manages to pry it away from the can so that it breaks dully at the end and falls into his curved hand. The pink and white marbled meat is exposed bit by bit through the slit that is lengthening slowly and spasmodically but at an increasing rate of speed, as each turn of the key thickens the roll of greasy and razor-sharp metal tape around its base. The top of the tin comes off with a sucking sound, and when he upends the bottom part and squeezes its sides together, the block of meat falls to the white plate below. The yellow gel that clings to its sides and top completes any imperfections in its shape, fills in any places where the meat did not touch the side of the can like the metal that finishes the forms of a prizefighter's shattered teeth and which seems to be an attempt to win back with its perfect imitation of shape the credulity it has lost by divergence from original color.

The gel forms lines piled successively on top of each other on the knife blade like the candle wax on the sides of the bottles in cafés, jelly through which run the lines of the thin scrapings of meat that his knife could not help but take. He holds its blade under the dribble of water. The soft deposit is pushed away bit by bit and joins the flow until its fragments plop onto the bars of the metal trap and begin oozing down through the round holes. Soon there is no sign of the substance on the knife save the faint whiskery line that still clings to the sharp edge and that he collects with a single careful swipe of his thumb which he then holds under the water and washes clean. The slices of meat fall pink and fat into a pile on the plate. When he is done, he presses them back into order and stands them back up as if reassembling the scattered leaves of a damaged book that can later be once more sewn securely together so that it can be perused in some sort of logical and straightforwards order. Holding the slices together, he runs them through with the knife whose tip peeks from one end.

He picks up the skewered loaf with the handle that extends from the other end. When he points the knife downward, the meat slices do not move, and he is obliged to extend two fingers which he places against the flat cool meat on either side of the knife blade and push them from their post. They fall off one at a time, like pearls popping in slow motion from the end of their string. He moves the knife across the surface of the plate as they fall; they overlap, so it is only in the uppermost slice that the short thin slit the knife has made is visible. The newly cut sides of these pieces of meat are sharper, flatter, and pinker than the edges that had come in contact with the can.

He picks up the potato peeler lying behind the plate and looks around for the cucumber. It is peeking out from behind a bowl like a pea-green moray eel waiting to strike at unwary passers-by, and he is forced to move the bowl in order to get at it. There are drops of water hanging onto this waxy surface that smear into streaks of smaller drops and make trails down the condensation that dulls its shine; he draws the enclosed blade across its skin very lightly and gets only a scum of the wax with which it is covered. The second swipe is less gentle, and a swath is cut that reveals the vegetable's firm yellow body, of which some still adheres to the underside of the green skin he has removed.

He digs the rounded point of the peeler into the exposed section and pulls out a small shallow core sample that is uniformly yellow throughout all of its short depth. He has not yet hit the softer core that is protected from the outside by the denser layer and the skin where pointed seeds packed together in rows like the inmates of a prison ship suffer their lifelong incarceration cut off even from communication with their fellows by a surrounding wall of protective gel that becomes thicker with the passage of time, as if controlled by the forces of nature that realized that as they age and become more weary of this eternal blackness, the restraints that guarantee their quiescence will have to become more powerful. **Note:** Unlike most prison boats, the cucumber does not bristle with rows of oars moving backwards and forwards in concert like the legs of a centipede to which the prisoners could devote their attention; the cucumber is not going anywhere. Indeed, it has no contact with the outside world at all that would allow it to control its own movements, and is in consequence completely at the mercy of all exterior forces that are able to buffet it about as they choose; the seeds are born into this penal vessel and grow mature and old in darkness.

The second time he digs the point of the potato peeler into the slit of skin, he is rewarded with a core sample that penetrates almost to the center of the vegetable. He touches the seeds and finds them slippery and cold; not even his teeth, it seems, can scrape off this jacket of thick slipperiness. He pops several in his mouth. In an instant he feels some of the gel clinging to his front teeth, then the strange papery cover underneath this coming off the two half-seeds that he worries with his tongue. **Thought:** It is a shame that the outer layer of this seed could not have been removed without halving the inner core as well, since except for its rough and blunt edge, it seems smooth and pleasant to touch. He would have been able to let it linger in the wet folds of his mouth for several hours like a single bead of grapefruit still trailing remnants of thread, a parcel that stays warm, unpunctured and tasteless on the tongue until finally it pops against the front teeth and releases a tiny hot packet of bitterness. **Randbemerkung:** Because of its immaturity no less than the fact of its being cut in half, there is little danger of this seed attaching itself like a fertile egg to the thick and soft interior of his mouth and bearing leaves and a tiny fruit that would grow at first unnoticed and then become so large he would have to give it the extra attention it required, opening his mouth for four hours a day in the direction of a light bulb and keeping the plant away from his chopping teeth during meal times. This investment of time and energy would have as its result not only that a living organism is preserved, which is certainly not without its value; he would also be able to show off the plant to his friends, fetching it from the side of his mouth on his tongue, being careful not to break its long and fragile stem in the process. The real problems would come later when the vegetable was grown so large that it stuck out and prevented him from eating. If the stem were long enough, it could hang from his mouth like a kidney coughed up from inside, still attached to its cords. A tooth or two would have to be knocked out to give the stem room to exit, and his acquaintances would simply have to get used to seeing him with a perpetual sneer where his lips curved around the green core.

Further: To protect the jointure of stem and vegetable, he might invest in a bag-like affair that supported the cucumber and prevented it from swinging free like the sacs in which the mourning members of some Semitic tribes encase their beards. **Note:** It is not likely that such an outlandish appearance would make his neighbors envious and desirous of becoming walking gardens. Nor would he want to multiply his troubles by planting corn in the dirt of his ears or tiny mustard seeds under a fingernail left uncleaned for the purpose, or a single castor bean in his navel. For he would be unable to guarantee that the tough yellow corn roots would refrain from filling his middle and inner ear and thus destroying his hearing as well as throwing him off balance, nor could he prevent them from entering his brain cavity and, forcing their roots into the grooves on the surface of the organ, squeezing it so unmercifully that he would soon become as much of a vegetable as the corn itself.

He pops the two bits of cucumber flesh into his mouth and swallows them without chewing, follows their progress closely about half the way down, and then loses them. Perhaps his esophagus, long jealous of the stomach which by the decision of an unjust fate has been made the organ to which all food automatically flows, has taken a nip at what passes it by as an expression of its pique. When he is finished peeling the vegetable, holding it straight up and down, each rounded end is capped with a tiny irregular patch of green so that the thing looks like a mountain seen in a clear lake mirroring it so perfectly and without any visible break that there appears to be only one rock mass growing identically in both directions.

They are sitting down. He feels the vibrations of his loud voice saying the prayer she has requested. He says it directly at her downcast eyes, leaning forwards slightly so that she will be able to hear. Her loose hairs flatten slightly against her head as if pushed back by the force of the monotonous sound that he is producing. The iced tea flows over his teeth and tongue, and the top ice cube pushes against his tongue, allowing him to taste the iron of the water from which it is made. When he tilts the glass back down and closes his mouth, the tea roils over his tongue and washes the cucumber taste from him like the waves that come hurrying up to obliterate a human footprint by the shore's edge.

He spreads his fingers out on the napkin and when he raises them, there is a pattern of sweat and the condensation from the glass, four rays where the uniform rough feel of the paper has been destroyed, the impressed pattern turned to limpid limpness that clings to the flesh a moment before loosening and fluttering back down. He could punch these wet spots from the napkin so that there would be a line of elongated moth holes with damp and irregular edges that would dry brittle and twisted. He scoops up a single lima bean in a pool of milk and unloads it into his mouth, all except for the drop of peppered whiteness that breaks against the plate, scattering rays of thin and blanched film and dots of black outward from its point of contact.

The bean squashes against his front teeth, its soft insides gushing from the encasement ripped at the edge like the strangely soft and yellow paste that spreads stickily across the floor from the hard black shell of a water beetle smashed by a carpet slipper. His tongue forces green purée across the inside of his front teeth and into the cracks between them, and when he makes a second sweep with it across the inside surface of his jawline, removes the fragments from the exposed surfaces of the teeth and leaves only a picket fence of green staves. He sucks the pool of saliva onto the hollow of his tongue and forces it between the cracks and back out again, feeling the scum rupture in tiny pops and then be washed completely away, save for a few bits that remain lodged at the extreme top and bottom of the teeth. He swallows, but this swallow is not so effective as one that follows it, cold and liquid, a mixture of tea and the dispersed clouds of the lima bean that must color it vaguely green.

She pushes the plate of canned meat at him. Her fingers, fluttering above it, urge him not to help himself. He jabs the fork into two of the pieces at once. The fork presses them together; abruptly the tines enter the firm meat and come to a sudden clinking stop against the ceramic. When he lifts them, the tips of the metal are not visible. Indeed, they seem not to have pierced the meat at all, as if the fork had instead jolted against something hidden inside the slice. **Reflection:** Perhaps this was the silver coin which, when discovered in his piece, would bring him good luck and fortune for the coming year, or the entire treasure trove of some insect pirate, a collection of the iridescent wings and delicate antennae stolen from the living bodies of captive gnats which had begged for nothing more than to be put out of their misery, buried in the flank of a convenient pig when it had felt its death coming on and lost to the world through the combination of the illegibility of the directions it had scratched on a faded piece of parchment and the unforeseen slaughtering and subsequent grinding into luncheon meat of the pig in which its treasure had been deposited.

He brings the meat slices closer to the surface of his plate; the bottom edge makes a greasy comb-shaped dullness on the smooth surface as it is drawn sideways. The slices have begun to rip around the impaling fork like the soft flesh of a gazelle around the iron-headed spear whose point is deep within its insides, kissing its life away, flesh that pulls and bleeds and breaks into wrinkles that widen into cracks under the weight of the great wooden shaft that bounces up and down in uneven rhythm as the delicate animal bounds through the wild grasses in a futile attempt to escape the pain which, contrary to its evident belief, is not following behind but instead is lodged within it. **Philosophical analogy:** This pain eats away at this poor animal as continuously and horribly as the emotional sickness of our civilization eats away at our own innards.

He is unable to let the slices down silently and smoothly onto the plate, to prevent the plop that the slice makes as it sucks against the surface of the ceramic, gluing itself to it with the airtight seal of its thin layer of oozing juices against the plate's perfect flatness as if never again to be separated from that which it had sought for so long. The fork pulls out of the first piece of meat without disturbing it; the second is lifted slightly into the air before it falls. When the piece does so, there remain in its smoothness the four large holes of the fork's tines, filled with shadow for the lower part of their depth.

Fantasy: The holes might be believed to be the tops of chutes that travel to dressing rooms under the table from which unannounced extras for the scene could pop, tiny peasants and shepherdesses that would climb nimbly from the shaft and do a clog dance on the plate before doffing their caps and disappearing as quickly as they came. **Note:** The seeming solidity of the plate cannot fool those of us who are aware of the myriad of tricks that stage directors have available to them, illusion devices that are capable of dumfounding us with awe and amazement by the sheer artistry and spectacle of the effects they produce and which are thus more than capable of making a plate which is actually riddled with exits and trap doors seem slick and unpierced. **Further:** Nor can the humbleness of the venue make us think that the production that could not be mounted here using for its platform two pieces of luncheon meat and the uncovered remainder of a dinner plate, that there is any reason why this arena cannot swarm with elaborately-coifed and -costumed Lilliputian actors offering in almost numbing profusion enactments of the greatest moments in the history of mankind, scenes of the deepest tragedy and those of the most strongly-felt love, the most enraged fury, the most biting wit and the most imposing intellectual beauty, all in a grand panorama in every color of the rainbow and full of your favorite songs.

There is a chip out of the edge of the plate, a nick where the gold-colored rim has been interrupted for a moment as if the painter at that point had had a particularly violent hiccup, or (as is far more probable) the machine applying this stripe had been jolted on its foundations by a sonic boom. He drags the fork towards it, leaving a trail of the grease that grows thinner and then disappears into the screeching of the unlubricated tines against the plate. As the fork moves into the slight depression, this sound becomes duller and rougher, and he feels the sudden change from the glazed to the unglazed. When he reverses the motion of the fork and swishes it sideways along the plate's edge, holding it limply at its end so that it is like an uncontrolled rudder moving back and forth smoothly and evenly in motion with the soft waves of a quiet lake, the alternation of smoothness and roughness in both sound and feel become soothing and almost hypnotic.

One sweep is too wide, and the fork slips off the edge of the plate. There is sudden silence.

"What are you doing, child?" asks the old woman, before taking another breath and beginning again on her discussion of the neighbor's baby-sitting activity.

It is a question to which she requires no answer, though one for which some sort of harmless response could have been invented. **Analogy:** In this way, it is like those great philosophical questions facing us for which there is no answer, questions that have been used to construct the bars of a prison that we cannot ever hope to be let out of by some kind keeper and against whose bolts and locks our ingenuity is powerless, our plans of escape doomed to failure. **Explanation:** It is we ourselves with our ingenuity who built the prison of words, thinking it intended for some other wretch about whose fate we could not stop our stone-cutting and steel-casting long enough to worry, as to do so would have been to divert our attention from our job. And then it was our own wails that filled the night, our own those fingers which bled from the fruitless scratching when we put in the last brick and discovered that we had been working unawares from the inside and had walled ourselves into the inescapable fortress, the prison in which we will certainly, barring some unforseen *deus ex machina,* end our days.

Truth: No one will ever find our battered and prematurely aged bodies, for no one but its inmates knows of the existence of this horrible catacomb. No one knows that in the heart of the most beautiful land in the world, hidden deep in the snow-capped mountains, there is a cell block in the bowels of which are rotting some of the most likable specimens of intellectually convoluted humanity in existence.

Their servitude, it is said (though we are merely reporting hearsay and cannot know for sure), is made the more bitter by the view they have from their windows of the sun that rises in the morning wrapped in a cloak of gold and sinks vanquished again every evening, its vestments and all the clouds around it covered with the scarlet blood gushing from the wounds in its lovely body shot through by the arrows of the gods who know that men are not capable of living continuously, that they must die each day and be reborn each morning. **P.S.** This servitude is made more bitter by the sight of the tiny and crisp yellow blossoms of the flowers outside the casements covered at dawn with shining layers of diamond dust that eventually become soft and old and then dry into brown wisps that rustle in the autumnal breezes. **Worse:** Not even those other prisoners at whom they must stare during the monotonous days and sleepless nights can provide comfort. Each of them is sunk into a reverie into which there is no intruding; their half-closed eyes cannot be made to flicker with a recognition of any other person, their stiff jaws cannot be made to move in any terms of succor or support. And thus even if there were one of these who, roused from his preoccupation with himself by he knows not what, attempted to establish some sort of contact with those around him, he would soon give up in disgust and sink once again into his narcissistic dreams.

In front of the dish of cucumbers is a vase of artificial flowers so dusty the greens have begun to resemble the yellows and the reds have begun to look as veiled and withdrawn as the eyes of meditating mystics. The shoulders of the container are draped with a cape of dust which reaches from the gilded neck down over the two filigreed hydria handles and down to the tops of the painted ovals in which Victorian naiads dance with orgiastic abandon, their free-falling drapes slipping from their white shoulders and from the tops of their firm round breasts and being caught up from their marble-white feet by tiny fists from which flutter white scarves through which the curves of their plump forearms and tiny dimpled elbows are visible. The vase is liberally decorated with gold porcelain lace around the bottom, the handles, and the top, where it seems like the ruffle of an Elizabethan noblewoman who has just lost her head to the executioner's axe and upon whose stump grieving friends have placed a mound of blossoms. The vase gives the impression of having been subject to a thorough going-over by borer beetles that have started the process of turning this bit of coy green and white bric-a-brac into a mass of holes that would crumble to dust at the first touch of a maid or a fastidious housekeeper. **Irony:** They had evidently not thought of the possibility of an old woman who would leave them untouched forever not from sloth but from an inability to see all the dust and cobwebs.

Question: How came these riddled edges to be gilded? **Tentative answer:** We would like to think that these insects were something more than ordinary bugs, that they wrought their destruction not for its own sake or to satisfy some organic need of their own: we cannot believe that this substance could actually contain any nutritive components for anything that was not itself as stiff and calcified as the vase. Instead, these bugs have disfigured the vase in an attempt to show us acquisitive humans through symbols that most of the ills of mankind are caused by the vicious and single-minded search for worldly wealth. To this end, they leave upon their ravages a coating of the purest gold that is the liquid which runs from their mouths like the tobacco-brown saliva of the common field grasshopper that clings to the thin stalks in the breezes. This substance is meant to convey the message that human beings who wish to clothe themselves in gold must of necessity become as riddled with holes as this porcelain filigree, as fragile and rotten as these handles and the trim around the neck and base.

Problems: We to whom the message was directed do not wish to admit to ourselves the meaning of the warning and consider this only a sort of decoration, a type of imaginative addition to something whose function is not to instruct us but merely to please our eyes. **Conclusion:** We are a guilty people whose culpability is made evident not by uneasy dreams of those whom we have wronged nor by our seeing in every smooth surface the faces of those whose lives we have snuffed out or ruined nor by our interpretations of what more placid people think of only as the natural sounds of the night, but which seem to us the moaning voices of the dead or the thunder and lightning that is the rumble of our sentences of damnation; our guilt is proven not by such propensity to see accusations in neutral parts of nature, but rather by our determination not to see them where they clearly exist, blatantly ignoring those messages that are actually there in nature and even going so far as to display these pointing fingers in public as if a show of bravado were sufficient to hide from others or ourselves that our hands are shaking and our voices cracking under the strain of trying to keep up the façade of innocence.

He raises his eyes to the picture over the table where the sister of these nymphs, or cousin, or perhaps even mother or grandmother (for creatures such as these never grow old), is staring meditatively at a flower upon which there remains but a single last petal, the one plucked the instant before fluttering from the perfect and round tips of her brownish-white fingers. Upon their smooth nails a sepia butterfly with tan wings has just landed, its antennae still quivering from its flight through the fading summer day. The nymph's beige breasts are cut off not by the knives that, it is said, performed mastectomies on Amazons so that they could draw their bows with greater ease, but by the less painful edge of the picture frame. Her round brown shoulders are shrouded in gossamer pierced with dark-edged holes like those that appear in the smooth bark of birches, eyes of doom set upon the trees to warn passers-by of the transience of their existence and of the fact that none of their actions passes unnoticed by the gods above.

Her beautiful cheeks and chin and forehead express only their own softness that damps the strength of whatever thoughts might be generated behind her puzzled eyes; the curled wisps of her hair sweep up into a coiffure coming charmingly to pieces and garnished with another daisy, the cousin to the one that her fingers have all but finished tearing to bits. **Objection:** No creature can really be as placid, soft, and thoughtless as this nymph seems to be. Perhaps her hair is the net in which her emotions are caught as they emanate from her skull, wrapped into silence and death as if by spiders that weave around the victims their silken shrouds, stilling their kickings and strugglings forever with a sharp bite that drains from their husks the body fluids without which they dry into fragments that are carried away by the wind.

He sees a blur of color in the glass, whose purpose here is to protect the nymph from the dust and deterioration of the outside world. The color can only be an intruding reflection from a similarly enclosed creature on another wall, sending a feeble image of greeting across the room only to have it repulsed by the covering. On the opposite wall hang two rectangular cross-stitch pictures of ample women in long dresses with round cats at their feet. They sit before stoves composed of black xxxxxes and glowing with flames of yellow and red crewel. Their coal black hair is pulled back from the outlines of their faces to reveal flat, ruby-red mouths and short blue slits of eyes, as if the human face were but an assemblage of discrete removable parts like eyeglasses that can be unhooked and simply lifted off, leaving behind the stamped pattern that comes printed on the cloth.

The cross-stitch women are not alone with their cats and their glowing stoves. They are kept company by scarlet block letters that hover over their heads, perhaps buoyed up by the heat produced by the threaded flames. Somehow, at any rate, the letters remain aloft and spell out comprehensible if rather flat sayings. THE HEART OF THE HOME IS IN THE KITCHEN, they say in one picture, and the other: THE PROOF OF THE PUDDING IS IN THE EATING. The corners of the plain brown frames are not well-aligned, and the tiny slits of the unfinished edges on the side pieces are visible. Splinters have begun to separate from the front edges of their sawed surfaces, leaving short exposed chips of white. He dips the edge of a spoon into the dish of cucumber slices.

They are coated with a thin white sauce that has slipped away from most of their wet surfaces without adhering, forming into round droplets. He lifts one of the slices that slips from his spoon and plops back into the sauce again, hitting a pool of the liquid and scattering the other slices with small dots of the sauce that quiver and then are still. The bowl offers a combination of two pale colors, one slightly gelatinous and the other a more opaque white of the liquid. If he had left the cucumbers unpeeled, there would have been circlets of dark green curving through the white liquid like the stylized backs of fishes in a Japanese print, cutting and slashing their way across the bowl as if a jumble of Moorish scimitars in the hands of invisible marauders.

Some of the seeds have come loose from the cucumbers and now float on the surface of the liquid, spinning lazily around from the shock of the dropped cucumber slice of a few seconds before. They are surrounded by their haloes of gel that keep the sauce from them, like the outspread gown and cloak of poor Ophelia who, medical experts tell us, must have remained substantially dry for some minutes before the water was able to change her velvets and satins to a mass of dark sodden death-wrappings. The spoon makes a hollow thudding clink as it scrapes the side of the bowl in an upsweep. It dredges from the bottom a pile of the slices that slip and slide sideways from one another back into the dish as they are lifted higher and throw off great gouts of the white sauce. The liquid forms into small lumpy sausages that break apart as they hit the slices beneath them. Clearly they are unable to obtain the traction on the air that is necessary to their earlier dissolution, like a caterpillar that, falling through the air, curls helplessly into a thick circle, its myriad of feet tucked into itself. Only upon landing is it able to unwind and spread itself out along a grass stem or a brown twig.

When the discs have stopped slipping, there are three left on the spoon, balanced in a more or less stable pile and stuck together by the white sauce of which a drop is clinging to the bowl that ascends from the dish in the process of describing the arch through the air over to his plate. In the next load, three more slices are brought over. Finally there is a disordered heap on his plate that is like an abstract pile of poker chips oozing from its sides a trail of sauce which flows down to the slight depression in the center of the plate and begins covering the painted pattern of leaves and flowers. In a few seconds, all that is left of the botanical motif are a few ends of pale plant sticking out from underneath like a color reversal of the white hands of a drowning man which pierce the wave that has covered him for the last time and then limpen from their flutterings and slip below the surface into the icy green water beneath.

The sauce approaches the edge of the pink meat slices and slips under. The sides of the trail between the pool in the center and the green slices of cucumber begin to pinch in at several spots, and almost immediately the sauce forms into separate paving stones that merely suggest the direction of the flow rather than plainly spelling it out, as if any other juices that were strong enough to wring themselves from the damp bodies of the vegetable slices could be expected to possess sufficient resources and power to hop in a series of flashing arcs from puddle to puddle like salmon climbing a run rather than taking the flatter trail of more earthbound liquids.

He offers the dish to her. For a moment she makes no reaction at all. She does not lift her hands from her lap, nor slow the speed of her voice. She comes to the end of a sentence and looks expectantly at him. As she ceases the movements that displace the wrinkled skin around her mouth and jaws, her hands appear over the edge of the tablecloth and move towards the dish. It is as if she were controlled not, like other people, by the movements of her interior bone structure, but rather by the contractions and loosenings of her skin that were moving someplace on the surface of her body at all times, her skin like a perpetual-motion ripple tank whose sides do not damp the effect the of a pebble dropped in so long ago that no one can remember when.

He answers her. He is not so much aware of the vibrations of his voice within his chest as of the sweep and fall of his inflection as it moves around the curved sides of a response given in answer to a question. Evidently it is acceptable. After all, not all pieces of the conversational puzzle must fit tightly; some buckling and even a few spaces are inevitable, almost part of the pattern. When her hands have curved around the bowl, her two index fingers hook into the air over its rim as they curve tighter than the others that are constrained to follow the more gradual arc of the bowl; her thumbs stick into the same plane of the bowl top parallel to her arms. It is as if her two thumbnails were the eyes of lobsters or crabs held out upon quivering fleshy poles and her hooked fingers their claws. When she sets down the bowl, she will pull back not hands but stumps that end at her wrists; the creature will scuttle sideways across the table and onto the floor with all the fingers outspread and scratching at the floor in a desperate attempt to gain traction on the linoleum.

She brings her arms behind her on either side as she approaches the bowl to their body. Soon it appears that she will have the elbows so far behind her that she could curve her upper arms around her body and touch them together at the small of her back, forming a circle that would sway gently back and forth around the central post of her torso like the great rings of a hoopskirt that can swing back and forth within a certain very narrow radius but always in virtually the same plane. When she has set the bowl down and her fingers have uncurled gradually from the bottom up and settled on the tablecloth at the sides of the bowl, they remain in the same position as when they held it, like flesh that separates from chicken bones during a too-prolonged period of baking, retaining on its inside surfaces the curves and impresses of the skeleton to which to which it has been bound.

She begins to talk again, and it is not until she pauses a minute or so later that she dips the spoon into the bowl and transfers two discs to her empty plate that she deposits carefully on one edge. She returns the spoon so carefully to the dish that it makes no sound, its bowl contacting the soft bodies of the slices and its handle gently kissing the bowl's plastic rim. He pushes the plate of meat slices towards her. She makes no movement to take any, and he lifts the cucumbers and moves the oval dish with the meat closer to her. At this point it seems that the rippling wrinkles get an extra dose of power, or perhaps her speech slows slightly to compensate, for as she talks, her hand comes up again from her lap and grasps the end of the fork handle. There it stays, her wrist resting just on the edge of the table and bending sideways with the weight of her arm.

He finds an empty space between his glass and the wall and fits the cucumber dish into it, as if placing a piece of the mosaic pattern into its proper position. The spaces around it could later be filled with smaller bits such as salt shakers, sugar bowls, and cream pitchers and then the entire surface smoothed off and filled in with a mortared paste of flour and water so that the level of the table top would be raised several inches and the bases of the containers would no longer be visible. At this point, the mouths of the different containers would be like holes opening up abruptly in an otherwise smooth surface into which an insect or rodent might fall and drown or be smothered, according to the nature of their contents. **Disadvantages:** Such an arrangement would put a serious crimp in the style of these utensils as well as in that of the people who had gotten the habit of using them. To use the salt shaker, for example, the entire table surface would have to be lifted from the tablecloth and overturned. The effect would be hardly less than catastrophic, what with the cucumbers sliding from their bowl and plopping in a gooey mass onto the cloth, the iced tea making a brown stain on most of the middle of the table, the sugar strewing in an arc that is dissolving on its bottom layer into the wetness, and the meat slices scattered over everything like dominoes flung onto the floor by an ill-bred child showing its displeasure at having lost the game. In addition, the accuracy of aim with such a contraption might leave something to be desired and the slice of tomato or whatever was to have been salted might not ultimately see so much as a single grain of salt, the deposit instead joining the other spilled food on the tablecloth.

Worse: The complexity of this maneuver necessary to using the salt would be nothing in comparison to the machinations required for using a fork or some other utensil that requires specialized movements. One's head reels, for example, at the thought of the gruntings and groanings that would come from those trying to scoop up something with a fork half-buried in a thick pad of cement-like substance, for we would have to turn the entire thickness belly-up and make blind scooping movements at the food that is, regretfully and once again, making a mess of the tablecloth. **Conclusion:** It is evident that we could not possibly be happy with such a system if the complex motions of the machinery of eating (the salt cellar that makes an arc and then returns like a high diver being bounced back through the pattern of his jump by the surface of a water turned suddenly and unexpectedly rubbery, the fork that levitates and then makes dipping motions with its tines like a seesaw being carried about by a tornado still bravely swinging back and forth on its non-existent fulcrum, the dishes that move sideways and turn like flat water beetles speeding in all directions just under the surface of a pool, the glass that curves up and back on the same track like coasting automobiles nearly attaining the peaks of hills and then falling back) were prevented by this sort of internal padding from exercising their motions in relation to one another. Our present system whereby we ourselves enter into the workings of the individual components of this larger system should remain unaltered.

He cuts off the corner of a slice of meat with his knife. Its serrations ratchet across the plate, their sound damped by the thick slice of meat above them. A triangular piece of ground pork parts from the remainder like a block of land separating quietly from another along a fault line. Two tines of the fork are stuck in this fragment while the other two hang stiffly off into the air as if too used to their usual position even to think of curving around to pierce the remaining meat. The cool tines slide across his tongue and then through the mouth; the after-effect of the fork's coolness make it seem as if a row of four canals has been drilled through his closed lips, canals through which any liquid held in the mouth must necessarily gush even without any pressure forcing it out.

He rests the end of the fork on the edge of his plate. It sticks out sideways, its handle resting by the base of his iced tea glass which is making a fuzzy wet ring on the tablecloth. His hand lies still a moment, and then his fingers curve up to stroke the frosty side of the glass before them, clearing the mist where they touch in wide horizontal swaths; the larger drops forming at their bottoms continuing on down the glass in thinner and more irregular horizontal columns. Suddenly he smells the biscuits in the stove. He pushes back his chair and crosses the room, where he pulls open the door of the oven. It releases a sudden blast of great heat that crinkles the skin of his face. He jerks his head back into the cooler air along the sides of the open door and feels the heat pull at the skin of his face as if it had been attached to thousands of tiny suction cups as soft as lips that stroke him as they pucker and fall away.

His legs are only an inch or two in front of the horizontal door. There is a sharp separation of temperatures above and below this boundary to which the hairs on his legs react by fluffing out within the lines of demarcation. As it disperses, the heat becomes less intense, and the height which the waves have been reaching on his leg decreases as steadily as if they were being slowly squashed by a huge flat candle snuffer until the heat band is only a few inches high, sharply drawn on one side and unclear and rippling on the other in the way that nothing can but heat and fire that throw off great undulating waves condensing to tear-shaped drops as they twist upwards and leap from the ends into the air.

Remarks: He has felt the coolness emanating from the refrigerator, and now the heat from the stove. Yet there are unlikely to be any more caches of extreme temperature to be revealed by opening doors in this kitchen. We can be sure of this not only from our knowledge of the structure of kitchens but also because there are no more extremes as far as hot and cold are concerned. **Second thought:** Yet who knows what other sorts of atmospheric oddities might lurk behind the various doors and cabinets that wait unopened along the walls of this room? Could we be sure that if he pulls open the white-painted wooden cabinets under the sink, he will not be hit in the face with (say) billows of tear gas that will blind him to the sight of the scouring powder cans grown rusty on their metal tops and somewhat soft and wrinkled on their sides from having been grasped too often with wet hands, the bottles of pink dishwashing liquid with crusts of no-longer-pink stickiness trailing down the sides, the boxes with the crushed skeletons of used scrubbing pads, once-delicate and intricate lattice-works that supported a frothy pink skin now matted and flattened, their detergent washed away and replaced with small dried fragments of scrambled eggs and fried chicken that cling to the maze of rusting wire like the brown hide of a dried sea-horse to its interior skeleton?

The bottles and jars of powders and liquid are all lined up in neat rows under the twisting silver-colored arm of the sink pipes from which hang washrags brown from frequent immersion in the iron-hued water and frayed at the edges, their rows of loose threads as stiff and awkwardly arranged as the tails of fish that have been washed upon the beach and are baking in the sun. Are we sure that, if he reaches above the counter to tug at the doors which she never opens, he will not discover a pocket of air marbled with thick yellow veins of sulphur gas that twine around the dusty cans and tins of food and disperse throughout the cabinet when he blows on them along with some of the cobwebs? Can we know that if he opens the drawer below the dish drainer, he will not have the unpleasant surprise of having to turn his head away from the piles of dishtowels and hand towels and handkerchiefs to avoid (perhaps) the pungent odor of burning rubber that pours forth without any visible explanation?

Reasoning: We know that there exist laboratories serving as the storehouses of the pure caches of various substances, warehouses that have along their walls elixirs and solutions of all the essences known to man. Though we have gotten into the habit of thinking of these as cold enamel palaces manned by attendants in white suits and rubber gloves, there is no reason why we should be unable to conceive of some of the more common elements being farmed out to more humble vaults such as to the kitchen of this old woman's house.

Perhaps, indeed, such pockets are all around us. It may be that the next book we slide from a library shelf will release a perfume made from a thousand flowers of the Pyrenees. Or that the next stone we kick from our path will reveal the mouth of a tube from which will gush strange undulating currents that twine around our arms and neck and make us fairly swoon with pleasure. Or that the feet of the next butterfly we sneak up on and pluck from its branch will turn out to be plugging four tiny jets in the wood that will squirt pink air at our face. Perhaps the world is nothing but a collection of hollow things serving as the storage chambers of the myriad vapors that can be dispensed into the air, existing for no other reason than to form the shells which enclose the air. **A puzzle:** It is hard to see why mankind has neglected to venerate to a greater extent the lungs as those internal organs most directly in contact with the air, to worship them as the true center of the body, that for which the entire exterior form was created. In fact, we humans are nothing but the elaborate coverings for the two balloons of our lungs, our arms and legs attached for the purpose of protecting and moving them.

The potholder is warmed from within by the metal bar it is enclosing, hot and hard inside the wrapping. He pulls the rack from the oven like a tongue that, by use of a hitherto undiscovered password, he has forced to pop forth immediately, bearing upon its surface the pan of biscuits that he lifts with his protected hand and sets quickly on the top of the stove. He neglects to push the rack back in before closing the over door; in quick succession he hears the hollow bang of the closing trap and the metallic and muffled clank of the rack falling back onto its guide rails. Fainter and as if in response, there is the quiet poof of the gas re-igniting to re-create the heat he has released. He twists the knob growing from the center of the stove and hears the flame die once again, its rattle a series of quiet clicks and pops.

The top of one of the biscuits crackles under his probing finger and exposes the soft white innards between the irregular pieces of brown crust floating on the surface of the fluffiness like thick shavings of chocolate on the outside of a dollop of whipped cream. The depression that he has made is still for a moment. Slowly it begins to fill in again; the brown covering begins to rise and its separated pieces move together again. Yet after several moments, the convex top of a moment ago is still not achieved. There remains a slight dip and, within the area of a small circle, cracks that stop at its edge as if this depression were the result of having buried something deep within the insides of the biscuits and having filled in the hole with loose dirt that sank as the rains came and packed it together. Soon it would be covered, not with the lush dense grass of the area surrounding it, but with sprawling spiders of crab grass and weeds that leave exposed veins of the soft earth spattered up onto this greenery by the force of the great thick raindrops of subsequent storms.

He crosses to the other side of the room and tugs at the handle of the second drawer. It glides out but comes to a sudden stop after several inches, pulling out crookedly and jolting against its frame. He bangs it back straight into its track with the heel of his hand that immediately begins to tingle. Again he pulls at the drawer, this time revealing an orderly rectangle of interior instead of a trapezoid that soon changes the proportion of its sides so that long becomes short and short becomes long as easily and smoothly as a piece of soap held in the fist can be made to metamorphose from sideways to lengthwise and then back over to sideways without much visible motion of the fingers enclosing it.

As he pulls, the handles of the silverware elongate and then blossom into the bowls of spoons, the tines of forks, and the curious blade-like flowers of knives that must open up like pods to reveal the organs of pollination within. One or two of the handles even produce great spoons pierced with holes or thick two-pronged forks. The product of each otherwise identical tuber is always something of a surprise, and he must simply wait until the drawer pulls out to see what they will make. He cannot look within these handles without pulling on the drawer and see the tiny infant forks and knives, soft and curled and harmless, and thus we cannot protect ourselves against the sharp-tongued creatures whose bites can be lethal.

Nor can we merely smash them all in infancy, for though most of the eggs produce the copperheads and coral snakes of sharp-toothed knives and forks, some bring forth only the benign rounded garden creatures of spoons that do us no harm. **Conclusion:** We would be doing ourselves a disservice by indiscriminately crushing all of these hard silver shells and scuffing them into the dust.

Before him lies a box of cardboard whose ripped edges have been sewn together with thread that is as faded and rotten as the paper it mends. When he lifts this doctored top off the base, he discovers a cache of spoons swathed in a gauzy white scarf, like the bodies of the recently dead beneath their shrouds, pale and shimmering as if seen through several feet of water that is roiled by the movements of sub-surface currents. When he tugs at the edge of the cloth, it pulls off to reveal a gleam of silver that soon covers the entire form of the uppermost spoon and the edges of those underneath. A string of morning glories curls its way in bas-relief up the handle of the topmost spoon, but his fingers are not sensitive enough to feel these bumps as metallic flowers without the aid of his eyes. Instead, all they sense is an indeterminate roughness framed by the smooth line of the edge, a long thin picture like that which the fair Melinda saw from her casement window as she stood in the tower room thinking of her lost lover.

The legend of Melinda and the morning glory: The flowers that had climbed up to the window frame, instead of opening to the sun, turned towards the darkness of her room as if to give light rather than receive it, and had opened their pale purple bells that seemed to say, Look at us, we too are without lovers, have nothing but the clean air and the kiss of the light, yet see, see how we blossom! Melinda's heart was lightened and she began to smile and sing; all too soon she had forgotten her lover and wanted only to be like the morning glory, to hang into the great expanse of blue heavens from its hold on the outside of the stones.

So she climbed upon the sill and, grasping the brown vines of her beloved flowers, stepped out into the air. Had it been able, the air would gladly have held up her lovely weight. Indeed, it is said, it managed against all laws of heartless gravity to support her for several seconds longer than it was supposed to anyway. But then, with a ripping and tearing of many small runners and roots, she fell to the earth, her great velvet skirts billowing out around her and the feelers of the morning glory twisting their brown fingers around her smooth white knuckles and its hard thick vine looped around her sweet throat. **End:** When she hit, it was in a bed of flowers that pressed themselves around her lifeless body, red flowers and yellow flowers and white flowers and blue flowers that surrounded her as if keeping watch, with the purple blossoms of the morning glory nuzzling against her pink cheek and twisting down upon her lovely breasts like great passionate leeches that were already beginning to limpen and to wilt as the blood in her limbs ran colder and become sluggish. Yet they are leeches that will not desert that to which they are attached or loosen their holds to go and seek another beauty from whom to draw their sustenance. For in the whole wide world there was no one so fair as the beautiful Melinda who is cold and dead in the flowers with her neck cricked slightly to one side like the tail of a cat upon which the door has been shut.

The front of the drawer is a jumble of exotic bits of metal twisting and curling into one another, the weed yard of an otherwise French-garden-like layout arranged into well-regulated rows and columns with spaces between them. This chaotic niche is allowed to exist not out of the laziness of the farmer, but probably because of her knowledge that the soil of the drawer is like all other things in being unable to maintain discipline forever, is absolutely incapable of sustaining any sort of rigidity and firmness of purpose for a long period of time without having to rebel and go through a time when no holds are barred, when all inhibitions are forgotten and when anything goes. For when this period is over, the things are usually ready to go back to work, to concentrate once again until they are overcome with primeval stirrings within. Her attempt has obviously been to keep this same proportion of control and its lack, but to do so spatially rather than temporally. She has assigned one portion to the production of whatever outrageous products the drawer can think up, so that it would be willing to devote the remainder of its energies to the cultivation of more conventional crops. The result is this tangled mass of corkscrews, bottle openers spotted with the rust dots of age, can openers to whose round blades still cling the remains of pineapple, green beans and hominy grits, and odd spoons with stains upon the metal of their bowls that look as if several drops of coffee had remained within.

He digs down between the bone handles of the larger knives and forks and finally manages to curl his fingers around what feels like a wooden sausage. When he manages to disinter it, it turns out to be the handle of a knife sharpener. He does a bit of closer inspection on the pile and tries again, this time managing to produce the pancake turner which carries up the rest of the pile on its spread hood. All of the other implements make a great clattering as they fall again, replacing themselves in a considerably less efficient pattern than that in which they had been previously arranged. As he tries to close the drawer, one of the knives digs its sharp point into the wood of the counter above it and props its handle against the front of the drawer. Only when he opens again and beats at the utensil with the pancake turner does it give up its grip and its attempts to escape and sinks back into the drawer.

He slips the corner of the flat metal under the edge of one of the biscuits and with a quick motion breaks its contact with the pan. Soon there is a basketful of steaming brown discs and a sheet of metal that bears a light pattern of circular brown shadows, as well as a pancake turner to whose edge there clings a row of crispy crumbs that he licks from the metal that is warm along its extreme edge and then cool. The half-sharp edges of the pancake turner bite into the corners of his mouth, and he tries to stretch his cheeks so that he can enclose it completely. He cannot do so, and he lays it back down on the stove, watching the tiny bubbles of his saliva pop and travel down its tilted surface. The wet circle from his upper lip glistens slightly; he feels the mark of the metal on the insides of his cheeks and the stretched tingling of his lips whose hard surfaces pucker into rows of hills like a piece of cloth to which a length of elongated elastic has been sewn that wrinkles back into an even succession of frills when the rubber is released.

He lays a biscuit on her plate by the pile of cucumbers and on his own beside the slice of meat and sits down. She has not stopped talking, and does not acknowledge his arrival any more than she has remarked his absence. He takes a biscuit and pulls part of its curvature away so that the soft fluffy inside is exposed. The filaments of dough pop as they are pulled past the limit of their stretching power, revealing tiny bubble caves that open behind them. He scrapes a sliver of butter from the end of the stick and wipes it from the knife with the soft surface of his piece of bread. The butter lies curled on the white oval, then slowly its edges liquify and it becomes smaller. His teeth find at first only the warm dry bread, and then are flooded with the melted butter caught in its tiny pockets and squeezing from the spongy layers as they are broken between the hard rocks of his teeth, the softness mixed with fragments of the crisp surface throughout that are divided until they are little more than soggy crumbs the same consistency as the rest.

He looks at her wrinkled mouth, caved in at the bottom into the space where her lower denture would be if she had not taken it from her mouth a decade ago and laid it away in the big drawer of her dresser, under her musty and carefully folded clothes and the gloves wrapped in tissue and the brown wrapping-paper parcel of the clothes in which she is to be buried. Her mouth pumps up and down. The lips curl outwards unevenly as she brings them together for sibilants so that they thin and seem for a moment like the pale ruffled edges sewn to the bottoms of slipcovers that by rights should not be able to flatten again and close upon the front of her mouth, remaining extended in a perpetual frill on her face, stiff and unwrinkled. As she comes to the end of a phrase, her eyes grow wide in emphasis and reveal the yellowed and bloodshot areas of the whites that the bagging lids had concealed. The flaps of skin that had provided gradual slopes down to the watery gloss of her eyes are now pulled up and back so that the eyeballs are surrounded with sharp banks that break off abruptly into sheer areas plunging directly into the stagnant pools below.

Remarks: We would be very unhappy if such a construction were to appear on a larger scale in nature. Though we might at first be fooled by the brownness of the banks into thinking that they were a good place to lie on our stomach and peer into the water, this would be wrong, as we would surely find out when the folds and flaps of the ground under us started rolling forwards under our weight, if we had not already discovered that something was wrong by feeling the peculiarly slimy surface of that upon which we lay. **NB:** All would go well if this larger counterpart of the eye had a pool that was not like caches of water in being penetrable but like the eyeball in being only just moist and slightly springy to the touch so that an athletic person might well find him- or herself able to exploit its trampoline properties to land back on the slippery and shifting banks.

There are a few eyelashes clinging to her skin like corn stubble missed by a wavering plow or the pinfeathers left in the skin of a fowl by a hurried cook. Unlike the long soft extrusions of young skin that, when pulled, produce at most a hill at their base that disappears when they are released, these hairs can be used to control the movement of whole masses of this older and more malleable epidermis. They can pull it sideways and upwards and even design circular sweeps in it that cause the skin further away from the manipulated area to pull straight back and forth.

She is silhouetted against a breakfast cabinet of dishes; behind her head is the rim of a plate standing up against its back that circles her skull like a flowered nimbus. She leans towards her plate to pop in her mouth a piece of the biscuit she has ripped off. In doing so, she loses her halo and acquires the handle of a cream pitcher that seems attached on the top of her head. For a few seconds there is only the sound of her chewing and of his voice. He is saying something about an Easter lily in her backyard and the best way to keep the dogs from trampling on it. His voice moves in a monotone which repeats itself in shortened form when she jerks her head up again and breathes outwards in a loud sign that indicates that she has not understood.

"Do you hear anything from Martha?" she asks suddenly.

Suddenly he is paying attention to her words, his skin flushing with hot anger towards his wife and towards his grandmother, who is bringing up the one subject that he will not think about.

One day out of what seemed nowhere, Martha announced that she was moving out. She did not like his graduate student existence, she said, and did not like the tiny apartment on the university campus.

"I had no idea you were unhappy," he said.

"I know," she said.

"What must I do to have you stay?" he asked, panic-stricken.

"I don't want to be with you," she said. And she left, her eyes determined.

For days he was rigid from the shock. Even now his feelings have not had time to fade to indifference; they are a mixture of poison and honey. Yet on the surface he is calm, functional.

What is his grandmother doing bringing up the subject? What does she mean by it?

Nothing.

She means nothing.

She leaves a space for response that he must fill. For once, she is waiting for him to speak.

"No, grandmother," he says.

She looks at him, and for the first time he feels that she sees him. Or perhaps, it is merely that she seems something other than a waxwork who sits before her, looking with her nearly blind eyes into his eyes.

Then the moment is over and already she is continuing on to the subject of the neighbor across the street who may or may not have cancer and on whom she spies through the lifted blade of the venetian blind.

There is a sucking noise as his spoon pulls from the applesauce and a hole that stays sharp and well-defined for only a moment before it begins to ooze over so that by the time he feels the cold granules against his tongue, he is almost unable to make out the mark of his spoon on its surface.

Now the plates are cleared except for two saucers, one with about half a slice of fallen and spongy lemon cake covered on its top side with bitter chocolate frosting and one that is strewn with pale crumbs and short smears of brown to which particles of the cake cling. He lays his fork down on his empty plate and gropes for the wrinkled paper napkin that has nearly succeeded in slipping from his knees. The meal is over.

III

The Field

THE BACK OF HIS HEAD IS COVERED with his fingers that pick in the thatched layers of his hair. He locates a strand rooted in the uneven white whorl of the crown of his head and follows it its length to where the jagged edges of his hair curve against the gaping pores of his neck. He drags his fingertips in the paste of dirt and wetness that oozes from the scalp there at that point where it rids itself of hair and becomes neck. He crushes an imaginary bug that is crawling across his neck and tickling him with its undulating feet which are as small, black, numerous, and as easy to destroy as the strands of his hair. Tiny insects inhabit greasy areas of the body, he had read, nearly invisible and noiseless. He tries to imagine that he feels them now, burrowing their ways into the layers of his fatty tissue, but he feels only the hotness of the vinyl car seat through his pants and the vague pressing of his loafers on his sockless feet. His fingers find a spot (scab? dirt?) on his white scalp and squash it blindly between them.

He is sitting on his right hand, palm upwards, and so is forced to disengage the left from the back of his head and bring it down to the level of the window so it can finger and nudge the cloth-covered rubber tubing which is shedding its fraying skin. He pulls at a brown thread and it, not so recalcitrant or so strong as his hairs, breaks with a snap between his thumb and index finger and sends them hurtling backwards in stunned reaction. These two fingers have picked at other discarded casings in other places: the fragile brown cicadas' outsides that are slit up the back and look like peanut shells through which the nut has escaped by osmosis, so perfect is their form; the ghostly skins of snakes that have been scratched against rocks and which bear the lateral pattern of their occupants' strainings like bedclothes molded and knotted under a recent copulation. Perhaps it was not these fingers at all that had picked at these secret droppings, perhaps it was the fingers of the other hand that are warm with sweat and body heat. This hand kneads the buttock above it gently, its knuckles sinking into the woven brown seat as the fingers press into the soft flesh. He tightens his muscles and the fingers are forced further into the seat, unable to penetrate any deeper than the surface fat layer. He feels the sun on the car side where the long white belly of his arm is slung.

He leans across the seat to open the window on the driver's side. The sun shines only on his side of the seat, where his elbow makes an indentation like that made by a certain sort of pincer beetle in beach sand. But his elbow is in the way of a perfect correspondence between the two. Surely no bug would be stupid enough to fall in a hole held down by an elbow. Maybe if he were to tie a knot in the end of a thread, stick the needle through the seat, and pull it from underneath, he could produce such a hole. Yet there would still be a knot in its bottom. He does not like the feel of a thread pulled as tight as this one would have to be, cutting a sharp red furrow in his thin fingers.

The asphalt in the parking lot has begun to get soft; if the sun were to stay lit that night as a surprise, this sticky black would bubble and boil, moving upwards to engulf the few cars that remained stranded underneath the bluish arc lights. But no: they would be eaten only as far as the white bands on their tires; then they would come to rest on stones and dirt which would remain unimpressed by the gratuitous overtime put in by the sun.

He can see the stripes of white paint that separate the spaces. The one on his right is covered by a car and so he looks out the back window, hardly having to turn his head. Evidently there had been some loose stones in the way when the painters came along, which had been coated white. Since then, they had rolled away, leaving blank spaces in the jigsaw puzzle. Perhaps he should look for these strayed children and return them to their own kind. That they were unrelated interlopers before the paint fell is no matter: catastrophe makes us all brothers. Perhaps a half-white pebble would wake up one morning in Duluth and become aware of its responsibilities to a white stripe of a parking lot in a small and faraway town. What would it do? It say? He sees a man in a white T-shirt coming out of one of the stores in the shopping center. He bends his head down and by moving his eyeballs to the top of their sockets reads: Ike Jones, Haircuts. He retracts his neck into the collar of his knit shirt to prevent a strain.

He is suddenly conscious of the itch that his three-day stubble is making on his cheeks and neck and, though he tries to remember the sensation he felt when he pushed up straight on one of the hairs on his beard and it bowed outwards and rotated on its axis and then finally popped from under the weight of his finger like a curved broom straw stuck in a crack in the floor that jumps its track and elongates, he cannot. He picks his left hand off the steering wheel and moves it to his chin to repeat the action. It is curiously slippery and not unpleasant. Again he tries to remember this now considerably more recent feeling, but is no more successful than before.

His left hand drops to his bare knee and his eyes move forwards to the window. The shopping center is long enough that the end past the supermarket crumbles off into the shimmering daylight. Another car pulls up opposite his and cuts its motor before rolling to a halt like a suddenly-disgruntled cat stopping a purr in mid-motion. To eyes that have seen cars sprout tadpole-like appendages and lose them in a twelve-year growth cycle, its sides seem offensively round. But it has not yet turned into a frog. Perhaps all the beautiful girls whose kisses are so necessary for this transformation are in hiding or, as the result of cost-benefit economic planning, had all simultaneously stood before their mirrors on a certain morning and disfigured their gorgeous faces with the acid from (wicked) a thousand automobile batteries, thus dashing to the ground any possibility of their ever being suitable liberators of creatures transfigured into vehicles. Now black hairs grow from their chins, their faces are fat and old, and they grin in awful glee at the steering wheels of their eternally-enchanted vehicles as they drive them to little-league fields.

The left door of the car flies open and a man shoots out. His hair is slicked back with grease that has curved it over the tops of his ears and left the long thin rows made by the comb.

His short sleeves are rolled up over his biceps, exposing his tattoo, perhaps in the vain hope that the sun would take a color cue and burn his entire arm the same fading blue as the ink and his jeans. The man turns in mid-arc and pulls a girl from the car. The row of curlers in her hair are pink and fuzzy like hollow caterpillars lined up and chained by their feet as if elephants in a carnival, her mouth opening and lopsidedly exposing her grayish and crooked teeth is like the rim of a confectioner's panoramic Easter egg melting in the sun. Her breasts are young but hang limply behind the thin cloth as if they too are overcome by the heat and are unable to draw enough moisture to stiffen along their entire length. Their tops are brown and flaking from too much sun, and her sleeveless shirt exposes the dividing line on her shoulders between bathing suit-protected white and the area intended for mass exhibit. Protesting, she turns her head. The man is advancing, grinning, one arm around her neck, the other draped over her shoulder and touching her back. She holds a paper bag filled with empty milk bottles between them but he draws her mouth closer to him and her misshapen lips are hidden from view.

When he looks up again they and their rusting Chevrolet are gone as if they had vanished into the torpid air. Had they a home? A child? A pair of jilted spouses? Dangerous to fill in their lives from a series of still shots. Perhaps they had no lives. Maybe they had hatched full-grown just seconds before with their seemingly rotting bodies like congenitally syphilitic children of Zeus and had fulfilled their destinies by appearing in the act of one putrefied kiss in the hot sun of a crowded parking lot, like insects whose life span is long enough to enable them only to emerge from their egg sacs and take the single action of laying more eggs themselves before they die. **Conjecture:** If the elephant graveyard is ever found, it may well turn out that its prize is not be the piles of worm-eaten and yellowing ivory, but the lost corpses of these young factory workers and beauticians they were produced to emerge from rusting automobiles and enact their wordless roles.

A bank stands behind the now-vacant parking space, a brick box whose starkness is relieved only by its drive-in window which bulges from its side like a pustule. An old woman comes walking in front. Her dress clings to her stubby legs and her laceless tennis shoes separate from her feet as she raises her heels the small amount necessary for locomotion. She walks slowly in the gutter of the curb that glows yellow like a phosphorescent python; her shoes leave amorphous indentations in the warm asphalt. He picks at the red scab on his right knee and looks at the dust on the dashboard and through the windshield onto the hood which radiates the lasagne-noodle rays of the heat of just past noon.

That night, in his room: he looks at the wooden crucifix frozen in and defining the four quarter panes of the dark window. The smooth layer that immobilizes it is glittering now. In the daytime it is alive with moving shapes of green trees and drops of residual dew. His face, his room, stare back from the window panes.

He turns his face slowly away, keeping his eyes on the same point. He is not able to get further than a quarter around. His pupils, squashed into the corners of his watermelon-seed eyes, ache like a woman's foot crammed into pointed-toe high heels. He swivels his head back to the window and then turns it again, this time aimlessly, and as noiselessly as the rows of plastic heads C-clamped onto the table of the hairdressers' school.

He lifts his left arm and drapes it over the horizontal bar of the lamp by his arm. It is metal, and he can feel the caloric rainbow that has formed in the rod: warm on the end towards the bulb, becoming cooler towards the point at which it drops abruptly to another level at the swivel joint. There is a thin layer of something on the silver-colored metal. Condensation? Grease? He drags his fingertips through it, changing the pattern that shows under the light, reversing the direction of shimmer.

His feet are jammed against the side of the metal bedframe, and the pressure is increasing in the soft arch of his foot. He tightens the muscles; they spring away from the metal. The white skin develops vertical wrinkles when he does this, making that long part between the hard ball of his foot and the heel look like blanched and rotting ivory. Perhaps the worms will come during his lifetime to bore thin tunnels into such unfeeling layers of his body; perhaps he will touch these marks of animal penetration with the same detached wonder with which he fingers the delicate lacy marrings of similar creatures on the outside of an abalone shell. Still, it may be that the process will not be so painless. A drill might be mere observation, were it to be focused on his fingernail. As soon as it exhausts that thin gelatin layer, as soon as the sharp point of its too-eager tongue darts at the soft underparts, it is a child of the total body and not a mere bastard of the eyes. But who knows? Perhaps, after all, he will be able to trace their paths as disinterestedly as he watches an ant farm arrange and re-arrange its patterns. He will follow them with colored threads, being one to whom their paths are object for nothing more than idle curiosity and concern. These threads will trail on the outside of this skin, the loops left inside the body quietly absorbing the seeping human juices which will make their dye run. **Note:** This presupposes, however, that the adventurous animal completed its trip by coming out at the surface again. And that is not a safe assumption, for the Minotaurs of the sub-cutaneous layers are fiercer than those of any other part or thickness of the body. Perhaps some day he will discover a tiny bump below the surface of his face or chest which, when squeezed, disgorges the half-digested milk-white paste of what must be the bones of some young and brash Theseus-creature that met its end far from its family, alone with an unforgiving monster.

He lift his legs from their tensed angle and puts his feet on the mattress, then lifts them again and, straining, jams a pillow under their heels. He leans back. The window is open at the top. It is cool outside. He feels the wind cut through the thick warmth of the air around him, brushing his cheek in furtive contact before its hands are snatched away by the reproving and apologetic mother air.

A moth which has been beating its furry body against the window for several minutes finds a crack in the top, zooms in and, disoriented, dives for the bedspread. It rests a minute, then it lifts itself suddenly and obliquely towards the lamp and narrows its orbit into the interior of the shade where it careens jerkily from one side to the other. Its body makes sharp thudding noises as it crashes into the white it must take for cloud. Perhaps it leaves a sort gray residue on the shade when it hits; some of the powder on its wings must shake off as it crashes into the barrier.

He leans over and pulls the lamp plug out. He had involuntarily closed his eyes and when the blink is finished, they are suddenly presented with darkness, as if, in the period of his twitch, he had been transported to a different place. He blinks again, but the critical mass is no longer present and the potential for catastrophe is once again zero: there are no more changes and the room remains dark. He hears the moth, disconcerted, fluttering against the ceiling and against the bookcases. This time its thuds are softer and less resonant. Perhaps it is tired, or the paper lampshade carried sound better. Suddenly the room is silent; the creature must have found the window opening through which it entered.

He leans his head back. The forms of the furniture are beginning to re-jell out of the slush of the night and become solid. In this way they are unlike the room when he wakes at midnight and lies rigid, thinking of Martha, his heart beating loudly and his eyes half-closed. When he does this the room has the rough consistency of an early photograph, though it becomes smoother as he lies there trying not to move. Only when it is like this are we able to conceive of ever being able to disperse our molecules enough to walk through the holes between the wall's atoms. Still, it must solidify a certain distance in, and the two bodies would penetrate the thickness of the grains in sandpaper and be stopped short by their cardboard backings. Would they lock together by the shock of impact, these two cobbled layers? A person could then be chipped from the wall, but his front would be nothing but a thin gray scab which would crackle and flake as he talked.

He closes his eyes again and when he opens them, the room is light, the lamp plugged in. If he is not back in his same world, at least it is as close a reproduction as can be expected of a conscientious but occasionally drunken demiurge.

The window shade is quivering slightly with the air. What is the process by which shades are suddenly broken loose of their position and sent flying upwards, curling like a cat's tongue gone mad? How would it feel to be pinned to a shade as it went spiraling upwards? The body can only fold at certain places. There would be lumps in the roll, places where the shade would wrinkle and bunch around his haunches and shoulders.

His eyes light on a speck of color on his desk. He leans over. It is the body of a tiny bug, shimmering green on its torso. He turns it over with his breath and reveals an uninteresting belly. He blows again and succeeds in righting his emerald particle. Was this small bit of fluorescent dust Night's payment for the escape of the moth? Perhaps it was dressed and chanted over in some of the infinity of time particles that make up one of our ungainly and obese seconds, beautified and sung to, a sacrifice to the great power that catches butterflies and lures moths. It seems to shake the sequins on its gown, but this is impossible, for it is dead and by now its half-drop of bodily juices has dried from it and it is his own eyes which, twitching as they blink, produce the iridescent shimmer.

He leans over it still, intrigued by its tininess. There were pictures in his childhood book of fairy tales of grinning giants' faces as they bent over thumb-sized people they were about to devour. He shuts his mouth now and so avoids looking greedy and underfed to any invisible pallbearers that might still be inching their way across from the corpse, hurrying silently across the desk surface to the dusty crevices behind the radiator.

He turns away and looks straight ahead, trying to see the jewel out of the corner of his eye. He is unable to do so and, it may be, embarrassed to be seen by the walls to be spending too much time on such a trifle, looks unconcernedly at the closet door and then over at his bookcase.

He stands before the bookcase and, removing a book, turns it upside down for examination. There is a dark smudge on the bottom of its outer edge of pages, a triangular soft patch, the pubic hair caused by the friction of book against dark bookshelves. He strokes it softly. Books, like people, only develop these marks of maturity when they have become old enough for the muscles of their bindings to be a bit slack, a tiny bit ripe. Only then are the pages allowed to traverse the short distance to the shelf where they light restfully, glad of the opportunity to place their weight on more powerful things and rub the flat cool shelf gently and clandestinely. He slips the book between its lesbic sisters, feels it slide between shelfmates which enclose it and expand slightly to fill the distance between their smooth bodies.

He casts a final glance at the dark-line spectra on his shelves, the diffused jewels of the inner light of inspiration that produced them. He turns away and, spinning around, lets his arm unfold from his side. It lights on a box of tissues and the body continues in its track momentarily before reversing itself and, diminishing in power, oscillating slowly until it comes to rest behind the appendage that stopped its motion. He clutches momentarily at the rim of the box and then, giving up all pretense at energetic movement, lets his fingers fall limply into the gaping pit below at whose bottom they are cushioned by a pile of tissue which receives the indentations from his fingers with barely a shiver. The fingers, stunned by the impact, quiver drunkenly and begin clamping at the white mounds.

He dispenses to the tissue a portion of warm semi-liquid which it ingests into its deep-running folds, and it retires to its resting place on the desk where it jerks and unwinds.

He stands now in the middle of the room, paying no attention to the silent motions around him of which those of the still-squirming tissue are merely the most obvious case. He walks towards the door, goes through it and down the hall to the bathroom. When he reaches the door, a hitch is inserted into his stride and his hands shoot out to overcome the sticky weight of the door so that his body need not take it upon itself. He almost trips over the threshold made of white stone that is black-streaked, partly because of its nature and partly because of black rubber soles which have deposited their wispy offerings upon it over decades. His knee buckles; his foot manages to sweep over the impediment and plants itself firmly on the cold tiled floor beyond. His hand has grasped at the shelves to halt his fall and knocked an aerosol can to the floor. It clatters sharply, and he may well admire the Stoic bearing that allows it to accept such jolts when it is filled with such raging internal pressure. With the pressure of his bladder is not a tenth, not a hundredth of that in the can, he must grit his teeth at lesser concussions.

He picks it up gently and sets it in its spot on the shelf, then with sudden decision plucks it again from its rest and, pointing it towards the wall, releases its wet mist until he is unable to stand its rapidly thickening sweetness. But the can makes no response; its sides do not show the relieved concaveness that would express its thanks better than any amount either of flowery phrases or its cool and cloyingly odorous breath. He clutches it and, his hand pumping in rhythmic annoyance, repays the remaining bit of liquid for the can's failure to re-adjust its exterior. Even now the can makes no reaction, and he throws it on the shelf. It bounces off the back panel and comes rolling towards him again, either a glutton for punishment or a scheming devil eager to have him lose his temper. He fools it either way by catching it quietly and then setting it firmly upright in the corner behind the razor blades.

He is in front of the shower stall. His clothes lie heaped by his towel; his left hand clutches the curtain while his right gropes for the stream. He feels it become tepid, then warm, then hot. He steps in and inhales the mildewed smell of the curtain that he pulls behind him. The water stands in droplets on the grease of his skin.

The hairs of his left arm are coated with rows of tiny clear parasites which gorge themselves until they become so large that they are unable to support their obesity with their invisible legs, at which point they gradually loose their holds and fall to the floor below where they are shattered into many pieces and washed down the drain. He opens his mouth under the sheaf of glassaline stems which break and twist as they hit his teeth. He feels the water welling in his throat and for a moment tastes the acid of vomit coming up to counter the downward force. Yet in a moment this is washed away and he tastes nothing now but the slightly metallic cast of the liquid that is trained on his face.

He turns once again and feels the pressure move around to the back of his neck. The spray divides itself on his shoulder and makes rivulets down his chest, dividing the hairs to serve as causeways and dikes. It gathers in the valley between his arm and stomach and builds up until it is unable any longer to bear the ever-increasing and delicious friction of new droplets on the surface of the lake or of the arm enclosing it that throbs gently and regularly, and it overflows suddenly onto his upper leg and foot. He breaks the enclosing seal and the pool disappears immediately, the parcel of its waters hitting the stream of his urine on its way down and splintering its shape. The yellow sweeps around the lip of the drain and then the color clears again and it is gone.

He picks up the soap and squeezes it with his thumb and index finger. It resists a moment, then shoots from its encircling ring and thuds against the floor. He picks it up; the soap has been flattened on its corner and has taken on the indentations of the rough-surfaced floor. In turning to replace it in the dish, he must grab the shower curtain for sudden support. His hand leaves a wet white print on the fiberglass, and he begins to flick droplets onto the cloth, watching them sit inviolate for a moment before their surface tension breaks and they stain the cloth clear. Soon the curtain is changed to a mass of heavy listless folds through which the light of the bulb shines more easily than before.

His movements are quicker now and more purposeful. He dries himself, limpening the towel. The toilet receives his offering; he sits quietly and lays his head on the paper roll which grips the side of the cubicle halfway up.

He is outside. He walks aimlessly, then seems to choose a path along the sidewalks. There is someone ahead of him. He passes the lamplights; his shadow revolves slowly around him until it is nearly opposite the lamp, at which point it speeds and lengthens suddenly, hastening to sweep forward, sacrificing density to size to be able to touch the still-firm shadow of the person in front with the fingers of sudden age, to hand it the wand of experience that it too might become frightened enough for its body to sweep nervously around its roller-coaster curve of maturity, giving up its tenure as an end in itself and becoming only the emaciated transmitter which stumblingly presses the fading cinder of its dark life on another younger being before it fades totally into uselessness and disappears into the light.

He is alone now, standing in a field. He cannot see the edges of flatness where it sweeps suddenly upward into the trees. The air is blue-black. He hears no sound in this place cleared of the habitat of animals which could fill the undergarments of the atmosphere with their tiny sounds and thus from which all possibility of noise has been eliminated. The field, like all empty things, is incapable of storing or sharing the thuds, moans, and cries of last year, last week, or even yesterday. He drops to his knees and, opening his zipper, strokes his penis which huddles tightly as if in protection against his cool fingers. It is half-flaccid as it ejaculates, the white drops catching on the grass blades below them, covering them thickly and slowly before oozing onto the sand.

IV

The Edge of the Water

HIS BARE FOOT SEPARATES from the linoleum and pads over to the kitchen counter, pulling along with it the other foot and the body that hovers over them both. He feels the soles shaping their soft bottoms to the flatness of the floor, their plump hills becoming wider and flatter as they press and then, as they lift, re-inflate to normal size. There is a slight slippage between bone and flesh as the body drifts forwards on its supports, and sand that grits under his heels when he comes on a spot that is not cool and smooth to the touch. The counter looms before him suddenly and, unaware of it as he is until the moment before he bumps into its edge, the strangely clear picture he had gotten as he felt it first brush his groin and looked down in startled awareness floats before his eyes for a few seconds, like the after-image of a bright light bulb in a dark room.

He sees, both in the image and now on the real thing, as he focuses his eyes and can look at it clearly, the shiny clear traces of what appear to be the dried trails of slugs, criss-crossing the surface that catch the light rays of morning coming in sideways through the window. He follows one of them with his finger and discovers that it leads nowhere in particular: it simply disappears, as if the animal that made it had suddenly sprouted wings and lifted itself vertically into the air. The window over the sink is slightly open and he leans forwards over the counter. Reaching up, he flattens the last two joints of his fingers down on the top of the open half of the window. This results only in frustration as the too-weak fingers become concave in helpless strainings and finally slip from the edge. He looses his other hand from the front edge of the counter and, folding himself at a 45° angle over it, pounces on the window with both hands and a good deal more force than before. He tightens his lips as the loud chunk of wood into wood vibrates the window frame and tickles his waist with the shiver of a slightly delayed echo.

With the closing of the window, he has cut off the cool morning breezes that seemed with their nagging curls around his elbows to be urging him to do something that he had forgotten. For the moment, their thin voices are still, and he feels once again the air of the kitchen that seems to protect him from harm rather than to keep him from anything desirable which may await him in less controlled and controllable climes. He seizes the damp washrag in one hand and the uppermost dish in the other and rubs one against the other. The plate begins to purr in porcelain contentment, or perhaps the noise is only the sound his fingers make as they hold onto the clean side the plate which is slipping slowly but perceptibly from his grasp. He transports the dish over the sink to its notched slot in the yellow plastic dish drainer where it is immobilized while gentle airy hands milk the moisture from its fat body and onto the collecting tray below.

The plates are now lined up on their sides in the drainer like the vertebrae of a very thick and stumpy boa constrictor that has suffered from a run-in with a predator at the point on its body where the line of dinner plates ends and that of matching dessert plates begins without horizontal pause. At one end, the rack bristles with the metal whiskers of the silverware. Here it looks like a horseshoe crab, upturned by the tides so that its grasping feet and furred legs wave in impotent appeal to the sun whose desiccating rays transform its waving innards to crisp motionless shells. Soon the scouring pad is having the last bit of its pinkness wrung from its unyielding center against the bottom of the black skillet, and is reduced to a squashed mass of tightly packed filaments. He adds it to the trash bag, which only two days ago fairly gasped with emptiness and followed each chicken bone and each potato peeling hungrily with its tiny hidden eyes. Today it seems to accept the wet scouring pad grudgingly, stuffed to the gills as it is, the jaws which were once opened in famished supplication now too full to close. **Lesson:** Gluttony is a fault with grievous consequences. Had the bag only closed its top after it had enough to satisfy the growling of its stomach—which he hears as the creakings of the floorboards—it would have ended up with a good full stomach and not be in the ignominious position of being so bloated that it must be carried out and thrown in the trash can. On the bottom part of this bag are two cans dripping tuna fish oil, the rotting remnants of a head of cabbage, and an extremely damp piece of discarded Scrapple. Any one of these would have served to render a less acquisitive bag more happy than it would be able to say; coming in troika, they should have sent it into transports of gastronomic bliss.

Insisting on keeping its mouth open for more, however, it acquired two glass bottles and the ample contents of the house's seven large ashtrays, all of which are quite indigestible.

He rinses the russet foam from the pan and arranges it carefully on top of the neat white rows of parallel plates, thus destroying any resemblance of the dish drainer to the skeleton of a snake. **Precept:** It may be pointed out that nothing resembles anything else except in the mind of man, for our reactions are based on descriptions that can be altered, through the change in a single word or at most two or three, from one thing to another, like the field of spit-weeds in the warm winds of Normandy which, when combing them in one direction, show the smooth green of the upper sides of their glossy leaves and then, shifting, upend the milk-white down of their underbellies so that suddenly it has snowed here on the rolling brown and gray hills, a snow which soon melts once again into patches of the green as the breeze separates and breaks the field into alternating blobs of the contrasting colors which move slowly downwind and across the valley as the plants undulate under its fingers.

He pulls the stopper from the sink's navel and watches the water form its own belly button into which it sucks itself dry. Soon the sink is nothing more than the skin and bones of the dirty bottom layer. Finally it accomplishes the impossible task of eating itself alive from the inside and disappearing, leaving nothing but a line of white scum which breaks up into its own separate bubbles and the dislodged particles of food from the pans that have collected in the strainer. He stirs these bits idly with an index finger, and is scarcely able to feel any difference between the textures of the pieces of putrid strawberries, the stringy bits of burned ham, and the soaked morsels of cereal which are mingling as friends now that the colors and tastes that made competitors and opponents of them have been sucked from their bodies and they are only gray slime that forms around the end of his finger.

He has got hold of the plunger in its middle, and is carrying it to the trash basket where it does not relinquish its catch until he loses patience and begins shaking it brutally up and down. All at once, a flattened donut of the food mush adds itself to the decoration on the side of the tomato soup can that already includes the dried driblets of bacon fat. When hot, these had saturated the colored pictures on the label of an impossibly neat table setting dominated by the red eye of the soup. Now, in hardening, the filmy streaks of the fat have become stripes of glaze that give the label the look of a miniature highway billboard left too long in the sun that has faded from glorious technicolor to uniform drabness.

He drops the strainer back into the sink and wipes the tips of his fingers on the dishrag as he rearranges it on the faucet. Soon, he is busily at work with the soap which is streaked lightly with the multi-colored additions of earlier dirty fingers which had merely patted the white bar several quick times as if thinking that contact alone with the pale purifying element would be enough to render themselves clean. His devotions now are somewhat more lengthy: he rolls the soap smoothly in his wet right hand, feeling it bumping past his joints and seeing the hand flatten and expand as it guides the bar expertly in a twirl of ever-increasing speed. This ends only when one squeeze is too tight and the flat bar flies from his fist and into the sink.

He shakes foamy white hands with himself. Apparently he finds a fist a good substitute for the bar of soap, and continues the kneading process. Soon both hands are coated in thick ermine gloves which disappear into the water as he turns the faucet on again and pokes the unrecognizably pale appendages under the stream. He watches them return to their normal hue, perhaps with a bit of regret for all his possible panic at having acquired hands of marble, for he has begun to like the soft sinuous feel of his soap-clotted epidermis, the thousands of tiny slimy bubbles that urge his fingers not to stay still but to dance, to stroke, to slide. Now, however, it is too late for regrets, for the water has turned the flesh at the end of his arms once again to hands, albeit hands with cleaner and less greasy skin.

He stands for a minute in the middle of the linoleum, listening to the clock's tick that emanates from a tiny face lost in the middle of a thick yellow plastic rim from which pop equally yellow bas-relief daisies. He notes the spots on the plastic tablecloth he has left unwiped in his haste, sees the pile of magazines and mail that spills out from their teetering perch against the wall to the middle of the table, the bottle of catsup with its bleeding mouth, the month-old advertisement section of the local paper and the fly swatter which rests on it.

He jingles the car keys in his pocket as he walks up the stairs, being careful not to step on the edges where the furry green of the carpet has begun to mat down and scab brown in a line that is not likely ever to heal. He grasps the knob of the newel post at the top in an attempt to obtain a pivot for the sudden turn he makes into the bathroom, then catches himself on the front of the sink. **Interpretation:** He spends his life, it seems, as a succession of more or less protracted careenings between collapses onto the inanimate things of this world. Not only is the day the white-bright interval between two embraces of his mattress and blankets, but each period when he is on his feet is only the time between that during which he is tossed between the strong arms of chairs. The periods in which he holds his balance and walks under his own power are the result of skillful juggling and re-arranging of the forces that, were he to let them, would throw him immediately to the floor or frog-walk him out the door. Finally, as he stands exhausted before a piece of furniture, these take over and push him—gently, if he has gauged their directions correctly, more forcefully if he has not—into the bodies of the things that have been waiting all day for his balancing mechanism to fail in correctly playing off one force against another.

He stands before the mirror with his head bowed slightly, as if waiting for it to marshall its forces and rub the film of sleep from its glassy eye before he asks it to take on the job of reflecting him. He looks at the swirls of the hairs that have fallen from the comb and are curled inside small puddles of water as if within sacs of amniotic fluid, and at the half-evaporated drops that spangle the silver-colored faucets in random patterns which will soon become ghostly two-dimensional arrangements of irregular circles. He shifts his support to one arm and clutches the faucet with the other. The faucet coughs and emits a quantity of collected irony phlegm; suddenly it seems to have emptied its lungs and be ready to breathe out air: in midstream it becomes clear.

He turns it down a bit, finding the drops with which it decorates his shirt sleeves annoying and the show of strength it has marshalled unnecessary. Yet he is not so piqued that he is rendered incapable of appreciating the furious weavings and knittings of the strands of the water in the translucent prop of water that seems to support the metal faucet. Nor does he fail to watch this tiny aquatic drama of jockeying for position in the structure of the tube that can be started and stopped at his whim, the jabbering actors in the play seeming to be totally unconscious of his power over them and continuing their petty quarrels and back-stabbings when he turns it on, as if they had never been interrupted by any previous closing of the valve from which they issue in such nervous profusion.

He fills a paper cup, coiling the gleaming tresses of the water in its bottom and watching them become still, shining, and clear, and feeling the cup sway and shiver in his hand from the force of the water as it hits the slick white inside of the cup and is deflected downwards. As he holds the cup to his mouth and tilts it upwards, the smooth inside becomes even smoother and wetter, and his upper lip raises itself not in a sneer of denial but in a pucker of welcome which is soon bathed by the waters that flow gently underneath. Soon the water comes spurting from his mouth in an explosion of particles that have been half-chewed and ejected in a hurry as if they contained worms or the crunchy white eggs of a beetle.

His steps down the stairs are slow, and he takes time to interject a few sideways kicks at the molding. When he reaches the back door, he turns and looks at the kitchen again, slamming the door decisively behind him. The screen slams a moment later as if in yet another echo. The grass is wet. It licks up around the bases of his shoes, leaving damp traces of kisses which will dry to invisibility and which he will not have to erase or hide with shoe polish. **Political question:**

Why are those grass blades which he has come so near to trampling on so effusive in cottoning up to him when their brethren but a few millimeters away are groaning under the heel of oppression? Have they no sympathy or feelings of loyalty to their fellow flora and no consciousness of the growing number of widow weeds? Are they so eager to keep their own chartreuse selves in a state of innocence that they are willing to prostitute themselves in teary gratitude to the monster which has chosen to spare them? **Answer:** There is no answer.

There are insects among these grasses that buzz and flit around his feet. A number of the less nimble of them join their unfortunate herbal comrades in becoming parts of the string of oval Victorian pressed flower tableaux that have spread out behind his retreating feet. Yet they remain flat for only a few seconds before springing up again and are nearly in full erection by the time he is a yard or two away. Had he thought about it, he might have been upset by the alacrity with which something he has destroyed and flattened refused to stay flattened, and had gotten right up and gone on with the business of existing. No one is fond of imagining that the things which seem to him lowly and unimportant are actually carrying on behind his back, mocking him by their ability to take his severest blows and remain unaffected.

The rose bushes by the door stretch out arms of welcome as he passes, hooking tiny demure thorns in his direction. **NB:** These thorns are not born hard and unyielding, but come from the ground as soft as dewy-eyed as the smooth sweet stalks they grow from. It is only when they have dried their wings and are about to fly off that the rose bush reveals that it has other plans for them: their lives are not to be among the tiny soft beauties of the world like the fluffy seed of the milkweed that floats free on the leisurely breeze. Nor are they to be like the new fuzzy fronds of the fern that uncurl slowly as if ready at any moment to change their hesitant minds and withdraw into the ground in tiny tight balls that resemble the pale white grubs sleeping by its roots. Instead of this, they are to become hard and sharp, the ugly addition to an already unattractive part of the plant so that the flowers may remain chaste and inviolate.

His shoes roil the dust of the garage floor mixed with the top layer of the dirt which underlies it. In the parallelograms of sunlight formed by the window panes he can see motes of dust ascending slowly to the ceiling. The rest of the garage is darker than the outside, and his shadow is thrown onto this soft floor, where it seems to burrow into the gray eiderdown. For a moment the smell is so soft that he feels it is he himself and not his shadow that is lying here on this floor in the foreshortened rectangle of light from the door, shimmering slightly as the musty air gently swirls the sand into a butterfly kiss. It seems his own body rather than the shadow's through which the glowing champagne bubbles of dust are rising, seems as if he would disappear into the blackness and become indistinguishable from it were he only to pick himself from the hot sun and glide into the cool corners.

This garage: childhood afternoons in the dust with the droppings of ants and mice. Upstairs in his bedroom, back in the house, is hidden a tan-gray booklet criss-crossed with darker filaments and spotted on the edge with a coffee stain. It is a ration card that he had found lying on the grass by the bonfire that his father was building one hot afternoon: military correspondence, the fading and threadbare patches of uniforms, the exotic purple and musty-smelling foreign money of occupation forces, more ration cards like the one he held clutched so tightly in his sweaty hand. As he watched the fire he felt a fear of losing something, something that he was able to remember only as an image of a pile of papers crushing into ashes and bits of cloth dissolving suddenly into flames. But when he later tried to wring its tan and aged secret from the card, he found that he had nothing between his fingers but a piece of stiff cardboard smelling only of the smoke that had billowed from the diminishing pile beside it on the driveway and from which it had escaped only by accident. And it was not until he was seventeen that he felt this feeling again, the cool summer morning when he walked up the sidewalks of the Cité Universitaire in Paris with his suitcase which was cutting a red ridge in his tightly clenched fist, squinting his eyes against the bright sunlight that turned the cement to liquid ahead of him, feeling the cool of the breezes from under the trees that lined the walk in this long quadrangle between the buildings, grinning in sudden uncontrollable happiness when he saw pairs and threes of self-assured young men with heavy two-day stubble and tortoiseshell glasses dressed in tennis whites that contrasted with their swarthy skins who crossed his path.

What was this feeling?

Perhaps the feeling of being poised on the brink of a world more solid than his own, a world from which he was forever excluded but that made his own formlessness solid by contrast.

And of course, this solidity that he could never attain was illusory. Moreover it was a solidity for him alone, an organizer for himself and no other, since a vision produced from the depths of his own need.

He sighs once, perhaps twice, but resumes normal breathing when he sees how he is filling his lungs with the dust and sending what remains outside into ever-dizzier twirls and leaps. He moves his limbs slowly, then faster until he has taken one step forwards, then two, then three, and he is at the car. Soon he has managed to wriggle through the tiny slit that is the maximum the lazy car can be induced to open its gills. This motion too distresses the dust in the air, which twirls in tormented patterns around the open car door.

The twirling particles: There was once a dying evening as the sun was beginning to take on the red mask it dons before disappearing as if attempting to disguise its identity. Four people sat on a sagging plank footbridge over a stream in the middle of a woods around a red and white checkered tablecloth feeding the bees and themselves drops of honey that caught the last moisture from the drying sun and glowed golden. They cut thick slices of crumbly yellow cheese that separated slowly from the rich dense bar, watching the wind dry the tops of the bottles empty of purple wine that attracted the dragonflies with their bodies covered with emerald dust and their wings the multi-colored and ever-changing translucence of soap bubbles stretched between hoops of gold wire. And then, underneath them, a fish glided silently into view from the lengthening shadows cast by the bridge into the still water. It swam over the last bit of sun-struck pebbled bottom and then stay still, fluttering its diaphanous fins slowly against the sub-surface currents, seeing the tiny bits of sand like these motes of dust in the garage that were fanned upwards into the crystal water by its heaving gills and fins.

Fact: The fish was irreparably lost and would soon swim into water so shallow it would die. **Lesson:** Nature is but a vast schoolroom, an educational display which teaches us something with each and every tableau. It teaches us that death is with us even in the middle of life, one is but half of the Janus face and is incomplete without the other, one opposite is not only logically but psychologically necessary for the other, and we are all of us attuned to the waves of death that float in the air around our heads.

The car moves out of the yard and onto the quiet street along which women sit on the front steps to their houses, barefoot and in curlers, watching their children who play in the street along which there are no sidewalks. The asphalt crumbles directly into a thin strip of pebbles and then turns into crabgrass. Some of the wooden houses are painted bright red or yellow or green; many are echoed by even brighter cars that have been hiked up over the rear tires and thus, when seen from the back, seem to be hitching their skirts above their backsides in lewd suggestion, or strangely-shaped cats raising their haunches against the invisible hands that stroke them.

A few houses away from the driveway is a lot-sized vegetable garden that, in the spring, is filled with short green corn plants. It will be fall before the thin corn will begin to crisp into monochrome versions of their current full-color selves, turning crackly golds and browns and then be reduced to short stubble with sharp edges that stick from the autumn ground like a four-day-old beard on a giant's face. The leaves are sharp along the edges and, if caught at the wrong angle, cut the skin more horribly than any knife, protecting the vegetables that are born in full, albeit infant-sized erection and that grow in length and become daily more engorged, kept in a state of perpetual tumescence by the soft silks and the downy thin husks that gird them, feeling the indescribably pleasureful swayings of the stalk which send shivers down their fat sides but which never seem to be enough to cause them to shoot from their insides any of the golden sap that must be packed within, save for the bit of dried liquid that has oozed from their ends and now clots the hairs of the brown silk. Not even when the hard metal hands of the machine husk it do they ejaculate, not even when smooth knives spread warm butter on their steaming sides which melt into rivulets of golden oil do they rid themselves of their great burden (though by this point they will have to think desperately of the shopping list for next week and of their multiplication tables which dissolve into meaningless figures in their rapidly blankening minds), not even when rows of small pearly teeth bite daintily into their sides and they feel the warm puffs of air from two tiny nostrils.

Across the field is a little store painted yellow with white shutters. Inside are thick jars of crackers in packages, a big floor refrigerator filled with bottles of soft drinks and carrying on its side the detachable canister under the bottle cap opener, a metal cylinder filled with the still slightly sticky caps that keep about them the smell of stale sweetness. Beside it are upended crates that offer blood-red apples from among leaves of green tissue paper, the showcase of candy and a jar of soluble aggies on the counter by the other jars of straight pretzels which lean stiffly against the walls of their prison, though they are popping out with the salty white pustules of some terrible salty disease. The sour balls melt in the puckering cheeks into pools of syrup that leave a smoothness on the spot of the inside of the cheek they have touched while dissolving, a small solid residue that wears off only after a few minutes of bathing it with the abundant mouth juices called forth by the candy. A fan whirs lazily overhead on hot afternoons; under it lies a wooden floor worn down to the naked boards by the rough shoes of the farmers who sat on the barrels in the corner. Yet the store contains none of this now. It is abandoned, and there are big chunks of concrete blocking the shallow driveway; only his brain supplies these still so-vivid pictures as he drives down the road past more wooden houses hovering over carefully-cultivated gardens with their rows of petunias or pansies or zinnias.

At the corner is a veterinarian's office turned florist. The new tenant has filled the front window, formerly decorated only with a brown curtain on which bulldogs and collies cavorted, with a considerably more eye-catching cataract of artificial flowers arrested in mid-fall by wooden posts of descending height that hold them steady and turn their stiff beauties to the eyes of passers-by. Across the street is a woodworking shop. He thinks of the big high-ceilinged room filled with fresh-cut lumber, of the smell that covered everything even more completely than did the sawdust he scuffed on the floor and which could be wiped from a smooth board with the flat of his small hand.

In the corner were piles of blond scraps bearing the marks of the lathe or jigsaw and which seemed perfect and inestimable carved gems, so that he could not begin to conceive why they had been thrown away and would not touch them for fear that they really were finished pieces that had been thrown here by mistake. He thinks of the great mountain-shaped heaps of sawdust in the corner bins in which he buried his arms, scarcely feeling the sharper nips of the coarser pieces in his joy at the handfuls of this fluffy sweet-smelling stuff that clung to his arms when he finally pulled them out, of the whine of the captive saws which could touch and mold only what they were fed, of the banks of fluorescent lights that hung down halfway into the room from the wood-beamed heavens like elongated spiders on observation lines and which glowed soft white on the silken surfaces of the completed tables and chairs that he was permitted to touch with timid fingers, to pat with his soft smooth hands.

There are more and more fields between the houses, gaps in the jawbone of the road coal black from the rain of the day before, some of which still stands in their thick furrows. The road runs thinner now, and soon there is no longer the even alternation of fields and houses, but solitary buildings set off alone in the middle of much larger tracts of land. These are not the huge peeling farmhouses with their outbuildings hovering about them usual to this part of the country; as often as not they are merely trailers that have been given some semblance of permanence by the metal awnings that stick from their sides to shade concrete slabs on which tubular metal chairs stretched with nylon webbing have lighted and seem only to be resting before fluttering away over the fields. Sometimes there is a small flower bed in front of the steps, though just as often there is not. Sometimes too there is a set of flamingoes looking only vaguely interested in the burned crabgrass they are about to peck, or a shiny orb that repeats in glossy green or red a biased version of what it sees, with the things close to it and of its world taking on gargantuan proportions while the things further off remain in a thin ring around the outside of the reflecting disc, given no more importance than the decorative frieze around the edge of an Oriental bowl.

The road winds on past ditches filled with rainwater in which mosquitoes have already deposited the clumps of black pinpricks that will soon desiccate to a bit of airy froth and not turn into the tiny black wrigglers that whip frantically back and forth in efforts to stick their needles through the water's skin. Even if they were permitted birth a day or two hence, they would not live past their infancy and would end their short lives as part of the layer of sludge that coats the inside of the ditch and the blades of grass so unfortunate as to grow there with its slimy blackness which would soon clog their tiny orifices with this jelly of decay and suffocate them, their wild thrashings barely disturbing the thick surface of the mud.

The inside of the car is beginning to feel close and stale. His groping hand finally finds the crank which bends his torso forwards and back and turns his arm and clutching fist around in a circle until the crank evidently becomes fed up with amusing this lost and seemingly helpless hand and it stops. The hand wanders vaguely in the air by his bare knee and then, seeming to get its bearings, lights on the seat by his pants. Through the open area produced by the crank's vigorous exertions, the cool air tumbles onto his face and legs, making the hairs rise to attention momentarily before settling down to parade rest, bathing him with a solid sheet of the smells of rain, wet dirt, and the woods.

He does not yet want to sense these smells or to feel the air that has ceased to feel uncomfortable and now blocks off his left ear to any sounds. He closes the window and drapes his hand over the wheel, looking at those houses and the fields which hang onto the sides of the black road like drowning people around a solitary log.

Soon he is on a dark ribbon down the middle of woods which draw back occasionally to let areas of the grassy fields touch the road. The woods are back, the grasses having receded and hidden around the skirts and feet of the trees which are bolder and not afraid to plant themselves at the very side of the asphalt. These are civilized woods, for all their desolation. There is no fear of sinking up to one's knees in marsh, or of having to battle one's way from a thicket of entangling brambles, no fear of coming in sudden contact with a particularly garish plant which one could not be sure to be harmless to the touch.

He appreciates this only out of the corner of his eye and through the windshield which is spotted with the uneven blotches of the dried remains of bugs. Some of these still stick to the glass, their dull wings askew in the position in which they were smashed. Other smudges have no dark centers, but are only the burst of colored juices of the bruised or maimed insect that blew immediately away or stayed stuck for just an instant by the smooth paste of its own innards before the wind pulled it from its position. There are other more elongated and thinner stains from bugs so fragile they had exploded on contact and distributed their thin bodies out over a larger area, small mosquitoes whose delicate legs never had a chance to bow themselves above the surface of the glass in support of the body that hung down between them on the tiny springs of its appendages, but which had been hurled into the rushing windshield and had at that moment disintegrated so that the smear they left, while containing all of the parts of the body that had produced it, is no more opaque than those made by the bugs that have been picked off after contributing only the drops of their body liquid, if a bit pinker from the blood freshly stored in their tiny stomachs. Insects must also be flung through the metal grill on the front and be plastering themselves against the sharp edges of the radiator vent, against which the wind will systematically break the thin supports of their wings and begin to press their bodies. Later he will find moths, bumblebees, and smaller bugs lying stiff and crucified in tortured positions and baked so hard that they cannot be removed whole but must be picked off piece at a time.

Houses start to appear in the trees, different from the ones he had seen earlier. They are redolent with ruin and age and speak of the fall of prosperity rather than a continuing subsistence-level life. They are tall and old, and their porches are enclosed with carved posts and shaded with stylized wooden filigree cobwebs that cling to the edge of their roofs. There is no paint to disguise their grayness, and in view of the great lengths to which the once white-colored wood has gone to assume neutrality, it seems almost unfair that the yards should not have taken the steps necessary to turning the same graying brown instead of permitting clumps of crisp chickweed to blotch them green.

In the driveways of these isolated farmhouses, there stand abandoned and rusting automobiles, and in the yards and on the creaking boards of the porches play small black children, their hair in braids and their bare feet gray from the dust that has been allowed to accumulate in the driveway under the car and to spill out onto the road where it forms two fan-shaped white patches on the black that are spread by the worn tires of the cars. On the sides of the houses, washing flutters from lines. Finally these houses disappear and the woods withdraw. Mown grass surrounds houses that are more modest in conception than the older ones he has just passed, but more carefully kept up. The children have vanished too, and occasionally a wrinkled white woman appears on a porch rocker, or a middle-aged man in a bright-colored chair who sits without moving and watches the road.

There is a church between the houses, completely without paint save for the few bright chips clinging to it like moths that have stayed behind to lay their eggs which will hatch soon into a new and brighter brood of insects, coloring the building once again with the sheen of thousands of outstretched and drying wings. Inside it are piled stacks of yellowed Bibles and mouse-eaten hymnbooks covered by the dust and touched by the faded sunlight that still lights the unused pews and abandoned pulpit with its pale rays, here in this run-down building or the houses around it.

The grassy marshes that lie around him now are flat and completely treeless and stretch out as far as he can see. They seem on the verge of humping together to squeeze out the road, to eject the sliver that is irritating their skins and that has infected it to the point that white oyster-shell puss oozes from both sides of the road. The sodden ground is slightly lower than the asphalt, and thus it cannot take the alternative course of sliding slow and slippery onto the darker surface and suffocating it; any more energetic schemes such as pushing it straight up and out are absolutely unthinkable because of the weak and ungovernable nature of mud.

The banks of high grasses sway and rustle their feathery heads in repeated denial of some accusation left unclear, and the slight wind here in the open makes the channels of the

Bay that run through the marsh ruffle in rhythm to the grasses. The birds that hang onto the tops of the grass are visible as spots of dark against the tan and the great body of water not a mile away, looming behind them. He would like to open his window now and feel the feels and smells of the salt air, but he knows that here over the water it will be cool again. He contents himself with the air blower under the dashboard which smells of nothing but the machinery of the car. As the knob for which he has groped leaves his hand and the rush of air flies up against his legs he looks up, sweeping his eyes up the dashboard before resting them once again on the visual shelf of the level of his temples.

A ghost of the metal and green persists in his eyes, overlaying itself on the reeds stretching out to the water and begging to be reinforced by another look. He is unable to resist this plea, incapable of leaving unfinished this half-strength impression. He drops his eyes in capitulation and stares at the row of dials and levers with his eyelids forced back in slight pain, as if this could increase the intensity of the object's effect on his mind and thus help make up for the brevity of the time he is going to be able to look at it. The air rushes at his eyeballs with sponges and he blinks.

The air that is blowing on his face issues from two elongated mouths with bared black plastic teeth that are peeking up from under the car pocket and hissing at him. Above them stares the Cyclopean eye of the button on the car pocket, its iris a sculpted gouge, as in certain classical portrait busts. The windshield, then, can be no other than the thing's forehead, clear so as to show all the activity taking place in its brain. The rear-view mirror that hangs inquisitively down on its stem like an angular orchid from a tree-growing vine must represent that faculty of the brain we call hindsight or memory, that which is considered the most important part by many people because it is so frequently appealed to for justifications of actions, for recriminations, for self-praise, and for simple pleasure. The odometer provides the psychic component of the dashboard, showing in its line-up of numbers that change at progressively slower rates the fact that what we take to be the rock-hard basal givens of personality are themselves changeable characteristics more long-lived than the more obviously temporary ones that can, with a drastic enough revision of the less important characteristics, be overturned as completely if not as easily.

The road has become thinner. He can no longer see the edges of the water behind the reeds, which now rise high on both sides. The sky is plated over with near-continuous clouds which are white and seem like a color-coordinated cover set down on the grasses to ensure that the captive animals within will not escape. Suddenly the road straightens and he sees the dark glimmers of something that is neither grass nor sky nor birds. The grasses gradually fall back as if beaten in their attempts to smother the road, and the dark blobs grow until it is clear that they are buildings by a wharf, ramshackle and deserted warehouses on the other side of a finger of water that glitters white as if sprinkled with mica chips. These buildings form the dark dot at the end of a long exclamation point of the road. Or is it a question mark? It depends on how much of the road one counts. Most likely, its entire length is no more than a squiggle; anyone who would attempt to see in it any specific shape would have to do a lot of editing. **Question:** Is this not true of life itself?

The car has stopped by the edge of the water where the reeds simply end, cut off suddenly by the thick gray boards covered with barnacles and algae which push back their roots from the tide. Their reflections shatter into hundreds of puzzle pieces on the tiny waves of the water's surface, corresponding edges lined up but not interlocked, as if the completed picture had suddenly been charged electrically and each piece had found itself repelled by its neighbor, some bits humping and buckling in their haste to uncouple, reflections only slightly disturbed by the pale green shadows of fish gliding by under them. The asphalt crumbles into the sides of the firm grassland, a few black bits having found their way down to the roots of reeds which have begun to enclose them like crickets in hearth cages. At the end of the road are a few pieces of oyster shells, but they have been dropped in someone's haste or carelessness and are not a part of the planned decorating scheme.

He is standing in front of the car's warm hood, leaning a hand on a dust-covered headlight. He kicks the shells two or three feet to the end of the asphalt, where they slide down the wooden ramp that sits half in and half out of the water like a resting frog. This is the ferry ramp; the road does not end here in the marsh at the water's edge. The ferry must be across the water and out of sight, for when he shades his eyes and looks out across the four or five hundred yards, he sees only the stray pilings that sprout the inevitable buds of silent seagulls, the brick side of a warehouse with its dark and shattered windows. The gas pumps set far out on the end of the pier look absurdly new against the gray boards aged by the wind and by time.

The few remaining boards of the pier seem like the last bones of what was once a magnificent prehistoric creature with beautiful sleek sides that, feeding one morning early by the water's edge, found itself trapped in the treacherous mud by its thick-set ankles. Trumpeting and lashing its huge tail as it might, it was unable to extricate so much as one colossal toe or even change its position to a more comfortable one. Then came the bone-winged birds that settled on its broad back and gouged out the beakfuls of living flesh so that the air rang with the impotent bellows of the pain-crazed beast.

Soon, mercifully soon, the once so-proud creature would be reduced to a skeleton which would bleach gray in the successive generations of summer sun and begin to crumble away one part at a time, until all that was left by the time he appeared was a rather bent backbone attached to the stumps of the thing's legs on which the birds leave their droppings that bleach brittle and bake on the hard surface until they too might as well be only discolorations of the bones. **Lesson:** The result of this pain and anguish is a useful and beneficial pier. But we cannot expect the creature to have thought of this in its throes. For it, like each of us, was but part of the great web of life that is built by the destruction and death of those of which it is constructed. He leans back on his car hood and, feeling the warmth of the engine soak through his shorts and tingle his elbows and the dust on the hood in which his fingers draw idle patterns, looks across the river at the silent oyster fishing village and the white sky.

Haverford—Chillum Heights 1974
Annapolis 1994-1996